T

GREEN

A **JAKE ELDERFIELD** THRILLER

DANGEROUS ART

ENDSLEIGH PRESS

Copyright

First published in Great Britain in 2026

Paperback ISBN 978-1-0682313-2-2

Typeset in Baskerville by Andy Barr
Cover design by twenty-five design

Printed and bound by Clays Ltd, Elcograf S.p.A.

HUMAN
AUTHORED

CONTENTS

To Sharon, whose love, commitment and red pen have made *Redline* and now *Dangerous Art* a reality. I am truly, madly and deeply grateful.

DANGEROUS ART

Last Chance? A Record Klimt
By Souren Melikian,
International Herald Tribune

Oct. 11, 1997

The last-chance syndrome is working wonders at auction, pushing up any major and fully documented picture by artists whose work is fading out from the market. This week at Christie's, it was Gustav Klimt's turn. *Schloss Kammer am Attersee II*, painted in 1909, almost tripled the highest expectations as it reached a world record for any Austrian or German 20th-century painting of $23.5 million. It represents the high point of landscape painting in Klimt's oeuvre. Painted in a pointillist style reinterpreting the technique devised 25 years earlier by the French artists, it is both strictly figural and stylized, making it equally attractive to traditionalists and modern-minded buyers. Hence the astronomical and totally unforeseen price.

1 | THE PHONE CALL – VERY EARLY ON MONDAY MORNING, 13TH OCTOBER 1997

When the phone rang in the middle of the night, my first instinct was to smother the bloody thing with my pillow and lob it out of the window. But I'm glad I didn't – it would have left my old friend, Liz, in a very bad place – the kind that generally ends up with your nearest and dearest dressed all in black and standing around a sacred hole in the ground.

I'd been staying at Burgh Island Hotel, an Art Deco delight off the South Coast of Devon, and this was my last night. I'd left the curtains open when I came to bed and now, rudely awakened, I took some calming breaths and stared at the view while the elegant chrome and Bakelite telephone trilled. The full moon was high, in a clear, midnight-blue sky, its reflection shimmering on the surface of the tranquil sea.

I counted to ten, took a deep breath, then reached for the handset before a neighbour banged on the wall. Flicking on the bedside lamp, I noticed the time.

'Jake? Jake, it's Nellie. I need your help,' said the rich, cultured voice I'd known so well since university.

I fought back the awkward feelings that welled up inside of me. 'And waking me in the middle of the night seemed like the way to get me onside?' I've always thought the best form of defence was to get stuck in.

'Ah – sorry mate. That explains why I had such trouble getting through the front desk. What time is it there?'

'Two in the morning. How did you know where to find me?'

'Liz left a message. That was before she decided she's not speaking to me. Again.'

'How can I help?'

'I'm stuck here in Singapore. Be a darling and go to Prague for me?'

I spluttered. Sometimes fate works in mysterious ways.

'We're mates, aren't we, Jake? And I know you care about Liz's happiness as much as I do. It's time I sorted this out once and for all. I'm going to ask her to marry me.'

Well, pass me a piano and call me Liberace. That was the first time I'd ever heard Nellie – otherwise known as Neville Bosworth – commit himself to anything. Must be the full moon.

How the hell was I going to sleep after this conversation?

2 | TWO DAYS EARLIER, SATURDAY 11TH OCTOBER 1997

Who'd have thought that a bloke from the back streets of Brum would find himself in a place like this? I shrugged into the white dress shirt, then concentrated on knotting my black tie into the perfect butterfly as demonstrated by the chap who sold it to me. Mine looked more like a terrifying moth but it would have to do. Anticipation bubbled as I headed downstairs and into the Palm Court Lounge.

I'd seen the lounge at lunchtime, but this evening it took my breath away all over again. Steel-framed French windows, set in a generous semicircle, afforded a panoramic view of the bay. Across the water, the rich, rolling Devon landscape dropped down towards perfect sandy beaches. With high tide approaching, the sea was creeping stealthily across the sand bar, cutting us off from the mainland.

The light outside was beginning to fade now but it was warm and welcoming in here. Atmospheric music from a long-gone era emanated from unseen speakers. The room was on two levels, the slightly higher one to my right. A fountain, backed by a low wall of aquamarine tiles, bridged the gap. Beside it, a short flight of steps linked the two floors. I picked out an unoccupied table on the lower level near the French windows, and headed towards it, passing the generously stocked bar. A collection of vintage cocktail shakers sat in a display cabinet in the corner. I supposed that in the event of a thirst emergency, some lively spirit would break glass and mix cocktails. Rapid relief for gasping diners.

I took a seat, looking up once more at the circular stained-glass roof that I'd first noticed at lunch. Blue, green and purple glass evoked the colours of a peacock's tail. A silver-gilt plaque on the wall by the entrance, displaying a male of the species, nailed the message home. This was truly a place to parade in all your glory.

'Good evening, Mr Elderfield. I trust you've had a pleasant day?'

'It's been hectic, Gary. Full of challenging choices. Like which way should I walk around the island? And shall I have the crab or the smoked salmon for lunch?'

The bartender's snazzy waistcoat broadcast his outgoing personality and made an excellent counterpoint to his smartly pressed black trousers and stiff-collared white shirt. A tartan bow-tie completed his outfit. His friendly yet respectful manner made him the perfect man for the job, as he cheerfully ensured that his customers wanted for nothing.

'Well, I'm going to have to press you for another wee decision. Which cocktail would you care for tonight?'

I perused the long list and made a snap decision.

'It has to be a Perfect Martini.'

'Coming up.'

I watched his straight back as he walked smoothly to the bar, stopping at a table to acknowledge a newly arrived couple.

I'd stayed over on the mainland, in a bed and brekkers in Bigbury-on-Sea a few times, as a kid, on holiday with my parents. Dad and I had built elaborate sandcastles on Bigbury's beach before pounding them in ruthless attacks. The wrecked hull of a ship had sat on the rocks below this building. I'd spent many happy hours there, daydreaming of pirate treasure and smuggler's caves – never thinking that one day I'd be staying in Burgh Island Hotel itself, like a time traveller, transported back to a world of Art-Deco-dence.

My martini arrived and I sipped, wondering how many glamorous film stars might have sat here before me.

'Jakey? What the hell?'

I placed my glass on the table and looked up into the astonished face of Liz Lowsonford, girlfriend of my buddy from university days, Neville Bosworth. The Blessed Liz had spent three years saving him and me from malnutrition whilst obtaining a first in Art History. Nellie and I, on the other hand, had occupied ourselves with the *real* business of a university education – that is, socialising – leaving just enough time to squeeze in a little Economics.

'Bugger me, Liz. What are you doing here?'

'That's a kind offer but I think I'll pass,' she said, a wry smile on her face.

The hint of laughter in her gentle, cultured brogue conjured an image of crystal-clear water tumbling down a stony highland stream. It was great to see her.

'I'm here with my parents to celebrate Dad's sixty-fifth. They'll be so pleased to see you.'

'No Nellie?'

Liz pursed her lips. 'His arse of a boss pulled out of some very important banking conference at the last minute and Neville volunteered to go in his place. I may forgive him one day.' She sighed. 'What are you drinking?'

'A Perfect Martini. Want one?'

'Now you're talking,' she smiled and sat beside me, slipping her arm through mine. 'I take it you're here on your own?'

I thought of my previous girlfriend, Ella; I'd had a spot

of bother with work – all resolved now – and she'd vanished faster than the proverbial Cheshire Cat, leaving no smile behind. And talking of cats, there was also Kat, AKA Katerina Dominova, who'd slipped into my life so easily in Ella's wake, creating companionship and domestic bliss where there had been, what? Survival? But she had then moved on too, leaving me wanting more.

I signalled to Gary and a martini appeared at Liz's elbow.

'That's me. Flying solo again,' I said.

'Poor Jakey. Well, perhaps you're better off that way. Relationships can be very trying. Listen to one who knows.'

We clinked glasses.

'Cheers,' I said.

'Mmm,' she said. 'I may need another of these.'

Liz turned in her seat to study our surroundings. 'What a place,' she murmured.

She looked stunning in her flapper-style cocktail dress. Its background colour was black but that didn't begin to describe it. Over a short, tight slip was another layer of something see-through, covered in a dazzling array of pale brown and gold sequins, forming diamond shapes with intricate infills. It was sleeveless and close-fitting and the hemline formed a racy zig-zag at mid-thigh.

'Like what you see?'

'Yep. Always wanted to see more of you.'

Liz grinned.

'My mother warned me about men like you. I'd forgotten just how smooth you can be.'

'I'm surprised that your Mum and Dad picked this place. It's a long way from Glasgow. I take it they're still living there?'

'Well, I'm surprised that you're surprised. Have you forgotten that my Mum comes from this part of the world? My grandparents, sadly no longer with us, brought Mum and Dad here to celebrate their engagement. Dad's been trying to think of an excuse to come back ever since. A genuine Art Deco hotel. Quite a gem.'

'Did you fly down?'

'What? No. Dad wouldn't hear of it. He drove us in his Bentley.'

Liz's short strawberry-blonde hair was combed flat. A black velvet band around her forehead had a peacock feather thrust into the side of it. Long drop marcasite earrings matched the bracelets she wore on each wrist, over ruched, silky-black elbow-length gloves. Her make-up evoked the high drama of a 1920s film set, bright red lipstick contrasting starkly with her pale skin, while black eyeliner, mascara and a dark eye shadow offset her bright, emerald green irises, seeming to make them sparkle all the more. She smiled warmly at me.

'It's wonderful to see you, Jake. I'm truly amazed you're here.'

She leaned forward and rested her hand on mine. A whiff of Lou Lou by Cacharel came to me, the perfume she'd always worn. I turned my hand over and gently took hers and looked up, into her gaze.

A muddle of emotions went through my head. The last year – the spot of bother with work – had been awful. I'd been accused of a crime I hadn't committed and had lost my job as a result. Although I'd subsequently been proven innocent, I'd experienced dark despair initially, and it had taken every morsel of my determination to carve out a new direction for myself. It was only now, as I looked into Liz's face, that I could come to terms with how alone I'd been feeling.

'Serendipity is a mysterious and wonderful thing. It's great to see you too. How've you been?' I asked.

She looked down, fiddling with a loose thread on her dress.

'Oh, you know. Busy. Networking. Building a career. That sort of thing.'

'And Nellie?'

'He's fine. Bastard that he is,' she said frowning.

She took another sip of her martini. 'Always disappearing on me.'

As I watched, she shrugged, then brightened. 'What about you? What have you been up to?'

'I'm very OK, thanks. Delighted to be here, obviously.'

Liz made a face and pulled her hand away.

'Don't be coy. I heard you'd been arrested. Last December, wasn't it? Was it horrible? Were you locked away with hardened criminals?' She laughed. 'Perhaps I should have visited? Them, not you, obviously.' She took another long pull at her drink.

I signalled Gary to get two more on the way.

'It wasn't that bad really. An open prison. They let me out when they couldn't prove anything against me.'

'How disappointing. You make it sound positively mundane.'

I looked up to see Liz's parents walking towards us. Shona was wearing a full-length silver and white evening dress, and her shoulder length blonde hair was pinned back behind a silver tiara. Liz was thirty-two, just younger than me, but the two might have been sisters rather than mother and daughter. Brian, on the other hand, looked his age with his lived-in face and thinning grey hair, but his twinkling blue eyes and ready smile betrayed a vibrant zest for fun.

We stood to greet them.

Shona hugged Liz and air kissed me within striking distance of each ear.

'Sorry, Elizabeth. Your father couldn't find his cufflinks. Isn't that dress a little short, darling?' she said, in her ultra-English accent.

'Don't fuss, Shona. She looks beautiful, doesn't she, Jake?' said Brian, shaking my hand. 'What a surprise to see you here, my boy. It's been far too long.' Brian's accent betrayed his origins in a Glasgow tenement, softened now by many years of climbing his way up to an ultimately successful business career.

'He's here on his own, Dad,' said Liz.

'Well, we can't have that. You must join us. I won't take no for an answer.'

'It would be my pleasure. Thank you.'

'We need Champagne,' said Brian, a broad grin lighting up his heavily lined face. He caught the eye of the ever-attentive Gary, who organised an ice bucket, a bottle of the good stuff and some old-fashioned Champagne "floats". Liz and I barely had time to breathe in our second martinis before the cork was out and the glasses filled.

'Jake is going to join our party for dinner. Could you organise that for us, please?' instructed Brian.

'Certainly, Mr Lowsonford, I'll have a word with the restaurant manager now.'

'You must be doing awfully well for yourself to be staying in this place, Jake,' said Shona.

'Yes, Jake, what are you doing here? Do tell,' added Liz, arching an eyebrow quizzically.

'It was a thank you from a grateful client.'

'At these prices? He must have been ecstatic,' said Shona, under her breath but not so quietly that I didn't hear.

'I saved his business from bankruptcy,' I said.

'Well done, you,' she said, between sips from her glass. 'And how long are you staying?'

'Just till Monday. Are you here for the week?'

'Och no,' interrupted Brian. 'We're away in the morning, driving across to the New Forest for lunch with some old friends of mine, then it's on to Southampton.'

'I've finally got him to book the luxurious cruise he's been promising me,' said Shona.

'Ran out of excuses, now I'm retired,' said Brian. He looked at me conspiratorially. 'Would your client's business be Race Engineering?'

I nodded.

'As you'll remember, Jake, the only cars that interest me were built before you were born. But one of the chaps at Beaulieu who's into moderns, and knows the Race family well, was telling me all about it. Congratulations.'

'Are you two going to talk cars all night? This is supposed to be a celebration,' complained Shona.

'Quite right, Mum.' Liz rapped her knuckles on the table and raised her glass. 'To my wonderful father on his special birthday.'

'And to good friends,' added Shona, smiling at Liz and winking at me. 'Can't you delay your trip for a day, Elizabeth, now that you know Jake's here?'

'Mum believes I work too hard.'

'Well, you do. Fancy having to go off to foreign parts so early on a Sunday morning. It's ridiculous.'

Liz turned to me.

'My boss asked me to make a last-minute trip. Once I knew Nellie wasn't coming, I decided to go but I played hard to get. It's cost him three nights in a rather lovely boutique hotel and a business class flight from Heathrow with a chauffeur-driven car to take me there. So, after having a fabulous time here with you three, I shall set out for the beautiful city of Prague.'

She pulled a face. 'The only bad news is that I'm being collected at six am tomorrow.' She picked up her clutch bag and stood. 'I need to freshen my lipstick. Are you coming, Mum?'

Brian topped up my glass. 'You know, we're very proud of her, Jake. She has a grand job with an old auction house in Glasgow, Matravers Fine Arts. Typical third generation business, mind.' He noticed my puzzled expression. 'Have you not come across that phrase? First generation works their socks off, the second looks after it, you know, rearranges the deckchairs occasionally but doesn't change a thing, then the third comes along and blows the lot. Nothing could be closer to the truth in this case. Langdon Matravers, the spoilt and entitled grandson of the founder, is running the place into the ground. If his brains were dynamite, there wouldn't be enough to blow the lid off a wee beastie's suitcase. It's a good job Liz is there to light a fire under his backside.'

Shona and Liz returned, Liz slipping her mobile phone back into her clutch bag and noticing me watching.

'I never go anywhere without this thing. It's my lifeline,' she said.

I grinned, patting my inside pocket, 'I'm as bad.'

Brian and I had stood respectfully when the women returned. There was something about this place that sharpened your etiquette to the standards of seventy or so years ago. The ladies sat; we sat.

A thought struck me. 'How are you going to get off the island at six am? Won't the tide be in?'

Liz laughed. 'Well, I'm not going to swim, you dope. Haven't you seen the bloody great sea tractor parked at the bottom of the ramp? It's all arranged. Cup of tea and a croissant at five, then I'm on my way.'

The room was filling up with glamorous couples. I was pleased that I'd now be with old friends and not a Bertram Lonesome attracting sympathetic glances from the other revellers.

A waitress arrived at our table, bearing a tray of canapés. She was stylishly uniformed in tailored black trousers, matching waistcoat and a well-cut open-necked shirt.

'Good evening, Mr, Mrs and Miss Lowsonford, Mr Elderfield. My name is Anna and I'll be serving you this evening. Chef has created these delicious canapés for you. We have oysters in tempura batter, miniature gruyère soufflés and ham hock croutons with a chilli dip for you.' She set the oval plate in the middle of our table.

'Thank you, my dear. They look delicious,' said Brian.

She smiled politely. 'I'll be back to take you through to the ballroom.'

I put down my glass and lifted the plate, offering it first to Shona.

'Such lovely manners,' she said, taking an oyster, 'You should keep this one, Elizabeth.'

'Behave, Mother,' said Liz, helping herself from the plate. 'These look good. I'm starving.'

The waitress returned some minutes later and escorted us into the next room. Gleaming cutlery and sparkling glassware adorned a sea of starched white tablecloths. About half of the twenty-odd tables clustered around the dance floor were already occupied, with more guests arriving. In the far corner of the room, a glossy black piano was parked next to a double bass, astride its stand. French doors along each side of the room offered views across the bay to the west and east of us. A huge, colourful mural of people partying decorated the end wall.

Once seated, our waitress unfolded and placed napkins on our laps. She poured more Champagne, discreetly asking Brian if he would like another bottle and promising to return shortly with our first course.

As the restaurant filled up, three young men wearing black tie strolled towards the piano. One carried a saxophone and took up position behind a music stand. He put the instrument to his lips and flexed his fingers on the tabs experimentally. The background music melted away as the second chap took up the double bass and waited silently. The pianist finished setting out his sheet music. He made eye contact with each of the other two, nodded his head three times and they started playing a jazz standard, "All of Me".

Conversation buzzed around us. Soup arrived. I sat across the table from Brian, with Shona on my left and Liz on my right. Liz chatted away to her dad, asking about his plans for retirement. I noticed Shona looking at me. She leaned in a little as she spoke.

'Did you make a lot of money out of that car company?'

I wasn't sure I'd ever get used to Shona's forthright style of making conversation. 'I did OK. They also gave me a rather nice car. Liz reminded me that you come from this part of the world.'

'I was born in London, but we moved down here when Father's posting came through. My older sister inherited the family house up near Tavistock and married a local chap.'

She lifted her Champagne glass and sipped knowingly as if she expected the whole room to award her marks for style.

'I'm surprised that a handsome man like you should be here on his own?'

'Are you flirting with my friend, Mother?' asked Liz.

Shona kept me in her steady gaze. 'You're not gay, are you?' she continued.

I narrowly avoided choking and put down my glass.

'Not that I've noticed. I just don't seem to have found the right partner yet.'

Shona looked pointedly at Liz.

'That makes two of you,' she said.

'Enough, Mum,' said Liz.

'What are your plans after this, Jake?' asked Brian.

'Good question. Before Race Engineering, I just wanted to clear my name and get back to work.'

Shona interrupted. 'Clear your name?'

'Jake was banged up in chokey with a bunch of old lags, Mother.'

Shona sighed. 'There are times when I find your manner of speaking tiresome, Elizabeth. Whatever do you mean?'

I decided to step in before they came to blows. 'An ex-client of mine committed a fraud and his accomplice tried to get off the hook by framing me.'

'Isn't that exciting, Mum?'

Shona drew back from me, putting her hand to her throat. 'How awful,' she whispered, shaking her head.

'It was very educational. I learned how to pick locks and crack a safe. I thought I might try out as a gentleman jewel thief.'

Brian roared with laughter, provoking smiles at the tables around us. Shona pressed her lips together and looked away. Liz's shoulders were shaking as she put her napkin to her mouth.

The doors to the dining room were opened wide by two smartly dressed waiters and a voluptuous young woman swathed in a low-cut, full-length, scarlet silk dress headed purposefully across the dance floor towards the musicians. Her long auburn hair tumbled loosely around her shoulders and her large brown eyes swept the room like radar scanners as she catwalked across the floor.

'Close your mouth, Brian,' said Shona abruptly, as the girl took up her station behind a bulky thirties-style microphone.

Liz's feeble attempt to disguise her laughter as a cough didn't fool anyone, and she fanned her face with her napkin.

I reached across the table and clinked my glass against Brian's. 'Happy Birthday. That's a hell of a wish you made.'

He chuckled discreetly.

'Good evening, ladies and gentlemen. Welcome to cabaret night at Burgh Island Hotel.'

The woman introduced herself and the other members of the band and a polite smattering of applause from the tables around us followed each name. The piano player counted them in, and the trio started to play once more. The singer – Diana – had a velvety voice that picked up the tune and caressed the words to "Pennies from Heaven".

Our soup plates gave way to a fish course.

'What's so urgent about this trip of yours?' I asked Liz as we tucked in.

'Someone has to wrap up my boss's tour.'

'What does that entail?'

'You've seen *Antiques Road Show*? Well, it's the same kind of thing. He set this up through a contact there. Everyone and anyone have been invited to bring along their curios to be evaluated. You know, is Aunt Magda's vase really a Ming Dynasty and what's it worth?'

'Does it pay?' I asked.

'It's a necessity these days, I'm afraid. We're in a global

market and it's becoming harder to compete with the big players. And sometimes we get lucky and turn up a real prize.'

'Great.'

She took a sip of Champagne before continuing.

'He's found some really nice Art Deco pieces but there's one particular item that's got him very excited.'

'Right.'

Liz frowned and shook her head. 'Could you perhaps show a little more enthusiasm? This is my career we're talking about.'

'Sorry, Liz, please do tell me about this treasure your boss has uncovered.'

'That's more like it. It's a Klimt.'

'Excellent. And that is?'

'A very exciting painting, circa 1914. Langdon says it could go for as much as five.'

'Five what?'

'Five million dollars, dimwit. I shouldn't be telling you, really. It's highly confidential until the deal is done.' She gave a lopsided grin. 'But I suppose I can trust you.'

'Did you say five million? I'm in the wrong business.'

'Not only will we land a healthy commission, but a successful auction will put us on the map.'

'What's your role in this?'

'Well, it's secret-squirrel. The plan is to hold a special, invitation-only, online auction but the client's demanding it happens quickly.'

'What's an online auction?'

'You need to keep up with the times, young man. Rather than struggling to physically assemble a bunch of self-important, crusty old collectors in a room, you can do the whole thing on the internet. Much easier for both the auctioneer and the punters. And better for the client too – it means geography is no longer a barrier to obtaining the best price for them.'

'Sounds like a winning idea.'

'It's part of our fightback. A rather clever chap has been building the platform under Langdon's direction, and this'll be our first online auction.'

'So, apart from having a great time at your boss's expense, what're your duties in Prague?'

'I've organised a top-class photographer to take some publicity shots for the pack we'll need to send to prospective bidders.'

'Can't a local photographer take care of that?'

Liz smiled. 'Photographing old masters is a specialist area and I'm an expert, darling.'

'I see.'

'And, while I'm there, I can check the paperwork and shipping details for the other items we're going to sell. They'll be in a different auction at a much later date. This picture is the *real* prize.'

'I suppose it could end up anywhere in the world?'

She sighed and shook her head. 'Perhaps, but that will depend on the new owner's ability to persuade the powers that be to let them have an export licence, and besides, it's more likely to spend its days boxed up in the nearest freeport.'

'How come?'

'For safekeeping. A lot of art changes hands without ever actually moving.'

'Don't people want to look at what they've bought?'

'It's all about security and investment; these sorts of pictures offer excellent returns with the minimum of fuss, provided they're kept somewhere safe.'

'That's where I should be keeping my cash then?'

'Perhaps. When you've amassed your personal pile of filthy lucre.'

I glanced up. Shona's attention had wandered as she studied the diners at tables around us. Brian's eyes were glued to the singer.

Our plates were cleared once more and replaced by the main course.

'This looks delicious,' said Liz, tucking in enthusiastically.

Shona picked up her knife and fork and pushed food around her plate, taking small mouthfuls. She looked at me thoughtfully.

'They didn't actually charge you with anything?'

'All charges were dropped,' I said.

She brightened visibly.

'Did they catch the man that did it?'

'They did. With my help.'

Shona relaxed and saluted me with her Champagne glass.

'Which makes you a good citizen.'

'I suppose it does.'

We talked further as we ate and then Anna, our waitress, collected our plates as Diana made an announcement.

'Ladies and gentlemen, we'll now perform the Charleston for you. The dance that goes with this music is great fun and easy to do. Could I please have some volunteer couples to join us up here, and Danny will demonstrate the moves for you.'

The saxophonist put down his instrument and moved to stand by the edge of the dance floor.

Liz gave me a meaningful look. 'Well? After all, we're dressed for it.'

'Why not. How bad can it be?'

We stood and I took Liz's hand. Three other couples

moved onto the dance floor with us. Danny showed us what to do, then the music started and we stepped forward on our right foot, kicking back with the left, whilst swinging the opposite arm. We repeated the manoeuvre but this time, leading with the left. After two cocktails each and a bucket load of Champagne, it was a mess.

'Did you enjoy that?' Liz asked as we left the floor.

'I'd say two out of ten for star quality but good fun.'

'And a gruelling workout too.'

Dessert was on the table when we got back.

'Well done, you two. That was fantastic,' laughed Brian, applauding.

I walked Liz around to her side of the table and pushed her seat in behind her.

'You're just showing off now, aren't you?' said Liz, raising an eyebrow.

Shona honoured me with a secret smile and a wink.

The waitress returned to offer coffee. Brian and Shona declined and said they'd call it a night. Liz and I stayed on to dance a few informal turns to some Frank Sinatra numbers. As the band concluded their set, Anna returned to offer refreshment in the lounge, which we gratefully accepted.

'Where is everyone?' asked Liz as she flopped into a chair.

'It got late.'

Gary appeared at my elbow to ask if we needed anything.

'Would you have a Speyside single malt?' asked Liz.

'Certainly, Madam.'

'Then you'd better bring us the bottle and a couple of glasses.'

'My pleasure,' he said, with a knowing wink.

Liz poured our coffee and a good measure of whisky for each of us. She raised her glass.

'*Slanj-a-var*,' she said.

'*Slanj*,' I responded. 'What does that actually mean?'

She took a good mouthful and washed it around her mouth, savouring the flavour.

'Cheers in Gaelic, my mother tongue,' she said, and she spelt out the words for me: *Slàinte Mhath*.

'I knew that.'

''Course you did. I've been thinking.'

'Oh yes?'

'There are two things on which I need your advice.'

'How can I help?'

'First one's my job. I'm worried. All this panic about me rushing off to Prague. My boss, that's Langdon Matravers, must be desperate – I'm sure that's why he's agreed to pay for the car, business class flight and a swish hotel. Anyone would think he was about to go bust.' She gave a short laugh, then looked serious. 'Actually that's not so daft. This chap he's hired, very bright, ex-Navy – submarines, I think – has loaded every feature he can think of onto this online auction platform and it's costing Langdon a fortune. It's a Concorde of a solution when we only needed a no-frills light aircraft.' She sighed. 'You know about business, Jake; what do you think?'

'I'm a nuts and bolts kind of man and this is hi-tech but everyone says the internet is going to be big business. I can see the logic in building the best solution you can, but I also know it's never wise to gamble with money you can't afford to lose.'

She frowned. It was late and we'd both had a fair bit to drink. This wasn't the time to attempt detailed analysis.

'Look, I don't have anything urgent on at the moment, so why don't I come up and spend some time with you and

Langdon when you get back? I'm sure we can build a case to bring in an investor to help get this rocket ship off the ground.' I smiled.

'Would you, Jake? That would be marvellous.'

'And the other problem?'

Liz took a long drink from her whisky. 'Nellie.'

'What's he done now?'

'I love him, Jake, God, how I love him, but he's so peripatetic. He won't settle and he won't commit.'

We were straying into dangerous territory. Liz and Nellie's relationship had always been pretty unstable. They'd broken up more than once and this wasn't the first time I was in danger of finding myself piggy in the middle. 'It's a tricky one, Liz; I mean, his job, you know, World Bank – the clue is in the title.'

She shook her head. 'He's never going to stand still long enough to have a proper relationship, is he?' She looked dangerously resolute. 'I think it's time I moved on.'

3 | SUNDAY 12TH OCTOBER 1997

I woke late and lay in a hazy stupor, wishing we hadn't finished the bottle, as the memories of last night drifted back to me. The conversation about Liz and Nellie's problematic relationship had continued after we'd reached my room. The pair of them had been together since university days and now I was complicit in their break up. Settled with a large, comfortable glass of malt each, we'd gone backwards and forwards over the trials and tribulations of their years together.

'Every time I try to pin him down and ask him where this relationship is going, he makes some joke and changes the subject,' said Liz.

I felt sorry for her but equally my heart went out to Nellie. Never one to nail his colours to the flagpole, Nellie was the archetypal good time guy. He kept his feelings deeply hidden but I knew that in his own way, whatever that was, he really cared about Liz. Business problems I could fix, but this one was beyond me. I loved both of them but try as I might I couldn't see how to keep them together. It was a bloody shame.

As the tide had gone out in our whisky bottle, the mood had lightened. I'd turned the radio on, at a modest volume, so as not to wake the neighbours, and we'd listened to some old dance tunes, until the inevitable desire to get up and have a go had snuck up on us. I shuddered at the memory. Eventually, still clothed, we'd both crashed out on the bed.

I put my head in my hands and let out a pathetic groan. Then, seeing the time, I bathed rapidly, threw on some fresh clothes and slunk down to breakfast.

The breakfast room had an engaging view towards the mainland. Nursing a sore head, I smiled sweetly at the waitress and secured a table by the window. Outside, fearless surfers were braving the wind and spray to take advantage of the waves. I marvelled as they returned determinedly to their boards following repeated wipe-outs. At least watching them took my mind off last night's farrago. A lifesaving cafetière of rich, dark coffee arrived with my requested copy of *The Sunday Times*. Bacon, eggs and toast followed, and my day felt as if it had truly begun. I wolfed down my breakfast with the paper's business section propped against the half-full coffee pot. I'd reached the toast and marmalade and started to feel more sanguine. Aided by a second pot of coffee, I stumbled on an interview with Allen Race. It was a full page in the Business Section under the heading, "Independent Sports Car maker races home". The picture that accompanied the article showed him as the entrepreneurial man of action, suited and booted, standing in the pits at Silverstone next to Race Engineering's Siren ST, their new car. I'd worked with Allen earlier this year, after the death of his father, when the business was close to bankruptcy. We'd managed to turn things around – and in doing so, had discovered Race Senior's death was not an accident. Allen had, understandably, been devastated by the news, but relieved and grateful I'd helped him uncover the truth. Thanks to his generosity, my own metallic silver Siren, registration J4KE.E, was currently sitting in the hotel's garage over on the mainland. *The Sunday Times*' piece glossed over the more gruesome details of the story. In this version, Allen's father had died unexpectedly, leaving the family to run the business as best as they could. With the help of an external consultant – yours truly – Allen had reorganised the company, solved teething problems with the Siren, brought in a new shareholder and signed a collaborative deal with a major German car manufacturer. All of this was true but fell a long way short of the reality that I'd faced when I got there. The story hinted at a direction of travel for the business, a market listing, perhaps? It would never do to rattle potential investors with stories of murder, kidnap, fraud and arson – and the fact that someone previously connected to the company was now serving a long sentence at Her Majesty's pleasure, would it? I wasn't complaining. All my debts had been cleared, and I could pause, take a breath and consider the future. Time enough to follow up all the leads I'd received for my next consultancy when I got home.

'Can I get you anything else, Mr Elderfield?' the waitress asked.

I thanked her and declined, leaving the dining room with my paper tucked under my arm. I returned to my room feeling as if I was on my way to rejoining the human race. I let myself in, drew back the sitting room curtains and opened a window to refresh the stale air with its whisky-fuelled undertones. The Malcolm Campbell Suite looked like someone – well, two of us – had partied long and hard. I suppose Liz and I had needed it after the deeply depressing discussion we'd had about her relationship. Try as I might, I hadn't been able to persuade her to change her mind.

A light rain beat sporadically against the glass. I retrieved cushions from their hiding places in the corners of the room. One of Liz's gloves lay draped across the back of the green leather sofa, and there was a sticky patch on the armchair where one of us must have spilled their drink. I wiped it with a damp flannel, smiling at the memory of Liz and I having another go at the Charleston in here – only this time, with a little less decorum. One glass stood next to the empty whisky bottle on the small round table between sofa and armchair. I discovered the second glass lying on its side next to the armchair with one of Liz's earrings inside it. I took the earring and glove through to the bedroom and placed them on the dressing table where I would remember to add them to my packing. That's when I noticed the postcard propped up against the mirror. I took it across to the bed and sat on the edge of the mattress, amongst the crumpled sheets, the smell of Liz's perfume lingering around me. She'd amended the picture of the sea tractor by inking in a figure standing on the deck and waving. I turned the card over to read the copperplate writing on the back.

> *Good morning, Sleepy Head. By the time you find this, I'll be well on my way to Prague. Thank you for a fabulous night – we had fun, didn't we? Come and see me in Glasgow – you promised, remember? You'll find all my phone numbers on my business card. RING ME. I'll be back in just three days. XX*

I scanned the top of the dressing table and saw the official looking business card. *Elizabeth Lowsonford BA(Hons), Art Historian*, it read, with an address for Matravers Fine Arts in Glasgow, office and mobile numbers. I already had her home number for the London flat she shared with Nellie but she'd put her parent's Glasgow number on the back of the card.

A knock came at the door, and I heard a key in the lock. 'Housekeeping,' a cheerful voice called. The postcard went back on the dressing table and the business card in my wallet. I grabbed a sweater and my newspaper, muttered good morning to the chambermaid tasked with bringing order to my room, and vacated the space.

It had been around 4.30am by the time I'd slept and although breakfast had helped, I still felt jaded from last night's heady mix of alcohol and "fun".

I went back to the Palm Court Lounge where Gary perceptively placed a Bloody Mary next to me, at the same table as last night. The rain had increased its tempo and now drummed a steady downpour against the roof and windows. Only the hardiest surfers remained amongst the waves. I leafed listlessly through the rest of my *Sunday Times*, giving the magazine a wide berth. Who bothers with that?

I put the paper down and looked out of the window. The idea of Liz and Nellie not being together was inconceivable. I mused about the how and where of the way they organised their time. Liz had two bases, London and Glasgow, staying with her parents when she was in the North but spending most of her time in London, where she shared a flat with himself. Nellie's office was in London, which was where you'd find him when he wasn't trotting the globe. That's how it had been since we all left university. My oldest, closest friends. We'd been inseparable during those years at Warwick and whilst I hadn't seen so much of them since, I always knew where they were if I needed them. Would I now be sending two Christmas cards to opposite ends of the country? It didn't bear thinking about. I loved them both and I wanted them to be together. And Liz should be talking to Nellie about her feelings, not me.

As a distraction, I tried phoning Allen, hoping to congratulate him on the article. His phone went to voicemail.

Gary brought me coffee and suggested I take a look downstairs where I might find something to interest me. I wasn't sure I was in the mood, but I put my head into the snooker room before moving on to the guests' library. Gary had mentioned that Agatha Christie had penned an Hercule Poirot novel, *Evil Under the Sun*, whilst she stayed here. I retreated to the lounge with the book and settled, with more coffee, on a sofa on the upper level. I was doing alright until I reached the steamy affair at the core of the story. Liz and Nellie, me and Kat? Two broken relationships. That's when I tossed the book aside.

By now, the rain had stopped and the tide was out. Fresh air would clear the last of the fug behind my eyes and maybe a walk would help me to think things through. I went across the strand that joined the island to the mainland, hoping to find the place where I'd stayed as a kid. Bigbury and its houses seemed smaller now than then. Whether the house had gone or I had misremembered its location, I couldn't tell, but my search proved fruitless. I stood and looked back at the island – joined, temporarily, to the mainland – and took a slow deep breath of rich sea air, which cleared my head and had a calming effect on my spirits.

It had been a great evening right up until the point when Liz had raised the Nellie topic. The business issue was my bread and butter but the personal relationship stuff was just too close for comfort and, in view of my own history, it had sent me into a tailspin. Just what had happened last night? Simply this: two old friends had been thrown together unexpectedly in a party atmosphere with too much booze. But I couldn't avoid a very scary thought. What if Liz was looking at me as a possible Nellie replacement? Shona had seemed to be pushing for that at the dinner table. Was she joking or was she not? And even if her mother had plans for me, surely Liz wouldn't be thinking along the same lines, would she?

It was getting cold, and the tide was on the turn. Time to wander back. As usual when I was wrestling with something – albeit it was usually a business problem rather than a personal one – it was as if my brain was directly geared to my legs. And so, as I walked, my cortex worked its way through this one, and by the time I'd got back to the hotel, I had a plan. I needed to talk to Liz, preferably face to face. And best if it was before she had any serious conversation with Nellie.

If only I'd known what was coming.

Back in my room, I took a bath, dressed and then went downstairs for a quiet, casual, much less formal dinner than the previous night. One small whisky and then early to bed.

4 | MONDAY 13TH OCTOBER 1997

So there I was at two in the morning, peering myopically at an atmospheric vista; moonlight over the briny, listening to a lovesick lunatic nagging me to get on a plane and plead his case to the girl I'd just spent a drunken night with. Mortifying. I listened in dumb silence.

His pitch continued. 'Her first message told me how pleased she was that you were there and I wasn't. And then, just a few hours ago, she announced that we should take a break. It's made me realise that if I don't act now, I'll lose her.'

'Why send me? Shouldn't you be the one to rock up on bended knee?' That conjured up quite a vision.

'Yes, Jake. Yes, I should. But I'm stuck here at this conference in Singapore deputising for my boss. I can't walk out. It'll be noticed. Livvy, my sister, lives here and I haven't even been able to find the time to have dinner with her. Honestly, the organisers watch me like hawks. I can't go for a pee without asking permission. Please say you'll go. I'm relying on you.'

'OK. You've talked me into it.' Never one to punch a gift-horse in the mouth, I accepted the opportunity with both hands. An early, grown-up conversation with Liz had to be my best route out of this for all of us. And there was an extra bonus: while preserving my long-term relationship with both of them, I'd be enjoying an extended break in the fine city of Prague.

'You will, Jake? That's brilliant. I'll be forever in your debt. I'll cover all your expenses, naturally. Just get her to phone me.'

I swallowed. 'I wouldn't hear of it, mate. This one's down to me.'

'You'll be my best man when she says yes, won't you?'

I woke at 7.30am, bathed, dressed and went down to breakfast. After that, I walked through the Palm Court Lounge and onto the terrace. Below me, two brave souls were swimming in the large natural rock pool. I checked my watch: 9.30am. It would be an hour later in Prague. I took out Liz's card and dialled her mobile. No answer. I left a cheerful message. I hoped she'd ring me back soon, otherwise how would I find out where she was staying? I could phone her office but they didn't know me from any old Herbert; how likely was it they would share her travel plans? I went back into the lounge. Gary caught my eye and brought me coffee. He raised a questioning eyebrow, and I shared my problem. A gleam came in his eye as he pondered for a moment.

'You know, when I first met Ms Lowsonford, she was returning from the residents' library with a broad grin on her face. She'd discovered that her next hotel was named after a small bird whose Latin name translated as *Petty King*. She'd be moving from a proud peacock to petulant monarch. It amused her greatly.'

I waited impatiently for the punchline.

'The Goldcrest,' he said.

'That's brilliant, Gary, thank you.'

I sought help at reception. They fired up Ask Jeeves and we found the hotel, close to the famous Charles Bridge and a short walk from the Old Town. I used my mobile to ring.

'Goldcrest Hotel. *Dobrý den*, how may I help?' said a melodious male voice.

'Good morning. Can you tell me, do you have a Ms Elizabeth Lowsonford staying with you?'

'Let me check, Sir, one moment.' He came back promptly. 'Yes. She arrived yesterday afternoon.'

'May I speak to her, please?

'I will try her for you now.'

The extension rang out and the call diverted back to reception.

'There is no reply. She may be in the bar or lounge. Shall I page her?'

I agreed and listened to a few bars of Strauss' 'Blue Danube' as my penalty.

No response. I left a message asking her to call.

'One more thing. Do you have any rooms available?'

'We are almost full, but we do have some small availability.'

'Great. I'll be in touch.'

I went back to reception and asked them to check flights whilst I packed my bag. In my room, I sat on the edge of the unmade bed and looked at the view. A hint of Liz's perfume still pervaded the suite. I remembered our first Christmas at uni, going with Nellie to buy it for her. The bedside telephone rang. It was reception.

'Mr Elderfield. There's a British Airways flight today at 5.05pm from Heathrow and they have seats available. Would you like me to book this for you?'

Could I make it? Say half an hour to check out and get across to the mainland, a long drive to the airport, parking, then check-in. I looked at my watch. Doable. Just.

I reached under the bed for my leather weekend bag. My passport was in the inside pocket.

'Yes, please.' I packed and went down to reception, where I asked them to ring the Goldcrest and book whatever room they had whilst I signed my bill. The receptionist summoned one of their two drivers – who would take me to the mainland, to pick up my car, telling him I was in a hurry to get away.

In the long, open fronted garage, J4KE.E was waiting for me, lined up amongst the array of residents' cars. I blipped the key, hearing the solid clunk of the locking system, and placed my luggage in the boot. Then I opened the driver's door and slipped into the form-fitting tan leather racing seat for the umpteenth time.

Every time I sat in this car, I felt myself apologising for leaving it alone for so long. My silver Siren demanded my attention and promised exhilaration in return. I put the key into its unusually placed slot in the centre console and pushed the red starter button next to the steering wheel; the engine fired and the exhaust note settled down to a comforting thrum. The monochrome dials in the piano black dash showed a nearly full tank and everything normal. The minute hand of the analogue clock ticked round to 11am. I put the car into gear and drove out of the garage and up to the exit. The gate swung noiselessly out of my way.

I drove cautiously at first, through the narrow, often single-track lanes, with their high hedges and passing places, until I reached dual carriageway where I could push on at speed. Piloting the Siren was a seductive experience. The handling inspired confidence and rewarded spirited, fast driving. The slick, precise gear change unlocked the engine's note, changing it from a powerful yet refined purr at normal speeds to an aggressive snarl when pushed hard. I watched rural scenes slip by me, cocooned in this beautifully trimmed and carpeted space, delighting in ignoring the envious glances of those I overtook. Motoring quickly across the countryside without a care in the world was a holiday experience for me. My mission gave it added spice.

My thoughts strayed to the little I knew about Prague. I remembered my charismatic history teacher fascinating us with tales of defenestration – the art of removing your opponents by shoving them through a convenient high window – a practice he claimed was invented at Prague Castle. I looked forward to seeing the place, from ground level at least. Liz hadn't returned my call as yet. Maybe it was better that way. I could just rock up and we could clear the air.

Was I right about Nellie and Liz, though? Did he deserve her? Whilst I'd been slogging away, training to be an accountant, he'd walked straight into a cushy number with the World Bank, courtesy of his public-school connections. He'd spent his time and taxpayer's money investing in big ideas whilst I'd been auditing the books of local businesses. The more I thought about it, the more I realised that workwise, Liz and I had more in common than she would ever have with Nellie. She might have enjoyed a comfortable upbringing, but she'd worked hard to carve out a career from her passion for art history. But compatibility isn't always about having things in common – and I knew Liz loved Nellie, even if he drove her mad sometimes. If they could just see inside each other's minds and hearts, they'd sort it out.

At the airport, I decided not to risk waiting for a bus to pick me up from long stay parking and opted for short term instead, wincing in anticipation of the bill at the end of this. I found a space three floors up with plenty of room around it: anything to keep my paintwork crease free. I grabbed my bag, and locked up, looking back at my car as I walked to the terminal. The silver paint still looked pristine despite the long drive. Good colour to hide road dirt.

The terminal was moderately quiet with only one person serving at the British Airways ticket desk. With no queue, I was ushered on to check-in, where a man of about my age did the paperwork.

'No time for duty free today,' he quipped, putting a cabin luggage label around the handle of my bag. 'They'll be calling your flight in the next few minutes, so you need to go straight to the gate.'

I thanked him and headed for security. The staff were standing around waiting for passengers and I was through in a matter of moments. I checked the screens. My flight had just been called. I risked a quick detour to pick up some Czech crowns, a guidebook, a take-away sandwich and a coffee.

The flight took 120 minutes. By the time I was through customs at Prague-Ruzyně Airport, it was 8.30pm local time. It had been unseasonally warm for October in the UK so it was a bit of a shock to step out into half-past Autumn temperatures. I turned up the collar on my faithful old leather jacket. We were old friends, this jacket and me – it was tidy enough to get away with smart casual but practical enough to get me through cold or rainy days.

It was already dark outside, limiting my view of the city from the cab. I had a fleeting impression of anonymous continental housing, apartment blocks and sleek modern streetlamps. As we approached the centre, the buildings became older and more characterful, with lots of Gothic architecture, and some front elevations painted in pastel shades. Many of the street surfaces were cobbled, creating a deep pitched *thrum* from the taxi's tyres as we crossed them.

Old fashioned streetlamps and elaborate statuary adorned every street. Couples took romantic interludes in horse drawn carriages and tourists strolled around studying menus outside bars and soaking up the atmosphere.

We crossed the river and turned left almost immediately. After a short distance we came to rest outside a mustard-coloured three-storey building with a red tiled roof. The driver and I both went to the back of the car, where I swapped money for my bag. It was just after 9pm and the square I was standing in was clean and quiet. The traditional-looking lighting cast a warm glow over the buildings and threw shadows over the cobbles. It all seemed very cosy and inviting, if a little Disneyesque. My guidebook had told me that the Goldcrest had been built in the fifteenth century, was family owned and had just twelve rooms. I walked up the front steps under a crazily painted, high ceilinged entrance porch and into a lobby with a sofa and massive stone fireplace. The highly-polished reception desk was overshadowed by a structure filling the back wall: a series of dark wood shelves housing a collection of elaborately coloured cut glass, which only a skilled high-wire artist would be capable of dusting. Below that was a bank of twelve pigeonholes, and I could see some had messages in, some didn't. Against each slot was a brass room number and hook, many with keys on them.

I rang the bell on the counter and heard a door open somewhere. A middle-aged man with dark hair and a thick, droopy moustache – the kind a bandit would wear in a Spaghetti Western – appeared. He smiled politely, so I introduced myself.

'Ah, Mr Elderfield. We spoke on the phone this morning. My name is Ladislav, and I am very pleased to welcome you to my hotel.'

He took my passport and filled in some documentation.

'I hope you had a pleasant journey?' he asked, as he handed across an old-fashioned room key with a large wooden tag bearing my room number and the hotel's logo. He also returned my passport.

'We prefer our guests to leave their key with us when they go out. It's better for security and also…' He looked round at the wall behind him. '…we can see at a glance who is in or out.'

I weighed the unwieldy key ring in my hand. 'I'll try to remember.'

'You're on the third floor. The service elevator is only for the staff and disabled guests, but it will be good exercise for a fit young man like you. I hope your friend returned your call?'

'Not yet.'

'Ah, I have not seen her today. Her key is not here so she is probably in; would you like me to try her room for you?'

Should I leave it until the morning? After all, she'd have been working all day. But it would be good to at least tell her I was here, wouldn't it? And who knows, maybe a few drinks and a late dinner?

He dialled her number. I noted the buttons he pressed: 105.

'I'm sorry, there is no reply. There are many things to do in Prague, fine restaurants, bars, the ballet, theatre and night clubs. I think perhaps your friend is having a very good time right now.'

'I'll catch up with her in the morning. Is there somewhere nearby where I could get dinner?'

Ladislav directed me to a restaurant around the corner and offered to ring ahead.

'Give me ten minutes to drop my bag and wash my face and I'll be on my way.'

I took the stairs up to the top floor and moseyed along the corridor. I thought I'd just try Liz's mobile. It went to answer machine again. Frustrating.

'Hi, Liz. I've arrived in Prague, and I have a room in your hotel. I'm about to go and eat something. If you're around, the chap at reception will tell you where I've gone.'

I'm guessing in far-off days, my room might have been servants' quarters. It was at the back of the hotel, right under the roof and not large. There were old beams where you could crack your head and a small window looking out over the city. The ceiling sloped down at a rakish angle – with lots of places where you could catch your head. The bathroom was extremely cosy; put it this way – you could pretty much use the shower, sink or loo without moving from the same spot. Having said all that, it was clean, comfortable and freshly decorated. I put my bag down and edged carefully around the single bed. From the window, I could see straight down into a modest, well-kept garden and a small car park. On the far side of the road was an area full of dense trees, with a path marked out by the soft glow of old-fashioned street-lighting meandering through the foliage. Beyond that, medieval buildings tottered up the hill to the foot of a brightly lit castle, illuminating the night sky. I was looking forward to exploring Prague, and hoping Liz could give me some pointers. In the meantime, though, I was hungry. I'd unpack later. And tomorrow, I'd need to shop for a few essentials.

I found the restaurant easily, selecting a veal escalope, creamy mashed potato, a selection of perfectly cooked vegetables and a local beer. It was surprisingly busy for the time of night. No sign of Liz but then she didn't know I was coming and had been pretty determined to enjoy herself. After a really good espresso, I pulled out my mobile and rang Nellie. I pictured him being woken from a satisfying slumber. He was seven hours ahead of me in Singapore. Sweet revenge.

'Jake? Is that you?'

'Sorry, mate. Were you asleep?'

'Too bloody right I was.' There was a shuffle of bed clothes and more swearing. 'It's four thirty in the morning here.'

'Thought I'd give you a progress report. I'm in Prague and tomorrow I'll get on Liz's trail.'

'I take it she's still not answering her phone?'

'No. But you know what a party animal she is.'

'Let me know when you've spoken to her, will you?'

'Of course. Sweet dreams.'

'Bastard.'

It was raining heavily outside. I had to leg it to avoid a soaking. Ah well, tomorrow was another day.

5 | TUESDAY 14TH OCTOBER 1997

I woke with Liz on my mind. I picked up the phone and dialled her room. It rang out. I tried her mobile which went straight to messenger, again. I checked my watch. It seemed early to be in a meeting. She was staying for three nights, so today would be her last day. I guessed she was trying to pack a lot in. I needed to run her to ground.

After a quick shower, I headed downstairs.

'Good morning, Ladislav.' I greeted him as I went in search of breakfast. 'I'm still trying to get in touch with Miss Lowsonford. Have you seen her?'

'I've not seen her at all,' he said, frowning.

'Is her key in?'

He checked the rack. The key for 105 was not there. 'I think she must have gone out very early. My colleague, Eva, checked her in on Sunday and she may know more about her plans. I'll ask her to tell you what she knows. Are you going into breakfast? I will send her to you.'

A few minutes later a slim, smartly dressed blonde woman in her late twenties came up to my table. Her high cheekbones and eyes that tilted up at the corner made me miss Kat even more than usual.

'Mr Elderfield? I am Eva. I remember Ms Lowsonford because of her lovely accent.' She had a pleasant, professional manner and was carrying a folded tourist map. 'Your friend asked for directions to a photographer's she had to visit on Sunday afternoon. I believe she needed to go there today also.'

'Could you show me where?'

'Of course.'

She cleared my breakfast things and laid the map across the table, marking one cross for the hotel and a second to show where Liz had been heading. She drew a line in black ink linking the two together, across Charles Bridge, through a large square and a couple of small streets.

'It was in Jakubska Street, number twelve. Here, I will write the details on the side of the map.'

'Did you see her when she got back?'

'Yes. She collected her key and I asked her if she needed a recommendation for a restaurant for dinner but she said no, she had been invited out and had only returned to change.'

'Did you see her go out?'

'No, but I was on the desk when she came in. It was quite late. My shift was just ending.'

'What time was this?'

'After midnight. She was wearing a beautiful cocktail dress, dark and covered in sequins.'

That sounded like the dress she'd been wearing at Burgh Island.

'I think she'd been drinking a little. She said Prague was wonderful and she'd had a really good time. She collected her key and wished me goodnight.'

I lapsed into silence while I thought this one through. What did I know? The last message she'd left for Nellie was on Sunday when she gave him the hard word. She'd checked in here, met with the photographer on Sunday afternoon, come back to the hotel to change, then out to dinner and back to the hotel at midnight. I had called her yesterday morning and again in the evening with no reply. And now, today, she was not in the hotel and not answering her phone.

'Have you seen her since then?' I asked.

She shook her head. 'I've just arrived. Maybe Ladislav?'

'No, already checked with him.'

Frustrating. Not answering her phone. Could she really be that busy?

Eva waited patiently while I considered further. There was one small niggle that didn't stack up.

'When I checked in, Ladislav said you ask guests to leave their key behind when they go out.'

Eva nodded politely. 'Yes.'

'And Liz did that on Sunday, collecting her key from you when she came back.'

'Yes.'

'When I arrived yesterday, she was out and must have taken her key with her and she's seemingly done the same thing again today – which is strange when she left it with you on Sunday night.'

'Maybe she was in a rush?'

'That must be it,' I said, not wholly convinced.

'Is there anything else I can help with?'

'I don't think so.'

Should I call the Embassy or the police? I wasn't sure I'd be able to stand the ribbing I'd get from Liz if she thought I'd overreacted. But I needed to speak with her to make sure she was alright. And if she really was that busy, maybe I could help her *and* slip in a chance to talk to her about Nellie? I looked at the map Eva had given me. It wasn't far to the photographer's. I could go, check it out and see where it led me. The route Eva had laid for me led through the most touristy part of Old Town.

I left some items of laundry in a bag on my room door and walked out of the hotel into bright sunshine, heading across the very Gothic fourteenth-century Charles Bridge. Although the many statues looked very old to my eyes, my guidebook described them as modern – by which they meant less than two hundred years old! There was no question that I was het up about Liz but I tried to relax a little and take in the sights as I walked towards my destination. It was pleasantly warm and hordes of tourists were following guides bearing brightly coloured, furled umbrellas above their heads; I had to squeeze past a large group of people gathered around a five-piece band knocking out jazz standards and flogging their CDs in the process. One or two couples were even dancing. I strode across and under the arch of Bridge Tower, where I crossed a busy road – still in the company of what seemed like a thousand holidaymakers – and continued along Karlova Street towards Staroměstské náměstí – the Old Town Square.

There were people everywhere, enjoying the fine weather and the spectacle, meandering slowly, studying the buildings, debating where to take coffee. As I walked through the large square with its myriad restaurants, each with its own tented forecourt, I had to edge around a crowd gathered to watch the hourly chiming of the Town Hall Clock. According to the guidebook, this surreal clock, with its rope-pulling skeleton, procession of twelve apostles and mysterious astrological symbols, had been commissioned by the town councillors, who were subsequently so anxious to prevent the clockmaker from recreating his masterpiece elsewhere that they had him blinded.

Leaving the square and its ubiquitous tourist-hauling, horse-drawn carriages behind me, I turned left when I reached Celetna St, then left again onto Jakubska St, looking for number twelve. This road was narrower than the previous ones I'd walked through, the four-storey buildings on each side leaning closer together with each floor. A little way along, I came to a shop front with a single word – *fotograf* – and the name Mikaela Venclová written on a plaque at the side of the door. I went in.

'*Dobrý den,*' said the young woman at the counter, '*jak vám mohu pomoci*?'

'Do you speak English? I think a friend of mine came here on Sunday afternoon. Her name is Elizabeth Lowsonford.'

'I am not here at weekends, but Mikaela will know. One moment please. Who is asking?'

I handed her a business card, and she went into the rear of the store. I heard voices in Czech. Not understanding any of it, I gazed around me: the shop was pleasant and bright, with a variety of arty photographs and sophisticated-looking portraits on display. The receptionist came back with another woman clad in black jeans, black t-shirt and an unbuttoned tartan shirt hanging loosely outside of her jeans. Her short hair was dyed a dark red and she wore work boots laced-up to mid-calf. She came towards me with a polite, enquiring smile on her face.

'Agata said you were asking about Liz coming to see me on Sunday?'

'I'm in town for a few days and I'm trying to catch up with her. I'm staying at Liz's hotel, and they said she came here. I was hoping that you might help me track her down.'

Mikaela studied my card. 'How do I know you're not a stalker?'

'Honestly, it's nothing like that. We're old friends who were at university together. We bumped into each other and had dinner with her parents on Saturday evening, but she had to dash here on business, organising the sale of a painting. I had a few days spare, so I thought I'd come and keep her company.'

She smiled. 'You don't look like an angry ex-boyfriend so I'm going to trust you. She was here to oversee a photographic shoot and the painting's owner came along too.' She frowned. 'I keep a bottle of wine or two in the studio, just to relax nervous customers before I photograph them. They each had a glass and then helped themselves to the rest of my bottle! Come.'

I followed her into a warehouse-like building behind the shop. In one area, the bare brick wall was obscured with white sheets, and a lighting rig stood in front of it, an empty easel resting in front. She led me to a small side room and flicked a wall switch, bathing the room in bright white light.

'This is where it all comes together,' she said.

The bench in front of us held an expensive-looking camera and various lenses packed tightly in protective black foam inside an open aluminium briefcase. A Polaroid instant camera stood on the bench next to it. But the main attraction was a white, glass-topped light box with a whole bunch of transparencies laid out on it. A magnifying lens stood next to it.

'I was just going through them to pick out the best ones for Liz. You're welcome to take a look but I think you'll be more interested in these.'

She handed me a wedge of instant prints, explaining, 'I

use the Polaroid to check each shot before I start. It saves time and film.'

'Isn't all this going digital?'

'It will. But some of us prefer a traditional high-quality analogue camera like this Hasselblad. Give it five years, when digital cameras have come of age and there's software to manipulate images and everyone will think they're a professional.'

The first print showed a painting on the easel, caught in a crossfire of bold lighting. A sullen-looking security guard stood in shadow behind it.

Then it got interesting. There was a picture of Liz, with an arm casually draped around an unknown woman, the two clinking full wine glasses. The other woman was quite striking: long jet-black hair; bold, sensual features; and wearing figure-hugging leather jeans and a long-sleeved cotton top, tight around her athletic profile. They were both laughing, enjoying each other's company. The next shot showed the other woman writing something with a marker pen on the back of Liz's hand and then, in photo number three, Liz held her hand up to the camera. The last picture showed the woman kissing Liz full on the lips. Liz had her eyes closed.

'What did she write on Liz's hand?'

'How is your Czech? Not so good, I guess? Let me translate for you. It says, *Admit me to the Dark Goddess – Temná bohyně* in Czech.'

'What's the Dark Goddess?'

'A fancy nightclub run by the picture's owner, Vanda Brazda; she even signed your friend's hand.'

'Liz went there?'

'Perhaps.' Mikaela smiled.

'Did she mention where she would be today?'

'No, but I'm due to see her later. I'll ring her as soon as I've finished going through the transparencies. Can I give her a message for you?'

'Just ask her to return my calls, please.'

Mikaela flicked back to the image of the two women kissing.

'She may have her hands full right now,' she said, raising an eyebrow.

Maybe Vanda Brazda would know what Liz was up to today? I asked Mikaela to show me where the Dark Goddess was on the map – and it turned out it was just five minutes' walk away.

It also turned out that the Dark Goddess was, in fact, a derelict-looking Gothic church in the middle of a small square. Was I in the right place? I looked at the map again. Yep – this was it. Large arch-shaped wooden panels covered the gaps in the stonework where the stained-glass windows would once have been, and clumps of green weed sprouted from the edge of the roof. It didn't bode well, I thought – but then I saw that the upper part of the bell tower was wrapped in a glass box, in a way that seemed both deliberate and striking. Perhaps the church wasn't abandoned, after all.

Walking around to the end of the building, I saw that the inside of the entrance porch had been spray-painted with mystic runes and pentagrams in what must have been the neatest piece of vandalism I'd ever seen. I tried the handle of the pair of sturdy-looking entrance doors, but they were solidly locked. A rustic iron pull hung next to them. I gave it a tug and was rewarded by the sound of ringing somewhere deep inside the building.

I waited.

Nothing happened.

Visiting a nightclub in the middle of the day? What did I expect? I tried again. This time I heard footsteps crossing a stone floor and bolts being drawn. The right-hand door opened with a piercing screech and a man in his mid-thirties stood there, wincing, clearly irritated by the noise. I'd half expected to be greeted by Count Dracula – you know, pale face, black cape and pointy teeth – but what I got was a healthy-looking, pleasant-faced bloke of medium height and build, dressed in crisp overalls. His clothes and blond crew-cut were dusty, as if he'd been crawling around in an attic.

'*Dobrý den*,' he said.

'I was hoping to see Vanda Brazda. My name is Jake Elderfield; here's my card. Would she be available?'

'Maybe,' he said, giving me a shy smile. 'It depends what you want.'

'She met a friend of mine, Liz Lowsonford, on Sunday. I'm trying to catch up with Liz and I wondered if Ms Brazda might have seen her since?'

'OK,' he said. 'Let me ask.'

He closed the door, and I heard him walking away. But I hadn't heard it being locked, and it felt strangely light when I pushed against it. On closer examination, what appeared to be old, grained oak, studded with handmade nails was, in fact, moulded fibreglass. I opened and closed it a couple of times, listening to the sound it made. The noise came from a small speaker tucked high up on the wall.

The inside of the church was a complete contrast to the outside: the founding fathers would be spinning in their graves. I was standing at the back of the building in what was now a reception area. Painted steel pillars supported a mezzanine floor above my head, and a tinted glass wall ran crossways through the space, dividing it from the rest of the building. Through the glass, I could see a large dance floor with tables and chairs around the edge of it. It was easy to imagine this place on a busy night, bustling with dancers strutting their stuff, the tables occupied by those more interested in drinking and gossiping. The well-stocked bars, lining each side of the floor, looked just the job – and, above each of these, a balcony led back to the mezzanine.

There was still no sign of the man who'd let me in and I figured that I'd come this far, so I might as well take a closer look. I leaned over the unoccupied reception desk and pushed various buttons there until the glass doors leading into the main part of the building swished open.

Moving to the middle of the dance floor, I got a 360 view of the place. Impressive. Clean, delicately carved stone pillars soared up to stout oak beams supporting a solid roof. On the outside, it looked forgotten and forlorn; inside, it was a funky, upmarket space. No way a casual visitor would chance on it – it was for people in the know, for the moneyed set, I thought, who liked something very out of the ordinary.

I looked up at the mezzanine, with its glass balustrade around the edge and saw it held a smug-looking restaurant; you know, blindingly white tablecloths, sparkling cutlery and glassware – the kind of place where the waiter looks down his nose unless you order from the pricey end of the menu. Above the restaurant, the bell tower, in its glass cubicle, provided an eagle's eye view of the dance floor and, on the outside, I guessed, the surrounding city. I noticed that from here, I couldn't see through to the reception area – there must be some kind of one-way coating that prevented light travelling through the glass wall, meaning all the celebrants in here could party on without being able to see new arrivals and lesser mortals gawping at them.

I glanced at the windows – boarded up from the outside, of course – and was surprised to see several backlit, contemporary artworks in stained-glass set into the masonry, each offset by the plain plasterwork that surrounded them. I counted twelve in total, six on each side; all similar but not identical. Each had a foreground of golden swirls and lattices – like an elaborate cage. Green stems wove up through gilded bars until they burst into vivid sunflower-like heads of magenta, violet or amber. Inside each of these decorative cells, a pale-skinned, androgynous figure was depicted, dancing, draped in a loose diaphanous robe, with a look of dream-like ecstasy on their face. Wraith-like but with richly coloured hair, dark eyes and bright red lips, their expressions were haunting. All in all, it seemed like a great place to entertain monied plutocrats, so long as they had a taste for the bizarre.

I heard footsteps approaching.

'You found your way inside then?' My guide had cleaned himself up.

'Curiosity got the better of me. I've never seen anything like this before.'

'Come and see the lady who gives her name to this place.'

A stage stood at the far end of the church, where the altar would have been.

'Meet the Dark Goddess.' The man motioned upwards.

The large window above the stage showed another bizarre artwork in stained glass: a stunning woman, clad in figure-hugging black, lounging on a golden throne, casually surveying the room. Pale-skinned with long dark hair, eyes as black as coal and red, red lips, she was the epitome of commanding female beauty, demanding total obedience from her subjects, and you got the feeling that her glass eyes missed nothing as they swept the room. She looked stern yet amused, enjoying absolute control of her environment. Like a dominatrix on a tea break.

'Ms Brazda will see you now.'

'This is quite a place. How many does it hold?'

'We've had as many as four hundred in here on a busy night. Follow me, please.'

Back we went through the glass doors to an elevator set into the bottom of the bell tower. Once inside, we ascended swiftly and silently.

The doors opened onto the restaurant and we curved around the edge of the immaculate table-scape and strode along the left-hand balcony until we reached a side door marked *private*. Our man knocked.

A low register female voice growled, 'Come in.'

We did as we were bid.

'Thank you, Tomáš,' said the woman sitting behind the desk. Frosty, I'd call my reception, as cold as a polar bear's favourite glacier.

Vanda Brazda put down my card and looked up. I could see where the artist had found his or her inspiration for the Dark Goddess.

'Jake Elderfield.'

She must gargle with iron filings steeped in treacle to have a voice like that. It was uncanny: the Dark Goddess made forty-something flesh. She rose to greet me. Her tight-fitting blue jeans and black t-shirt with closely cropped sleeves showed off her physique. She was slim but strong and the way she gripped my hand in greeting, I wouldn't fancy my chances in an arm-wrestling contest.

The room was sparsely furnished, with oak panelling and

a plain grey carpet. The large, steel desk was uncluttered, just a pocket-sized notebook and pen in front of where she'd been sitting, and a desktop computer at forty-five degrees to her. The way she hit a couple of keys, blanking the screen, made me slightly curious – but what she got up to in her spare time was her business. There was just one splash of colour to break up the plain, light grey walls: a painting on the chimney breast opposite her desk. It was a large, frameless picture and I went over to it and stared, mesmerised. A haughty-looking female, looking down on the world, dressed in red and gold, wearing a golden collar and bangles, and what looked like a gold snake wrapped around her elevated right arm. In her left hand she held a glass saucer – containing who knew what – high in the air.

'Is this the picture you're selling?'

She waved me to the chair in front of her desk.

'No. It's a reproduction of Hygieia, Goddess of Health. She was the central character in one of Klimt's most famous works, 'Medicine'. The original was created as a triptych – 'Medicine', 'Philosophy' and 'Jurisprudence' – for the University of Vienna. His work was described at the time as perverted excess and all three pictures were burned by the Nazis.'

I'd seen such frameless prints before. Modern copies of famous pictures. This one was truly massive. I raised my eyebrows, impressed, and sat in the chair Brazda had indicated.

'I am very fond of Klimt's work. He was the inspiration for our windows downstairs. I saw how you were drawn to them.' Her fingers went to her computer keyboard and she swivelled the screen around to face me. A single image filled the screen; me on the dance floor staring fixedly at the windows.

'Very striking. Particularly the one above the stage.'

She shrugged. 'It needed to be dramatic, to create atmosphere, and theatre.' Her computer screen reverted to showing images from cameras dotted around the club. The dance floor, the bar, seating area, the restaurant. They flicked through, one after the other – more cameras than space on her monitor – all empty but immaculate and awaiting guests. She clicked a button and the screen blanked. 'How may I help you?'

'I'm trying to catch up with Liz.'

'Ring her.'

'I have. She's not returning my calls.'

'Maybe she doesn't want to see you.'

'I'd be surprised. We've known each other a long time.'

'She's very outgoing. I expect she's made friends here.'

'You met her on Sunday?'

'Yes. In the afternoon and later we had dinner here.'

'What time did she leave you?'

'It was early.'

'Early? She didn't get back to her hotel till after midnight.'

Her smile was as bright as a camera flash and over just as quickly. 'This is a night club. Midnight is when things get started. But she excused herself after dinner and drinks.'

'Is the club always open that late on a Sunday?'

She shrugged. 'Always. We have many customers every night.'

'Have you seen her since?'

'No. If there's nothing else…?'

I rose. 'Thanks you for your time.'

She pressed a button on her desk phone. A voice came through.

'Tomáš. Mr Elderfield is ready to leave. Come and fetch

him, please.' She turned back to me. 'How long will you be in Prague?' she asked.

That was a good question. Unless she'd changed her plans, this was Liz's last night. Finding her was becoming more urgent. 'Not sure yet. Maybe a few days.'

Vanda Brazda's sunburst smile came back for a brief action replay as she passed across a handful of tickets. 'Take these. And come and see us when the club's open – if you get the chance.'

The door opened and Tomáš stood quietly, waiting to show me out.

'I'm staying at the Goldcrest Hotel. If you hear from Liz, will you let me know?' I said.

She nodded briefly. 'Enjoy Prague.'

Walking out, I noticed how many CCTV cameras they had around. It was an intriguing place, like something from a very Gothic fairytale. I wondered if it was frequented by vampires?

This was baffling. Eva had been the last person to see Liz on Sunday just after midnight. No one since. I pulled out my phone and tried her again. It went straight to answer machine. Was she just not talking to me? I thought she saved that for Nellie.

My stomach growled as I walked past all the cafés and bars in Old Town Square. The place was buzzing. Everywhere seemed to be full. I'd only had coffee and half a piece of toast for breakfast, distracted by concern for Liz and my conversation with Eva. It was time to refuel.

I stopped abruptly, outside a place called Reuben's, a small, friendly-looking café-bar where a solitary older chap was bustling around energetically, taking orders and shmoozing customers. All the outside tables were full but there were a couple of free spaces inside, and I peered at the menu displayed by the door. I was aware of tourists wandering past, pointing at things and consulting guidebooks and, for some reason – instinct, perhaps – I glanced towards my right. There was a guy in front of the next café along. Nothing exceptional about him; his nondescript appearance blended perfectly into the scene. But *something* was making my hackles rise. He was staring blankly through the café window; then – there it was again – a shifty glance in my direction. Probably a pick-pocket looking for a mark. I took a seat inside Reuben's and selected a drink and a toasted sandwich. My mobile rang. Might it be Liz?

'Jake. It's Mikaela. Liz isn't returning my calls.'

This was the excuse I needed.

'Let me speak to her office.'

'Thanks.'

I took out Liz's card and dialled the number.

'Matravers Fine Arts. How may I help you?' said a smooth, young male voice with an upper crust Scottish accent.

'I'm calling from Prague. We're trying to get in touch with Liz Lowsonford to approve the transparencies that she commissioned but she's not responding.'

'Ah – then I'll put you through to Mr Matravers.'

Insipid music leaked out of my phone as I was put on hold.

A louche, educated voice came on the phone.

'Langdon Matravers speaking.'

'It's about your transparencies, Mr Matravers,' I said.

'Ah yes, I'm glad you rang. We need them in a bit of a hurry.'

'I understand but Ms Lowsonford is not returning our calls.'

'Don't you worry about that – just get them over to me as soon as you can.'

'We haven't spoken to her since Sunday afternoon and we are concerned for her. Has she been in touch with you?'

'What? Yes, yes – we've been in constant communication. Now, about these transparencies…'

'Do you have another number we could reach her on?'

'Look, old chap. Liz can take care of herself. This is a rush job and we need to get on. What's the quickest way to get them to me?'

Selfish bastard. I hung up. A couple at the next table were clinking their cocktail glasses together. There was a Noilly Prat bottle on their table, which put in mind a description of Matravers.

Next door's café voyeur was nowhere to be seen. I finished my sandwich and hurried back across Charles Bridge towards the hotel. It was then that I picked up my tail again, walking maybe twenty metres behind me.

I stopped, turned and stared. With all the tourists around, he stood out like a cooking apple on a tray of exotic fruit. He looked quickly away and strode over to the side of the bridge, peering along the river. I left him there and strolled on.

As I walked, I mulled the situation over in my head. Mikaela was expecting Liz to go and see her today before returning to Glasgow – so why hadn't Liz been in touch with her? That just didn't make sense. This was Liz's job and she loved it. I couldn't imagine her ever being less than 100% professional. And now I had a stalker – a pretty incompetent one, but a stalker nevertheless. Who was on my case and why? I sighed. That was one for later; right now, I needed to find Liz.

***

Eva was on reception when I got back to the hotel. I didn't waste any time.

'Were you on duty yesterday morning?' I asked. The days were blurring. Yesterday was Monday.

'No. It was Ladislav.'

'When I checked in, he told me he hadn't seen Liz all day.'

'He may have been in the office when she was on her way out.'

'I still don't understand why she didn't leave her key given that she dropped it off on Sunday?'

'Sometimes, if there's no one at the desk, guests prefer to hold on to them.'

'And you definitely haven't seen her today?'

'No.'

'Then I need a favour.'

She looked at me enquiringly.

'I want to get a look inside her room.'

She frowned and was about to object.

'What if she's lying ill in there, unable to call for help?'

'Housekeeping would have found her.'

'Even so, I'm worried. There's no trace of her movements today or yesterday and it's not just my calls she's not answering. I need to see inside her room; there may be something that tells us where she is.'

Eva hesitated.

I nodded towards the rows of pigeon-holes. 'And it looks to me like she has quite a few uncollected messages up there.' The space for room 105 held a thick wedge of notepaper.

She came to a decision. 'I'll come with you. Housekeeping will have a master key.'

She was back in a few minutes.

'They say her bed has not been slept in.'

She unlocked the door and I followed her in. Liz's ground floor room was bathed in sunlight from French windows leading onto the gardens. Large and airy with a four-poster bed, it was much posher than my broom cupboard.

I checked the wardrobe first. Coat hangers tinkled noisily as I ran my hand along the short row of jeans, a jacket and dress. Next, I opened a couple of drawers in the dressing table. Underwear. I tried the bedside table. Usual hotel paraphernalia in the drawers but nothing of Liz's. I checked the bathroom. Cosmetics, toothbrush, as you'd expect.

I sat on the edge of the bed and glanced around the room. My eyes rested on the dressing table mirror. My anxious face stared back at me. Everything seemed perfectly normal. Was she just having a good time somewhere, now that she was off the hook from Nellie? *Pull yourself together, Elderfield.* I made an effort to relax my careworn features and stretched, straightening my back. What was that? My heel had brushed against something under the bed. It moved. I lifted the valance. It was Liz's clutch bag – the one she'd been using at Burgh Island. Her mobile was inside, dead, the battery exhausted.

Eva sat down next to me, a second room key in her hand. 'I found this lying under the chest of drawers.'

Liz's room key. I took out my own phone and re-dialled. 'Put me through to Matravers. It's Jake Elderfield from Prague.'

'You again. How soon can you get the transparencies over to me?'

'You said you were in constant communication with Liz; was she on her mobile?'

'Of course. It's the only number I have for her.'

'That's bullshit, Matravers, and you know it.'

'What is this? And who are you to talk to me like that?' There was a pause. And then: 'You *don't* work for the photographer, do you?'

'Liz and I are old friends and I'm here to meet her.'

'Listen Elderberry, or whatever your name is. I don't give a damn about your social arrangements. I need those pictures urgently. Give me the photographer's details now.'

I stayed silent and moved to the French windows, peering sightlessly over the garden. 'You'd do well to be polite if you want my help,' I said. Eva was staring at me. My left hand brushed against the cool glass, helping to take the heat out of the conversation.

Matravers coughed a ham-fisted apology. 'Well, er, yes. Sorry. It's this new client, important job. It's got me rattled.'

I slid my fingers across the pane, reaching the edge. The putty holding the glass in place was soft and tacky. It was clumsily done. Matravers was still blathering away as I lowered the phone. Most of the glass in the doors was striated and discoloured with age. All except for this one crystal clear pane right next to the lock.

'Elderfield? Damn… we've been cut off again.'

There were fine scratches in the brass surrounding the keyhole. I tried the handle. The door was locked.

'I'll call you back, Matravers.' I cut off his protests.

I turned to Eva. 'I need to get this open.'

She brought the room key she'd found. There was a second, smaller key on the ring, which unlocked the door.

'Thanks.' I showed her the repair. 'Can you find out when this was done?'

She picked up the house phone and started speaking as I went into the garden.

A moment later, she followed me out.

'What are you thinking?' she asked.

'There's no keyhole on the outside of this door and the putty around the replacement glass is very new. I'm wondering what's gone on here.'

'No breakages have been reported anywhere in the hotel during the past month.'

That was as I expected.

'If someone wanted to get in,' I said, thinking aloud now, 'they'd have to break the glass, stick their hand through and pick the lock from the inside. Awkward but doable.'

'Surely your friend would have heard them. She'd have had time to run out of the room or call for help?'

'She could have been asleep, or maybe they were waiting for her when she came in.'

'How would they know which room she was in?'

'Good question.'

I studied the ground around the outside of the door. 'Nothing here.'

'What were you hoping to find?'

I knelt down for a closer look. 'I was hoping whoever did this might have left us a footprint or two.'

'It rained heavily last night,' said Eva. 'Which could have washed any prints away.'

I slapped my forehead. 'Yes. I forget about the rain last night. I had to run back from the restaurant.' I looked around. The shortest route to a waiting car lay across the grass under some trees. 'Let's take a look over there just in case.'

'Wait – what's that on the fence?' said Eva.

A small sliver of something was caught there, flapping in the breeze. I walked across and claimed my prize: flimsy, black and see-through, with a few gold sequins attached.

'What is it?' asked Eva.

'Let's go back inside.'

Eva took the swatch of material from me. 'This matches the dress she was wearing on Sunday night.'

Liz's evening bag was where I'd left it, lying on the bed. The inside pocket contained one of the hotel's check-in cards – the ones that state the hotel's address, the guest's room number and the dates of their stay. I thought about the guy who'd followed me in town earlier – it would have been easy enough for any semi-competent pickpocket to have got a quick look inside Liz's handbag on Sunday night.

I checked the wardrobe and confirmed that her Burgh Island outfit was missing, then I dialled Glasgow again. 'It's me, Matravers. I'm standing in Liz's hotel bedroom. All her things are here, including her phone. No one's seen her since Sunday night and she's due to check out in the morning. What's going on?'

'I'm sure there's a perfectly rational explanation.'

'Really? And what do you think that might be?'

'She'll have had to go out of town to follow up on some of the other auction items.'

'For two days? With no change of clothes or mobile phone? That's not Liz and you know it.'

'Well, ah. No. I see what you mean.'

'It looks to me as if Liz has been snatched from her room and is being held somewhere against her will.'

'Who'd do a thing like that?'

'I don't know but I'm going to find out.'

'There's just… I hate to ask… but…'

'Spit it out, Matravers.'

'My new client. It's imperative that I run this auction on Monday and for that I *must* have the transparencies.'

'How important are they to you, Matravers?'

'Important and urgent.'

'Well, if that's the case, I'd like to hear the truth from you. When was the last time you spoke to Liz?'

'Sunday morning. On her way to the airport.'

'Where is she, Matravers? Do you know?'

'No. No, I don't.'

'Do you know who's got her?'

He hesitated just a beat too long before replying. 'No. I…'

'Then I'd better phone the Embassy and get the police out here.'

'No. I beg you. Please, if you can get the transparencies to me, I can sort all this out. It's just a misunderstanding…'

'Best I get the police…'

'No! You mustn't. Just get me those damned pictures. I *must* auction the painting on Monday and I can't do it without them. Everything depends on it.'

'Everything? Including Liz? Look, Matravers, what do you know?'

There was a deep sigh from the other end of the phone. 'Please, I can't say any more.'

'Here's what we do. I'll bring your pictures to you, but you only get them if you level with me. No bullshit and no lies. Do you agree?'

'What choice do I have?'

'None. I'll call you later.'

I dialled Mikaela. She answered in two rings.

'It's Jake. I need those transparencies.'

'They belong to Liz's employers. At least, they will when they pay me.'

'I'll pay you. I'll take them to Matravers and get my money back.'

'Why would you do this?'

'I'm one of Liz's oldest friends. It's my job to look after her interests.'

I asked Eva to find Liz's phone charger and to check today's flights to Glasgow for me before legging it back to Mikaela's and handing over my credit card.

'You'd better see what you're buying.'

Six transparencies were spread out before me. She handed me a magnifier and flicked the switch on the side of the light box.

'I think Liz would be very pleased with these. It's disappointing that she couldn't pick them up in person,' she said.

'Tell me something,' I said. 'With all the technology around these days, wouldn't it have been easier to take these images digitally and transmit them to Glasgow electronically?'

'Sure – and if Liz had been happy to have soulless pictures that didn't capture the artistic merit of the painting, that would have been fine. But we both agreed that there's something about an analogue image that can't be reproduced digitally. It'll come, but we're not there yet.'

I felt stupid inspecting the transparencies. Was I supposed to be playing spot the difference? I tried to keep my inane comments to myself and focus on what I was looking at – which was a bare-chested woman with long dark hair and a cloak draped around her shoulders. She'd catch her death like that. She was holding her hands out in front of her and there seemed to be a snake wrapped around her right leg. The crown she was wearing made her look like a minor royal who'd been caught out before she'd had time to get properly dressed. I didn't understand art. One thing, though, struck me as particularly odd. 'Where's the artist's signature?'

'Not all artists sign every painting every time. Sometimes they forget or maybe they didn't want the recipient to sell it on at a profit. The signature doesn't matter as long as there's provenance to support the sale.'

With an envelope stuffed with the transparencies tucked safely inside my inner jacket pocket I set out for the Goldcrest. That's when I picked up my tail once more. He was about ten metres behind me as I came up to the pedestrian crossing that would get me over to Charles Bridge. Before the lights changed, I made a dash for him, but he slipped away before I could get close. I'd better keep my eyes peeled.

Ladislav greeted me at the door.

'Eva told me what happened. I'm devastated. We must call the police.'

'Not yet. I want to know the who and the why of what's behind this before I involve the authorities.'

'You sound like you know what you're talking about,' he said.

I nodded, figuring I should explain a little. 'I investigate cases of financial fraud and fix failing businesses. I've learned a few things along the way.'

'If there is anything I can do, please ask. I've arranged to have a twenty-four-hour security service on duty from today.'

There was a flight that evening to Glasgow via Amsterdam and a return at the crack of sparrows next morning. I asked Eva to book them for me and to keep my room on for the time being. Matravers answered on the first ring.

'I'll be in Glasgow tonight.'

'And you have the transparencies?'

'Of course. But you only get them if you're straight with me.'

'Come to my office in the morning.'

'You'll have to meet me this evening. I'm on the first plane back to Prague tomorrow. Come to the airport.'

'Better than that. Stay at my place and I'll run you back in the morning. I'm only fifteen minutes from there. What time do you land?'

'Nine forty-five.'

'Here's my address. Get a taxi and Mrs Mac will have something hot waiting for you and we'll take a bottle of fine old whisky to wash it down.'

Eva summoned a cab for me. I climbed into the back and peered out at the traffic as we headed for the highway and the airport. To say I felt wound up like a coiled spring was an understatement – more like a bomb with a dodgy timer. I closed my eyes and breathed through my nose, relaxing the tension in my body.

I'd thought I was coming here to head off an awkward situation between my two oldest friends. But this was like wrestling a ghostly playwright – all words and no substance. I mustn't let emotion cloud my judgement, though; Liz's freedom relied on my ability to see things rationally.

I forced myself to think things through. What was certain? Answer – very little. Back at Burgh Island, Liz had said Matravers was to put Vanda Brazda's painting up for sale at five million dollars. Liz had been tasked with dotting the t's and crossing the i's or vice versa. That's all I knew. I'd need to get the rest out of Matravers. In the meantime, though, I had plenty of questions. Was this linked to the auction? If not, then why would anyone snatch Liz? I guess her dad was worth a few bob, but she'd only been in Prague a few hours and this had been a last-minute trip. Surely, if someone was planning a ransom demand they'd put a bit more planning into it? And besides, with her parents on a cruise, how were they going to press their demands? But then Matravers was desperate to get his hands on the transparencies, which definitely made it sound as if this had something to do with the painting. Was someone trying to get their hands on the proceeds from the picture's sale? I can't say I'd taken to Matravers from our dealings so far and Liz's father clearly didn't think much of him. Was he behind all this? Could he sell the painting, keep the cash and tell the owner that the kidnappers had forced it out of him? Liz's dad had said he was a lousy businessman; was he that desperate for money?

I needed to dial down the heat and shine a light on the truth on this one and I knew just the man to help me: my old friend, mentor and ex-boss, David Lansdowne. He'd set up the opportunity with Race Engineering that had paid off my debts and cleared my name when I'd been accused of fraud.

'I need a favour.' The line was crystal clear, like David was sitting next to me in the cab, not back in his office in Stratford Upon Avon.

'How can I help, Jake?' he said, his smooth delivery and crisp diction immediately reassuring.

'I'm on my way to meet a fine arts dealer, Langdon Matravers, in Glasgow tonight. I hear his business is on the ropes and I need to know everything I can about him.'

'Of course. Tell me what you have. Where shall I send the report?'

That was David – no whys and wherefores – just *give me the details*.

'I get into Glasgow Airport from Prague at quarter to ten this evening. Could someone from your partner office in Glasgow meet me with it?'

'Twenty-one, forty-five.' David was writing it all down. 'Consider it done. To be put in your hands on arrival.'

I took Liz's phone out of my bag and switched it on, then went through her stored numbers and dialled her messenger service. A bunch from me and an increasingly pissed off Nellie. Nothing from Matravers and one from her mum sounding put out that she hadn't been called but hoping Liz was *having a nice time*. Liz's last outgoing call was to Nellie on Sunday morning. So much for the lifeline she never went anywhere without.

Back at Prague airport, I checked in and sat in departures with a coffee. Time for a good ponder. My working life was all about unpicking the remains of dead or dying enterprises. It had taught me a lot about resolving complex situations, but I was going to need everything I'd learned for this one. And more besides – a kidnap was not something I'd come across before. Time to rope in a professional. Detective Sergeant Guy Cooper was the copper I'd found myself working closely with on the Race Engineering palaver and we'd got along well – like a factory on fire, in fact.

'Do you ever do any work?' I asked him, over the sound of screaming engines in an outdoorsy environment.

'I'm up at Donnington on a day off.' He shouted. 'Hang on – let me find somewhere quieter.'

'That's better. Motorbikes again. Are you racing or watching?'

'Watching. As usual. What can I do for you?'

'I'm in Prague, about to get on a plane to Glasgow.'

'What a glamorous life you lead.'

'My friend, Liz, has been kidnapped and I'm going to find out why.'

'That's got my attention. So why are you getting on a plane? Do you think you're next?'

'It's complicated. I'm on my way to see her boss, who knows more than he's telling.'

'You need to speak to the local force in Prague.'

'And I will. But Liz's boss is either scared or a bloody good actor. He's being tight-lipped so I'm going to extract the truth from him.'

'Try not to leave any bruises.'

'Thanks for the tip. I'm hoping I can use you as a sounding board as I pick my way through this.'

'Kidnap is *not* my specialist area, but I can dial into the relevant expertise when required. But no heroics this time – let's do it properly.'

I sipped at my lukewarm coffee and threw it away in disgust. I reeled off my mental checklist. I was confident that the report I'd get on Matravers from David would tell me all I needed to know about his finances and now, through Cooper, I had access to any police expertise I might need. But I'd keep him at arm's length so he couldn't interfere if I had to do something that was not strictly legal to sort this mess out. What about local knowledge? Eva was proving really helpful, and I reckoned Ladislav would lend a hand if I needed him to – but I had a better answer. If I could find her.

Never far from my thoughts, Kat was smart, incisive and she'd grown up in Prague, knew its people and its ways. And from what I knew of her history, she'd trodden some of its meanest streets. If anyone could help me, she could. But would she?

We'd got to know each other whilst I was sorting out Race Engineering. She'd been seeing Carina Race – Allen's sister – when I first met her, but circumstances had thrown us together in a way I was truly grateful for. She was shrewd, intelligent and tough-minded. The kind of ally I could rely on. We'd been there for each other. For a while, anyway. But then she'd gone back to London, and I didn't have a number for her. The only thing I did have was the name of the hotel she used to work in. Maybe they could help? I found a smartly uniformed chap at the information desk.

'I need the phone number for a London hotel. Can you help me?'

'Of course, Sir, give me the details.' He was back in less than a minute. 'Here you are.'

'Thanks.'

The number rang.

'I'm trying to trace Kat Dominova. She worked with you before she moved to Stratford Upon Avon. We've lost touch. Can you help?'

'Kat, yes. I'll put you through to personnel.'

When the extension was answered, I explained myself again.

'You're in luck,' she said. 'I'm sure you understand that I can't hand out an employee's details without their permission but if you give me your number, I'll pass it on.'

'She's back with you? Thank you, that's very kind. Would you also give a message to her please? Simply this: I'd really appreciate her advice about an important matter – a situation in Prague, where I'm staying. Things have turned ugly.'

It was after 10.30 in the evening by the time I reached an almost empty Arrivals Hall at Glasgow Airport. Just one person was waiting there. Her black motorcycle leathers were sprayed-on tight and her long, fair hair was loose around her shoulders. Her silver helmet rested on the floor between the toes of her tightly laced biker-boots.

'Jake Elderfield?' she asked in a broad Glaswegian accent.

I nodded.

'May I see some identification, please?'

She studied my passport before grinning and handing over an envelope. It felt a little like being served with a writ – a process I'd initiated against others but never experienced myself.

'Thank you,' she said. 'This may be the closest I ever get to a part in a spy film.' She blew me a cheeky kiss and in one neat move, swept up her hair and pulled her helmet back on.

I followed her out into a black, breezy night. A sleepy driver in a lonesome cab was reading his paper. I handed him the address, and we moved off at a leisurely pace. I put on the reading light and tore open the envelope. The leaves of A4 made grim reading. I finished just as the cab swung between a pair of stone pillars, each with a rusting iron gate hanging drunkenly from it. The driver swore as we slalomed along the pot-holed gravel driveway between a forest of pine trees.

The stately house at the end of our journey was backlit by moonlight, which was more than sufficient for me to see that the old building was in dire need of some TLC. It was a large property, four floors and two considerable wings. A hexagonal tower stood at the left-hand end, with a stonking pile of rubble marking the spot where the one on the right used to be. Lights blazed from every window on the left side of the building. The ones on the right remained in utter darkness.

The driveway swept around a large circular pond in front of the house. A statue of some ancient laird stood on a plinth in the middle – pleased, I'm sure, to be facing away from his crumbling mansion. We parked up between the pond and the imposing porch with double doors and worn stone steps, and I paid the driver and clambered out.

Ancient coaching lights, either side of the doors, flickered then glowed dimly as I approached the steps. The left-hand door opened.

'Good evening, Mr Elderfield, and welcome to Matravers House.' Langdon Mungo Matravers – as I now knew him from David's report – spoke loudly, in a cultured accent, an ingratiating smile on his face. He was tall, well over six foot, and slim, wearing an old-fashioned velvet smoking jacket in a decadent burgundy. His white-collared, green pin-striped, open-necked shirt was paired with a dark green silk cravat, grey trousers and brown leather slippers. I estimated him to be fiftyish and, with his bushy eyebrows and greying sideburns under a floppy mop of collar-length, dark hair, he looked like his description on the page I'd just read: a man of privilege, an ex-public-school boy more focused on his hedonistic lifestyle than the things most people would consider important.

My jeans, loafers, sweater and reasonably smart but comfortable leather jacket made an excellent contrast to his outfit.

'Come in, come in,' he said eagerly.

He took my bag through the oak-panelled hallway and up a flight of stairs. He seemed in a hurry.

'Hope you'll be comfortable in here.'

The room was old-fashioned, high ceilinged and huge, with a definite nip in the air. It occurred to me it could be straight out of a full-on baronial Scottish set piece – the kind of thing Sir Walter Scott would have pictured if he was writing in a high fever. A large stone fireplace held a grate bearing a couple of smouldering logs, and the four-poster looked like a genuine antique, although it was difficult to tell if there was actually a mattress and pillows under the pile of blankets and sheets or just a handful of planks and a couple of breeze blocks. The mouldering, depressingly patterned floor covering had shivered away from the skirting boards, leaving a couple of rows of gnarled floorboards around the edge.

'Bathroom's next door. I'll be in the dining room – back downstairs and in front of you. Hot food and whisky await you as promised.'

I left my bag on the bed and freshened up, then went in search of my host.

'Ah, there you are. Sit ye down. Mrs Mac has dug out haggis, neeps and tatties and made us some onion gravy to go with. Let me pour you a drop of the good stuff.'

The dining room could best be described as faded-stately. A collection of offensive weapons – long shiny swords, short, evil-looking knives, muskets and pistols – filled one wall, in a kind of Catherine Wheel of arms, while a massive, gloomy painting over the fireplace showed a large number of brave clansmen being slaughtered by a line of cowardly Redcoats as Bonny Prince Charlie looked on. At least it was warm in here, though, with a hearty fire in the grate.

Two places had been set at the near end of the long, but otherwise bare, dining table of polished oak. My host was already seated, glass in hand. He looked at me searchingly as he poured scotch into a cut-glass tumbler in front of me. I put my hand over the glass when he reached a quarter full and topped it up with water from a nearby jug. He filled his glass to the brim. There was a profound falseness about his cheerful bonhomie. 'Tuck in, tuck in.' He cast aside the metal cover from his crest-bearing plate to reveal a mound of steaming food. I followed his lead.

'Help yourself to gravy.'

As I poured, he spoke anxiously. 'Have you got them?'

I patted the breast-pocket of my jacket.

'You know the score. I want full and frank disclosure first.'

He took a long pull at his drink, emptying half his glass in one swallow. I swooped on the plate of hot food like a hungry seagull.

'OK. But if you breathe a word of this to anyone, I'm finished.'

I said nothing, obliging him to fill the silence.

'I was doing an antiques sweep in Prague when I was asked to look at a painting…'

'A Klimt,' I said.

'It was the right age, good work, but unsigned and when I looked more closely, I decided it was probably painted by one of his students, perhaps helped along by the master himself.'

'Liz said it was worth five million.'

Matravers had both his hands around his whisky glass.

'I needed her to believe that.'

'Keep talking if you want the transparencies,' I mumbled between greedy mouthfuls.

He waved the whisky bottle in my direction and topped up his own glass when I declined.

'When I met the picture's owner, I told her I estimated its value at twenty thousand dollars.'

'Rather less than five million – what were you up to?'

He dropped his head, blinked his eyes and sighed. 'I'll tell you the whole story. She said she'd think about it. Then she invited me for dinner and drinks. Well, one thing led to another, and I found myself in a private members' area of her fancy nightclub. I met a couple of provocatively dressed young lassies. They offered me some of their Colombian marching powder and I thought it'd be rude not to. After that, I kind of lost track…'

'What happened?'

'I woke up in my hotel room next morning, on top of the bed, fully clothed. My posterior hurt like hell. It's not felt like that since I was at school having it warmed by the headmaster. My back and rear were covered in slash marks and bruises. I racked my brains, but I couldn't remember what had happened.' He refilled his glass and drank thirstily.

'And then?'

'As I was pulling myself together, my phone rang. I was asked if I'd enjoyed myself last night. After I'd stopped swearing, there was laughter, and I was told a car would pick me up in half an hour for a private screening of a new video about to be released. I could collect a set of souvenir stills to remind me of the hospitality I'd enjoyed. They'd be keeping the master. I'd also find out what I would need to do to stop the next screening being less private.'

'What can you tell me about the person who phoned you?'

'Male, spoke excellent English with an accent. I think Russian or something Eastern European.'

'What did he want you to do?'

'To falsify a provenance and to put a sales pack together for a newly discovered, authentic painting. And then to organise its auction.'

'And I suppose he said you'd have to sell it for five million.'

'That's right.'

'What if you refused or couldn't manage it?'

'He'd release all the material he was holding, and I'd be ruined.' He studied his empty glass and shook his head slowly before reaching for the bottle.

'I can't believe that would be enough to persuade you to commit a major fraud like that. What on earth made you think you could get away with it?'

All his bluster had evaporated. He was raw now, the

layers of bullshit and bravado blown away. 'I don't think you understand how this business works. The Matravers name means something in this business. We have a fine reputation built over many years. My father and grandfather built this company and made it what it is today. It could all be wiped away by the merest hint of scandal.' He put his head down and swallowed, wouldn't look me in the eye. 'I'm desperate, nearly broke and he said he'd pay a commission. And there's something else. Something I did in my younger years that I'm not very proud of. If that ever came out, I really would be finished in this business.'

I let that rest for the moment – I could have asked what the *something else* was, but I already knew the answer, thanks to David's notes – and moved the conversation along. 'Weren't you taking a big risk sending Liz? She might have taken one look at the painting and agreed with your first valuation.'

He still couldn't look me in the eye. 'I briefed her very carefully; how the picture was a rare find and told her the provenance proved beyond all doubt that despite first appearances, it was entirely genuine.'

'So you lied.'

He hung his head again, like a five-year-old caught with his hands in the biscuit barrel. 'I didn't think she'd have any problems. It was just a question of photographing the picture, agreeing the details and getting the contract signed.'

'You couldn't face going back there, could you?'

He took another pull at his whisky and squared his shoulders, but remained silent.

'You made Liz an accessory to fraud.'

He stared at me balefully.

'What happened next?'

'I got another phone call on Sunday morning when Liz

was en route. A Klimt had just sold for twenty-five million dollars in the States. That weekend's *International Herald Tribune* covered the story.'

I reached for my drink and gulped down a deep swallow. 'Same chap?'

'Yes. It was pretty obvious what he was thinking. I said it was ludicrous to believe this picture could raise that kind of money. I'd be a laughing stock if I tried. He asked why I wasn't one already.'

The whisky was working on him like a truth serum.

'Go on.'

'My instructions were to sell the painting through an internet auction next Monday, whilst there was still a buzz in the market. I told him I needed longer.'

'Was that true?'

'He'd been sniffing around. My new website is fully developed, tested and ready for its first auction. So, no, he knew I was lying.

'Monday was my deadline and he said I'd regret it if I didn't comply. Then the line went dead.'

'Why didn't you call the police?'

Matravers opened and closed his mouth, like a dolphin parted from the sea, before spluttering a response. 'The potential for reputational damage was too great. If any of this got out…' He lifted his glass again, spilling a little as he put it down. 'I was naïve enough to think I'd convinced him. After all, five million is a lot of money. The market is buoyant at the moment and I was confident I could put something convincing together to justify the price.'

'Liz was snatched from her hotel on Sunday night.'

'And on Monday morning, I received another phone call. From the same gent. He said Liz would be his guest until after the auction. Unless I did as I was told, they would transport her back to Scotland and make me watch while they tortured her. They'd make me write a note confessing to her murder and I'd be found hanging in the same room as her body.'

'I take it you agreed to his wishes after that.'

'What choice did I have?'

I took out my sheaf of papers summarising Matravers' personal circumstances.

'They chose their mark well, didn't they?'

'What do you mean?'

'You excelled at school, didn't you? Bullying, gambling, drinking and cheating at your exams. It's a wonder you weren't expelled. As it is, you left with no appreciable qualifications and joined Daddy's firm. When your father died, you inherited everything and set about spending it like a hero. You must be very proud.'

Matravers looked somehow older and more frail now, and his hand shook when he reached for his glass.

'And there's that other matter you skipped over.'

'What do you mean?'

'The *something else* you mentioned earlier. The fact that when it comes to forgery, you have form.'

He stayed silent.

'My researchers are very thorough. Just after you joined the firm, someone paid a significant sum for a picture that proved to be a fake. It cost the business a considerable amount of money to keep the matter quiet. Photographs of your sexual peccadilloes might be personally embarrassing for you but tangible proof that you're a forger and a cheat would be the end of Matravers Fine Arts, wouldn't it?'

He looked miserable; I thought he might even cry.

'Last chance. All bets are off unless you're *completely* straight with me. Tell me about this private members' area.'

'It's in the club's basement. Vanda Brazda took me down there after dinner. Lighting was low, there's comfortable seating and quiet booths around a small, brightly lit stage. Two women were pole dancing.'

'Did Vanda stay with you?'

'No. She left after she'd taken me down there. The girls came over and introduced themselves.'

'Your last memory before the blackmail incident was inside the club?'

'It's all pretty hazy but yes I think so.'

'And they offered you cocaine. Were you still drinking as well?'

His guilty look said it all.

'No wonder you're hazy about the way it unfolded. And you might easily have been slipped something extra to make sure you didn't give them any trouble.'

He slumped in his chair and ran his hand through his tousled mop of hair.

'How much were you promised if the auction was successful?'

'Beg pardon?'

'You might as well tell me. If the kidnapper shares the proceeds, you'll be guilty of aiding and abetting. He'll probably keep his hands on all the blackmail material for extra leverage. Who knows what he might tell you to do next?' I was reminded of the stained-glass windows in Brazda's club. 'You'll be like a dancer in a gilded cage – doing your best to look like you're enjoying it but locked up with no way out.'

He reached for the whisky bottle. I was quicker, moving it to my side of the table. He sighed.

'Five percent on a minimum sale price of twenty million,' he mumbled.

'One million dollars,' I said through pursed lips.

'I'm being short-changed. I'd normally expect a buyer's premium and a commission that would come to rather more than that.'

'Have you heard what you're saying? Liz is locked up, God knows where, and you're complaining about your share of the booty?' I bit back my anger and reasoned aloud. 'We can't be sure of the extent of Vanda's involvement. But she put the painting up for sale and your two seductresses were in her club. She may not be the ringmaster, but I'd say she's in the circus.'

Matravers nodded thoughtfully.

'What about your private screening; who did you meet there?'

'Just the driver. He kept his mouth shut and showed me to a basement office with a video screen. The stills were in an envelope on the desk, and my instructions came through the voice-over.'

'What a mess you've made. The question is what are we going to do about it?'

'Please, without those transparencies I can't set up the auction,' he whined.

'We could get Vanda pulled in for questioning.'

Matravers looked like he was about to protest.

I held up my hand to stop him. 'But I don't want to alert the kidnappers that we're on to them.'

Matravers closed his eyes and sighed. I put the whisky bottle back within his reach. He nodded gratefully and drained the bottle.

'For Liz's sake, not yours.'

'Of course, of course,' he said, hurriedly.

'Tell me about your website. You say you're virtually bust

yet you hired a top-flight designer who has built in all sorts of bells and whistles that must have cost you a fortune.'

'It's my last chance. Look, I may have done some shady deals in times of need but I know my way around this business. The internet will be the future of auctioneering – you wait and see. And I wanted to be at the forefront of that, to really put this business back on track. That's why I sought out the best man I could find to do the job. And of course he was available – he's a consultant these days and he'd just finished a contract for the Navy up at Faslane.'

'Let's hope it doesn't send you on your way to the bankruptcy court. For Liz's sake, we need to keep the kidnappers believing you're committed to delivering your end of the bargain. I'll need to talk to your developer and satisfy myself that your internet site will deliver.'

'That's no problem.' Matravers reached into his pocket, took out his wallet and passed a business card to me. 'Here's his details.' The strain showed on his face now and he hadn't touched his food.

It was time, I thought, to put him out of his misery. I took the transparencies from my pocket and placed them on the table in front of me. 'How do you contact the kidnapper?'

His eyes followed my every move. 'He said he'd call every day for a progress report.'

'When's your next call?'

'Tomorrow some time.'

'Tell him you have a silent business partner who's now in charge of this. Me. You give him my phone number and from now on he talks to me and only me. I'll take his calls at six pm each day. I'll expect a progress report from you every day before I speak to him.'

'He won't like that.'

'I don't care if he likes it or not. If he wants his twenty million, he'll do it.'

'I can't agree. It's too big a risk.'

'You *will* agree. If you attempt this auction without my backup, I'll make sure the blackmailer is the least of your worries.'

He reached for his whisky, draining the glass dry.

'And you only get these transparencies if you play by my rules. Agreed?'

He looked down at the table with furrowed brows, squared his shoulders and, for the first time, looked directly at me. 'Agreed.'

I pushed the envelope across the table, so it landed just this side of his hand. 'You'd better run that damned auction to the deadline or you'll have me to answer to. I'll see myself out.'

I phoned for a cab, I stomped upstairs, retrieved my bag and went outside to wait for it.

6 | WEDNESDAY MORNING 15TH OCTOBER

I spent an uncomfortable night at the airport lying across a bank of seats in Departures. My phone rang at 4am. It was Nellie.

'People will talk if you keep calling me in the middle of the night.'

'What's happening, Jake? Have you spoken to Liz yet?'

I told him the whole sordid tale. He was understandably horrified.

'I'll get on the next plane to Prague.'

'How long have you known me, Nellie?'

'What's that got to do with anything?'

'It's got to be what? Fifteen years? And have I ever let you down?'

'No, Jake, never. But…'

'Listen, my friend. I'm good at this stuff. Let me do the groundwork and as soon as I have a good reason to bring you to Prague, I will. I promise. In the meantime, stay positive, do your job and let me do mine.'

'But…'

'It's cool, Nellie. As soon as I have any news I'll tell you straight away.'

It took a while to convince him to stay put, and in the end, it was being honest that did it. 'Look, Nellie, I don't want you there, OK? Not yet. You'll get in the way and I don't want you doing anything that might put Liz in further danger. If you stay put, and let me handle it, I'll let you know as soon as it's OK for you to come.'

'I'll be ready as soon as you say the word.'

It seemed like I'd just closed my eyes when the phone rang again. I looked at my watch. It was 6.30am.

'Hello?'

'I got your message.'

I sat up and rubbed my face into wakefulness. 'Kat – it's so great to hear your voice.'

'Sorry to call so early but I'm on breakfasts today. What's happened?'

'My friend Liz, we're close, I think of her as my sister – she's been snatched from her hotel, and the kidnappers won't release her unless her boss runs a crooked auction.'

'That's awful. How can I help?'

'The whole thing seems to centre around a nightclub called the Dark Goddess and the woman who runs it.' I paused. The line had gone silent. 'Are you still there?'

'You mean Vanda. Vanda Brazda.'

'Yes. Do you know her?'

'I used to. A long time ago.'

'I need everything I can find out about her and her associates if I'm going to get Liz out of this situation.'

'These are dangerous people, Jake.'

'Just tell me what you know.'

'It's time I faced up to what happened all those years ago. I'll sort a flight and call you back.'

The line went dead before I could protest. I was awake now, so I thought I might as well use the time productively. I fished out the business card that Matravers had given me last night.

The phone was answered after two rings. 'Good morning. Quentin Bailey speaking.'

'Morning. I'm Jake Elderfield; call me Jake. Hope you don't mind the early call but I'm sitting here waiting for a plane with time on my hands.'

'No problem, I'm in the office. What can I do for you?'

'Langdon Matravers gave me your card last night. His auction on Monday has become pivotal to resolving a situation I'm working on in Prague and I thought I should brief you.'

'I'm listening.'

I outlined things in as few words as possible. 'So, you see why I can leave no room for failure.'

'That's understood, Jake. And it's probably just as well that Matravers chose me to build his site. I trained with the Royal Navy's CIS team – that's communication and information systems. I'm used to making things bomb proof, just in case.'

'I'd like to get a demo when we can,' I said.

'Say the word and I'll set it up.'

'I'll be in touch.'

The plane ride back via 'Hamster-Jam' was half-empty and pretty relaxed, a good time to think through a plan to deal with the complicated situation I'd put myself in. OK – here we go. The kidnappers were holding Liz. To get her out, Matravers would have to auction a painting for twenty million dollars that he estimated to be worth twenty thousand dollars. Ridiculous. David's papers suggested he was a talented auctioneer – when he stayed off the booze and focused on the job. So, maybe there was a chance. Next problem, given Liz's skill for ferreting out the truth and telling it like it is, I could easily imagine the kidnappers deciding it would be better not to risk letting her share whatever she'd learned about them with the authorities – which meant it would be good to get her out as soon as possible. But I wouldn't be able to do that until I knew *where* they were keeping her. And, even if I did discover her location, the kidnappers would be at their wariest now, wondering if we would go through with the auction. That in turn meant that, as long as I could convince them we would cooperate, the time to rescue Liz would be just after the auction. With the picture sold, their guard would be down. And that of course gave me a bit more time to figure out where they were holding her. Which left three questions: how could I guarantee they would keep her safe until after the auction; make sure she didn't annoy her captors too much; and facilitate the successful sale of a fake painting without ending up in jail myself?

Still, even if I didn't have the answers to those questions, nor a plan, exactly, at least I knew what I was up against. With that, I fell into a troubled sleep, worrying about what Liz must be going through and dreaming of Kat, feeling guilty at dragging her into this mess. I woke with the captain's announcement of our imminent arrival in Prague ringing in my ears. Better for a sleep, I was feeling much more bullish. With Kat's help, I'd crack this. Besides, I'd had my first big idea. And this one wasn't any old firework that would whizz, bang and phut. Oh no, this was a loud, proud, fly-me-to-the-moon rocket of an idea.

It was half twelve and I was on the right side of passport control at Prague-Ruzyně Airport and gagging for a coffee. I switched on my phone and dialled my answer machine.

Kat's voice came through. 'I'm on the next plane from Heathrow landing early this afternoon. Will you meet me at the airport?' I left a message agreeing to her plan.

The Arrivals board showed I'd got plenty of time for caffeine, so with a trusty mug of the hot stuff in front of me, I got on the dog and bone once more. First call was to the Goldcrest to see about a room for Kat. It was Eva who answered, and we agreed she could use Liz's for the time being. Next was Detective Sergeant Guy Cooper, sounding very official this morning. I briefed him on what I'd learned last night.

'Let me see if I've got this straight. The kidnappers have Matravers over a barrel. They've given him a strong incentive to succeed and promised a nasty end if he fails. He's to run his online auction on Monday, having knocked up a false provenance and recruited a bunch of potential bidders and he's got to raise at least twenty million dollars. And now you've put yourself right in the firing line by becoming the chief negotiator with the kidnappers. What's your game plan?'

'I've thought of a way to keep Liz safe while she's in the kidnappers' hands.'

'Nice one. What are you thinking?'

'I'm going to sell them an idea – a way of turning their one-off dodgy profit into an ongoing revenue stream – and stress it's an option as long as I have a healthy Liz to help me make it work.'

'Not sure I want to hear this.'

'There's no intention of actually doing it; it's just a way of building trust to make sure they don't do anything I might regret.'

'OK – so what follows?'

'Today's Wednesday. The auction has to run on Monday. I'm thinking we go in straight after the sale, round up the kidnappers and get Liz out of there. That gives me four clear days plus a few odd hours to find out where they're keeping her.'

'Where will the auction be held?'

'Glasgow. It'll be hosted from the auctioneer's office and that's a problem for me. I can't be in two places at once, minding Matravers and getting Liz out.'

'Let me have a word with the boss. Maybe I can go and hold Matravers' hand while you rescue your friend.'

'Might that be possible?'

'Absolutely. And if the boss objects, I'm owed leave.'

'Thanks, man. There's something else too. I really want these people to suffer for their offences. I'm assuming that intent to perform a crime wouldn't be treated as harshly as an actual crime.'

'That's right. Although I'm not an expert on international law. But if the crime is carried out, actual harm will be caused and that carries a more severe sentence than intent. And stealing twenty million dollars will add a significant penalty.'

'That's what I thought. Another good reason to resolve this *after* the auction has taken place. I'll ring you when I have some more news. The next week will be tough on Liz. But she'll survive. She captained the women's hockey team at uni and I watched some of her matches. God help them if she gets her hands on a hockey stick.'

My phone rang almost as soon as I put it down. No number showed on the display.

'Jake Elderfield?' It was a pleasant-sounding male voice, speaking accented English.

'Yes. Who's this?'

'You are expecting my call.'

Time to put the first part of part of my plan into action. 'If you're who I think you are, I said six tonight.'

'I understand. But I know you met Langdon Matravers last night and I have spoken to him. I thought we should speak as soon as possible.'

'Future calls need to be each day at six.'

'You understand my requirements?'

'I do. Now you need to hear mine.'

'You're an interesting character, Jake. May I call you Jake? You trained as an accountant, and you specialise in business turnarounds. You have had brushes with the law and have also enjoyed a recent major success. But I am intrigued. What do you know about Fine Art?'

'Nothing. But Liz does and she's an old friend.'

'Ah, so that's how you have become involved with Mr Matravers?'

'His is a classic failing business and that's my subject. But your plan interests me. Take a fake painting, add a false provenance produced by an expert, sell it to the highest bidder through a third-party internet auction, make a lot of money, rinse and repeat?'

'Rinse and repeat? I don't understand.'

'Simply this. Wait a while, then do it again.'

'Turn a one-off into an ongoing income stream? Yes, why not?'

'It's an excellent idea and if we became partners, it would allow me to turn Matravers' Fine Art around.'

'You would like to be part of this future plan?'

'For a different deal, of course. Liz provides the expertise, you source the pictures, Matravers sells them. We split the profits.'

'The way this picture came to us was sheer luck. How could we source more pictures?'

'Liz has the knowledge and the capacity to identify the opportunities. It will be a question of which artists, what subjects and market appetite. With Liz's help, you'd identify painters who were both capable and prepared to create pictures that could have been produced by great artists and Liz would oversee their work to ensure it meets her specification. Matravers would front the auctions under my direction.'

'Would this not get you into trouble with your police?'

'I wouldn't be rushing to tell them.'

'What about your friend, Detective Sergeant Cooper?'

'Why do you think he's my friend? I keep him sweet.'

'Ah. I'm beginning to understand. This is a very interesting idea.'

'I only need one thing from you to make this work.'

'Please, what is that?'

'Liz's safe return. As soon as she's back with me, I can brief her and get her working on the next picture.'

'You have a good idea, Jake, but you go too fast. You and I don't yet know each other. We need to do this first transaction and if it goes smoothly, we can talk more. Miss Lowsonford stays with me until then.'

'I understand. But I need your absolute guarantee that you'll keep her safe and well until we have done business together.'

'You have that.'

'As you say we don't know each other yet. I need evidence that you're keeping your word.'

'What do you suggest?'

'A daily fax showing Liz – fit, healthy and holding a copy of that day's newspaper.'

'Where should I send this?'

'Fax it to Matravers.'

'This I can do.'

'Then I will speak to you at six pm.'

'I will call you on this number.'

I kept an eye on the Arrivals board. When Kat's plane landed, I moved to where I'd be able to see her come through from the baggage area.

There was a small rush of Brits piling through – you could tell by their dress, their luggage and the way they were brandishing guidebooks. And it helped that they were speaking English in loud voices too. But no Kat. I guessed she must be in the loo or pursuing a lost bag. I was about to ring her when a woman wandered past then turned back towards me.

'Say, do you know where I can catch a bus into town?' she drawled in a Midwest accent.

She wore bootcut blue jeans, black ankle boots and a stylish black leather jacket over a Chicago Bears sweatshirt. I could hear the tinny rasp of rock music leaking from the skinny headphones draped around her neck. A Sony discman was clipped to a pouch on her belt. Her only luggage was a well-travelled khaki canvas shoulder bag. Large sunglasses and a dark bob of hair covered most of her face. I was about to reply when she came in close, pulled her glasses down her nose and looked up into my eyes. She spoke quietly, her lips curving into a discrete smile. I thought I'd remembered every detail of her face, but it gave me goosebumps to have her standing right there in front of me. Her pale, smooth complexion and grey-blue eyes took my breath away…

'What's this? You don't recognise me, Mr Jake. After all we've been through together?' She put her finger to her lips before I could respond. 'Why don't you offer me a ride in the cab you're going to hire?'

She'd got me again. Her talent for changing her appearance – and persona – had slipped to the back of my mind: when I'd first met her, she'd had dark hair (which turned out to be a wig) and was acting as Carina Race's maid, complete with uniform; the next time, she was blonde and dressed to seduce.

I gave a grin as I remembered that particular evening, and replied in a voice loud enough to be overheard as we walked, side by side to the taxi rank, like two polite strangers who'd just met. I offered up the occasional polite smile as we waited in the queue. It was a relief to ditch our bags into the boot and settle into the back seat of the cab. We'd been close; she'd even lived with me – albeit staying in the spare room – for a short while, before she decided to move back to London. Should I hug her? Shake hands? Give her a kiss? I was no good at this stuff.

'How did you get through passport control looking like that?'

She laughed. 'I only put my wig and sunglasses on after they'd seen my papers. I waited in the bathroom until everyone who was on the plane would have cleared through with their baggage.'

'Why the disguise?'

'Vanda was connected with some sort of syndicate and I got on the wrong side of them. There's a good chance they have people at the airport who might remember me.'

'Well, it certainly fooled me.'

She rewarded me with another smile, much larger than the last. 'Anyone can put on a wig, sunglasses and a different outfit but if you really want to become someone else, you have to think yourself into their life, their personality and back story. You know, the people who are best at this are like chameleons; they don't need props. They might change their hair style, but they will stand differently, use facial expressions to project a new personality, change their accent and use an altered vocabulary. One day I will be this good.'

'Right.'

'I only had a little time, after you called, to prepare, so I browsed a local charity shop for inspiration. I met a girl from Chicago after I escaped to Dresden. Martina Novotná, she had a Czech father and an American mother, and when I saw these boots and shirt, I knew that's what she'd be wearing to travel. She was a big fan of rock music, so I picked up some Billy Idol and Aerosmith CDs and the player. Everything else was already mine – you'll remember the black wig from Carina's.'

'You're really good at this stuff, aren't you?'

'I should have been an actress or a spy,' she beamed.

'How have you been?' I asked.

She smiled. 'OK,' she said. 'Really OK.'

'Great.'

She put her sunglasses in her shoulder bag. 'Suppose you tell me what's going on.'

I ran through the whole story – Liz, Nellie, my mission of mercy and what I'd learned so far.

'Vanda was my dance instructor. The one I fell in love with.'

'She was why you left Prague all those years ago?'

She patted my hand. 'I'll tell you the whole story some day, I promise.'

She put her glasses back on and looked out of the window, silent until we reached the hotel.

***

They were waiting for me inside. Two men in "business casual" clothes. Both young; in their twenties, one guy built for comfort not speed, although it was nothing a diet and a little exercise wouldn't fix. I'd nearly met the other chap on Charles Bridge – my friend, the cooking apple.

'Hello again,' I said to him, offering a friendly smile. I glanced at their official-looking, photo ID cards and their unpronounceable names.

Apple-man's English was excellent. 'Jake Elderfield? Please come with us. We have questions,' he said, scowling back at me.

I thought of him as hard and sour: perhaps Bramley would be a good name.

'What's this about?'

'We'll talk at our offices.'

I left Kat with Eva and went outside to the waiting Skoda, where Comfort Man opened the rear door for me. They got in the front and spoke to each other in calm, quiet Czech as we drove along busy streets passing ambling pedestrians and bustling shops.

It was difficult to know how this would go. I wasn't prepared to level with them just yet, figuring it would be best to work out my lyrics once they gave me the tune.

The Skoda swung into an underground car park, and we took the lift up to the third floor of a modern office block. I followed them through a bright open plan space, and into a ubiquitous meeting room with beige walls, grey carpet, a wood-grain effect table, four very average office chairs and a distant view of the castle. They were formal yet polite, leaving me there while they went off to do something far more important. I sat. Then I got up and stood by the window to admire the nondescript view of this modern, drab part of town. The hands of my watch took flight, seeming to spin round while I contemplated this waste of valuable time. Still, it was a good chance to mull over my priorities for when I got out of here.

After a couple of centuries, Bramley came back in with four coffees and took a seat. I sat next to him. The door opened again and two further men came in. They were both older and obviously more senior; the first, who made me think of a schoolteacher, in his crumpled brown suit, seemed content to let the other guy take charge. The latter, dressed in a smart grey double-breasted suit, black shirt and pale striped tie, looked like an interesting character. Maybe in his fifties? He had jet-black hair that I guessed was dyed and the kind of luxuriant moustache I'd always imagined adorning the face of First World War pilots. He took the chair opposite me. Moustache-Man introduced himself as Gabriel Lambert and the other man as Chief Inspector Jakub Havlíček.

I took a plastic cup from the tray, tried it and waited. Lambert picked up his coffee and sipped cautiously, put down the cup and flicked an immaculate white handkerchief across his moustache. He spoke in slow, heavily accented English. Havlíček took his turn at the coffee and said nothing.

'Most people who come to Prague stay for a week or so, view the sights and go home. But not you, Mr Elderfield. You flew in on Monday night. On Tuesday morning, you visited a night club – an odd thing to do in daylight hours, wouldn't you agree? In the afternoon you caught a flight to Amsterdam and on to Glasgow and now here you are again.' He stared at me inquiringly. 'My colleague followed you as far as Old Town Square. And later, Charles Bridge. When we received the arrivals submissions from your hotel, we put a name to your face and checked your travel arrangements.' He looked at me expectantly.

'Are you Belgian?' I asked politely.

'Why? Because I'm an investigator with a moustache and a French accent? Why are you British so obsessed with a fictional Belgian detective? I'm French. Do you want me to sing "La Marseillaise" to prove it?'

'Sorry I asked.'

He sighed. 'Suppose you tell us what you are doing here?'

'Well, let's see. Currently I'm enduring your hospitality but I'm finding the conversation less than entertaining.' I turned to the man who I'd identified as Bramley, 'And whilst we're on the subject of lacklustre performances – what was all that about earlier? My uncle Sid could have done a better job of following me discreetly and he's so tall he stands out like an aardvark up a gum tree.'

Bramley sipped his coffee and didn't respond.

Lambert spoke again. 'He only needed to ensure he could recognise you from your passport photo. Once we had the hotel's documentation, we could verify your identity. I will ask you again. Why are you in Prague?'

'I came to catch up with a friend who's working here. I thought we could spend a few days enjoying this beautiful city together, but she's been too busy. She even had me run an errand to Glasgow for her.'

Bramley opened his pad and started taking notes. Havlíček kept watch and enjoyed his coffee.

'Why would you visit a nightclub when it's closed?'

Bramley looked at me, his pen poised.

'All part of the errand. A painting has been put up for sale with the auctioneers my friend works for. I was just checking some final details.'

'Vanda Brazda is selling a painting?' asked Lambert.

'You know her?'

'We're keeping an eye on her club. Why did you need to go to Glasgow?'

'The auctioneer urgently needed some publicity shots of the picture to be collected and delivered to him.'

'And your friend can confirm this?'

'Of course. But Liz is out of town for a few days.'

'And we should take your word for this?'

'Little choice until she's back on the scene next week, I'm afraid. What's your interest in Vanda Brazda and the nightclub?

Lambert cleared his throat. 'Right now, I'm interested in you, Mr Elderfield. Why is an accountant who grubs around in failing businesses visiting Vanda Brazda? Could it really be for something as mundane as transporting some photographs? Or another reason?'

'No mystery – just as I've told you.'

'Then I shall say this. This club and Vanda Brazda may be connected with certain currency irregularities, perhaps even money laundering. I would advise you to stay away from the Dark Goddess and Ms Brazda. It would be unfortunate if my colleagues found they needed to detain you as part of our investigation, wouldn't it?'

Lambert passed a business card across the table. 'Call me if you find you have anything more to tell us. We'll be keeping an eye on you.'

He put his papers back in his file and got up from the table.

'I will say *au revoir*, Mr Elderfield. You are free to go for now.'

Bramley ushered me from the room and out of the building. I hailed a cab. Once inside I checked the time. I'd better catch up with Matravers before my call with the kidnapper at six. Lambert's card came out of my pocket with the phone. It seemed I'd made a useful contact. He was a Criminal Intelligence Officer – Interpol no less – on attachment to *Policie Ceske Republiky*. If I'd known, I'd have tried to be more fascinating.

I dialled Matravers to take his report.

'I got lucky with the research for the provenance document and picked up a thread I've been able to exploit. The printers are staying on all night to typeset and produce the sales pack. Q, that's Quentin Bailey, will put everything into a document we can send over the web, and I'll courier a hard copy to each bidder over the weekend. The high-definition prints from the transparencies you brought across are costing me a fortune.'

'You spoke to the kidnapper this morning?'

'Yes, he called you?'

'He's going to send you a fax every day showing a healthy Liz – forward it to me at the hotel as soon as you receive it. Is there anything else?'

'No. All is good.'

'Just stay on schedule for Monday's auction.'

Back at the Goldcrest, I hesitated outside Kat's room. After the whole Race Engineering saga, she and I had become close as we started to rebuild our lives. I had thought our friendship might develop into something more but one night, I'd come home to a casserole in the oven, an affectionate note and an empty house. But now, she'd answered my call for help – with no questions or prevarication, just when I needed it most – and that had to be a good sign, didn't it? And I liked her. I *really* liked her. But perhaps it would be best to try to keep a lid on that till this little adventure had been dealt with.

A ripple of female laughter came from behind the door. I knocked and Kat answered it, her short blonde locks on display. She'd put her dark wig on the dressing table, next to a saucer of milk. One thing I loved about this girl was our shared sense of the ridiculous.

Eva was lying sprawled on the four-poster and there was a Kat-sized impression in the quilt next to her. Liz's things had been cleared away somewhere.

'I see you two have got to know each other.'

'Meeting Eva was a big surprise. We grew up together. I didn't recognise her at first but then it's been eight years. There was a lot to catch up on,' said Kat.

'Same old Kat now she's put aside her disguise and dropped that dreadful American accent,' laughed Eva.

'But you're completely different from the last time I saw you, with your dyed hair and curves. I didn't recognise you until you spoke,' said Kat.

'I only went blonde to be more like you,' retorted Eva.

'Now, we could be sisters,' said Kat.

A shadow passed over Eva's face.

'I'm sorry, I didn't mean…' said Kat.

'It's a long time since Ana left us and I've learned to live without her,' said Eva. 'But I'll never forgive Hendak.' She summoned up her efficient, professional persona once more and brightened, looking at her watch. 'I must relieve Ladislav for his break. Why don't we meet in the bar in an hour?'

As she left, I noticed that locking bolts had been installed on the French doors. 'Those are new.'

'Eva said Ladislav had them installed on every window and outside door,' said Kat.

I took Eva's place on the bed and Kat sat back down on the edge. 'What did the police want with you?

'They'd noticed that I wasn't behaving like a good little tourist. Who's Ana?'

'Eva had a twin sister. They were very close. Ana was always the serious one whilst Eva was full of mischief. She was devastated when Ana died. I couldn't see how she'd get through it.' She paused, reflecting. 'She's become much more like Ana now.'

'I guess that's what losing a sister must be like.' I thought of Liz then; she felt like a sister to me, and I hoped I wouldn't have to find out what it would be like to lose *her*.

Kat must have seen the wheels going round in my head. She reached out and touched my hand. 'It will be OK,' she said.

I nodded, then, to change the subject, said, 'I can't believe you and Eva know each other. What a coincidence!'

Kat explained, 'Eva, Ana and I were at dance school together. After I left Prague, Eva decided to change her life completely. She started working for Ladislav here at the Goldcrest. He has helped her so much. She used to be such a silly little thing; I almost didn't recognise her at first – she's so… sleek, so professional. I can't get over bumping into her like this.' She shook her head in disbelief.

I smiled. 'Life's funny that way. I used to work with a guy in Oxford and we were having a beer in a pub one night and got chatting. We discovered that we'd both been in Bristol two years before, on the same floor of the same building, through a set of double doors. It was the weirdest thing. He was convinced that there are fewer people in the world than they say because he kept bumping into the same ones.'

As we sat there, Kat was close enough to touch. I wanted to reach out, to stroke her hair, hold her in my arms…

'What's next?' she said, breaking into my thoughts.

I pulled myself back on track. 'We have to work out where Liz is being held.'

Kat looked thoughtful. 'There's a basement at the club.'

'I don't think she's there. Matravers says that's a private members' area for naughty goings on; you know the kind of thing – pole dancing and lots of quiet corners.'

Kat gave a wry smile. 'It was full of smoke last time I saw it. Vanda's business partner was using the basement to make drugs. He was a gangster, smooth but hard as nails.'

'What was his name?'

'Andel Hendak. And there was another guy, Dmitri – I never knew his last name; I always thought he worked for Hendak, but Tomáš told me it was the other way round. He carried a gun.'

'I met a Tomáš working at the Dark Goddess.'

'That would be him. Tomáš Novák. He was a friend. I would never have escaped from Prague all those years ago without his help. Him and old Reuben. I wonder if Reuben's still around? He ran a café.'

'On Old Town Square?'

Kat's eyes lit up. 'Is it still there?'

'Can't miss it. I've been there. I'm pretty sure Reuben must have served me. Looked like the owner, anyway. Not very tall, scrawny, lots of energy, smartly dressed.'

Kat clapped her hands together. 'I can't believe it. After all this time. That's Reuben. How wonderful. I have to see him.'

'And what about your friend, Tomáš? Would he help us?'

'I'm sure he will.'

I looked at my watch. The last hour had flown by.

We headed for the bar where Eva was waiting for us. 'I'm starving. I've not eaten all day,' I said.

'Then let's go to Reuben's,' said Kat.

Eva went to fetch her coat and we regrouped at reception. Now she'd left the safety of the hotel, Kat was back in her black-haired, leather jacketed, American persona again, Martina Novotná. 'My Dad escaped from Prague in the fifties,' she drawled. 'He brewed beer in Chicago – he's just retired.'

'You have a real ear for accents, don't you?'

She winked and put her arm though mine. 'I'm so pleased you gave me a ride from the airport. Now I can take you to one of my dad's favourite haunts and our new friend can come with us,' she said loudly.

Eva put her arm through mine on the other side, and we set off together in pursuit of a square meal.

It was warm and cosy in the café, and the man I assumed to be Reuben was standing behind the counter polishing glasses. His carefully pressed white shirt, black trousers with their knife-sharp crease, and his quick, watchful eyes and ready smile all served to reinforce the impression I'd had of him as the proprietor of a smooth running, popular café – although his neat moustache and closely cropped dark hair belied his age.

'You were right; it is him!' Kat whispered to me, excitedly. She gestured to us to wait while she approached, greeting him in Czech. He studied her politely at first, fooled by her disguise, then his face broke into a big grin and he threw his arms around her. Kat waved us over and did the introductions.

'My favourite girl has come home.' He pointed to the pinboard behind the counter. 'See, the postcard you sent me is still there.'

Kat grinned and hugged him.

'This calls for a celebration. Let's go in the back room.'

'What about your customers?' asked Kat.

'I have an assistant these days.' He opened the door behind him and called out, 'Pavel?'

A crisply dressed young man in an outfit matching Reuben's appeared at the door. 'Yes, sir?'

'Take over, will you? An old friend has come a long way to see me. Bring coffee, sandwiches and brandy for four.'

The boy nodded formally. Reuben ushered us through into the back sitting room. He added a couple of logs to the wood burner and we settled into the armchairs and sofa. Pavel bustled around, bringing plates, cups and glasses.

Reuben listened eagerly as Kat told her tale of escape from Prague and her life for the last eight years. She started in English but switched into rapid Czech as she responded to his questions. She gestured towards me and the old man smiled and put his hands together in silent thanks and I guessed Kat was telling him of our time together in Stratford Upon Avon. She introduced Eva then, and Reuben looked at her solemnly, saying in English, 'I am sorry for your loss.' Finally, Kat explained why we were all here together. The old man's face took on an unforgiving expression.

'I have never forgotten the way those people hounded you out of Prague.' He looked at me solemnly. 'You have been so kind to Katerina. Anything I can do to help shall be done,' he said, offering the plate of sandwiches to Kat and adding, 'Tomáš is a good boy. He still comes regularly to see how I'm doing.'

My phone rang. It was Cooper. I got up and left them chatting, going out into the small yard at the back of the building.

'What do you know?' he asked.

'I've got three names for you. First there's Vanda Brazda; she runs the Dark Goddess nightclub and she's the one who's put the painting up for sale. Interpol and the police here are watching her club. I reckon they suspect there's some kind of tie up with a money laundering racket. Then there's Andel Hendak, who was Vanda's business partner eight years ago and may still be. The last one is called Dmitri. He used to be Hendak's boss but that's all I have on him for now.'

'I'll see if anything comes up on them that might be useful. In the meantime, I've briefed the boss and he's authorised me to contact the Metropolitan Police Art and Antiques Unit.'

'I think the guys in Prague are way ahead of us.' I told him about my visit to the local cop shop.

'That'll come in handy.'

'Tell me about your Art and Antiques Unit?'

'They're part of the Specialist, Organised and Economic Crime Command. That's my next call.'

'OK – ring me when you know more.'

When I went inside again, there was a glass of brandy waiting for me.

'Reuben's going to get a message to Tomáš for us,' said Kat.

Reuben came back in from the café, pulled up an old dining chair and sat next to me. 'You know, it makes me so mad. First the Nazis, then the Russians and now these gangsters occupying my country.' He looked determined. 'My friends and I, we may be old, but our fighting spirit is intact. We are ready to assist you.'

He put his hand on my arm, and I smiled at him gratefully.

After the meeting broke up, Kat and I returned to the Goldcrest and Eva headed for home. At the hotel, a uniformed security guard opened the door for us. Ladislav was on the desk.

'I'm sorry we've brought all this trouble down on you, Ladislav. I expect Eva has explained to you what I'm doing about it?'

'I am happy to help you in any way I can.'

'Kat and Eva are old friends, and I'm concerned that may put Eva at risk. Would it be possible for her to stay here until this is over?'

'Certainly. The room next to yours is free. I will get a message to her.'

I went and lay on the bed for a nap. It seemed just a few minutes before there was a knock on my door.

'It's me, Jake,' said Kat. 'Tomáš is here.'

'Give me five. I'll meet you both in the bar.' It was 6pm, time for my call. My phone rang promptly. 'How has your guest been today?'

'Hello, Jake. I would say as well as can be expected. I will send your first photo of her this evening.'

'I'll look forward to seeing it.'

'Good, good. I must tell you, I have been talking to my colleague about your idea, and we are very keen to explore it with you when this business is over. Do you really think Miss Lowsonford will cooperate?'

'Liz and I have been friends for a long time. Once I talk to her, there'll be no stopping her.'

'Excellent. And how are things progressing with the auction?'

'All on schedule. The information packs are being put together as we speak, and a list of potential bidders has been drawn up. It's being handled very professionally, of course, and our auctioneer is very confident.'

There were only two people in the bar, huddled in the corner. Kat was back in her blonde, undisguised form, sitting next to Tomáš, who was now in jeans and sweater. They had their heads together, making up for their lost years.

Tomáš stood to shake my hand. 'Hello again.'

'I've been hearing how you saved Kat from the bad guys,' I said.

Tomáš smiled. 'And you – you have been a good friend to our Katerina also.'

'And she to me.'

Ladislav fetched us some drinks and moved out of earshot.

'Tomáš – we wanted to ask you what you know about Vanda and the painting she's selling,' said Kat.

'The painting was mine. It was hidden in my attic.' He took a sip of his beer. 'I know nothing of such things, so I asked Vanda for her advice. An expert was in town, and he offered to sell it on my behalf. I agreed and she advanced me the money so I could press on with my renovation work.' He turned to me. 'I have a house I'm renovating, bit by bit, but cash is always a problem, of course! She'll get her money back when he sells the picture.'

'How much did she give you? I asked.

He smiled. 'Five thousand crowns.'

'The auctioneer said the picture would raise twenty thousand dollars and now he's being blackmailed to sell it fraudulently for twenty million dollars,' I said.

Tomáš swore in Czech.

I continued. 'I came to the club to ask Vanda if she'd seen my friend, Liz, since they met on Sunday. She said not. I'm certain that Liz was taken from this hotel against her will on Sunday night. Her boss – the auctioneer who has to sell the painting – received a phone call on Monday to say Liz would be released after the auction, as long as it's successful.'

Tomáš shook his head. 'That's terrible.'

'What's your role in this?'

'I know nothing of it.'

He looked sincere. Was he telling the truth?

'I trusted Tomáš with my life eight years ago. I still would,' said Kat.

He smiled gratefully.

'Vanda Brazda lied to you about how much the picture was really worth. What about this Andel Hendak and Dmitri – do you know Dmitri's last name? Are they still around?'

'Andel yes, all the time. Dmitri is Dmitri Petrov. I haven't seen him for years.'

'Could Hendak be involved in this conspiracy?' I asked.

'I'd put money on it.' Tomáš smiled ruefully. 'Twenty million dollars, in fact. If I had it.'

'We need to know where they're holding Liz.'

Tomáš shrugged helplessly. 'Andel Hendak has contacts all over the city. She could be anywhere.'

'What about the nightclub?'

Tomáš thought hard. 'I can think of nowhere.'

'No private rooms, store cupboards, anything like that?'

'No – apart from Vanda's office, kitchens and toilets, dressing rooms for the stage, it's all public spaces.'

Kat looked at me. 'What about the basement?'

Tomáš grinned. 'It was refurbished after you set fire to it. It's now a club within a club.'

'You set fire to the basement? That's a story I *have* to hear,' I said.

Kat grinned.

'There's been no need for me to go down there since they fixed it up,' said Tomáš. 'But I saw the layout they were planning and there was no space in which you could hold someone.'

I thought about Reuben's offer of help. Could I get him and his old military friends to set a watch on Hendak and Brazda? They might just lead us to Liz. I'd sound him out.

'Vanda and Andel have always been close. There's sure to be something in her office that will tell us more. Could you get me a job at the club, Tomáš?' said Kat.

'Too dangerous. You'll be recognised,' I said.

'I agree with Jake. If Vanda or Andel see you, there'll be trouble. Maybe I can take a look around?' said Tomáš.

Kat arched an eyebrow. 'You could, Tomáš, but everyone knows you and they'll see where you go. I'm a mistress of disguise. Ask Jake. No one will notice me if I'm a member of staff.'

I thought about our meeting at the airport. She was right – it was more than just her hair and clothes; she really was good at this stuff. Her posture, mannerisms, facial expressions, even the pitch and tone of her voice had been different.

'I'll give you that – but I don't want you to take any unnecessary risks,' I said.

'Do you have a better idea?' That determined jib was showing on her chin. 'I know my way around the club. And I'm the perfect employee; I can work the bar, be a waitress, even be a dancer for the night.'

'I guess it could be OK, as long as you're careful,' said Tomáš. 'And you won't need to come face to face with Vanda or Andel. He doesn't come in to the club at night these days and Vanda has an assistant who deals with hiring and firing and all the staff issues. I'll get you an interview.'

'You could say you saw me help out at Reuben's – he'll back you up. Tell them I'm from Chicago and I understand American ways – I'll be a useful addition to the team,' Kat suggested, before adding, 'even you won't recognise me, Tomáš. I'll have dark hair and lots of make-up.'

I still didn't like the idea, but knew it was impossible to stop Kat once she'd decided on a course of action.

Just then, my phone rang. It was Cooper again.

'The Met's Art and Antiques Unit are in. They've agreed with my boss that I should be the link man between you and them, and he's cool about me going up to Glasgow and liaising with my opposite number. They'll send him all the paperwork and I'm officially on secondment as of tomorrow.'

'Wow,' I said. 'That easy? If you run that end of things, I can work with the police over here.'

'Secondments happen all the time and to be fair, after the Race Engineering business, as soon as I mentioned your name, the boss put his head in his hands and said *what's he done now*? We'll need to brief Glasgow CID as the auction is on their turf. Anything else?'

'We're about to plant a spy into Ms Brazda's camp.'

'That sounds dangerous.'

'You've met Kat – still think it's a problem?'

He chuckled. 'I guess not. That one can look after herself.'

I hoped he was right.

7 | THURSDAY 16TH OCTOBER

Thursday dawned bright and clear. I woke with the desire to check up on Matravers. I swung my legs off my narrow single bed and reached for my phone.

'What's happening?' I asked.

'The kidnapper sent his first daily fax over late last night.'

'How did Liz look?'

'Angry.'

'Healthy?'

'Hardly leaping in the air with joy but, yes, absolutely fine.'

'Good. You have the hotel's fax number; send her picture across to me, will you? I want to see if there are any clues to her location in there. Anything else to report?'

'I've had a message from Vanda Brazda asking for sign-in details for the auction. She wants to monitor the bidding from her office.'

'Which means she must know about the twenty-million-dollar price tag and what's behind it. Which also means she's in this up to her neck; there's no doubt now,' I said.

'And I'm ready to start contacting potential purchasers. The electronic information pack is ready, hard copies due tomorrow.'

'You're still on schedule for Monday?'

'It's tight but yes. I'll be on the phone today. It's time for the hard sell. I want at least half a dozen participants.'

'What happens if you fail?'

'I'm not going to.'

'I hope so, for both our sakes.'

I dressed and met Kat for breakfast. Tomáš had already called her to say the club's assistant manager would see her at six that evening.

'I need to buy more clothes,' she said. 'Something more suitable for an interview.'

'I'll come with you.'

'If I'm going to work in the club I don't think we should be seen in town together from now on.'

'No problem,' I said, taking out my wallet. 'Is that enough?'

'More than,' she said, handing half the notes back to me.

I tried to refuse. 'Keep it, you might need it.'

'No. If I land this job someone might go through my bag. Bar work doesn't pay that kind of money.'

'Say if you need more.'

'Thank you,' she said and gave me a peck on the cheek.

'Are you sure about this job?'

'My mind's made up.'

I was expecting her to say that, but wasn't sure whether to be grateful or anxious that she was going to go through with it. She finished her coffee, and black wig on, headed out on her expedition.

Having her here had really boosted my confidence. Involving her had been an unexpectedly great move. I thought I'd benefit from her knowledge of Prague and whatever she'd experienced of its darker side but the real bonus was her network – Tomáš, Eva and Rueben. Eva was on side and I'd sent a note back with Tomáš last night asking Reuben if he and his old soldier friends would keep tabs on Brazda and Hendak for me. A positive response had been waiting for me at reception this morning.

I reached for my phone. I checked my watch and worked out the time in Singapore. I'd missed my chance to call Nellie in the middle of the night but he deserved to know what was going on, even though I'd denied myself the pleasure of spoiling his beauty sleep. I poured my coffee and he answered in two rings.

'What news?'

I told him where we'd got to.

'I never dreamt I'd be involving you in anything like this when I asked you to go to Prague.'

'It's just as well you did.'

'I want to be there.'

'I know you do, mate, but honestly, for now, you're better off where you are. My plans are taking shape and there's nothing here for you to do right now. At least if you're there, you're occupied and doing something useful. And anyway, as I said before, the last thing I need right now is a clumsy ruffian like you practising his posh boy boxing skills on any passerby that crosses him. No, stay where you are and let your uncle Jake sort out the detail then you can walk in and look like a hero.'

'Thanks, Jake. You're a good pal.'

I disconnected the call. The phone rang straight away.

Cooper had beaten me to it. 'Those names you mentioned – Andel Hendak and Dmitri?

'Hendak's on Interpol's database. He's a person of interest but nothing hard and fast. Loads of Dmitris – can't do much with just a first name.'

'Then you're in luck: I've discovered his last name is Petrov. I'll ask the Interpol guy here if he knows anything about him.

And Kat has her interview at the club this evening. With luck, she'll be working there tomorrow night,' I said.

'What's your plan now?' asked Cooper.

'It's time I levelled with the local police – that's today's priority. And I'll need to introduce you to Matravers. I'll have to come over so we can brief his bankers on what we need them to do. Suppose we meet in Glasgow tomorrow afternoon? I can fly across in the morning.'

'We can catch up with the local CID at the same time.'

'And I want to see this web auction working – I'll organise a demo whilst we're there. It'll be good to go face to face with Q, his techie; there's a lot riding on his work.'

'You'll stay in Glasgow tomorrow night?'

'I'll organise a hotel for us. I'll book you in for the weekend and I'll fly back on Saturday.'

With Eva on the case for flights and accommodation, I fished out Interpol Man's card and rang the number.

''Allo?'

'Monsieur Lambert – this is Jake Elderfield. I have things I need to tell you.'

'I am pleased to hear it, Jake. Are you at your hotel? I will send a car for you.'

Half an hour later I was back in the same room as yesterday with Gabriel Lambert and my old friend Bramley.

'Last time we met, you mentioned money laundering. Can you explain to me how that works?' I said.

Lambert studied me for a moment before he replied. 'There are three stages: placement, layering and integration. Placement is where you feed the dirty money into the banking system in small amounts so as not to arouse suspicion. Nightclubs can be a good place for this as they generally take a lot of cash. With more significant operations, a large number of individuals will each make modest payments into an account in their name before the money is transferred to another account where it's under the gang's control. Once aggregated, the money will then start its journey through the banking system, becoming progressively cleaner as it travels.'

'Sounds complicated.'

'There are many stages, which makes it very expensive – as much as thirty percent of the face value of the currency. It's often carried out by a specialist organisation.'

'That's really useful. I haven't come across anything that would suggest money laundering. This looks like a major fraud underpinned by blackmail. Let me tell you what I've learned over the last few days.'

Lambert leaned forward. 'I'm listening.'

They looked serious as I spoke. It was some moments after I finished before Lambert looked up from his notes and said, 'This is a very serious development. You are telling me the truth this time?'

'Why don't you check my story with Detective Sergeant Cooper?'

Bramley took Cooper's phone number and left the room.

It was only a few minutes until he returned and spoke softly into Lambert's ear. Lambert looked at me with new respect. 'Detective Cooper has verified your story and told us something of your previous work with him. I am glad that you have shared what you know but I must inform you this is now a police matter and you must step aside.'

'No.'

'What do you mean, *no*?'

'I can't agree with you. This is a completely different type of crime from money laundering, which is the reason you're watching the night club. This one's much simpler: they kidnap Liz, they force Matravers to auction a fake painting, they make a pile of money. It's a snake of a crime, with its head in Prague and its tail in Glasgow. There are four victims: Liz, Matravers and the "mark-in-waiting" who'll be defrauded of twenty million dollars on Monday.'

'Who is the fourth victim?'

'Tomáš Novák sold the painting at the centre of the fraud but was paid a lot less than it was worth. Brazda led him to believe she was advancing him the amount he would get from a legitimate sale.'

'I see. I'm sure you realise that Interpol and the police here are well used to handling complex crime.'

'Of course. But my friend's life is at stake, and I know more about this situation than you. I've put resources in place that will help you bring this affair to a satisfactory conclusion.'

'I don't accept your proposition. We will take it from here.' Lambert turned to Bramley. 'Please show the gentleman out.'

Bramley got up from his chair and opened the door. I didn't move.

'I suggest your friend here does what he's best at and fetches more coffee whilst you and I have a little chat.'

Lambert bristled visibly before making an effort to calm himself, ushering Bramley on his errand.

'I really must protest, Elderfield…'

'I'll stop you there. Just listen. We can all get what we need out of this if we work together.'

Lambert hesitated. 'Go on.'

I spoke again. 'Here's how we do this. We let the auction run and as soon as it completes, we strike. They'll be so busy congratulating themselves while they wait for the money to be transferred, they won't see it coming. You'll have smashed a major international fraud, put right a number of injustices and rescued an innocent kidnap victim. All I'm asking is to be allowed to help you with what and who I know.'

'What about the proceeds of the sale?'

'Under the supervision of the British police, it'll be held by the auctioneer's bankers and then returned to the would-be purchaser.

'We'll need to know where the criminals will be at the time of the auction and where they are holding your friend.'

'I'm pretty sure Brazda will be in her office watching the auction. I'm expecting the kidnapper, whoever he is, will be with her, but I'll try to make certain of that. And I'm working on a way to find where they're keeping Liz.'

Bramley came back with the coffee and resumed his seat.

Lambert beamed and rubbed his hands together. 'I can live with this. And you are right, with Detective Sergeant Cooper seconded to work on the UK end of things I can liaise with him as well as the police here. We can keep you involved as long as we're clear that the police here give the orders in Prague.'

'My priority is to bring Liz out safely. As long as we can do that – the rest is up to you. Tell me, what do you know about Hendak?'

'He visits the club at least twice a week. We suspect he has links to an Eastern European hospitality syndicate. As you know, my specialist area is money laundering and this group appear to be operating in this arena, but nothing has so far been proven.'

'Another name has been mentioned: Dmitri Petrov.'

'Very little is known about Petrov. We believe that he was an important member of the syndicate, but he has not been seen in this country for some time.'

***

It was dark by the time I got away from Lambert. He laid on a car and driver to take me back to the hotel. I was battling hard to keep my anxiety for Liz under control, but kept reminding myself there was no percentage in losing it now. Everyone was relying on me, and I could see the pillars of a robust plan coming together. I sat in the back of the unmarked Skoda and watched the driver's suited back as he made his way through the evening traffic.

I took out my phone. It rang almost immediately.

'Good evening, Jake. I trust you've had a productive day?'

'Good evening. Yes, thank you. All is going according to plan. I've arranged to go back to Glasgow tomorrow to check everything at that end.'

'That's good. We don't want any slip ups.'

'I will make sure of that. How's Liz?'

'She is in good health. I will call you tomorrow. Goodnight.'

I breathed a sigh of relief and settled back in my seat to watch the traffic for the rest of the journey, jerking awake as we pulled up outside of the Goldcrest. My watch said I'd lost twenty minutes.

Eva, bless her, was being a huge help. My trip to Glasgow was all confirmed.

As I turned away from the reception desk with my key I had a thought. 'Is Ladislav around? Could he spare me five minutes?'

Eva smiled. 'I'm sure he could.' She picked up the phone. 'Let me show you where his office is.'

'Come in, take a seat,' he said through the doorway. He stood to greet me and put two glasses on the table, splashing brandy into them. '*Na zdraví*,' he said. 'What can I do for you?'

'Cheers,' I responded. 'I'm conscious of how much trouble

I've put you to and I just wanted to say how grateful I am for your support with all this.'

Ladislav studied my face before he replied. 'My family have owned this hotel for many years and nothing like this has ever happened before.' He banged his clenched fist against his heart. 'It hurts me here to think what your friend must be going through.'

'We're doing everything we can to keep her safe,' I said. 'You've been a tower of strength, Ladislav. I can promise this will all be over on Monday. In the meantime, if we are putting you to any extra costs…?'

He held up his hand in protest. 'I wouldn't hear of it. My guests have not been inconvenienced in any way. And they find the twenty-four-hour security very reassuring – so that will stay.'

I finished my brandy and stood. 'Thank you, Ladislav. You're a good man.'

He stood with me, placing a companionable hand on my shoulder, 'I consider it my duty to assist.'

Eva spoke as I walked back through reception, 'She got the job.'

'Great,' I said.

Kat opened her bedroom door wearing a towelling robe. Her short hair was wet and spiky.

'Come in,' she said. 'I'm there tomorrow night.'

'I heard. Did you see Vanda?'

'No. Just this new manager who looks after all the staff. I thought you'd be pleased.'

'I am. It's just… I've got one good friend who's in trouble because of this, I don't want you going the same way.'

'I'll be careful, Jake, I promise.'

'See you are. You're too valuable to lose.'

'What about dinner? I'm starving.'

'Me too. I went to a great place when I got here on Monday night – I can't believe that was only four nights ago. Get dressed, I'll ring for a table.'

The restaurant was quiet this early in the evening, which suited us well. We asked for a table furthest from the bar – best to keep a low profile.

Over a bottle of wine and some good home cooking, Kat told me about her interview.

She beamed. 'She asked me lots of question and I'm to do a trial shift tomorrow night. Easy – the job's mine.'

'Vanda must have upset you pretty badly for you to set fire to the basement?'

She shuddered slightly, her expression hard to read. 'Not a great time in my life.'

I poured more wine for us.

'When are your shifts?'

'Friday and Saturday evenings from seven till three and Sundays, seven till two.'

'Nothing in the week?'

She grinned. 'I'm not sure they'll want me after Monday.'

'What's your plan?'

'A good look around Vanda's office at the first opportunity I get. I'm sure she'll still walk the floor every hour or so to see what's going on. I'll just slip in and out.'

'What if she locks her office?'

'Tomáš is copying the key for me.'

'A useful guy to have on the inside.'

'Yes. He's managed to tread a fine line with Vanda – using his practical skills to her advantage but steering clear of all her schemes. I don't know how he's done it.'

'Even master criminals need people they can trust. He has integrity. Vanda will regret conning him over the painting.'

'He only stuck with her because of his mother,' Kat's expression softened. 'She was quite ill for some time before she died and Vanda pays well. He got used to turning a blind eye to things he didn't like. I'm sure he wouldn't still have a job if Vanda had ever realised he helped me get away from her. After his mother died, it was easier just to carry on. There was no one left for him to worry about with me gone and Eva having made herself scarce. Vanda has never asked him to do anything he didn't want to do.'

'With you, Tomáš, Reuben and Eva on my team, Vanda's in for a jumbo surprise.'

We walked slowly and companionably back to the hotel after our meal, under a starlit sky. It reminded me of our brief time together in Stratford when Kat had stayed with me in my little house in Old Town: we'd often walked together into the centre to visit the Vintner, one of my favourite restaurants and, afterwards, we'd stroll home again to our separate beds. It had been a time of recovery for both of us, and it made my heart ache to remember how much I'd wanted our relationship to be something more – but I'd lacked the skill or the courage to ask. And besides, I wasn't convinced that either of us was ready for another long-term relationship. As it turned out, I didn't know the half of it.

In our comfortable olde-worlde hotel in its quiet cobbled square, neither of us felt quite like sleep, so we helped ourselves to more wine from the bar and went to Kat's room. There, we sat on the floor, side by side, our backs against the end of the bed.

'I'm glad you called me,' she said.

'It seemed like the right thing to do, for so many reasons,' I replied.

She looked into my eyes. 'You understand that I'm doing this for me as well as for you.'

Silence is a powerful tool when you want someone to speak.

'I was very young when I first met Vanda,' she said. 'She was my world. I fantasised about her night and day. And when she asked me to move in with her, it was a dream come true. She swamped me; I was the centre of her world, I couldn't think, I couldn't breathe, I couldn't move without her approval. I loved the way it made me feel. And then, little by little, it changed. Once she'd possessed me, all her attention returned to her ambitions. I was useful for my dancing, housework and sex. She stopped seeing me for who I was. Thrown off my pedestal, I'd been replaced by a nightclub. Just another push, another squeeze, another questionable act ignored and she'd be where she'd always wanted to be. It wasn't love; it was control.' She gulped her wine. There were tears in her eyes.

I tried to think of something to say. I wanted to hug her and tell her it would all work out.

She looked so unhappy. 'I was ashamed of what I'd become. I ran from Prague to escape myself as much as my pursuers. England was a fresh start. And for a while I experienced independence. But being someone's pet can be very seductive. No need to think ahead or worry about little things like money. As long as you please your Mistress, that is.'

'I never realised...'

'It all started with my mother. She wanted me to live the life that she'd always craved for herself but failed to achieve. I ran from her to Vanda and from there to Carina.'

She shrugged and wiped the tears from her eyes with the back of her hand.

I passed her a paper tissue. Carina had treated Kat like a plaything, to be picked up and discarded at will – I'd seen first hand how fickle she could be – but I hadn't realised it was something of a pattern for Kat.

She smiled. 'Thank you. You're always so kind to me.' She sipped her wine. 'So, you see; this is not just about Liz for me. I'm vanquishing my ghosts by helping you. My mother is dead, Carina is out of reach in South America, but Vanda is here and it's time she paid.'

'I was so disappointed when you left me,' I said.

She smiled again, this time sadly. 'It couldn't last. You knew that.'

'I really thought we had a chance.'

'I never lied to you, Jake. You were sweet, looking after me the way you did. But after Carina…'

I finished the sentence for her.

'After Carina lied to you? Let you down? Hurt you? You couldn't trust anyone else?'

She sipped her drink.

'I was going to say… after Carina, I didn't know what I wanted from a relationship and I still don't. That one night we spent together, the night before you went to the Isle of Man, was very special. And this I do know. You are my friend. You were there for me when I needed you and that's a good reason to be here now.'

The night she mentioned was etched in my mind; it was partly that, I suppose, that had given me hope that, in time, we might have become *more* than friends. But if friendship was all that was on offer, I'd take it.

'Well, that's something anyway.'

Kat put her hand out and stroked my cheek. 'Don't be like that. We're a good team, Jake. The best.'

I pulled myself up. What was I thinking? I knew that I loved this girl. I'd made myself vulnerable to her, hoping for a long term *let's-live-happily-ever-after* relationship but she'd walked away from me. That did not give me the right to punish her for not feeling the same way as me.

'OK,' I said.

'OK?'

'Pals. Good pals.'

Unexpectedly, she leaned forward and kissed me lightly on the lips.

'Thank you,' she said. 'Now can we go to bed?'

8 | FRIDAY 17TH OCTOBER

I was awake before the alarm. I'd slept surprisingly well, considering the disappointment I'd had. Oh, we'd gone to bed when Kat suggested it – she to hers and me to mine. Not what you thought, eh? Me neither. Still, we both knew where we stood. And I was happy to play the long game – for now. In the meantime, we had a job to do.

I showered and dressed quickly, packing my bag for another overnight in Glasgow – this time in a proper bed rather than an airport departure lounge. By the time I'd finished, Ladislav had slipped last night's fax from Matravers under the door. Liz was pictured sitting on the edge of a large bed holding yesterday's international edition of the *Financial Times*. She looked tired but well. There was a fiery look in her eye – I'm glad I wasn't the cameraman. No clues as to where they might be holding her.

I skipped breakfast and slipped out of the hotel, vowing to grab something at the airport. The taxi Eva had organised for me was waiting on the corner. There was little traffic at that time of day, meaning I didn't have to wait too long to get my caffeine fix.

I was an old hand now. The flight to Glasgow via Amsterdam passed without incident. For the last stage of the journey I took a taxi from the airport into the centre of Glasgow. It was driven by a guy whose accent was so strong

I understood him less well than any of the cab drivers I'd used in Prague. He dropped me outside the Central Hotel, a beautiful old building in Gordon Street, fronting the railway station.

I checked in, dropped my bag in my room, splashed some cold water on my face and went to grab another cab. I'd arranged to meet Cooper at Matravers' offices after he'd finished briefing Glasgow CID.

This cab driver was the strong, silent type, concentrating on getting us through the heavy midday traffic in one piece, handing me a breathing space in which to focus on the meetings to come.

We'd arranged it so I'd have half an hour with Matravers to set him up for this afternoon's proceedings. Cooper would then rock up with reinforcements from Glasgow CID, and we'd run through the game plan for Monday. Matravers' bank manager would join us to be informed of the part we expected him to play. Cooper figured that having the local plod here would ensure everyone behaved themselves. I'd arranged for Matravers' tech man, Q, to provide a demonstration of the auction site for Cooper and me tomorrow morning. I wanted to know how exactly the damn thing was supposed to work, what might go wrong and what options we had if it did. Liz's life and the kidnappers' arrest would depend on a slick, faultless performance. After the demo, I'd head back to the airport and reach Prague in time to catch up with Kat before her Saturday evening shift at the Dark Goddess. Phew. I was going to need a holiday after this. So would Kat. Maybe I could persuade her to come away for a few days? I smiled to myself, and thought *we'll see*, as my Mum would say.

***

We pulled up in Sauchiehall St outside a terraced stone-fronted Georgian property. It was exactly the sort of building I'd pictured Matravers working from. In contrast to his palatial country ruin, it looked in good nick, prosperous even. But then, I supposed, like a bank, it would have to inspire confidence in its clients. There was a brass plate next to the door that proclaimed *Matravers Fine Arts* in Times New Roman. Inside was entirely predictable: high ceilings, plush carpets, oil paintings and hordes of antique brown furniture.

A smartly dressed young man rose from behind his desk and ran a hand through his luxuriant blond hair. His light-grey houndstooth three-piece suit looked expensive and his pale blue silk tie matched his breast pocket handkerchief. As he stood, the light caught his long blond eyelashes.

'Mr Elderfield? Good morning, I'm Mr Matravers' personal assistant. I'll take you in. Would you care for coffee?'

Matravers' office was fronted by a pair of highly polished dark wood doors with intricate brass fittings. My new companion led me over to them, knocked formally, opened one and announced me. He promised to come back with my coffee, closing the door behind him.

Matravers sat behind his massive desk, staring blankly at the tooled-leather surface. The wall behind him held a be-whiskered, head and shoulders portrait of a man I took to be his grandfather in the prime of life – the enterprise's founder watching over his grandson's stewardship. The disapproval showed on his face. Matravers turned his bleary eyes on me. He was doing a good impression of Macbeth on the morning after he'd seen Banquo's ghost.

'Good to see you,' I said.

His cheeks were hollow and I'd swear the grey had

swept up his sideburns to engulf more of his dark hair since Wednesday.

He stood and shook my hand, his face expressionless. I took a seat on my side of his desk as his P.A. came back in, balancing a tray bearing a silver coffee pot and two china cups. He set it on the leather-clad desk and poured.

'Milk? Sugar?' he said.

I wondered if he ever smiled. 'Just milk thanks,' I responded.

He poured our coffee and left the room.

'He knows something's going on,' said Matravers. His hand shook slightly as he lifted his coffee cup.

'Can he be trusted?'

Matravers frowned but didn't speak.

I went to the door and called the young man in.

He joined us with an eager-to-please expression lighting up his face.

'What's your name? I asked.

'Andrew, Sir, Andrew Blair.'

'Well, Andrew. We're going to take you into our confidence but every word I say must never be repeated. Do I make myself clear?'

'Profoundly, Mr Elderfield.' He said, with the eagerness of someone reading a compelling spy novel.

'Mr Matravers is central to an undercover operation that will expose a gang of professional art fraudsters. Lives and a lot of money are at stake. The police will be joining us shortly and will back up everything I've just said. I need your absolute guarantee that you'll keep this matter to yourself.'

Blair struggled to master his eagerness to hear more. 'You have my word on it, Mr Elderfield. Is there anything I can do to help?'

'Almost certainly. We'll get back to you on that. For now, I'd like you to write me a letter confirming you've agreed to keep this matter confidential. Include all of your contact details, just in case.'

He raised an eyebrow in silent question.

'If information does happen to be leaked, the police will want to talk to you.'

'Of course, Mr Elderfield. I'll do it right away.'

He left the room.

'Can't have him gossiping to a friend or the local paper, can we?' I said.

'That's a weight off my mind,' said Matravers. 'How much trouble am I in?'

'That depends on you,' I said. 'This could go one of two ways.'

'I'm listening.'

'How good an actor are you?'

'Why?'

'In option one, you're humble and contrite in front of the police' – I looked at my watch – 'who'll be with us shortly. When they tell you how stupid you've been, you listen carefully and reassure them that you'll cooperate fully with their investigation.' My turn to try the coffee. 'If you do that, you just might avoid jail provided that we get Liz out of this in one piece.'

He watched me attentively.

'In option two, you try and fail to somehow bluff your way out of this. Go that way and I can pretty much guarantee you'll be leaving this office in handcuffs.'

I leaned forward and placed my elbows on his desk. I hoped he'd hate that.

'Of course, whatever you do, you're going to lose this place. Wouldn't your Grandad be proud?'

'Something will turn up, surely?' he bleated.

'Last chance saloon and you're out of bullets. I predict an imminent fire sale.' I had a sudden thought. 'Unless…'

'Unless?' he asked hopefully.

'I can see one possibility. Let's get this business out of the way first though. How are you getting on with setting up the auction?'

Matravers sighed heavily. 'It's not going as well as I'd hoped. I've been emailing out packs and making phone calls all morning. No takers yet, but a few possibles.'

'How far are you through your list?'

'There's still plenty to go. I've saved the hottest prospects for this evening.'

'You said before, you needed six players for the auction to work.'

'That would be best, but I'd settle for four.'

There was a discreet knock and Andrew Blair appeared around the door. 'Two gentlemen to see you, Mr Matravers.'

D.S. Cooper's open, guileless smile and wide-set blue eyes had their usual disarming effect on Matravers as his slim, six-foot-four frame darkened the doorway. His Scottish CID colleague followed him in.

'Detective Sergeant Cooper,' he said, introducing himself as if we were mere acquaintances but directing a smile at me, and a nod that made his longish hair bounce.

Cooper's colleague was a different matter. Short, stocky and with a high facial colour, he looked like a man who could easily take offence and use his fists to settle the argument.

'Jake,' said Cooper, 'may I introduce Detective Inspector Rob McCloud?'

I shook McCloud's hand and introduced Matravers to them both.

Blair followed them in with more coffee and brought extra chairs over. Before he left, he handed me an envelope, which I discreetly placed in my pocket.

Cooper opened the batting. 'As I understand it, the auction takes place at eleven am on Monday. How long do these things last?'

'This will be the first internet auction I've done and, you know, these things are very new,' said Matravers. 'And there's a lot riding on this.'

'You're not kidding,' I said.

He looked at me before turning his attention back to Cooper. 'But to answer your question, to a large extent the auctioneer can drive the pace.'

'Can you wrap it up inside half an hour?' I asked.

'Half an hour maximum it shall be.'

'Good,' I said. 'There's one other thing I need. The kidnappers must be completely relaxed after the auction completes, believing their money will be with them speedily and securely. It needs to be a complete surprise when we arrive and arrest them.' I handed around copies of an official looking contract I'd had my solicitor draw up. 'I'll need an autographed copy from each bidder faxed across before the auction starts. It commits the lucky buyer to paying up promptly in cleared funds. We'll send signed copies from every bidder across to the kidnappers before the auction.'

'Consider it done,' said Matravers.

I looked at him sharply. I'd expected more resistance to such an unusual request. Was he saying what he thought I wanted to hear? We'd need to keep a close eye on him.

McCloud was looking increasingly unsettled. 'This is all very well, but you people need to recognise that this is my patch, and I already have enough to arrest you,

Matravers' – and, looking at me – 'and you, you're treading very close to the edge.'

I was all set to give him his answer, but Cooper headed me off, sighing heavily and making a placatory gesture with his hands. 'Calm it, Rob. Remember, the kidnapper said he'd bring his victim back to Glasgow and do away with her before disposing of Matravers. There's an opportunity to get these people for a stack load of crimes if we play along with Jake's plan.'

McCloud took his time but reluctantly conceded. 'Aye, I guess you're right.'

'The Art and Antiques Unit tell me this type of fraud is on the increase, so it'll be a feather in all of our caps if we help Interpol lock up the protagonists,' said Cooper.

'It's a huge relief to me that you're both here,' said Matravers. 'I really don't know what I would do without your advice and support.'

I nodded my approval at him.

'You'd be going to jail,' growled McCloud, with a look that suggested the handcuffs might be coming out at any moment.

There was a knock on the door and Matravers' bank manager, Jeremy English, joined us. Young Blair did the coffee/chair trick again.

'I'll take this opportunity for a wee break,' said McCloud as he got up and left the room. Cooper mimed smoking a cigarette to me. 'He's trying to give up and it's giving him a sore head. He'll fit in with us.'

I set out the bank's role. Cooper and I had agreed to keep things as simple as we could, since that way lay fewer possibilities for mistakes.

'On Monday morning at eleven am, Mr Matravers will

open an auction to be conducted over the internet,' I said. 'A painting, reputedly by Klimt, will be put up for sale with a reserve of twenty million dollars. The winning bidder will be expected to pay the auction sum and any fees in cleared funds into Matravers Fine Art's bank account in trust for the painting's seller. Under the terms of the contract, payment is to be initiated before close of day. The contract states that the bank will hold the funds and transfer them to the seller once the buyer confirms receipt of the painting.'

I paused for coffee intake. McCloud came back in looking much more content.

'But the painting in question is a fake, the seller is a fraudster, and we're going to catch them in the act. We'll keep you fully informed on the sale day so that you know what to expect and when to expect it. Detective Inspector McCloud and Detective Sergeant Cooper will be here throughout the day to ensure everything happens as I've outlined. It's vital that you let Detective Sergeant Cooper know as soon as you receive the funds. He'll ensure that you have all his contact details. I'd like you to place the money in an escrow account where it can't be touched except on the combined instruction of the two police officers here present. We'll be asking you to hold the money until it can be returned to the buyer.'

'Twenty million dollars is lot of money…'

'It is, Mr English, but at no time will your bank be out of pocket. You'll simply be holding the funds until their release has been authorised by these two officers, acting with the authority of the Art and Antiques Unit, a division of the Met.'

'I'll have to obtain clearance from head office for a transaction of this nature.'

'By all means. Just make sure you have it by ten am on Monday morning.'

Everyone stood and shook hands. First to depart was the near speechless bank manager.

McCloud got to his feet next and cleared his throat. 'I'm glad you're taking this seriously, Mr Matravers. We're grateful for your cooperation and our gratitude will prove to be of inestimable value to you. See you don't offend us.' He turned to Cooper. 'I'll see you tomorrow evening, Guy.'

It was great to know Cooper would be up here over the weekend to keep an eye on these two – especially as I was sure there'd be a little social drinking involved.

Blair popped his head around the door. 'It's after five, Mr Matravers. I'll be off now if that's OK?'

Matravers nodded his agreement.

'Best you don't come in Monday. The office will be shut,' I added.

'Right you are, Mr Elderfield. I'll see you on Tuesday, Mr Matravers.'

The office door closed. Matravers looked drained. 'If I still have a business on Tuesday. What happens to me when all this is over?'

'Liz will be free and you'll be off the hook.'

He looked down and shook his head despairingly, 'But I'll be ruined, won't I? I've still got to pay Q for all his work on the auction site, I've no money and I'm not going to make anything from this sale.'

'This isn't a sale; it's a criminal fraud. First, we get you through this, then we can think about the future.' Why did I always do this? Take responsibility for someone else's problems. One look at his solemn, grey-toned face told me. Because I could, that's why. For me, it was as simple as seeing what building blocks were lying around and looking at the different ways they could be assembled. All that was required was a little imagination, a pinch of innovation and a big dollop of sheer bloody-minded determination. But now it was time for simplistic bravado. 'Cheer up. Let's get the auction out of the way, then see where we are.'

I studied his face. He'd become an oily prat again – too nice, too cooperative.

'We'll see you in the morning, Matravers, for the auction demo. Be ready,' I said.

I'd insisted that the demo was a complete dress rehearsal, with all the same kit that would be used on Monday and I was looking forward to meeting Q – the man supplying the tech brain behind Matravers' good idea – in person. The demo was set up for 8am.

'Of course,' he said.

Cooper and I got up to leave.

'Shall we see if we can find a cab?' he asked.

'Let's take a stroll.' I'd picked up a street map from the hotel. I liked to walk places I didn't know – it was the best way to get the measure of a city, and a chance to review all of its sights and sounds. There was some fine architecture here, Victorian, Edwardian, even some Art Deco and of course famous touches of Rennie MacIntosh. And besides, I really needed some of the fresh stuff after all that hot air.

'Don't worry about Matravers,' said Cooper. 'I'll keep him revved up till all this is over.'

'It's what happens after this that's really worrying him.'

'Sounds as if he's going to find himself in the bankruptcy court.'

'I have an idea as to how I might fix that. But first I need to know – will he be prosecuted?'

'He's helping us prevent a major fraud and sort out a kidnapping. Up here, it'll be the Procurator Fiscal's decision, but it seems to me it wouldn't be in the public interest.'

***

Back in our hotel, we went to our rooms to freshen up. It was approaching six o'clock, time for my call with the kidnapper. He was prompt.

'You are there with your police friend.'

Interesting. A statement not a question. 'Well, you know what they say. Keep your friends close and your enemies closer.'

For a moment I thought he was choking but I realised the croaking noise was a hoarse laugh.

'Everything is in good shape for Monday and I'll make sure there won't be any hitches.'

'And you had a member of Glasgow CID too.'

'You're well informed. The two policemen are spending time together this weekend.'

'Does he have the same outlook on life as Detective Sergeant Cooper?'

'Cooper will manage him. It'll be important for us to have friends on the local force when we go into business together.' I explained about the binding contract and proposed funds transfer.

'I'm impressed. I like you, Jake – you manage the detail. But I need your advice. Your friend Miss Lowsonford. She gets restless and she is quite angry. How can I keep her settled until after the auction?'

'Give her a message from me.'

'And what should I say?'

'Tell her to remember the words of our old friends Sam and Dave.'

'What does this mean?'

'When we were students, Sam and Dave were always quoting that old wartime phrase, *keep calm and carry on.* She'll know that message could only come from me.'

'And this will work?'

'I guarantee it.'

'I will speak to you tomorrow.'

The line went dead. I checked my watch. Too late to ring Kat. I left her a message saying I hoped everything had gone well and I'd see her tomorrow. It was nearly 7pm now, which meant 2am for Nellie. He answered in three rings.

'I was awake,' he said. 'What's new?'

I briefed him on the day's events.

'I should be there.'

'Glad you said that. Can you be here on Sunday? I'd like you to be with us when we go in to get her.'

'Are you sure Kat will be able to find out where they are holding her?'

'Definitely.' I crossed my fingers and looked at the fax Matravers had handed me.

I'd been putting off speaking to Liz's parents for days, not knowing what to say. And the last thing I wanted to do was make them anxious when they were on a cruise ship and supposed to be enjoying themselves. But I knew Liz and her mum were close and guessed Shona would start to worry pretty soon if she didn't hear back from her daughter. There was nothing for it. I'd just have to lie. I breathed a sigh of relief when Liz's mum's number went to answer machine, crossed my fingers firmly and started speaking, wondering what would come out. 'Shona. Hello, it's Jake Elderfield,' I said brightly, 'Hope you're enjoying your cruise? I'm in Prague with Liz. She's fine, but she asked me to get in touch as she's been so tied up with work, she's not had a chance to return your call. Things will calm down after Monday and she'll ring you then.' I reasoned I'd bent the truth, rather than broken it.

First fact: it *was* work that had caused this problem. Second fact: the situation *would* be happily resolved – I hoped – on Monday. Outright lie: as far as I could tell, Liz had not been tied up at all. Everything I was doing should see a happy, healthy Liz contacting her mum soon.

It had been another full-on day. I splashed cold water on my face, finger combed my dark mop of hair and let my brown eyes study the tired but confident smile in the mirror. I'm a great believer in the idea that if you want to improve your mood, crack your face. Time to grab a bite to eat with Guy Cooper.

Trying not to droop while I waited for him in reception, I picked up a leaflet and read a little of the history of the place we were staying in. Built in 1883, it had been one of the poshest hotels in Glasgow and at its peak had hosted a whole bunch of notables – Winston Churchill and Frank Sinatra to name but two, although they hadn't shared a room. Its other claim to fame was the work of one John Logie Baird, who transmitted the world's first long-distance television pictures to the hotel on 24 May 1927.

Cooper talked motorbikes through dinner, and I made polite efforts to stay awake. He was still sore at having missed the Isle of Man TT this year because of the Race Engineering business and he boasted that he'd made his boss sign off his holiday for next year so he could be there with his bike.

'It's just one week, so whatever trouble you get yourself into, you are not, repeat not, to call me.'

I grinned. 'Problem is I never know when some twisted plot is going to engulf me. You wouldn't want to miss out, would you?'

He laughed. 'Do us both a favour and take next May off.'

On that note we said goodnight and I was away to my bed.

9 | SATURDAY 18TH OCTOBER

Cooper and I had a quick breakfast at seven the next morning and then went out to find a taxi to get to Matravers' office.

I feared the worst when we found the door locked, but a swift jangle of the bell brought Matravers scurrying. He peered through the glass, seeming to hesitate before opening it.

'It's you,' he said, once the door was open.

'Did you think it was someone in urgent need of a Picasso?'

'Come in, come in,' he said, glancing both ways down the street before closing and bolting the door.

'What do you make of him?' said Cooper quietly as we followed him through to his office.

'He's strung out after another sleepless night and maybe…' I gestured a drinking motion with my hand.

'I may have a had a wee tipple last night but I'm perfectly sober now,' said Matravers, hovering in the outer office.

Cooper and I exchanged glances.

'Q is setting up in there.' He gestured towards his office. 'But I wanted to have a quick word first.' He hesitated.

'What's on your mind?'

'I don't know how to tell you this.'

I smiled sympathetically, 'A problem shared and all that…'

He took a deep breath. 'I made over a dozen calls to

collectors or their representatives last night. All over the world.' Another deep breath.

'How many have you signed up?'

He passed a hand over his forehead. 'That's just it,' he said. 'Not a single one. I've got four possibles but...'

'But no probables by the sound of it,' I said.

'No,' he said. 'As things stand, it's a washout.'

Matravers' office door opened and a clean cut, fit-looking chap in his forties, dressed in a pair of navy trousers, white shirt with a button-down collar and a navy crew-necked sweater, stood there. I noticed the contrasting suede patches on the shoulders and elbows, and the shine on his black brogues was almost dazzling. His closely cropped dark hair, clear blue eyes and sober expression completed the look. Everything about him inspired faith and confidence. I half expected him to salute rather than shake hands.

'Gentlemen, may I introduce Quentin Bailey, known to one and all as Q.'

I was on automatic pilot after what Matravers had told us. I shook hands and walked into the office feeling completely numb. Was there any point in going through with this? Just listen and think, I told myself.

'There's coffee and bacon rolls, over here on the side table,' added Matravers, whose mood seemed to have lightened now he'd shared his bad news. Cooper followed my lead and said nothing. 'Help yourselves and grab a seat. Q will warm up the works.' Matravers poured himself a coffee.

Bailey's equipment was set out on Matravers' desk. Every piece of electronic hardware was squared precisely with carefully bundled cables running in parallel lines. Cooper and I sat; Matravers stood, coffee in hand, at the back.

Bailey pressed switches and things warmed up. He stood

to one side of his kit and started speaking. 'Langdon's brief was quite clear. We were to build a solution that would take advantage of technology to modernise the way auctions are conducted. He won't mind me saying that others are investing in similar solutions, but what we have here is a robust approach that utilises the latest developments in coding and has been thoroughly tested to ensure its reliability.'

Matravers joined in. 'Rather than trying to get all these high-net-worth individuals or their representatives together in a room, it's so much easier if they can relax in their own space, in front of their computers, letting their soaring imaginations stoke up the price they're willing to pay for the unique thing on offer.'

'It's a shame we don't have any of them for this auction then, isn't it?' It had to be said. I just wish I'd said it. Cooper – who *had* said it – looked apologetic. Bailey had stopped dead and was staring at us.

'Langdon's just informed us that he has no takers. But,Q, please continue,' I said. Instinct was telling me to listen carefully. Maybe there was a way of using what we had...

'The auction software is installed on this desktop. The dashboard will show an overview of which bidders are logged in as well as their last bid and the current leading bid. The two laptops are here to mimic bidders. I'll just log them into this demo.'

I leaned in so I could peer at the desktop screen. The layout was quite simple. Along with the bidder information that Bailey had told us about there was a box labelled *current bid* and alongside it were two clocks showing the current time and time of the last bid. Below that there was a large area of blank screen labelled *dialogue box*.

Matravers chipped in again. 'We developed this together.

It shows everything the auctioneer needs. The quantum of the last bid is on show to everybody, but only the auctioneer can see which bidder made it. When the pace slows, I can broadcast a message to all bidders to encourage them to go higher. And they can individually message me back.'

With Bailey manning the two laptops and Matravers playing auctioneer, they imitated the auction process. Bailey's final bid was twenty-one million dollars.

'Very impressive,' I said, looking at Bailey. 'How bomb-proof is it?'

'Everything has been thoroughly tested,' said Bailey equably.

'Power cut?'

He pointed at a box on the table. 'This is an uninterruptable power supply. In the event of a failure, it'll provide power for up to twenty-four hours.'

'Virus?'

'We have the very latest anti-virus software, and the code has been structured to resist attack.'

Matravers helped himself to a bacon roll.

'What happens if he gets ketchup on the keyboard?' asked Cooper.

'Or someone spills coffee over it?' I said.

'I'll show you,' said Bailey, picking up a coffee.

'These are military grade keyboards, impervious to most things,' he said as he poured the coffee liberally over the keys.

'Mind my desk,' said Matravers, grabbing a pile of napkins, 'I've only just had the leather renewed.'

'And I carry a spare keyboard just in case.'

'What if the desktop won't boot up or it freezes in operation?' I asked.

Q smiled, knowing I was clutching at straws. 'Unlikely, but

as I've done today, I'll be running a second machine in parallel and in the event of a crash, I can switch to it seamlessly.'

Cooper's frustration boiled over. 'That looks great Q. And if only we had some punters, we could have a great auction.'

The first glimmer of an idea was forming. 'Q, we've just seen you run a fake auction with two bidders. Could you do it with four?'

'I could set it up for a dozen if you like,' he said.

I looked at Matravers. 'You said six was ideal, didn't you?'

He nodded. I went back to Bailey. 'Would it convince the kidnappers?

'From where they were sitting, it would appear just like the real thing.'

'And we could send fake contracts for each of the dummy bidders guaranteeing the prompt payment from the winner.'

'A fake auction for a fake painting. I like it,' said Cooper.

'It'll work. We've no intention of the kidnappers ever getting their hands on the actual cash, so we don't need real money. Just as long as they believe it,' I said.

'OK,' said Bailey. 'If Langdon comes up with fake names and typical profiles for each collector, I'll set up an email, web presence and digital footprint for each of them, online searches, previous auctions they've bid in, a few purchases, that sort of thing.'

'Would it stand up to a thorough search?'

'Yes,' he said confidently. 'I'll make sure of it.'

'How soon can you do this?'

Bailey looked at Matravers. 'What do you say? A few hours? This afternoon?'

'We can start straight away,' said Matravers.

'I'll be here at oh eight hundred on Monday morning to set up, if you think of anything else,' said Bailey confidently.

'You'll be here all the way through the auction?' I asked.

'I'll be here,' he said. 'Well, gentlemen, if there's nothing else, we'd better get on.'

Cooper helped Bailey pack up the bulk of his kit, leaving one laptop for him to work on.

I checked my watch. Time to hoof it back to the airport. 'Well, Matravers. Next time I see you, your fake auction will be over. You'll be free of these people and so will be Liz.'

'That will be a relief.' He looked awkward. 'Don't think I'm not grateful.'

'See you do your job.'

He looked at me shyly and spoke tentatively, 'That other thing. You won't forget? You know, you thought there might be a way…'

'I've not forgotten. Once this is all over, we'll see if we can't get you out of this financial hole.'

'Thank you.'

Cooper saw me out to the waiting taxi I'd called. 'If the auction's a fake, we won't need the bank to do anything. I could make a call and take the pressure off English?'

'You could but I'd rather you didn't. I've got a funny feeling about the kidnapper. He always seems to know what I'm up to and who I'm with. I wouldn't be surprised if he had someone at the bank who'd tell him if we cancelled things. Let's leave it as it is.' I hesitated before I got in the cab. 'You know, I'm really grateful to you for all your help with this.'

'Least I can do. And don't worry, I'll keep an eye on things here and make sure everyone plays their part. I'll have dinner with Matravers and McCloud this evening and I've booked them into the hotel for the weekend so I can keep an eye on them. I won't let either of them off the hook until after the auction.'

'You're a good pal, Guy.'

He grinned, 'What do you mean? I'm still chasing that promotion we talked about.' He turned serious. 'Your most important job before Monday is to find out where they are keeping Liz.'

It was after 5pm when I got back to the Goldcrest. I picked up my key then headed for Kat's room. She gave me a fashion parade, showing off the clothes she'd bought with my cash: smart trousers, stylish but practical blouses and footwear that looked good but wouldn't have her in agony after a night on her feet.

At 6pm on the dot, my phone rang. I put my finger to my lips and put the call on speaker so Kat could hear what the kidnapper said.

'Good to speak to you, Jake.'

'And to you.'

'You are safely back in Prague now?'

'No problem at all. How's Liz today?'

'Much calmer. She was so pleased to get your message.'

'Good to hear.'

'Is everything on track in Glasgow?'

I put my hand up and crossed my fingers. Kat smiled.

'All good. We currently have six bidders lined up and they've all provided the requested references, so we know they're good for the guide price. And I'm satisfied the auction technology is robust.'

'Excellent. I must say, I'm glad to be dealing with you.'

'And I you…I'm sorry I don't know what to call you.'

There was a hesitation before he answered. 'Call me Andy,' he said.

Kat looked as if she would explode. I put my hand across her mouth, and she got up and moved away from me.

'I'll ring you tomorrow at this time. Have a good night, Jake.'

'I will, Andy; goodnight.'

Kat took a bottle of vodka from the fridge and poured two healthy measures into shot glasses, passing one to me. She knocked hers back. I did the same. She poured two more.

'That bastard,' she said, shaking her head.

'Did you recognise his voice?'

'Andel Hendak.'

'Vanda's partner. How sure are you?'

She frowned. 'It's been eight years but I'm pretty sure. But I don't understand – why the hell are you being so polite to this man?'

'He's got Liz. But I'm playing him. I need him to trust me right up to the point when someone slams the handcuffs on him.'

'Now it makes sense.'

'What was the message he mentioned?'

'Liz was losing her cool and he didn't know what to do, so I asked him to remind her of the words of two old friends, Sam and Dave. He asked what that meant, and I made it sound as if they were two characters we used to know; I said they always used the phrase *keep calm and carry on*.'

'And that worked?'

'Like a charm. But the *actual* message was *remember the words of Sam and Dave*.'

'How did that help?'

'Liz and I didn't know anyone called by those names – the only pair we knew of made a recording of one of Liz's favourite tunes back in the 60s.'

'So?'

'It was called "Hold on, I'm Coming".'

Kat took my glass, placing it next to hers. Folding her arms around me, she hugged me close before pushing back to arm's length so she could look into my eyes. 'You wonderful, clever man. Hendak has no chance against you.'

It was all I could do to keep my mind on the job. 'How did it go last night?' I asked as she made coffee.

'Typical trial shift – they watched me closely to make sure I knew what I was doing. But everything was good. I'm to use my discretion and fill in where I see the need. The perfect opportunity to check Vanda's office.'

'Tonight's the night, then.'

'I'll need to get my head around Vanda's routine. She likes to keep her finger on the pulse, you know, make sure the team are managing the detail.' She frowned. 'I'll need to keep a close eye on her and her movements so I get a sense of how long I'll get in her office.'

'When I visited the club, she gave me complimentary tickets. Why don't I rock up and give you a hand?'

'Great idea,' said Kat. 'And Eva could be your date for the night. It'll look more natural if you have someone to talk to and dance with.'

'Sounds risky. Wasn't Eva part of your dance troupe all those years ago?'

Kat laughed. 'Even I didn't recognise her, and we were best friends. And back then, Eva was a scrawny brunette getting over the loss of her sister. Look at her now – a ravishing, sophisticated blonde with a sense of purpose. I'll do her make-up, just to be sure. As long as you two are careful.'

'It'll give me the chance to confirm Hendak is our man,' I said.

'How so?'

'Vanda's in this up to her neck. And the kidnapper told

me he'd talked to a colleague about my idea. So if Vanda knows about the kidnap, it'll prove that she and Hendak are in this together.'

'She's not stupid. Be careful.'

'Always.'

'Why are you frowning?' she asked.

I'd left my dinner suit in the boot of my car back at Heathrow airport. 'I have nothing with me that's smart enough for a glitzy night club at midnight.'

Kat smiled. 'I can fix that.'

Kat sought out Eva, who willingly joined our conspiracy, getting straight on the phone with a determined look in her eye, speaking in Czech. At first, she stood in front of the mirror answering the rapid-fire questions coming to her, then she studied me, conversing with Kat – still in Czech – and speaking into the phone. She scribbled on a piece of paper, shooed me from the room with instructions to go to the address I'd been given to make a collection. As I was leaving, Eva was heading into the shower and Kat was laying out a selection of cosmetics. I checked the time. Good job Kat was a quick worker.

I checked my watch again as Eva and I waited in the Goldcrest's reception. I'd brushed up well in the hired pinstriped, black velvet Hugo Boss suit, black shoes that went to a point at my toes, and a crisp white shirt with a discreet pattern on it. The hire shop had been well stocked. And Eva looked amazing, wearing a close-fitting, long-sleeved dress in shimmering silver, with a hemline that left little to the imagination and glossy natural-coloured tights. A short grey, velvet-hooded cape completed the look. I'd better watch myself; there'd be a queue of gallant young males fighting to take her home. With moussed up hair and lashings of war paint I'd say her chances of being recognised as the old Eva were zero. She'd even come up with a new name for the night – Mia – which we both needed to remember.

'How far will you be able to walk in those?' We looked at the towering silver heels she was wearing.

'These are nothing. Remember, I'm a trained dancer. I could Lambada in these if I needed to.'

A cab drew up. She shivered as we stepped out into the night air. It was another cool, clear, starlit night. I opened the waiting car's door for Eva before installing myself in the seat next to her.

She was the perfect distraction – amazing to look at and, according to Kat, more moves on the dance floor than Madonna: as every good magician knows, if you're going to pull a stunt, you need a powerful way to misdirect your audience. I caught sight of us in the rear-view mirror, me looking pretty suave and Eva in full-on glam, draped in her grey velvet. I thought about Kat's attitude to disguise – maybe I'd do well to spend a few minutes thinking through my role as a soon-to-be partner to a bunch of kidnappers and extortionists?

I checked Eva's cape into the cloakroom and flashed our tickets. We went through to the main area of the club. It was buzzing. The dance floor was full of smartly dressed couples strutting their stuff and trying hard to be noticed. The tables around the two bars held a mixture of chatting guests and voyeurs who'd come to watch the show and soak up the atmosphere. Six professional dancers set the pace from the stage whilst, from her place above it, the iconic Dark Goddess cast an amused eye across them all.

The sound level felt just right, loud enough to make you want to dance but low enough to allow conversation. Kat was serving and greeted me like any other customer. She poured a couple of sparkling waters into Champagne glasses – we needed to look like we were partying while staying sober.

'As it's your first time here, let me show you around,' said Kat.

She gestured with her arms, pretending to point out the club's features, whilst we spoke in low voices.

'From the balcony you'll be able to see when Vanda leaves her office and when she's on her way back there.' A row of small tables was arranged along the edge of the balcony, some of which were occupied by couples chatting or watching the dancers. 'The third table from the left is empty and would be perfect; you'll have a good view of the ground floor. I'll station myself in the bar on the opposite side of the dance floor, so you'll be able to signal to me discreetly. Use Vanda's first two trips to see how long she's out and I'll come up on number three.'

'What if she only comes out twice?'

'Trust me, she won't. Her exact routine might have changed, but I know her, and I know she likes to keep a close eye on things. She'll want to check on everything at least three times.'

'OK – once you're in, I'll have Eva keep watch from the table and I'll move back and lean against the office door. I'll keep an eye on the time and warn you when I reckon you have five minutes to go. As a make-sure, I'll have Eva signal me when Vanda's on her way back and I'll rap on the door.'

'Great. When I come up to go into her office, be having a conversation with Eva, hold your hands up for emphasis and use the number of fingers you show for the number of minutes you think I have. Don't talk to me up there – too many people may be watching.'

Kat returned to the bar and Eva and I went back through reception and into the lift, which swooshed discreetly up to the first floor. The doors opened onto the glitzy dining terrace with its view over the dance floor. We walked through the tables of diners to reach the balcony in front of Vanda's office.

'Someone's got in ahead of us. What shall we do?' said Eva.

The couple at the table we'd picked out looked as if they were there for the night.

'Wait here,' I said to Eva. 'Be ready to move in as soon as they get up.'

I grabbed a napkin and a *Reserved* notice from the nearest vacant dining table. I put the napkin over my arm, adopted an ingratiating smile and walked across to the young couple sitting at the target table. They were speaking to each other quietly in up-market East Coast American accents. I gave a half bow and spoke in the poshest English accent I could convincingly manage. 'I'm terribly sorry, Sir, Madam, but this table is reserved.'

I received a polite smile back but no attempt to move. The bloke had a bored expression on his face as he reached for his wallet. 'I'm sure you could find another suitable table for the other party?' he said, holding out a handful of high denomination notes.

I gave a small cough. 'That's very kind of you, Sir, but you see, this gentleman is a very special guest. It appears that his lawyer rang us to reserve this particular table this afternoon, but my colleague neglected to put a notice on it.' I put the sign down on the table.

'You say his lawyer booked it?'

'Yes, Sir, apparently the gentleman is celebrating having escaped a jail term for grievous bodily harm, and he and his lawyer are going to celebrate his good fortune here tonight.' Eva was close enough to hear every word. Out of the corner of my eye, I could see her lips twitching.

The guy took more notes from his wallet, waving the enlarged bundle towards me.

'That's most kind of you to offer, but I'm advised that the gentlemen in question only got off the charge because the witnesses to the crime refused to testify at the last minute. I don't believe he's the sort of chap you can say no to.' I looked at my watch. 'He's due to arrive in the next five minutes. Best I get the table ready for him.' I moved their glasses and started to wipe the table with my napkin.

'C'mon Brad, we're leaving,' said the woman, rising and grabbing Brad's arm and marching him back towards the lift, ignoring his protests.

Leaving the *Reserved* sign on the table, I dropped the napkin on the floor and pulled out a chair for Eva. She put our glasses down and I sat alongside her. Kat looked up from the bar below and gave me a discreet wink.

Eva was staring at me. 'I didn't know you were such an actor.'

'It just came to me. The only English accents they ever hear in America invariably belong to smooth TV villains. I copied my friend Nellie's accent – you'll meet him tomorrow, although he's no villain – just a rogue.'

Kat sent a colleague up with fresh drinks and some canapés.

We'd arranged our chairs so that I could look out over the balcony while Eva was at my side, facing me. She'd be able to keep an eye on Vanda's comings and goings, and I'd have my back towards Vanda's office, making me indistinguishable from every other bloke watching the eye candy on the dance floor. Eva nudged me just after 9pm and I started timing. I risked a quick look across the restaurant towards the lift, following Vanda's progression through the busy restaurant. It was peak trough time – lots of diners getting stuck into their fancy cuisine. Vanda stood in the lift and, as the glass doors closed behind her, I turned away before she could spot me. Looking over the balcony, I saw her walk from the reception area, stopping at the bar on each side of the dance floor and chatting to the staff. I saw Kat busying herself at the back of the bar, keeping out of sight. Vanda waved and smiled to regular customers, exchanging a few words as she edged around the dance floor, heading for the DJ. She moved gently, in time to the music, as she watched the professional dancers. It all seemed pretty relaxed.

Her next foray was similar, at around 11.05pm. I did a quick mental calculation of how long she'd been out on each occasion. The average was near enough twenty-two minutes. When she came out for the third time, just after 1am, we were ready for her. I caught Kat's eye and nodded. Vanda strode towards the dance floor and, once she was past the bars, Kat made for the lift. I started a conversation with Eva as Kat walked towards us. Eva shook her head, pretending she couldn't hear. I held up both my hands, fingers spread wide, closed them into fists and opened them again. Twenty minutes – keeping two minutes back, just in case.

I got up from the table, briefly facing Kat. She blinked once as she walked past me, inserted her key into the lock of Brazda's door and was in. I took up my station, leaning back against the door.

Eva looked towards me and gave a discreet thumbs up.

The hands on my watch seemed to have sped up. At twelve minutes, a member of staff accosted me – could he be of assistance? I adopted a pissed-off expression and told him my girlfriend and I had argued and we were cooling down. His expression said *we've all been there, mate*. I slipped him a middling denomination note, and he left me to it. My watch put on a spurt and, at eighteen minutes, I saw Eva reach for her evening bag: our prearranged signal.

When Vanda moved back towards the bar area, Eva was to take out her compact, open it up and pout, messing with her hair and make-up. I saw the compact come out of her bag several times before she opened the small circular steel case and the mirror caught the light as she teased her hair. I rapped the knuckles of my right hand against the door behind me. Nothing happened. Had Kat heard me? Maybe the door was sound-proofed? I should have checked.

I kept an eye on the lift doors. Another minute and I saw them slide open. I drummed with both my hands this time. No response. Vanda came out of the lift and stopped in the restaurant for a chat with the head waiter. He'd been busy earlier but was chilled now it was a bit quieter. Vanda, I could see, was asking questions, listening intently to his answers. I glanced at my watch. Twenty-one minutes had passed.

Eva mouthed *what's happening?* at me and I shrugged. I rapped on the door again as loud as I dared.

Come on Kat, what's keeping you?

Vanda put her hand on the head waiter's arm, gave a last decisive nod and started walking towards me. What the hell was I to do? Having Kat caught red-handed in Vanda's office wasn't part of the plan. I walked smartly across to Eva and whispered discreetly in her ear, 'Stand and turn. We're about to bump into Vanda. And remember: your name's Mia.'

I put my arm around her and laughed. 'Well I can't say I'm a great dancer, but we'll give it one last go.' We made as if to head towards the lift just as Vanda reached us.

'Good evening, Jake. It's a pleasure to see you again.' Interesting. When I met her on Tuesday, her manner had been much cooler. 'It's good to have you here when the club is open.'

Wow – a warm smile from her.

'And you have a friend with you.'

'Ms Brazda…' I said.

'Call me Vanda.'

'Vanda. This is Mia. We met in a bar last night and I invited her along. I hope you don't mind?'

'Not at all. It's a pleasure to meet you, Mia. Are you from Prague?'

'Oh no,' Eva replied, 'I'm originally from Průhonice. But it's dead there. I wanted more action, more life. And now I've met this rather nice English gentleman.'

The door of Vanda's office edged open. I half-turned and moved towards the balcony's edge, looking out across the space below us. 'What a place, Vanda! It's a great big party down there. You really know how to set a place alight, don't you?'

She stepped closer to me and, with Mia waiting just behind her, the possibility of her noticing what was happening at her office door was eliminated. I saw, from the corner of my eye, Kat emerge, close the door softly and move towards the lift.

Vanda was close enough that I caught the faint aroma of her fragrance; difficult to make out, there was something musky going on, confused by cigarette smoke and warm bodies. Her lips were close to my ear. Then came that low, gravelly voice again. 'I believe we may be doing business together in the near future. You must meet Andel, my business partner, next time you're here.'

'I'd like that. We have a lot to talk about.'

'I'll be with him on Monday for the auction. He's looking forward to meeting you in person.' She stepped back and spoke in a louder voice once more. 'Now Mia – you seem familiar. Have we met before?'

How would Eva respond? Out of the corner of my eye, I saw the lift doors close behind Kat.

Eva shook her head. 'No. I don't think so and I've never been here before.'

'No matter. You remind me of someone I used to know.'

'Well, you must be busy. We mustn't keep you,' I said.

'Yes, I should get on. I hope you're both enjoying your evening with us?'

'Mia and I have had a great time, thank you. She's dragging me down to the dance floor one last time and then we'll be on our way.'

It was 3.30am by the time we three regrouped in Kat's room. Ladislav had provided very welcome cold plates – whether they were meant as a very late supper or an early breakfast wasn't clear but then it's pretty rare that you wash your breakfast down with a decent brandy.

We'd each gone to our rooms to 'de-glam'. I was back in jeans and a cashmere sweater. Eva had swapped the silver dress and towering heels for a bathrobe and lost the moussed-up hair and war paint. Kat's wig was resting in a drawer somewhere and she'd ditched the staid slacks and blouse in favour of faded jeans and the baseball shirt. She smiled as she noticed me admiring her toenails: immaculately manicured and painted a striking claret in colour. She wiggled her toes and blew me a kiss.

The three of us lay in a circle on the huge bed, the food in the middle, brandy glasses perched on plates, as if we were having a picnic in the middle of the park. And now with everyone settled, it was time to see where we were. I looked expectantly at Kat.

'All the time I knew Vanda, she carried around a pocket notebook. It used to contain all her notes about everything she was working on at the time. I knew she wouldn't be carrying the notebook around the club so I assumed it would be somewhere in her office. I was sure that if I could get a look inside it, we'd find what we needed to know,' she said. 'Her desk was clear, so I went through the desk drawers.'

'They could have been locked.'

'They were.'

'How did you get in?'

'I just did.'

'You can pick locks?' I persisted.

'Of course. What did you think I was going to do?'

'Good point.'

'Nothing there, so I turned my attention to the filing cabinets…'

'And?'

'Just bills and receipts.'

I sighed.

'But then, I found it.'

'Where?'

'In her jacket, hanging on the back of the door.'

'Don't keep us in suspense.'

'Nothing useful. A few current notes about things in the club, some phone numbers for suppliers, some stuff crossed through as dealt with and a whole bunch of missing pages. The only interesting thing was the sign-in details for Monday's auction.'

'Where does that take us?' I asked with a sinking heart.

'Her computer.'

'Of course,' I said. 'Why didn't I think of that before?' I remembered the CCTV image of me studying the windows around the dance floor. What better way of monitoring a captive than putting a camera on them? 'What did you find?'

'Nothing. It was password protected. I tried everything I could think of. That's what took the time, and it's why I was late coming out.'

'You were nearly caught.'

'I know. I'm sorry.'

'One good thing came out of our little conversation with Vanda.'

'What was that?'

'Confirmation. Andel Hendak is definitely our man.'

'Big surprise,' said Eva.

'We're no closer to finding out where they're holding Liz, are we?' I said, with a heavy heart.

'Can't we just force it out of them when they're arrested?' said Kat.

'Last resort. There's sure to be others involved and who knows what might happen to Liz while we're asking questions,' I said.

'What *can* we do?' asked Eva.

We all pondered for a moment.

'I see two possibilities,' I said eventually. 'Reuben and his friends have been trailing Hendak and Vanda – maybe they've spotted something? Our only other option is to crack Vanda's computer.'

'I'm sure that if Reuben had seen anything, he'd have been in touch,' said Kat, shaking her head. 'What happens if we can't find anything?'

'She *has* to be somewhere.' I paused. 'There's no other option,' I said then, half to myself. 'We'll check with him tomorrow.'

Kat's expression changed.

I frowned, looking at her. 'What are you thinking, Kat?'

'There might be something in Vanda's apartment. I could get in there and take a look around.'

'Now you're a Kat burglar?' I said, trying to lighten the mood we were sinking into.

Eva had been listening quietly. 'It's not possible. I know, I've tried to get in there before.' A wave of frustration swept across her face. 'I thought I might find something that would link her or Hendak to the drugs racket that killed my sister. I wanted someone to pay for Ana's death.' She shook her head. 'But Vanda put in a new security system and has guards in the lobby.'

Kat put her arm around her. Eva wiped her eyes on the back of her hand, angrily.

I looked at my watch. 'That's enough for tonight; let's get some rest. We have a couple of possibilities, and that will do for now. Eva, can you get a message to Reuben and Tomáš for us all to meet at the restaurant at midday? And, Kat, can you and I meet at ten? I need your help with a call; I want to ask an expert how we get into Vanda's computer.'

10 | SUNDAY 19TH OCTOBER

Kat opened her bedroom door just as I was about to knock on it. She made coffee whilst I dialled Bailey.

'Quentin Bailey.'

'Morning, Q. I need your advice.'

'That's no problem. How can I help?'

With Kat next to me, coffee in hand, and the phone on speaker, I explained the situation. 'So, you see, we need to get into Vanda's computer. I'm hoping that we'll find a video image or something that'll give us a clue as to where they're holding Liz.'

'Kat, please talk me through the computer set-up.'

I was astonished when Kat was able to reel off the exact detail, including the make and model of the computer and modem. 'I didn't know you had a photographic memory,' I said in a stage whisper.

She smiled. 'You don't know all my talents. Yet.'

'We'll need the telephone number they use to hook up to the web,' said Bailey.

Kat reeled it off. Just like that. She saw my astonished expression. 'I found the phone bill when I went through the filing cabinet.'

'I don't suppose you found the internet service provider's invoice as well?' asked Bailey.

'I did,' she said and trotted out their name.

'That's going to save us a lot of time,' said Bailey.

We heard the thump of the keys as he worked the keyboard on his laptop. 'That provider's in Prague.'

'Why do you need to know who and where they are?'

'Every time a computer goes online, their service provider allocates an IP address to the phone number being used – it's like a postcode, allowing messages to be routed to and from it. But the IP address isn't fixed; it's randomly allocated from a block they hold. I'll need the service provider to give me the IP address the first time I hook up to this machine. After that, with the software I'm going to install, I'll be able to find it whenever it goes online.'

'How does it work?' I asked.

'If Kat can get into the office again this evening and make sure the computer is switched on and connected, I'll need an undisturbed half-hour to download my software and run some checks. If you can stay with the PC, Kat, in case I need you to do anything, that'd be grand.'

Kat looked doubtful. 'Half an hour? What if Vanda comes back and I'm still in there?'

'Don't worry. I'll keep her occupied,' I said.

She raised an eyebrow.

'What happens next?' I asked Q.

'Another session, longer this time. I'll need up to a couple of hours to download everything from the target machine to mine,' said Bailey.

'A couple of hours?' exclaimed Kat.

'Yes, but I don't need you to be there for that, Kat. If you can just make sure the machine is still on when everyone leaves the building tonight, I'll have all the time I need. What time will the place be empty?'

'Two in the morning. I'll hide in the toilets till everyone has left,' said Kat.

'And the CCTV will spot you as soon as you come out,' I said.

Q cut in. 'The only person that will see her on the CCTV footage is me. I'll doctor it.'

'I need to know where Liz is before the auction finishes,' I said.

'Plenty of time. The auction doesn't start until eleven. I'll have downloaded everything by four am, which gives me a solid seven hours. It'll be like being in the service again. I'll ring Matravers now. If I set up in his offices this afternoon, I can be there all night.'

'Better have some strong coffee to hand.'

'Jake, you'll need someone to twist the service provider's arm to provide me with the IP address for that first look-see. They won't like it.'

'I know just the man,' I said, thinking of my contact at Interpol.

'Kat, I'll be waiting by the phone this evening when you get into the office.'

'No problem. I'll speak to you later.'

'Let me speak to my Interpol contact, Q, and I'll call you later to let you know what we agreed.'

'Speak later.'

Kat made more coffee whilst I dialled Lambert.

''Allo?'

I filled him in on the details.

'This man Bailey sounds interesting.'

'He trained with the Royal Navy.'

'Very impressive. Fortunately, we had a similar situation a couple of weeks ago so if you can let me have Monsieur Bailey's contact details, I can put him in touch with our expert who will apply the necessary leverage to the service provider.'

I'd just finished the call when the room phone rang. Kat answered it. 'Thanks Eva, I'll let him know.' She turned to me. 'Your friend Neville Bosworth is here.'

I looked at my watch. Excellent timing. 'First thing is a room reorganise. This room goes back to being Liz's and now Nellie's. Eva's single is otherwise occupied tonight but a double's come free which you two can share.'

'Yummy, a little girl-on-girl action. Shame we won't be getting an early night.'

I shook my head in theatrical prudishness. 'Let's go over to Reuben's for lunch and a team meeting, when you two have become reacquainted.'

I left her laughing at her own joke and went to find Nellie.

He was chatting with the duty security guard when I reached reception – or, more accurately, Nellie was doing the talking while the bloke in uniform hung on every word. Nellie always said it was his natural leadership qualities, but I figured they took one look at him and saw a chump with more money than sense. Good job he had me to look out for him. He stood as I approached. The security guard hung on to Nellie's briefcase as if it contained the Crown Jewels. He seemed reluctant to let it go.

'How're you doing, me old mucker?' Nellie looked like he hadn't slept for a week. To be fair, he probably hadn't, given how worried he must have been about Liz.

'Just the man I need. I've got a job for you.'

'Tell me more.'

'Let's get your gear to your room and you can meet the team over lunch.'

'Great plan. I'm starving.'

'Yeah,' I said. 'You look it; didn't they feed you on the plane?'

'Oh, you know how it is, canapés, Champagne, foie gras. It's such a trial being in first class.'

'My heart weeps for you. Well, today you get proper food and then I'll tell you what I need you to do.'

'I just want to say, Jake, how grateful I am to you, for taking this on.'

'All part of the service.'

Eva and Kat were waiting for us in the bar. Eva stood to shake hands with the Honourable Neville Bosworth, whilst Kat appraised him quietly.

'I'm hungry,' said Kat. 'Let's go.'

'Good idea,' I said.

Coats were grabbed and we met in reception. Kat, in her black wig, came up to me for a quiet word.

'Why don't you walk with Neville and Eva and I'll follow separately? In case anyone recognises me from the club.'

We took over Reuben's back room again and Tomáš met us there. Reuben and Pavel served goulash with fresh bread and a good red wine. With the bowls cleared and strong coffee served, I brought everyone up to date.

'The auction will start at eleven am tomorrow and will last for up to thirty minutes. Then we raid the club.'

'Do you know where they're holding Liz?' asked Nellie.

'We'll find out tonight,' I said.

Reuben raised his hand. 'My friends took on the task of following Hendak and Brazda whenever they were outside of the club. Something strange happened yesterday. Hendak was seen going in at ten am yesterday morning and then again at two pm.'

'No one saw him leave in between times?' I asked.

Reuben shook his head.

I looked at Tomáš. 'What other exits are there? I asked.

'There are only the fire doors and they're alarmed.'

Reuben put up his hand again. 'My colleague did some research yesterday evening. He has a friend in the Catholic church who has made a study of our oldest religious buildings here.' He leaned forward in his seat. 'That particular church was rumoured to have been built with a tunnel. Prague could be a dangerous place in the Middle Ages, and sometimes priests would need to protect valuables and themselves.'

'Do we know where the tunnel led?'

'We were lucky and my colleague was thorough. It led from the crypt to a nearby house. Unfortunately, this map fell into his case while he was looking at it. He will return it later.' He drew out a musty old parchment and spread it on the table in front of us, weighing down the corners with empty coffee cups. The map showed a dotted line leading from the church to a building on the edge of the square. The building faced out of the square, meaning anyone leaving it would not be visible to someone watching the church.

'I never knew there was a tunnel down there,' said Kat.

'No one ever said anything about a tunnel to me,' agreed Tomáš.

'I hear you both but,' I said, pointing at the map, 'Hendak left the club by some means and there's no other way than the tunnel. But the question is – why leave that way?' I turned to Reuben. 'Could he have spotted your watcher?'

'An old man, sitting on a bench feeding the pigeons? Not a chance.'

'Then he had another reason.' I pointed to the map. 'What's this building?'

Reuben responded. 'A three-storey house.'

My mind went back to the image of Liz sitting on a bed

with the newspaper in front of her. A bedroom in a house? I'd bet on it – in fact, I *was* betting on it, in a way. 'Then that's where they have Liz.'

'We could set up a raid right now. Talk to your contact at Interpol, and we could have Liz out this very night,' said Nellie.

'No,' I said firmly. 'Liz is safe where she is right now and the last thing we want to do is storm the building and put her at risk. No, we'll stick with our plan. We'll go in tonight and confirm this on the computer. I bet their CCTV will cover all the entrances and exits for both buildings. We'll be able to use the tunnel to access the house tomorrow morning. Whilst Hendak and Vanda are being arrested, we can rescue Liz.'

'That's all very well but what's going to keep Vanda out of her office for half an hour while I play with her computer?' asked Kat.

'Simple,' I said. 'Nellie and I will have a fight.'

'What? Have you lost it?' said Nellie.

'Hear me out,' I said. 'Eva and I go to the club again, like we did last night. Nellie, you'll come in after us. You'll need to look like you've had a few drinks. Can you manage that?'

'I've had plenty of practice.'

'Eva and I will be on the dance floor. As soon as Vanda comes down from her office, Nellie, you'll leave the bar and cut in with Eva, edging me out of the way. We'll have a slanging match and do some pushing and shoving,' I said.

'Vanda will get her tough guys from the door to throw you out,' said Kat.

I smiled. 'I've thought of that. Vanda thinks I'm in league with her and Hendak, so she'll want to keep things civilized and me happy. We'll make sure she's occupied until you're back downstairs. And I'll have the police on standby just in case.'

'Great,' said Nellie. 'I get to knock you about in public. It's been a long time coming, mate.' Looking at Eva, he added, 'And I'd say she's worth a few cuts and bruises, wouldn't you?'

Eva giggled girlishly while Kat considered him coolly.

I spoke again. 'Are we clear what we're all doing tonight? Good. Now tomorrow morning – Tomáš, can you make sure the doors are open for us by the end of the auction? And can you put the camera on the main entrance out of action? Maybe turn it off and on a few times in the morning so they think it's on the blink, then off completely just before eleven. We'll have two raiding parties: one to arrest Hendak and Vanda, the other to go through the tunnel for Liz. Nellie and Tomáš, if you go with the group to get Liz, then Kat and I will go with the first group. Reuben, could you and your friends be our long-range sweepers? We'll need you outside both buildings and we'll want a description of anyone you see leaving who might be trying to make a getaway.'

'What about me?' said Eva.

'We couldn't have got this far without your help, Eva and we need you again this evening. But tomorrow, you can take a break and I'm sure Ladislav will be glad to have you back on his team a hundred percent,' I replied.

She looked disgruntled but said nothing. I took five minutes at the end of the meeting to update Bailey on our plan for tomorrow. I also alerted him to the tunnel and the likelihood of Liz being held in the house.

Sunday night started like an action replay of Saturday, with Eva and me pouring ourselves into our rented finery, catching a cab and rocking up to the club. Nellie put on the dinner suit he'd brought with him – flash bastard – and took a later cab. Kat left before all of us to be in time for the start of her shift.

So there we were: Kat behind the bar, Nellie propping it up and Eva and me strutting our stuff on the dance floor. Although it was a Sunday in October, it was still pretty busy. Not quite as crowded as the night before but there were plenty of blokes in smart suits with expensive watches worn like medals and women in short dresses. I kept an eye on Kat who was on the lookout for Vanda.

We'd been there about an hour when Kat looked me squarely in the eye and nodded. A minute later Vanda strolled out from the direction of the lift. As she walked towards the DJ, Nellie followed her but then changed direction towards Eva and me. I hoped he wouldn't overplay the stage drunk. I pretended to ignore him, smiled at Eva and concentrated on dancing. I felt a tap on my shoulder and turned.

'I say, old chap, you'll let me dance with your beautiful partner, won't you?'

'No,' I said, turning back to Eva.

'Oh, go on,' he slurred. 'What's happened to Prague hospitality? You people are supposed to make visitors welcome.'

'That lets me off. I'm not from these parts.'

'A fellow Brit, eh? Even more reason why you should let me dance with your girl. She's bound to prefer me to you. After all, I'm properly dressed.'

'Why don't you just clear off and leave us alone?'

Nellie put his hand on my arm and pulled me around. 'Not cricket, Fella. You know the rules; the best man has to win.'

I moved as if to turn back but Nellie stopped me. I pushed him. He pushed me back, harder. A space cleared around us. Eva stepped away, leaving the two contestants facing each other. We crouched forward and stared into each other's eyes.

'How'm I doing?' said Nellie, out of the corner of his mouth.

'It's working,' I whispered. 'Vanda's coming over. Count to ten then swing for me.'

Vanda arrived on the scene. 'Is this man bothering you, Jake?'

With perfect timing, Nellie aimed a blow at my head which I ducked. Vanda grabbed his outstretched arm and twisted it up behind him. Nellie grimaced and stood very still.

'You can let him go, Vanda, just a misunderstanding.'

She dropped his arm and I grabbed his hand as if to shake it, then spoke softly in his ear, 'I had a great night with Liz at Burgh Island. She didn't leave my room until four in the morning.'

The colour drained from his face and he bared his teeth. Then he came at me. His first swing delivered a stinging blow to my jaw; the second knocked the wind out of me. I managed to parry the third only to suffer a clout to the side of my head. He was swearing under his breath as his hands pummelled me, his human punch bag. I put both my arms up in front of my face, saving me from the worst of it. But he kept the punishment coming.

'Bastard,' he said. 'You're going to regret this.'

Vanda had stepped back, silenced by the frenzied attack.

I stepped in towards Nellie, keeping my arms up to block his jabs. In close, I hugged him with my left and swung with my right.

'That's good, keep it up,' I whispered.

'Oh, you want more do you? See if you like this.'

Nellie redoubled his attack, his hands spinning like windmills around my head. Just as well that two familiar "off-duty" coppers chose that moment to grab him by the arms and pull him back. With Bramley's mate holding a quietly-simmering Nellie, Bramley got out his notebook.

'Ms Brazda, can you tell me what happened?'

I checked my watch. We'd been twenty minutes, so that meant we needed, say, another fifteen to be on the safe side. The DJ had stopped the music, and everyone was standing there, distracted by the spectacle.

Eva came over, putting her hand up to my eyebrow. 'That's a nasty graze.' She turned on Nellie, and shouted at him. 'You bully. You deserve everything you get.'

A member of staff brought a first aid kit and Eva made a drama out of the incident by insisting on daubing ointment onto a large plaster and sticking it above my right eye.

I checked my watch again. We were good to go. Bramley was still questioning Vanda. I caught his eye and scratched my nose. The agreed signal. He brought Vanda over.

'I'm pleased to say that despite the disturbance you've caused, Ms Brazda is prepared to let the matter drop if she sees you two shake hands and apologise. Would that be acceptable?'

Nellie was tight-lipped as he took my hand. 'You've not heard the last of this,' he goaded, before standing back and broadcasting a sincere-sounding apology.

I could see he was still angry but there was nothing I could do with Vanda Brazda watching us both. 'It's forgotten. C'mon, I'll buy you a drink,' I replied.

'That's kind of you but I think I've had enough. I'll say goodnight.'

'Are you satisfied, Ms Brazda?'

'Completely. Jake, Mia, come up to my office for Champagne – just the thing to take the sting out of your bruises. I'll find someone to bring it to us.'

We passed Kat on our way to the lift. My heart rate climbed as we approached Vanda's office door: would everything be just as she'd left it? We went in and made ourselves comfortable. A knock came on the door.

'Come,' said Vanda, in her strong, gravelly voice.

No! It was Kat, carrying a loaded silver tray. She looked completely professional as she placed it on the desk.

'Please pour for us,' said Vanda without so much as glancing in Kat's direction.

Kat took off the foil and removed the cork, poured three glasses and returned the bottle to the ice bucket. She handed a glass to each of us then turned to go.

'Just a moment,' said Vanda.

Kat hesitated and my blood ran cold.

Kat turned to face the music, her expression neutral. 'Yes, Ma'am?' she drawled.

'I haven't seen you before, have I?'

'No, Ma'am. I only started yesterday evening.'

'That explains it. You may go.' And, just like that, Kat was dismissed. Vanda turned to Eva and me. 'Cheers,' she said, raising her glass.

We couldn't have been in Vanda's office for more than thirty minutes, and she, of course, was on her best behaviour now she thought I might provide a new income stream for her – but even so, I breathed a sigh of relief as, bottle emptied, we said our goodbyes.

Eva and I returned to the bar and Kat came over as soon as she was free.

'How did it go?' I asked.

'All good,' said Kat. 'I had a confirmation from Q. I just have to go back in and turn everything on at closing time.'

'Won't they be suspicious if the machine's still on when they come in tomorrow morning?'

'Tomáš will get in early and make sure everything's off.'

***

Eva and I took a cab back to the hotel, where we found Nellie in the bar, glass in hand.

'Not sure I'm talking to you,' he scowled.

'C'mon. You know nothing happened between Liz and me, don't you? I just needed you to make our scuffle look convincing.'

'Is that right?' he said. 'I'll just have to believe you until we see her, won't I? Still, it looks like you've taken a good beating, mate.' He grinned.

I put my hand up to my jaw and felt the bruise developing there. 'I've had worse.'

'How's your plan developing?'

'All good so far. Just need Kat to get back and confirm she's got the PC turned on again.'

Nellie looked at his watch. 'What time will that be?'

'Club closes at two am.'

'Nothing to do but finish this wine then.'

'Haven't you had enough?'

'Only my second tonight and there's a bottle to finish.'

'I'll get some more glasses.'

Kat came in at 2.45am, by which time Eva had gone to bed. I poured the last of the wine into a clean glass and handed it to her. 'I salute you,' I said.

She smiled and sipped from her glass.

'I think I'm about done for the night,' I said.

'What time's reveille?' said Nellie.

'Breakfast at nine am,' I said.

'Oh good. A whole six hours. Better get your girl to bed,' said Nellie, gesturing towards Kat, who was asleep in her chair, her half-full wine glass precariously gripped in her hand. I gently removed the glass and placed it on the table.

'C'mon, Sleeping Beauty. Time for nite nite.'

She murmured something I couldn't catch as I put my arm around her and walked her along the ground floor corridor to the room she was sharing with Eva. The only problem was that Eva was already asleep and the door was locked.

With nothing else for it, I took her to the lift, squeezed us both in and up to the top floor and my miniscule room. Now what? I slipped off her shoes and dress and eased her into my bed. I grabbed a spare pillow and blanket and prepared myself for a night on the floor when the murmuring sound from the bed formed into barely intelligible words.

'C'mon, it's cold in here.'

I didn't need to be asked twice. Modestly keeping my Calvin Kleins on, I budged up tight on the narrow bed, pulled off her wig and threw it across the floor. Settling down, I wrapped my arms around her warm, slumbering body. Exhausted, I was asleep in seconds.

11 | MONDAY MORNING 20TH OCTOBER

My mobile rang at 8am. I levered myself out of bed and reached for it, sitting on the floor.

'Morning, Jake. Enjoyed your lie-in?' It was Bailey's now familiar voice.

'Makes a change for you to be giving me a wake-up call.'

'I have news. I've been through the video. First thing I did was to edit out the sections with Kat going in and out of Brazda's office and her late escape from the building at the end of the night. I then went back in and overwrote their file copy and back up. Their stored footage shows they have cameras just about everywhere. I've been able to piece together a rough layout of the building – or should I say buildings?'

'Could you see the tunnel?'

'Clear as day. The basement camera showed someone entering it at 12 noon on Saturday.'

'And what about Liz? Any clues as to where they're holding her?'

'Your hunch was right. They have her in what looks like a luxurious suite at the back of the house on the first floor.'

I breathed a sigh of relief. 'That's brilliant news. I didn't fancy going up to the front door of their little pad and asking to see her. Tunnel's a much better bet. Only issue now is how we get access to the basement. Kat tells me there are two options – an alarmed staircase designated as a fire escape, or the lift. We'd need a four-digit security code to take the lift. But if we use the fire escape, the alarm will sound.'

'Then you're in luck. There's a camera inside the lift that picks up everything. I'll fax you my map of the place with the four-digit code written on the side.'

'Great, Q, thank you. We'll speak later.'

I filled the kettle and made a strong coffee in the one available cup. I took a swig and sat on the edge of the bed.

'I'm awake,' came a muffled voice from under the tangle of bed clothes. A hand came out and grabbed the cup from me. 'I need a shower,' Kat said, sitting up, sheets and blankets falling around her waist. 'Don't gawp. It's not like you haven't seen all this before.'

At some time in the night, she'd removed her bra and knickers. She kissed my forehead and handed me back the cup. 'Stop looking so gormless and finish the coffee while I wash.'

I nearly choked on the dregs as I watched her head into the tiny bathroom, and I tried – and failed – to resist watching as she stood behind the glass door of the shower, water pouring over her naked form as she applied creamy bodywash. Now I *was* awake.

She dried, dressed and kissed me on the forehead again before skedaddling downstairs to the room she should be sharing with Eva. She was to meet me for breakfast in half an hour. I had just enough time for a rapid shower before I caught up with Lambert on the phone.

Nellie, Eva and Kat were already tucking in when I reached the dining room. Kat pulled out the seat next to her, looking full of energy, and her smile dazzling like the bright morning sunshine outside. She was laughing at me. 'My turn to get you a coffee, now I'm dressed.'

I nodded my agreement and watched her walk across to the buffet, fill a mug and add just the right amount of milk. She took toast, butter and scrambled eggs, loading the egg with black pepper the way she'd seen me do it, carrying everything back to the table and placing it in front of me.

'Now eat. It's a big day and you'll need your wits about you.'

Nellie took it all in with an astonished half-smile on his face but, unusually for him, didn't comment.

I turned to Kat as she sat down again. 'Thank you,' I said.

'You're welcome,' she replied.

Oh, I'd got it bad. Just a short time ago I'd had this girl in my arms. I could get used to this. If only… She was looking at me expectantly. *Quick. Think of something to say.* Just faster than a slow-moving train, I came out with, 'No disguise today?'

'I think we're past that, don't you?'

I was walking back through reception when my phone rang. It was the kidnapper, Hendak. I looked at my watch: forty-five minutes to go.

'Good morning, Jake. How are you? It's a fine day. I hope you'll have time to enjoy Prague in the sunshine today?'

'Morning, Andy. Are you ready for the auction?'

'Yes. I'm looking forward to watching it and that's why I'm ringing you. I need a favour. I have a last-minute bidder for the painting. He's very keen. Would you please organise access for him?'

'He'll need to sign the paperwork to say he'll pay up promptly if he wins.'

'That won't be necessary. I can vouch for him.'

'What if he refuses?'

'He won't. I guarantee it. Let me give you his details.'

'Hold on, I'll grab a pen.' There was some headed paper and a pen on the reception desk.

'His name is Andre Luganov. Here is his email address.'

I jotted it down. 'We'll organise this straight away.'

'Excellent. I will call you this afternoon so that we can meet to transfer our guest to you and discuss our future together.'

'I look forward to it.'

'Thank you, Jake. I'm grateful. We will speak later.'

'We will,' I said, terminating the call. 'We certainly bloody will.'

I dialled Bailey. 'I've just had the kidnapper on the phone. He wants us to enrol a late bidder. Here are the details. It may be some kind of test. Can you fix it?'

'Consider it done.'

I phoned Guy Cooper on his number and filled him in. He listened silently. 'Interesting,' he said. 'A late runner for a fake auction.'

'I'm wondering if it's some sneaky way of checking it's a real auction. But I can't see how it would prove anything. Or maybe this guy, Luganov, has the cash but needs to see that other people want it before he'll commit.' An idea occurred to me. 'Pass me across to Q, will you?'

Two unmarked cars pulled up outside the hotel. Lambert was in the back of the first, Bramley in the second. Lambert signalled: time to go. Eva called the others and gave them the message that I'd meet them outside in two minutes. Q came on the line.

'That trick you pulled the other night to get into Vanda's computer. Would it work in reverse?'

'Explain,' said Q.

'This guy, Luganov. We only have his email address, but

we know he's going to be online at the start of the auction. Can we use that information in some way to find his phone number and from that get his location?'

'Yes. Luganov's email is supplied by a service provider in the UK that I know well. I'll speak to my contact there now and as soon as Luganov goes online I'll have the number emailed to me. If it's in the UK, I can get his address from here. We'll need Interpol if it's overseas.'

'We don't have much time.'

'I'll get onto it now.'

I joined Lambert in the first car and briefed him on this latest development. The journey gave us time to detail our plans for the club. There'd be two heavily disguised wagons waiting in the square: one would be a telecoms and control room; the other would house Raid Response Officers who'd split into two groups. Lambert, Kat and I would lead the group tasked with arresting Vanda and Hendak, while Bramley, Nellie and Tomáš would go with the others to liberate Liz. That reminded me – the policeman I knew as Bramley had a real name, which he'd flashed at me on his ID card. I must remember to ask Lambert what it was when we had a quiet moment.

'There is one other thing I must say, Jake,' said Lambert. 'Chief Inspector Jakub Havlíček will meet us there. Interpol's role in all this is liaison; we coordinate an orchestrated approach to policing across nations. In each country, the authority rests with the local police force. Chief Inspector Havlíček is the officer assigned to this case.'

The cars dropped us at the rear of one of the houses that fronted onto the square. Bramley guided us through the yard and into the house. It was 10.45am. Chief Inspector Jakub Havlíček nodded to me and we shook hands. Try as I might to think of him otherwise, he still looked like a geography teacher on a field trip to me: a slim, serious man in a brown tweed suit and sensible shoes.

Two removal trucks were parked at the front of the house. I laughed when I realised these were ours. Removals – very good. Three men in overalls were making a slow job of pretending to move some furniture. Bramley's radio squawked.

'The ambulance has arrived,' he said to Lambert. They've parked out of the way in the next street.'

'Just in case,' Lambert explained to me.

The comms van bristled with screens, microphones and boffins wearing headsets. The other wagon contained ten fit-looking officers seated along the sides. They were dressed in black overalls with helmets parked on the floor by their booted feet. And they were armed: each had a holstered handgun while two nursed automatic rifles. One man cradled an evil-looking steel battering ram.

My phone buzzed. A text from Tomáš told us he'd disabled the outside cameras. I showed Lambert and he signalled it was time to move. I was surprised by the slick, silent way in which they surrounded the club's entrance.

I dialled Cooper. It was 10.55. 'We're in position.'

'Good. Q wants to speak with you. I'll hand you across…'

'Jake. Luganov's on a London number and my contact at BT has provided the address.'

'Amazing. Pass it to Cooper, will you? And put him back on?'

I paused while the phone changed hands.

'Yes, Jake,' said Cooper.

'Q has just handed you Luganov's address. I think we

should pass it to your friends in the Art and Antiques Unit. They should plan to visit him as soon as the auction's over.'

'Good idea. Stay on this line and I'll hand you to Q while I ring them on the other phone.'

10.58. I was standing in the middle of the entrance porch surrounded by police officers. Lambert, Bramley and Havlíček were wearing the same bulletproof vests as the Rapid Response guys, and carrying sidearms. Bramley brought out more vests and insisted on putting them on Nellie, Kat and me. My heart was beating like an overworked steam engine and I was jumpy as hell, but my dander was up. We were going to pull this off.

Cooper came back on the line. 'They're sending a car to that address in central London but they won't move in until I give the signal.'

11.00. Lambert called for everyone's attention, then spoke in a soft voice. 'Please follow your instructions carefully. Lives will depend on it. No one is to move until Jake gives the signal that the auction has finished. Everyone knows the importance of this operation. Today we will break up a dangerous gang and rescue an innocent victim. Do your duty, gentlemen.' Then he turned to me and spoke in an even softer voice. 'I have only been able to involve you in this operation because of your specialist knowledge; you are a financial investigator and Mr Bosworth also has financial expertise. I have been able to include your other friends because of their familiarity with the premises. Please be very careful and don't take any chances.'

Like I was going to listen to that.

***

11.05. I put my phone to my ear. 'What's happening?'

'Matravers has made his opening pitch – you know the kind of thing – *a very rare and valuable painting, with all the interest in the period, it's bound to be a good investment*. Now, he's asking who'll start the bidding at twelve million dollars.'

Silence for a minute.

'Now he's suggesting ten million.'

Silence again, then: 'First bid's up at nine million. Another at ten millions, now twelve million. Matravers is doing a good job and he's nodding to Q for the next bid as he goes. The newcomer, Luganov, has jumped in at fourteen million – Q's come straight back with fifteen million. Luganov again with seventeen million, Q with seventeen and a half million and Luganov with twenty million.'

There was a pause.

'No more bids, that's a rap.'

'We go,' I said to Lambert. He nodded.

'Guy? We're going in,' I said into my phone.

'Right. I'll relay that to the Art and Antiques Unit.'

I pushed past the officer with the battering ram who was making his way towards the doors and turned the handle, mentally thanking Tomáš for his presence of mind in silencing the artificial door squeak.

He was waiting inside for us, of course, and as soon as he saw us, he leaned over the reception desk and pressed a button. The glass doors leading through to the dance floor swooshed apart. I introduced him to Bramley, carefully evading the use of Bramley's name. Bramley produced another bulletproof vest.

Nellie gave a thumbs up as he followed them into the lift. Bramley studied the code on his copy of the layout and input it to the keypad. The doors closed and the lift disappeared downwards.

As we waited for the lift to return Kat spoke softly, 'Vanda's face will be a picture.'

We piled in and Kat hit the button for the mezzanine. The doors parted and we moved quickly and quietly through the restaurant. The officer with automatic weapons led our group, followed closely by Lambert and Havlíček, looking warily around them. We clustered outside Vanda's office door and Kat edged forward using her pass key to get in. The door swung inward.

Vanda stood. 'What's the meaning of this?' she demanded angrily.

The man on the other side of the desk from where she'd been sitting took his time to react. He must have been in his late forties but was trying to look younger. Judging by the Champagne glass in his hand, the vintage bottle that stood on the desk and the fat cigar smouldering in the ashtray near him, he had a taste for the finer things in life – which was probably why the stylish, sharply-cut suit he was wearing was a little tight in places. His improbably black eyebrows and hairline looked as if they'd been parting company for some time; he didn't have much left on top but a virulent bunch of grey curls were trying to escape from his open necked shirt. His eyes followed each of us as we entered the room and he leaned forward to put down his half full glass but deposited it too close to the edge of the table. It rolled away and smashed on the floor. This must be Andel HasBeen – I mean Hendak.

'You are both under arrest,' said Havlíček in Czech. He turned to one of the Rapid Response officers. 'Advise them of their rights,' he ordered, this time in English.

'You have no right to come barging into my office in this way.'

'We have every right, Madam,' said Havlíček. 'And this piece of paper explains why.' He handed it to her and she read it silently.

'Hands on the table where we can see them,' said Lambert. 'Both of you.'

Vanda noticed Kat for the first time. Her mouth dropped open. 'You! What the hell are you doing here?'

'How'dy boss,' drawled Kat in her American accent. Then she switched into her own voice, suddenly tinged with both bitterness and anger. 'I wouldn't have missed this for anything. To see you finally face the consequences of your actions. It's been my pleasure to be part of your downfall.' She bowed theatrically.

Vanda's eyes were cold and she stepped sideways then lunged towards Kat, making a grab for her. But I'd seen what was coming and stuck my foot out. Vanda sprawled across the floor and the two closest officers lifted her to her feet and held her between them.

Kat had sprung back when she saw Vanda coming towards her, and Hendak clearly saw his opportunity. He jumped to his feet, grabbed Kat and, holding her in front of him, took a pistol from his pocket, pressing the barrel against her temple. I thrust forward, ready to dive at him but Lambert put a hand on my shoulder.

He spoke to Hendak. 'You are only making things worse for yourself. Put the gun down and let her go.'

'Stay back,' said Hendak, gesturing at us with his pistol.

'There are marksmen all around the building,' I said. 'They'll shoot you on sight and ask questions later.'

He smiled. 'Well, well, Jake. I believed in you. A great shame it was just a lie. You would have made your fortune.'

'If I'd been serious, I would have made both our fortunes.

But you know, sometimes wealth comes at too high a price. Integrity, fairness and not ripping people off come higher up my list.'

'Here's what we're going to do,' Hendak said, curtly. 'I will count to three and everyone except me will put down their guns. It if doesn't happen, I will shoot this woman.'

'Do as he says,' said Havlíček. 'That's an order.'

'One,' counted Hendak.

All eyes were on the senior officer. He nodded and put his pistol on Vanda's desk.

'Two.'

There was a clattering noise of weapons being laid down.

'You,' said Hendak, gesturing towards me with his gun, 'Clear my path to the door.'

I carefully shifted discarded weapons, chairs and people out of the way, taking my time and trying desperately to come up with a plan. If I could only get my hands on the bastard. Kat's face remained impassive, but her gaze followed my every move. I tried to communicate with her with my eyes: *don't worry*, they were saying, *I'll get you out of this*. I willed her to stay calm. She seemed somehow to understand my message, and I sensed we were both ready to act if we saw an opportunity.

Vanda was still being held firmly by the two officers. Hendak stepped forward, pushing Kat towards the door. He eyed me cautiously. 'You need to keep your distance, Jake, for the sake of your girlfriend.' I kept pace with him but moved no closer.

As he neared the door, he turned towards us, keeping Kat in front of him. He stepped cautiously backwards, risking a quick look over his shoulder to check his path. Then he was outside the office, on the balcony, reversing slowly towards the restaurant.

Just then, a blonde head appeared from behind a table. Eva stood, a neutral expression on her face, her right hand hidden behind her. Hendak couldn't see her from where he was, but I watched, almost numb with fear for Kat – and yet somehow removed from what was unfolding in front of me.

When Eva and Hendak were about two metres apart, she ran forward, closing the gap between them. Her hand came out from behind her back, brandishing a gleaming, long-bladed kitchen knife.

'Andel?' She spoke quietly, calmly. He half turned in astonishment, releasing Kat and raising his gun. 'This is a present from my sister, just for you.' Her face changed as she spoke and her voice went up an octave, a banshee set on vengeance. She plunged the knife into the side of his neck with strength I wouldn't have guessed she had.

Hendak's left hand closed around the blade as he tried to wrench it out. At the same time, he levelled his gun at her and fired it at point blank range. Still feeling at one remove from it all, I watched as she crumpled to the floor silently. Hendak staggered three steps and slumped down. Kat rushed to Eva, pulling at a tablecloth and scattering the place settings on the floor.

Vanda made use of the distraction to bring her arms together in front of her suddenly and dig her elbows into the chests of the two men holding her. They staggered back and she made a run for it.

I jolted into action. 'Get the medics,' I shouted at the top of my voice, chasing after her. She made a dash for the edge of the balcony, grabbing the top of the wall that ran round it with one hand and leaping into space. I reached out for her, but she was too quick. I looked over the edge in time to see that she'd performed a perfect parachute jump, landing on her feet, bending her knees to absorb the impact.

'*Au revoir*, Jake,' she shouted, running towards the nearest emergency exit.

'Vanda's getting away,' I yelled to no one in particular. I heard the crash of breaking glass and the clang of alarm bells as she forced her way through the doors. A couple of officers charged to the lift to see if they could overtake her.

I turned back and ran towards where Eva was lying, with Kat crouching over her, pressing the tablecloth – now soaked in blood – firmly against the wound in Eva's chest.

'The paramedics are coming,' said Lambert.

Eva's eyes fluttered and closed.

Kat let out a small scream. 'She's stopped breathing,' she cried. 'Do something, Jake.'

I looked at the seemingly lifeless woman lying on the floor and Kat's desperate face. I'd seen it done but never tried it – yet this was no time to hesitate. I knelt down and leaned in, pinched Eva's nose, took a deep breath, covered her mouth with mine and blew steadily for about a second. Kat checked for a pulse as I kept breathing air into Eva. I wasn't sure how long I could keep going, but knew Kat would never forgive me if I gave up.

Just then, two ambulance crew arrived and took over. One coupled her up to an oxygen cylinder and massaged her chest while Kat maintained pressure on the wound. The other medic examined Hendak, quickly stood back and shook his head.

I'm not sure how long we stood there, stunned and shocked by how events had played out. It could have been mere minutes or much longer. Eventually, though, as the paramedics attended to Eva, I found myself looking at Kat, and thinking how relieved I was that she was OK. I could never have lived with myself if anything had happened to her.

God, I'd have a hard enough time if Eva died, knowing it was at least in part due to me.

I reached for Kat and, for a moment, we clung to each other.

I was still processing everything when Eva recovered consciousness and, after giving her some shots and applying a temporary dressing, the paramedics gently lifted her onto a stretcher to carry her away.

Kat turned to me. 'I'll go with her.'

'Keep me posted,' I said.

She nodded and reached up and kissed my cheek before following the stretcher.

'Thank you,' she said, looking at me meaningfully.

My phone rang. It was Cooper. 'No time now, I'm on my way to check on Liz,' I said.

'I'll be quick. The Art and Antiques Unit have been on. They got no reply at Luganov's front door, so they went round the back: kitchen door open and nobody there.'

'How odd.'

'But just before his computer shut down, they caught sight of an exchange of emails with a bank in the Cayman Islands – timed literally as the auction finished – requesting an immediate payment in cleared funds of twenty million dollars in favour of Matravers Fine Arts.'

'So he paid up then hoofed it. Weird.'

'That's my news. Good luck with Liz.'

'Thanks, man.'

Havlíček stayed in the club to supervise the team as they conducted a sweep of the building while Lambert and I passed Hendak's body and took the lift down to the basement, hearing gunfire as soon as the lift doors opened.

'That doesn't sound good,' I said.

'Let's find out what's going on,' said Lambert.

This was the first time I'd been down here. I suppose the polite description would be a discrete space for adult entertainment and intimate encounters – but where I grew up, it would have been called a knocking shop, complete with low-level lighting, cosy booths built for two and wipe-clean bench seating. And, for those who preferred more privacy, there were areas at the rear, behind curtains. In the middle of the room, in a place where it would command the attention of everyone who was not otherwise occupied, there was a small, low level wooden stage with two steel poles running up to the ceiling. One of the curtains at the back of the room was pulled to the side and someone had strong-armed a false door disguised as wooden panelling, exposing the mouth of the tunnel.

Lambert and I looked at each other and headed through the door, the sound of gunfire getting louder as we drew nearer. Along with the smell of cordite.

We peered ahead cautiously: there was a bend in the tunnel about thirty metres away, half-hidden by a haze of smoke. Our squad were there, returning fire. Nellie saw us looking and nudged Bramley and they kept low, running back to us.

'What's happening, Svoboda?' said Lambert.

So that was Bramley's proper name. I mouthed it a couple of times.

'Not good,' said Svoboda. 'They've put up a barricade across the other end of the tunnel.'

'Show me,' I said.

Tucking into the nearside wall and crouching down, Svoboda and I ran up to the corner in the tunnel. As we did so, spent bullets ricocheted off the opposite wall. Most slid along the ground towards us but one or two slammed into the wall nearby. It was scary but there was no choice: we had to keep going.

The sound of sporadic gunfire from the far end of the tunnel grew louder still as I approached the corner. From there, I could see that the barricade was another thirty metres or so further on. A haze of gun smoke hung in the air between it and us. Two of our Rapid Response team had made a shield wall of sorts across the tunnel and they, Nellie and Tomáš were sheltering behind it.

'I sent the other three up to wait outside the street door in case they tried to leave that way,' said Svoboda.

'How many are there?' I asked.

'Two, armed with pistols,' said Svoboda. 'We could force the street door and go in behind them?'

'No. We need to act now before they start thinking how to use their hostage as a bargaining chip,' I said.

I gestured to one of the team who was holding an automatic weapon. 'How accurate is he with that?' I asked Svoboda.

'A Hechler and Koch MP5? At this range? He can group his shots to four centimetres.'

'What about these shields? Will they stop bullets at close range?'

'Yes.'

I looked at Nellie. 'Are you thinking what I'm thinking?'

'Murder ball,' he said. 'Like I used to play at school.'

I turned to Svoboda. 'I need helmets, two shields and some kind of defensive weapons.'

'Whatever you are thinking, I can't allow it.'

'I'm not asking. Don't make me assault a police officer.'

Lambert came up behind us. 'These are crazy Englishmen, Svoboda, you won't stop them. Give them what they want.'

Svoboda took us back to the tunnel entrance and found us what we'd asked for. As well as the bullet proof vests, we now had helmets with full face visors, ballistic shields and hard rubber batons. In five minutes we were back behind the shield wall.

I turned to Svoboda and he translated my words to the officer with the Hechler and Koch.

'Your officer is to keep up a barrage of fire. When he says *go*, Nellie and I will move towards their barricade, keeping to the left. He shoots to the right, keeping the bastards pinned down until we get over there.'

The guy with the gun nodded and grinned. He said something I couldn't catch.

'He says good luck and he promises not to shoot you in the bum,' said Svoboda.

I was grateful when the second Rapid Response Officer said he'd lead the way.

'Ready, Nellie?'

He put up his thumb. 'Ready.'

Our man raised his gun and started shooting. '*Běžte*,' he said quietly.

'Run!' said Svoboda in a stage whisper.

We took off, Mr Rapid Response, me, then Nellie following closely behind. It was hard to move quickly, encumbered with all our gear, whilst also staying low and hugging the wall – but move we did. I did my best to keep up with the officer in front as Nellie scuttled along behind. Friendly bullets zinged past us as we crawled along the tunnel, holding our shields in front of us. A less friendly bullet slammed into my shield, then another. It seemed the bad guys had worked out what was going on, and our man must have adjusted his aim, firing at the two points above the barricade where the bullets had come from. This was exhausting and not a little terrifying: here we were crawling along in damp semi-darkness, being shot at, pushing heavy shields in front of us and wearing bulky bulletproof vests.

I stopped for a moment to put up a hand to wipe the misted-up visor of my helmet. We were about a third of the way along. More shots were coming at us now. Were there more guns? I couldn't tell. Our man with the automatic rifle renewed his fire to the right places. I started crawling again, Nellie following close behind. That's when I felt it, like a hot knife against my shoulder.

'You're hit!' shouted Nellie.

'It's nothing, keep going.'

A loud *crack!* sounded in my ears. Something had hit my helmet. My ears were ringing but I was OK. Got to keep going. I caught up with the officer in front of me. Their barricade was chest height, about five metres.

'Ready? Let's get the bastards!' I shouted.

I charged and put my shoulder to the barricade. Nellie and the policeman were alongside me. We heaved as one and their barricade collapsed. We pushed through, Nellie and I swinging our batons and our policeman brandishing his gun in one hand and a baton in the other. We were greeted by four astonished faces, twice the number we were expecting. I guessed they'd all started firing when they saw us coming forward. Two of the bastards turned and ran, closely pursued by our Rapid Response man. Behind us Svoboda, Lambert and the other officer ran forward. I came face to face with a man I recognised as one of the bouncers who'd been in the club last night. He raised his pistol, pointing it towards me.

I adopted a fencing pose I hadn't used since university and lunged at the pistol with my baton, knocking it down as he fired. The bullet struck the floor. He raised his gun again and I raised my baton. Hard rubber against lead. I didn't fancy my chances. I looked into his eyes as he stood impassively in front of me. Could I strike him before he shot me? I feinted a couple of times, swinging my baton. He stepped back. I lunged and he retreated again, firing and knocking the baton from my hand. As he raised his gun for another shot, I dived to the floor and put everything I'd got into skimming my shield at his ankles. He stepped sideways, giving me just enough time to get back on my feet and face him. His gun was coming up once more when I ran towards him and kneed him in the groin. He bent forward – straight onto the punch I landed on his chin.

I leaned back against the cool tunnel wall and took off my helmet. The top of it was cracked and splintered where it had been struck by a bullet. I looked around. Nellie was sitting on the floor on the far side of the tunnel looking pleased with himself. He waved a mock salute at me. Svoboda was questioning the guy Nellie had neutralised. The one I'd tangled with was sitting on the floor looking dazed with our other Rapid Responder standing over him.

Lambert came up. 'We should get that arm looked at.'

'Just a scratch,' I said. 'Let's go and get Liz.'

As my recent opponent was pulled up to his feet and led away to custody, the other prisoner replied to Svoboda's questions in querulous Czech.

'What did he say?' I asked.

'That it was all Hendak's idea. Your friend has not been harmed in any way.'

'She'd better not have been,' growled Nellie.

'Are there more men in the building?' asked Lambert.

He replied in halting English. 'Is just four of us.'

'Do you believe him?' I asked.

'We'll have him lead the way, just in case,' said Lambert. 'Take the cuffs off and let him carry an empty pistol. Keep him covered with your gun.'

The second Rapid Response officer came back grinning and reported to Svoboda in Czech, who translated for me: 'He says, he opened the street door and let the others in and all the bad guys have been rounded up. And he says well done, would you like to join the Rapid Response Unit?' He was grinning from ear to ear.

We set off in a line up the narrow stairs in the old house. The air was cool and a little fusty but all the surfaces were swept clean. The decor was plain but in good condition; not a residence but a place people passed through.

At the top of the stairs was a small landing with three doors leading off it. At the far end, another even narrower staircase led up to the next floor.

'What's up there?' said Lambert.

'No one else. I promise. Storage.' Our captive pointed to the door nearest the back of the house. 'She is there.'

Svoboda sent the two officers upstairs to take a look while he opened the other two doors and peeked inside. 'As he says,' he reported.

The key was in the lock, so I turned it, anxious to liberate Liz.

Nellie was first into the room, which was warm, comfortable and surprisingly spacious. The barred windows looked down over the empty back yard. Liz was sitting at a desk under the window, wearing the sort of designer jogging bottoms and top that I'd only previously seen in the Sunday supplements, with suitably expensive trainers on her feet – but she stood and blinked, owl-like, as Svoboda, Lambert and I followed Nellie in. I noticed her bedraggled cocktail dress from Burgh Island, hanging up in the open wardrobe. Tomáš and the two officers, with their semi-automatic weapons, stayed outside. One led the prisoner back downstairs whilst the other tried to look like he had something important to do.

Liz stood. 'So that's what all the noise was. I've been expecting you.'

'Hold on, I'm coming,' I crooned, doing my impression of a sixties pop star. Lambert watched, an amused and slightly puzzled expression on his face.

She hugged Nellie and then me. 'Thank you,' she said to me and then, glancing at Nellie, 'I can't believe you brought *him*, though.'

'Charming. I've come half-way round the world only to find that you two spent the night together in my absence.' Nellie wasn't going to let this go, I realised.

'What? Well, love of my life, I confess. Strictly speaking Jake and I did spend the night together at Burgh Island…'

'I knew it. Call yourself a friend, Jake? Let's finish what we started.' Nellie said, putting his fists up.

Liz started laughing. 'Oh, don't be so ridiculous. Nothing happened, except for some pretty appalling attempts to dance whilst under the influence. Then we both conked out.'

'I knew it, really,' said Nellie. He dropped his fists and looked embarrassed, turning to me. 'Why did you suggest otherwise?'

'I told you. Because you were mincing around like a fairy princess last night when I needed our fight to look real.'

Nellie turned to Liz, 'Is there someone else?'

'You oaf,' said Liz. 'Wrong as usual. I just wanted you to stop buggering around and get on with proposing to me.'

Nellie's expression changed to one of earnestness, 'Do you mean it?'

'With all my heart.'

'Everyone move, please,' said Nellie, ushering us out. We did as we were bid, but clustered around the open door, watching Nellie go down on one knee.

'I accept,' said Liz with a glint in her eye. She pulled Nellie to his feet and planted a lingering kiss on his lips. 'Well, thank the Lord that's over. Now perhaps we can get on with the important stuff. Jake, will you please introduce everyone to me? And update me on all that's happened since I've been here?'

How like Liz, to bring everything back to reality.

Lambert squeezed back into the room. 'We should have the medical people check you over.'

'No need. I've been treated very well. The worst thing has been being confined in this rather lovely room.'

Liz was right. In contrast to the basic decor in the rest of the house, this room was warm, spacious and tastefully furnished, with an ensuite bathroom next door.

'My hostess was much more forthcoming after Jake's intervention. She explained that this room was sometimes used for special guests and their – how shall I put this? – hired-by-the-hour companions. I've a feeling I'm the first one to actually *sleep* in this bed. So, I'm rested, well fed and ready for action.'

'What sort of action do you have in mind?' I asked.

'Don't we have bandits to catch? And what about the painting – did it sell?'

'We have one deceased bandit but Vanda got away, and we have a buyer whose money is on the way to Matravers' bank but who then did a runner when the police called to see him. Criminal connections, perhaps? And one of our team has been badly wounded.' I explained Eva's role in things. 'And Tomáš here is the rightful owner of the picture.'

'Where is it now?' Liz asked.

'That I don't know,' I said.

Liz ruminated. 'When we'd finished at the photographer's on Sunday, Vanda instructed the security guard to bring the picture back to her office. She said it would be perfectly safe because she had CCTV everywhere.'

'I've been in her office and I didn't see it. Tomáš, do you know where it is?'

He shook his head.

'Let's go and look,' I said.

Liz, Lambert, Nellie, Svoboda, Tomáš and I trooped down the stairs, through the tunnel and back up in the lift – past the blood stains on the restaurant floor where Hendak's body had been.

I scanned Vanda's office. Everything was just as I'd remembered it, including the overturned chairs and the almost full bottle of fizz in the ice bucket, one half-empty shampoo glass on the table and one lying broken on the floor. My eyes swept the room.

'Liz. How big is the painting we're looking for?'

'Approximately one metre and forty-two centimetres high by one metre and ten centimetres wide.'

Where would you hide something that big in here? Filing cabinets? Not a chance. Under the desk? I had a quick look, nope. Floor? Ceiling? Clutching at straws. And then inspiration struck. I turned back to confront the large print, noticing for the first time how far it stood off the wall. I went up to it.

'That's not it, you lummox,' said Liz.

I lifted the modern print off the wall and there she was again, hanging behind it: the bare-chested young woman with long dark hair and a wine-red cloak draped around her shoulders, no longer peering out from a small transparency but in front of us in all her glory. She didn't look any warmer than last time I'd seen her. And I swear that vicious-looking snake had moved further up her leg. It was true, I still didn't understand art.

'It's not the first time this picture has been hidden away,' said Tomáš.

'She's beautiful,' whispered Nellie.

'It's exquisite,' Liz said. 'But it's not a Klimt.'

'You knew,' I said.

'As soon as I saw it at the photographer's. It's the right period and it's certainly a similar style to his but it doesn't feel right. *What's old Matravers up to?* I asked myself. I decided to play along and see what would happen. Hadn't bargained for any of this, though,' she added with a smile.

'Do you know what it is if it's not a Klimt?'

'I have a fair idea and now we have it, I can complete my research.' She turned to Tomáš. 'You said she'd been hidden away before. Where did you find her?'

'Behind a false wall in my attic.'

'Can you take me there?'

'Of course.'

'Now?'

Half an hour later, with the flesh wound in my arm dressed by the ambulance team, Tomáš, Nellie, Liz, Lambert and I were standing in Tomáš's kitchen while he made coffee. Tomáš stood close enough to hear while I rang Kat to check up on Eva.

'Is it over?' said Kat.

'Liz is here with us now. She's completely fine. Vanda got away and they've taken Hendak's body to the mortuary. How's Eva?'

'She's in surgery. They're saying she lost a lot of blood, but she's been very lucky.'

Tomáš's tense expression relaxed a little.

'Where are you now?' asked Kat.

'At Tomáš'.'

'The doctor is coming to speak to me. I'll ring you later when I have more news.'

'You risked everything for me. I'm truly grateful,' I said, trying to keep the emotion out of my voice.

'When your best friend asks for your help, what else can you do?'

'Am I your best friend?'

'I have to go,' she said. There was a pause and then: 'Yes.'

It was warm and bright at the top of Tomáš' house, with the afternoon sun blazing in through a row of newly installed Velux windows. The attic had originally been a series of rooms with lath and plaster walls in between, and I guessed it would have been the servants' quarters, back when this now dilapidated house had been grand. Tomáš explained that he wanted to restore the whole thing but was starting up here to create a luxurious penthouse apartment that would command a high rent, to give him the money to work on the rest of the building – or, at least, that had been his plan before recent events. Now, with the Dark Goddess likely to be closed for the foreseeable future, he'd probably need the income from the penthouse to live on. Assuming he'd got the money to finish it.

I walked over to the nearest window. The view was splendid, with the Old Town and the castle on the hill beyond. He'd stripped back most of the room to a bare shell before starting his rebuild. New flooring, a healthy slab of insulation to the outside walls and a new plasterboard inner wall. Skeletal timber frames, new partition walls in the making, showed how the space would be divided into rooms. He was doing a top-class job. This end of the attic had been laid out as a large kitchen, diner and sitting room. All the services were in and the new kitchen units, still wrapped in polythene, sat around, contemplating their final resting place.

I helped Tomáš move tools, boxes and rolls of insulation to make room for the others to come up. Voices on the stairs told us they were on their way. Liz was first, followed by Nellie, then Lambert. Once they were all in, Tomáš became our tour guide.

'This was my family's home for four generations before I was born. That is, until the communists divided it into self-contained apartments. My mother and I shared the floor below after they took over. After the Velvet Revolution, we were able to apply for ownership to be restored to us. Before my mother died, I promised her that when I could, I would restore the house, and this penthouse is my first phase. Beyond this living room there will be a study, two bedrooms and two bathrooms. This room is nearly finished but as you will see, I have much left to do.'

That was the longest speech I'd heard Tomáš make since he'd got worked up over how Vanda had ripped him off over the painting. Liz was getting twitchy, reaching the limit of her polite patience.

'Yes, yes, and you're making a fine job of it, Tomáš. But could we please get on and see where you found the painting?' she asked.

'Of course, everyone, follow me, but watch your step. Not all the floorboards are in place yet.' As he walked, he pointed out the new plumbing and wiring that was being installed. If he couldn't afford to complete the renovation, I could see a career for him as an estate agent.

Liz bustled beside him, trying to hurry him along, with an artificial smile locked in place. 'I'm sure it'll be lovely when it's finished,' she said.

'This is going to be the master bedroom,' said Tomáš, his eyes sweeping the space as he spoke. I could tell he wasn't seeing the uneven floor, crumbling plaster or cobwebs hanging from the ceiling; instead, the expression on his face suggested he was picturing the future, his grand vision finally made real.

Liz's attention wandered to the chimney breast on the end wall and the gaping, soot-infested space where the grate used to be. She ducked down, under the mantelpiece to look up the chimney, coughed and stepped out again with a smear of smut on her face. 'Did you find the painting up there?' she asked pointedly.

Nellie pulled out a handkerchief and did his best to wipe the soot from his fiancée's cheek while suppressing a smirk.

'I should think that very unlikely,' said Lambert.

'You are quite right Mr Lambert,' said Tomáš. 'No, I found the painting quite by accident. I wanted to construct a private roof terrace with a pair of glass doors over here for access. I took down part of this wall so I could examine the building's structure, to make sure it would take the changes.' He tipped a large screwdriver into a jagged cut in the plaster, levered it, then lifted a section clear, revealing a dark space behind the wall that was just large enough for someone to crawl in on their hands and knees.

Liz rushed forward to peer inside. 'Do you have a torch, Tomáš?'

'Of course, I will get it for you.'

By the time he came back, Liz's top half had already disappeared from view. He switched on the torch, alerted her and squeezed it through a gap near her right shoulder. It was a few minutes before she shuffled back out again and turned off the torch.

'I can't see much; it's packed with straw.'

She smiled at Tomáš, disarmingly. 'I wonder, would it be possible to take down a larger section of wall? I want to get a proper look at the whole area. And, Nellie, why don't you do something useful and make more coffee?'

Nellie gave a mock bow, 'Of course, your ladyship. Anything to oblige.' He turned on his heel and disappeared down the stairs.

'He is a love,' she muttered in an aside to me. 'But he's always better if I give him something to do.' Her orders delivered, she took a seat on a nearby packing crate and started to pick straw and cobwebs from her clothes. 'Ugh. Spiders,' she shuddered.

Tomáš came back with tools and set about enlarging the hole. Liz hovered beside him issuing instructions. Nellie returned with a jug of coffee and topped up everyone's mug. As soon as she was happy, Liz grabbed the torch and disappeared inside again: all we could see of her were the soles of her expensive trainers and the odd flash of torch light, although her voice drifted back to us through the sound of scrabbling.

'I'm going to start passing some of the rubbish out. There's a lot of straw and quite a few newspapers. Nellie and Tomáš, can you please make two piles, papers in one and straw in another. Don't bugger around with it and be careful with the papers. They're very old. I want to examine it all before we get rid. And Tomáš, find me some refuse sacks, will you?'

I sipped my coffee and pondered Tomáš' situation. Matravers had told Vanda that the painting was worth twenty thousand dollars and she'd only paid Tomáš five for it. If Liz could evidence that, we could claim that the painting still belonged to him; Vanda had paid a deposit but title wouldn't pass until full and final payment of the whole value had been made. Otherwise, I could see him losing it to a police investigation that might take aeons to resolve.

Liz reversed out of the hole, dragging some kind of cloth bundle behind her. 'Where's my gear when I need it?' she muttered.

'What would be useful?' asked Lambert.

'I left it in Glasgow. I didn't think I'd need it on this trip. For this, just a pair of gloves, a small knife and, ideally a magnifying glass,' said Liz.

Lambert fished in his jacket pocket. 'I always carry a few useful items with me, just in case. Would these do?' He produced a pair of latex gloves, a pocket knife and a small, neat, fold-out magnifying glass.

'Perfect,' said Liz, taking them from him.

She carried the bundle over to a work bench under one of the new windows and placed it down. She put on the gloves, slipped the magnifying glass and knife into her pocket, got down on her knees and started sorting through the pile of straw. As she finished with each tangled clump, she'd pass it to the guys, who manoeuvred it into a rubbish sack. With no finds emerging and all the straw bagged up, she then took out the magnifier, sat on the floor and moved on to the papers. She took one from the top of the pile. 'This is the Národní listy, dated March 1939.'

Tomáš knelt next to her to translate the foreboding headlines, alerting the populace to the imminent arrival of German troops. They went through the rest of the pile together, pulling out odd details about the impending occupation.

'These provide a firm date as to when and why the painting was put into hiding. I'm sure the Nazis would have branded it degenerate and burnt it.'

'You're looking decidedly grubby, darling,' said Nellie.

'Thank you for that insight,' she responded and sniggered. 'This is FUN.' She looked pointedly at Nellie. 'You'll be able to run a hot bath, provide warm towels and free flowing wine for me when I've finished this, won't you? After all, you can't leave your soon-to-be wife *grubby*, can you?'

Well, that was a first: Nellie, looking embarrassed.

'Just one more job, then we can go.' Liz returned to the workbench where the anonymous cloth parcel waited, bathed in Autumn sunlight. She took out the pocket-knife and magnifying glass and prepared to operate. First, she turned the bundle and examined it, removing the loose outer layer of damp, fusty cloth. The parcel inside was tightly wrapped in oil cloth, held in place by twine. Liz inspected it carefully then sliced through the twine, unwrapping the cloth to reveal a small leather chest that was kept closed by a simple knob and loop, like the fastener of a duffle coat. We crowded around to see as she opened the lid to reveal two bundles of envelopes: cream in one pile, pale blue in the other, each packet held together by a loop of scarlet ribbon, tied in a bow.

Liz picked up the cream stack and unknotted the ribbon. She took a small envelope from the top of the pile.

'It's addressed to Oskar Kaintz, in Vienna,' she said. She spoke as if we'd been debating the matter and this proved she'd been right all along.

The flap had already been slit open. Liz took out the letter and showed us the date from the top – 3rd May 1914 – before handing it to Tomáš. The paper was crisp and the writing, small and neat in bold, clear copperplate blue ink. It looked as if it could have been written yesterday.

He studied it carefully. 'It's German. I can understand most of it but it's very old-fashioned.'

'We'll need to get it properly translated,' Liz said, turning to the second page. 'But I'd say we have a very emotional, personal story here. If you look at this area, where the ink has run and dried, it's as if someone was crying when they wrote this.' She carefully refolded the pages and returned them to the envelope. 'Would you have something I can put these in, Tomáš?'

'Of course,' he said, retrieving a plastic carrier bag from amongst his tools. 'It's clean,' he said.

'I'll have these photographed and translated. I'd also like to take the newspapers to have all the headlines and dates checked.'

I could see Tomáš was desperate to ask but wasn't going to. I decided to put him out of his misery. 'So, Liz, what do you think it's worth?'

'Well,' said Liz, turning to Tomáš. 'What did Vanda Brazda pay you for it?'

'Five thousand dollars!'

'Now my real work starts... Tomáš, I'll need you to dig out whatever family papers you have. A picture of this age and quality, with some form of provenance attached – which I suspect the letters will provide – is certainly of value. I'm not sure of the exact amount yet, but I think we can safely say it's worth more than five thousand dollars. Substantially more.'

Now was my chance to get Lambert's opinion. 'What do

you think, Gabriel? Vanda short-changed him. And there's no receipt.' I looked at Tomáš meaningfully, cutting him off before he could contradict me and produce the piece of paper I knew he had in his wallet.

Lambert pursed his lips and mused, before speaking. 'If the painting were still yours, would you sell it?'

'Yes. I could use the money to finish this.' Tomáš gestured around him.

'And you would handle the sale?' Lambert asked, looking at Liz.

'Yes, if that's what Tomáš wants.'

Tomáš nodded emphatically.

'Then my report to the Czech police will say that as long as I have written statements from Tomáš and Liz, together with copies of the photos of the picture and provenance that you certify Liz, the painting is the property of Monsieur Novak and the sum of five thousand dollars should be held over from the sale proceeds until the investigation is completed. And I'll need a statement from you as well, Jake,' he said.

Tomáš looked relieved.

'My pleasure, Gabriel,' I said. Overcome with gratitude, I gave him a man hug. Fortunately, he didn't plant a peck on my cheek.

'Good, then I'll get back to my office to start on the paperwork. Jake, can I ask you to organise a time for the three of you to come in?'

'Of course.'

'And I'll also be in touch with Detective Sergeant Cooper to tie our stories together,' he added.

I nodded. 'I'll let him know.'

We all shook hands with him and he departed.

Tomáš looked relieved and a little numb. 'What will happen to the club?'

'It'll stay closed for a while, but will be put first into administration and then, I'd imagine, up for sale,' I replied.

'How quickly can you sell the painting?' he asked Liz.

Liz spoke slowly, thinking through her answer. 'Now that Guy Lambert has confirmed the previous sale was invalid and you're the rightful owner, I can organise a photographer and contact the National Gallery to take their advice on safekeeping. I'll need time to bottom out the provenance and then we'll know exactly what we've got. And we'll need enough lead time on the auction to drum up a posse of eager bidders – say six weeks or so?'

We split up. Liz, accompanied by Nellie, was eager to get cracking. Tomáš and I, meanwhile, set off for the hospital to see how Eva was doing. When we got there, she was out of surgery and in the ICU. Only one person was allowed to be with her, so Tomáš took over from Kat and I whisked the latter away in search of coffee. Over steaming mugs, in the hospital's café, I updated her on Tomáš' painting. She smiled limply.

'You're exhausted,' I said.

'I'm just worried about Eva. After her sister, you know…'

'She's in the best place but she needs a reason to recover,' I said.

'Yes. Without that she might not feel like trying.'

'But perhaps what she needs just walked into the hospital with me.'

She looked puzzled, then brightened. 'You mean Tomáš?'

I nodded and she smiled.

My phone rang. 'Is now a better time?' said Cooper.

'Perfect.' I brought him up to date with everything that had happened at this end.

'You've had an action-packed morning. I'm just waiting for Matravers' bank to confirm receipt of the money and in the meantime, we've put out an alert to pick Luganov up.'

'I don't get it. Why would you pay all that money and then hoof it as soon as the police arrive?'

'If Hendak knew him, there has to be a reason. Maybe he's an illegal?'

'Maybe. We won't know until we talk to him.'

12 | TUESDAY 20TH OCTOBER

Liz, Nellie, Kat and I got together at Reuben's for a late breakfast. Tomáš was still with Eva, having spent all night at the hospital, but Reuben sat with us.

'I saw Vanda get away,' he said apologetically. 'I only realised it was her when she was getting into a car on the other side of the square. She was in a police uniform with her hair pinned up under a peaked cap. She walked through the police cordon as cool as a bottle of iced vodka and was driven away. It all happened so quickly, I didn't even get the registration number.'

'Description of the car?' I asked.

'I gave it to the police straight away but I'm not sure it did any good.'

I took a moment to take stock. Eva down, Hendak dead, Vanda escaped and our buyer Andre Luganov mysteriously missing. We were doing well.

Liz saw my expression and put a hand on mine. 'Remember there's good news, too. You sprang me, you've defeated a major fraud, Eva is recovering and, because of you, I'm sure I can get Tomáš enough money to do up his house.'

'What's your gut feel on the picture, value-wise?'

'Would you ask your doctor for a diagnosis before she's run all her tests? Between you and me, I would say six figures, in sterling. But that's a guess at this stage so please don't tell him.'

'He'll be very happy to hear that but OK, I'll keep it to myself,' I said. 'And this is an opportunity for you, too. Matravers Fine Arts is on the edge of extinction. A successful auction of this painting using the new online facility could put you on the map. But if Matravers stays in charge he'll throw it away. This is your chance to take over and really make the business fly. Matravers knows lots of potential clients and rivals. You could keep him on as a "glad-hander" and as an auctioneer – which he seems pretty good at.'

'That's not a bad idea, Jake. How do you see it working?'

'Leave Matravers to me. You've a painting to research and a deal to agree with Tomáš. And I want to see you successfully drag my old friend down the aisle. I think that's enough for now, don't you?'

Liz smiled warmly and put her arm around me. 'What would I do without you?'

'What are you two up to?' asked Nellie.

'Art darling, just art,' said Liz. 'But I have a question for you. When are you going to speak to my father?'

'He's on this blasted cruise.'

'Gabriel Lambert will set up a shore to ship telephone call for us. How does two pm this afternoon sound?'

'When did you organise that?'

'While you were snoring.'

'Excellent. In the meantime, let's head out and buy a ring.'

'And whilst we're out, I can see how the translation of all those lovely letters is going.'

Liz winked at me before prodding Nellie. 'Right, let's get on. Finish your coffee, my husband-to-be.'

The door closed behind them.

'It's been quite an adventure,' said Kat.

'And it's not over yet. There's a best man's speech to write and I'm going to need your help.'

'Will there be a part for me?'

'Depends…'

'On what?'

'You'll have to be my plus one at the wedding.'

She smiled. 'Well, I'll have to consult my diary…'

'We don't know when it is yet.'

'That's OK then,' she said, linking arms with me.

My phone interrupted us. It was Guy Cooper.

'What do you know?' I said.

'There's no sign of Luganov yet. But his money is safely at Matravers' bank. The team did a quick check around his house before making it secure but there's no clue as to where he's gone.'

'Strange.'

'And Rob McCloud's been in touch. They're taking the view that Matravers has suffered enough. He thinks there'll be no further action taken against him.'

'Does Matravers know yet?'

'It'll be a few days before it's made official.'

'Good news. In the meantime, I think I've worked out a way to get him out from under his financial mess.'

As I finished my call, Kat's phone rang.

'Hi, Tomáš. How is she?' Her expression changed from concern to relief. 'Really? That's great news. Can we see her? OK, we're leaving now.' She ended the call, a big smile on her face. 'They're really pleased with her and she's being transferred to a ward.'

We grabbed a cab to the hospital, where Eva was sitting up with no wires attached. There was a rosy glow in her cheeks and, considering what she'd just been through, that was surprising.

'You look well. Have you had lots of visitors?'

'Just one. Tomáš has only just left. He's been here all night,' she said, frowning. 'He needs his sleep, poor love.'

Kat and I exchanged glances. We stayed with Eva until her mother arrived, then we headed for a quiet dinner at a place Kat knew.

Nellie and Liz were in the Goldcrest's bar when we got back, and there was a dazzling diamond set in white gold on Liz's ring finger. We paid due homage to it, heaping praise on Nellie for parting with what must have been a significant outlay. They were drinking fizz. Nellie got two more glasses and topped up all four till they were brimming.

'Nellie's had the dad call so now it's official,' said Liz. 'Which means the wheels of the wedding machine are accelerating to full throttle.'

'Congratulations,' I said as we clinked glasses.

'When are you thinking?' said Kat.

'Oh. It's all set,' said Liz. 'December tenth. A Christmassy wedding. And a Yuletide honeymoon.'

'So you'll be auctioning Tomáš' painting after Christmas?'

'Not a bit of it. Both auction and wedding are in hand. And all I have to do for the latter is issue my instructions to the groom and best man, choose my bridesmaids and have our dresses made.'

Nellie looked like a man who'd found himself on the big dipper – he was enjoying the ride but was slightly shocked as to how fast it was going. 'Let me know if you need a hand with your speech,' he said to me.

'I have plenty to work with, thanks.'

'How will you ever get everything organised in time?' asked Kat.

'I have a secret weapon. My splendidly sensible aunt has been volunteered for the task,' said Liz. 'She's very active with Saint Eustachius, the church in Tavistock, and she's already been in touch with the vicar to organise the date.'

'Tavistock. That's where your mum grew up, isn't it? You were telling me about it when we were at Burgh Island,' I said.

'That's right. Lovely little market town, full of Victorian splendour. My parents married there all those years ago and Aunt Siobhan inherited the family house when my grandparents died. She's had it completely restored.' She lowered her voice. 'And with Nellie's posh parents coming it will be good to be able to entertain them in style.'

'Do you have relatives around there?'

'Not many but it's a big house with nine bedrooms and a brace of cottages, so plenty of space for close family and friends to stay. And there's a barn where we can have the reception.'

'Sounds very grand. I thought you had to live in an area to be married there, though,' I mused.

'Siobhan's squared it with the vicar. Apparently, I'm living with her at Wychtor House, in Wychtor Ferrers, a couple of miles out of town.'

'So where is Tavistock?' Nellie asked.

'In a valley on the Western edge of Dartmoor, between Okehampton and Plymouth.'

I was conscious of Kat sitting next to me, sipping her drink and watching Nellie, Liz and me chattering away.

'Kat's agreed to be my plus one,' I said.

Liz grinned and reached for Kat's hand. 'Then perhaps you'd also consent to be my first bridesmaid?'

Kat nodded her agreement and they hugged.

'And,' Liz continued, 'I wanted to ask your advice, Kat.

Do you think if I asked Tomáš and Eva to come to the wedding, Eva would be my second bridesmaid? Having you two there when you have done so much for Nellie and me would be wonderful.'

'I'm sure she will,' said Kat.

We four talked for a bit longer before Kat came in close and whispered in my ear, 'Without Eva, I'll be all alone in that big empty bed. Don't be long.' She kissed me lightly on the lips.

Nellie and Liz left soon after, leaving me all alone with a full glass of fizz. Well, it would be rude not to finish it – although I was mindful of Kat waiting for me upstairs.

I was facing the French windows. The curtains were open and it was dark outside. The main lights in the bar were off, leaving only the lamps aglow on each table, each throwing out a soft, low circle of light. I relaxed for the first time in what felt like a month, I sipped my expensive wine and reflected. This last week had been quite an adventure, but somehow, we'd got through it. Luck or hard work? I smiled; I'd opt for a judicious mix of the two.

I was just about to finish my drink and sneak off to join Kat when I froze. With my back to the door, I couldn't see but I'd swear that someone was edging round behind me. They'd been very quiet, but some sixth sense had tipped me off. Was it Nellie playing a joke? No, it was too subtle for him. I didn't turn but kept a relaxed outward appearance whilst staying on high alert. Reaching forward, I gripped the top of the bottle as an impromptu weapon, ready to use it if needed.

I wasn't prepared for the hint of a familiar perfume. Then she took the seat opposite me. Vanda in a police uniform. She removed her peaked cap and shook out her hair. I reached forward and emptied the last of the fizz into one of the recently discarded glasses – but kept the bottle close just in case.

'You look like you need a drink.'

Her smile held something extra: humour with a sprinkling of unquenchable self-belief.

She picked up the glass and studied the lipstick marks. 'This is not clean.'

'I thought you'd enjoy the taste.'

She made a show of it, putting her head back and running the precocious little number across her tongue. 'You love her, don't you? I could see it in your face when Hendak grabbed her.'

'Yes, I suppose I do. She's become part of my life now.'

She closed her eyes and sipped from the glass. 'I loved her once. I was very angry when she left me.' She put the glass down and met my gaze. 'My anger has gone now. I realise that you and Kat, you have both done favours for me. When Kat set fire to the club's basement, Hendak was forced to move his drug-making factory, which was good. I never wanted it there. And now, because of both of you, Hendak is dead and I am free of him.'

'On the loose for now but not free. The police are after you.'

'They won't catch me. I can change my appearance, obtain new documents – good forgeries and life goes on.'

'That takes money.'

'Which I have. And besides, I've done nothing wrong. This was all Andel Hendak's idea and he made me go along with it.'

'The authorities might take some convincing of that.'

'I'm not so sure. Hendak's dead so he's not here to say otherwise. And the buyer will get his money back.'

'What do you know about the buyer? He seems to have vanished without the painting and he's making no attempt to claim it. Odd, don't you think?'

'How would I know? I've never heard of him.'

'Interpol think you're involved with money laundering.'

'Where's their proof?' She sipped her drink. 'Don't you want to know why I'm here?'

'I'm guessing you're about to tell me.'

'I like you, Jake. You're imaginative, inventive and you get things done. I can't go back to the club now, so it's a fresh start for me. And as Kat will tell you, I'm ambitious and will put one hundred percent into any project I commit to. You and I, we would make a great team. Together, we could take on the world.'

I studied her face. Did she seriously believe I would go into partnership with her? And doing what, exactly? At the very least, she was an accessory to a bunch of pretty serious crimes and the way she'd treated Kat was abysmal. I didn't doubt her driving ambition, but she was one book I was going to judge by its cover.

'No, Vanda. That's not a path I want to take. Why not give yourself up?' I said. 'I could negotiate a deal for you. I'm sure they'd waive prosecution in exchange for you sharing everything you know. They'd probably organise a new identity and everything.'

'They'd find out. Hendak's precious syndicate, I mean. My life wouldn't be worth living.'

'Then I think there's very little we can do for each other.'

'Won't you even consider my offer?'

I'd had enough of this. I was tired, and Kat was waiting for me. 'Look,' I said. 'You have me wrong. I have no interest in working with you.'

She saw my resolute face and shrugged. 'Goodbye then, Jake. I'll be seeing you.' She got up, pushed her hair back into her peaked cap, blew me a kiss and headed out, back the way she'd come in.

I finished my drink. I didn't quite like the implied threat in that *I'll be seeing you*. First stop, then, the security guard on the door: no more admittances – apart from residents or guests with bookings, of course – without checking with me first. Even if they claimed to be with the police.

Upstairs, I knocked gently on Kat's door. No answer. Maybe she was already asleep? I hesitated. Should I knock louder? But she was exhausted, after everything she'd been through, and if she *was* asleep, then she must need it.

I let out a deep sigh as I climbed the stairs to my lonely single bed in my doll's house sized room.

13 | WEDNESDAY 21ST OCTOBER

I didn't sleep well. Meeting Vanda last night hadn't been *entirely* a surprise because I'd guessed I'd not seen the last of her – but even I hadn't expected her to be quite so brazen as to turn up at the hotel.

I went down to breakfast at 9am. The dining room was pretty full. Kat was already there, sitting on her own at a two-person table in the middle. She didn't look up when I came in. I helped myself from the buffet and took a seat opposite her.

'Morning,' I said.

She looked around the room as if I wasn't there. I threw my unbuttered croissant at her. She put up her hand in one simple, graceful movement, deflecting it onto the table. Of course. When was I ever going to tell her that I loved her?

Her mood softened as she made a show of wiping her hand on her napkin. 'Where were you last night?'

'I had a visitor. Afterwards, I knocked on your door but there was no answer.'

'And I suppose your meeting was more important than spending the night with me?'

'It was Vanda.'

'Vanda? You have to be kidding.' She lifted her hand again, this time in a *stop* gesture. 'Tell me in a minute. I'll get you another croissant first – if you promise not to throw it at me.'

'I swear.'

'You do. I've noticed.'

She went to the breakfast bar and brought back an assortment of pastries and a fresh jug of coffee. '*Now* tell.'

'She thanked me for ridding her of Hendak and offered to cut me in as her partner in crime.'

'And?'

'Not a chance. I offered to mitigate with the authorities if she gave herself up. Then she left.' I shook my head.

'What?'

'I can't get over it. The cheek of the woman turning up here, after everything she's done, expecting me to welcome her with open arms.' I took a bite of the warm, soft pastry. 'You're quiet.'

'I'm just not surprised. She thinks all she has to do is pout her lips seductively and we'll all come running.' She reached across the table and took my hand. 'Be careful, Jake, she'll be back. What are you going to do?'

'I have to make some phone calls.'

'Let's go to my room. It's a bit crowded in here.'

Upstairs, she sat on the bed and I paced restlessly in front of the French windows as I dialled Cooper's number. He answered on the third ring.

'Don't tell me you've lost the painting?' I could hear him chuckling to himself.

'I had a visit from Vanda last night.'

'Do you always attract the complicated ones?'

I smiled to myself, thinking of Kat. *Yes, yes, I do.* 'She told me this whole thing was Hendak's idea.'

'Do you believe her?'

'Maybe, but he's not around to deny it.'

'Still if it's true…'

'If it's true, she's still been a very naughty person.'

'And she's on the loose. Watch yourself, Jake.'

'Oh, I shall.'

I caught Lambert between meetings and updated him on the Vanda meeting.

'I think you are right not to trust this woman. Is that what she really wants? I wonder. We would be very keen to talk with her and yes, your idea of a deal of some sort is certainly worth consideration. I would love to know what she knows. Be careful, Jake, and keep us advised of your movements.'

I put my phone down and sighed. All these people warning me to take care. What did they expect me to do?

'Jake?' Kat's voice broke me from my reverie and I noticed her clothes were piled neatly on a stool, and she was under the covers of the freshly made bed.

'We need to make up for lost time,' she said.

'I ought to just check in with Liz.'

'No need. I saw them at breakfast before you came in. They've gone researching, won't be back till later.' Her expression changed to a kind of lean and hungry look as her naked foot and calf slid out from under the quilt. Then her knee. And thigh. Wow. That was quite a leg. And I knew there was another one next to it.

I didn't need asking twice.

I piled my clothes on top of hers and climbed in beside her. We kissed and then some.

It was sometime later, with her arms around me, that she whispered in my ear, 'I'm still not entirely convinced, you know.' I could hear the smile in her voice.

'Of what?'

'That there is a worthwhile alternative to my previous sexual orientation. It may take a number of further attempts to convince me.' She smiled. 'One way or another.'

'Well, there's no time like the present.'

'Oh no,' she said, getting out of bed, and walking slowly and seductively across the room. 'It's time for a shower,' she added as she walked into the rather grand bathroom. I heard the tap start running and her face appeared around the door. 'Care to join me?'

I followed. Like a squirrel who'd found a long lost hoard of nuts.

It was midday when I got around to looking at my watch. My phone must have been waiting because it rang immediately.

It was Liz. 'We're in Reuben's. Care to join us?'

I muttered something.

'What's that you said?'

Kat snatched my phone. 'He'll have to get dressed first.'

I heard Liz chortle. 'What *have* you two been up to?'

I snatched the phone back. 'None of your business. We'll see you in an hour.'

'That's good timing. I've booked a meeting room at the National Gallery. Tomáš and Gabriel are going to join us.'

'Have you heard how Eva is?'

'I'll put Tomáš on.'

'The doctors are very pleased with her. She needs to stay in a few more days, but she's making good progress,' he said.

The others were already there when Kat and I were shown into a rather anodyne meeting room at the National Gallery. Lambert caught me for a quick word about Vanda. Apparently, they'd allocated extra resources to the hunt for her and Svoboda would be on hand if she came calling again.

He'd also heard from Cooper: Luganov's disappearance was baffling and no trace of him had yet been found.

I thanked him for the update and sat down. We were spread around a large rectangular table, with Liz at one end. I was at the front, on her right, and Nellie on her left. Kat was on my right; opposite Liz were Lambert and Svoboda; and Tomáš was next to Nellie. It felt a bit like end of term at school: with the pressure off, everyone's mood was light and jocular.

Until teacher got to her feet and started talking.

'Time, I think, to call this meeting to order,' said Liz, standing next to an easel and waiting for us all to settle down and give her the attention she expected. She whipped up the blank sheet of paper covering the easel to reveal a full size, full colour copy of the painting I had come to think of as Snake Woman. And there she was again: the beautiful, full breasted, largely naked figure with a claret-coloured cloak draped around her shoulders, exposing her sculpted curves.

Her life-like appearance and the artist's use of colour and texture had me believing that if I reached out to touch her cape, my fingers would meet soft, rich velvet. Her long black hair cascaded around her shoulders. She held her hands out in front of her at waist height, palms upwards. A serpent was entwined around her right leg, its tail just above her foot, its head close to her groin. The snake's eyes were directed towards the viewer, and it seemed to me that the reptile both possessed and protected her. The woman's eyes were black, and she was standing straight-backed and proud. A blue jewel adorned her belly button and a gold circlet containing blue, green and red stones sat around her forehead. Swags of metallic gold with interposed patterns of small black and white squares decorated each side of the picture.

The photograph had a profound effect on all of us, and we fell silent, mesmerised. It had only been two days since we'd recovered the original from Vanda's office but now, in this setting, with the drama of the last week or so behind us, this reproduction seemed even more vivid, more vibrant. It held our attention like a magnet.

'This painting dates from 1914,' said Liz. She spoke calmly and with confident authority. 'Although it bears a superficial resemblance to the work of another, more famous man, I'm now certain that it was created by a less familiar artist, Oskar Kaintz. We can thank these letters for that knowledge.' Here, she waved photocopies of the originals that she had retrieved from Tomáš' attic.

Pointing to the picture again, she continued. 'We now know that the sitter was Tomáš' great-grandmother, Liliana Cercy. She and Kaintz were intimates, enjoying a violently passionate relationship. They fought, they made up, then fought again. It was only after this painting was completed that Liliana found herself to be pregnant. She rushed to his studio, expecting to delight him with the news. Instead, she found him in someone else's arms. They argued, he threw her letters back in her face – which is why there were two packets of letters in Tomáš's attic: one stack were the ones she wrote to him, the other pile were his to her. Liliana picked up the fallen envelopes and, whilst he was distracted by his current *inamorata*, she took the painting from the easel and left. She returned to the family home in Prague to bring up the daughter she subsequently bore. I've been unable to find any record of Kaintz completing another work after this painting. In 1916, he enlisted in the army and was later killed in action.' Liz sipped some water from a glass that Nellie placed before her. 'Thank you, darling. Tomáš has been through his family papers and I'll ask him to summarise what he found.'

Remaining seated, Tomáš took a paper from his pocket and unfolded it, reading from his notes. 'Liliana was born in 1890, when the Cercy family owned a large department store in Prague. Liliana's daughter by Kaintz, Helena, was born in 1915. Helena had a daughter, Marie, my mother, who was born in 1940.'

Liz cut in to Tomáš' flow, holding up one of the newspapers retrieved from Tomáš' attic. 'This headline from 17th March 1939 reads "Hitler declares protectorate". The article reproduces a speech he gave at Prague Castle announcing the annexation of Bohemia and Moravia in the name of the German peoples.'

Tomáš continued. 'Liliana died in 1947, as the country became a communist state under Soviet control. The family's department store had been closed by the Germans, leaving Liliana, Helena and Marie in reduced circumstances. The family home was then seized by the authorities and divided into apartments. The Cercy family retained the use of the upper floor and attics.

'In 1957, Marie married my father and I was born in 1958. My grandmother, Helena, died in 1959, my father in 1968 and my mother in 1996. So, I am the last in the line.'

We took a break and grabbed a coffee before returning to our impromptu classroom.

Liz resumed her station. 'So far, we've identified the artist's name, his relationship with Liliana and understood the Cercy heritage. We also know that Tomáš is the rightful owner of the Cercy house and its contents – including this painting.'

Lambert nodded his agreement.

'Thank you, Monsieur Lambert. I'd like us now to review how the picture travelled through time from its completion in 1914 until it reached Tomáš' possession in 1997. From the letters she wrote to Oskar, we know that Liliana was a headstrong and vivacious young woman who left the family home at the age of twenty for the bright lights of Vienna, then the capital city of the Austro-Hungarian empire. She found work as a waitress, which is how she met Oskar, in 1911. We are lucky to have so much correspondence between them and therefore both sides of their story. He was besotted and begged her to sit for him.

'Then, in 1939, with the Nazis practically on the doorstep, Liliana, with her family's agreement, arranged to put her prized picture beyond their reach. We're fortunate that she was far-sighted enough to think of placing this exchange of letters alongside it. It must have taken a great deal of determination to do this. When I went through them, I realised that there was one still sealed and addressed to the rightful heir of her painting. I'd like to read it to you now. I have the translation here. May I, Tomáš?'

He nodded his agreement and she picked up another paper.

'*It is with a heavy heart that I say goodbye to my Prize. My one consolation is that, in reading this, you have found it and my sacrifice has not been in vain. Save for my parents, there are only two things in this world that remain dear to me, my daughter, Helena and this painting. I suspect, by the time you read this, Mother, Father, Helena and I will be beyond care, in another place. My Prize is all I have left of the only man that I ever loved. He was flawed as are we all, but he possessed a rare talent. Even now, as I look upon his work for a final time, my heart flutters and my breath is taken away. I am fortunate. It has hung on my bedroom wall since I rushed home in 1914 until this moment in 1939 when I leave it to your tender care. I hope that it brings you joy and good fortune.'*

The room was silent when Liz stopped speaking, and there were tears in her eyes when she put the paper down. She remained still as we all considered her words. Tomáš blinked and looked down at the paper in front of him. Kat dabbed at her face with a tissue, offering me a watery smile. I rubbed my hand across my eyes and pretended I was above such things.

'And now we must consider the picture and its value,' said Liz. 'We have an original painting by a talented artist with an incontrovertible provenance. Until now, little has been known of Oskar Kaintz. These letters will prove to be an invaluable source of information providing a window into his life over a five-year period. He was an esoteric individual with a hedonistic lifestyle. Born into a good family and inheriting wealth from a distant relative at quite an early age, he was very gregarious, enjoyed fine food and wine to excess and had many lovers. That is, until he met Liliana, when, at least for a while, he focused on his art. He was known to be a perfectionist, with a shocking temper. If a picture didn't meet his expectations, he would shred it and begin again. He staged a number of exhibitions in Vienna, and a modest catalogue of his work has been recorded. With the recent popularity of artists of this period, I would expect there to be considerable interest in this painting.'

She paused for drama. 'When this picture was placed in its last auction it reached a price of twenty million dollars but that auction was a sham. I need to be clear with you that we are not talking about such a large sum of money. Equally, the five thousand dollars that Ms Brazda paid to Tomáš on account does not reflect the value that I would place on this picture. So, we are somewhere between five thousand and twenty million dollars. Would anyone care to hazard me a guess?'

'Ten thousand,' said Lambert.

'Twenty-five,' I contributed.

'This is not an auction, gentlemen,' admonished Liz. 'But it is interesting to get your views. We have a number of factors to consider: oil on canvas is the most sought-after medium; the picture is of excellent quality and condition; its story is supported by unquestionable provenance. Also, we mustn't forget the human-interest angle: we have an unprecedented insight into the artist's life and, although he's relatively unknown, in the current market, I believe there *will* be considerable interest in his work. The last issue is scarcity. The price this picture achieves must reflect the fact that there are so few pieces to his name.' She looked around the room and smiled. 'Final bids, please, gentlemen.'

Lambert smiled too. 'Fifty thousand dollars.'

Liz looked at me.

'Seventy-five,' I said with a shrug.

'Far too low,' said Liz.

Tomáš was stunned.

14 | A LONG WEEKEND 22ND – 26TH OCTOBER

Kat and I decided to stay on in Prague for a few days – we both needed a break and Kat was keen to show me around – but it was time for Nellie and Liz to get back. They had a wedding to organise, Liz had an auction to publicise and Nellie had an office in London to haunt and a whole bunch of restaurants to frequent.

Nellie hired a limo to take us all to the airport, where he'd also booked a private room so we could say farewell in privacy. As Tomáš, Kat and I piled into the limo after Liz and Nellie, it occurred to me that if I'd accepted Vanda's offer to work together, perhaps I'd have that kind of money too.

At the airport, the happy couple dumped their luggage and an older gentleman with bushy eyebrows and wispy hair, dressed in a white chef's coat, led us away to serve vintage Champagne and canapés. He didn't say much but we did get a brief smile when Nellie invited him to stay for a glass of the good stuff.

At this point, Nellie turned serious and, with a stern look on his face, raised his glass. 'To new friends and old. What we six – I'm including Eva in this – have been through together will bond us for life. My wife-to-be and I will be forever in your debt, and we hope you'll join us for our wedding in December, as our guests of honour.' Nellie looked gravely into each of our faces. 'To new love and old. May it last for all eternity.'

We all, including our chef, raised a glass to that one – just as a smartly suited British Airways flunky came to escort Liz and Nellie to their flight. Having waved goodbye, the three of us who weren't flying took a taxi back into town. It was then that I noticed Tomáš hand Kat a piece of paper. She unfolded it, read it solemnly then slipped it into her pocket.

The cab dropped Kat and me at the Goldcrest before taking Tomáš on to the hospital to see Eva.

The next few days were a bit of a blur. Kat was as good as her word. Prague Castle, Obeckni Dum (the municipal hall), Prague Museum, the Mucha Museum, ballet in the National Theatre and a couple of jazz clubs. By the end of it, I felt like a proper tourist. There had been no further sign of Vanda.

Eva came out of hospital on the Saturday and she and Tomáš joined us for afternoon tea on the Sunday. Eva told us shyly that she had taken Tomáš to meet her parents that morning and was planning to move in with him. Neither Kat nor I were remotely surprised and joked that theirs might be the next wedding we'd be attending.

After they'd gone, Kat reached over and took my hand. 'There's something I have to do before we go home.'

'OK. What's that?'

'I've been putting this off. My mum and dad both died in the flu epidemic of 1995. Tomáš found out where they were buried for me.'

'I'm so sorry, Kat.'

She was close to tears. 'My mum and I were never close, but I miss my dad.'

I hugged her and she sobbed a little. Her voice was

muffled. 'I didn't dare contact them after I left. I thought I would just bring them trouble, but now it's all over…'

'I know…'

'Can we take flowers?'

'Of course.'

While Kat nipped to the florists, I made a quick phone call. Then it was a cab to Olšany Cemetery. We were there in a few minutes. I noticed an unmarked car near the entrance with two men sitting inside it. One of them was Svoboda. I returned his nod of acknowledgement, paid the cab driver, and Kat and I went in. It was a huge place, and it took some time to locate Kat's parents' modest, somewhat overgrown grave. We got down on our hands and knees to pull out the copious weeds with our bare hands. Kat placed her flowers on the grave and I left her to have a quiet moment, kneeling there, by her parents' side.

As I walked, a familiar figure in a police uniform stepped from amongst the trees. She fell into step beside me.

'You're following me,' I said.

'Have you thought any more about my idea of working together?'

'Not a chance. But my offer still stands. I'm sure there's a deal to be done if you turn yourself in.'

'Such a nice view from here. And so touching: just look at Kat, kneeling at her parents' graveside. She looks so alone, doesn't she? And yet, do you see the couple standing just a few metres away? All I would have to do is give them a signal and they could have her out of here in seconds.'

In that moment I was glad that I'd rung Lambert and told him where we were going. I'd been relaxed when we were amongst the crowds in touristy places but here, in a graveyard, I was less confident. I looked beyond Kat. There was

Svoboda and the other guy, keeping a low profile. They were closer to Kat than I was. As I watched they split up. Svoboda walked towards me and the other guy went to the grave next to where Kat was and studied the legend on the stone.

I stopped walking and turned to face Vanda. 'So, run this past me again. What is it you think we can do?'

She smiled. 'Now you're listening to me. That's good. I'd like to return to the idea you presented to Andel. I…'

'Freeze.' Svoboda was standing close by with his gun held in both hands and pointing at Vanda.

She looked up and turned to run. I grabbed her in a kind of rugby tackle, forgetting what a tough nut she was: though I hung on like a smoker to his last cigarette, I couldn't stop her. She dragged me along for a few metres before my grip gave out. Svoboda ran after her but was back in a few minutes.

'She was fast,' he said breathlessly.

'Definitely,' I agreed. 'I'm sorry we didn't get her but I'm glad you and your colleague came out here. I was worried she was going to snatch Kat.' I put my hand out in a friendly gesture.

His handshake was cool and firm. He gestured towards the other officer. 'Let's see what he found out.'

The other man had been interviewing the couple Vanda had pointed out, but now they were walking away. We moved towards him and he to us.

Svoboda searched his face expectantly.

'They were here to visit a relative's grave. I took their details just in case.'

Svoboda nodded curtly. 'Wait for me in the car.' He turned to me. 'Ms Brazda is a slippery customer. You need to be careful, Mr Elderfield.'

'I agree and I'm grateful for your help.'

'Goodbye for now.'

As he strolled off back to his car, I knelt down next to Kat at the graveside.

She'd been crying. She saw my face. 'Is there a problem?' she said.

I looked at her tear-stained cheeks. Bless her. She'd missed all the action – and I wouldn't have it any other way.

'Nothing at all but it looks like rain. C'mon. Let's get out of here.'

Vanda was nowhere to be seen.

Back at the Goldcrest, I rang Lambert.

'We checked up on the couple and they were completely innocent,' he said.

'Yes. She was trying to spook me into working with her.'

'I think it's time for you to leave Prague, Jake, at least for a while. As long as you're here, Ms Brazda may seek you out again and that just makes life more complicated for both of us. Go home and let us wrap things up.'

I booked flights for the next day.

15 | MONDAY 27TH OCTOBER

My three day trip to Prague had lasted fourteen days. With Eva out of hospital, she and Tomáš saw us off at the Goldcrest and Kat and I caught a Czech Air flight to Heathrow, where my Silver Siren would be waiting patiently in the car park.

It was only on the flight back that the thorny subject of our future together came up. I had to confess, I'd been dreading this moment. I thought I was very clear about what I wanted but I always became totally lost when trying to work out Kat's view on the matter. It started well enough.

Gin and tonic in hand, I kicked off. 'What are your plans when we get back?'

'An interview at the hotel. They want me to be Restaurant Manager.'

'Oh, would you be interested?'

'Kneeling to standing – an excellent elevation.'

Kat's English was excellent – she spoke mostly like a native – but now and again… I sipped my drink and said nothing.

'You're quiet,' said Kat.

'Sorry. It sounds like a great opportunity.'

'It is. Good salary with accommodation and it would put me on the path to further opportunities across the group.'

'Ah.'

'You don't approve?'

'I'm not saying that. And I don't want to hold you back. It's just…'

'That you don't want me to have a career.'

'It's not that at all. Just, maybe not this career.'

Our voices were getting louder and the jib in her chin was back.

'First, it was my mother, then Vanda, Carina and now you. It seems like everyone wants to tell me what to do.' She was angry. The tip of her nose had gone white and there were two high spots of colour on her cheeks. I needed to sort this out right now.

Making an effort to stay calm, I took her hand gently in mine. 'Do you remember the night we first met?'

She looked at me suspiciously but didn't snatch her hand away. I took that as a positive.

'How could I forget? Carina was trying to get the better of you, and she made me part of her plan.'

'And do you remember that moment when she had you serving dinner to us, as if you were some servant she didn't care about.' I remembered it well: Carina had persuaded Kat to dress up as a maid, and had spent the entire evening trying to wrongfoot me – and she'd succeeded. Even then, though, I'd found Kat intriguing. 'I said something that made you stop and think.'

'I remember every word. You said that every relationship – business or pleasure – needs trust and commitment to stand any chance of working. And you told her off for not listening to her employees.'

'How did it make you feel when I said that?' Kat looked at me thoughtfully.

'Like a door had opened and a brilliant light shone down on me. I was shocked. I realised that until that point in my life, the only reason I'd been listened to was to have my words twisted and my intentions manipulated. I felt as if you were speaking directly to me.'

I thought hard before I spoke again. 'I'm not going to say *I liked you from the moment I met you* because I didn't know you then. But when you reacted to those words, I *saw* you. I mean *really* saw you. There was understanding in your face and fire in your eyes.' Now I was holding both of her hands in mine. 'Kat, I would never, ever issue orders to you. And if you and I are going to have any sort of a relationship together then it has to be one of equals, where two intelligent, caring people communicate openly with each other and come to mutually beneficial decisions.'

'That I like the sound of, but what do I do about this job?'

'That has to be your call. Have the interview, see if they like you, and if you like them, then decide if it's what you want more than anything else.'

'How will you feel if I take it?'

'Honestly? Disappointed for me, but happy for you and hopeful that I'll still see you sometimes.'

'OK.'

We kissed then. She was tired. I let her sleep and peered out at the clouds below us and the sky above.

We landed. I put her on the train to Paddington before heading back to the Siren, paying the extortionate parking fee and hitting the road.

16 | TUESDAY 28TH OCTOBER

I felt tired and not a little depressed when I got back to my little house in Stratford on Monday night. I collected the pile of post waiting for me inside the door and dropped it on my naff dining table – that'd wait until tomorrow – and shuffled off to bed.

In the morning, with a first cup of black coffee inside me, I rifled through the bills, direct mail pieces and advertising nonsense, leaving a bunch of envelopes to one side that looked worth opening. One was particularly interesting: an expensive-looking cream A5 envelope with Liz's immaculate copperplate on the front. I slit it open and pulled out the crisp, goldleaf edged card addressed to *Kat Dominova and Jake Elderfield*. It was a wedding invitation, a hastily scrawled note with it. We were invited to stay in a cottage on her aunt's estate. Liz was suggesting that we come down by the 5th, the Friday before, so that we could enjoy a combined Stag and Hen do – she called it a 'Stendo' – on the Saturday night. Tomáš and Eva would be there as well and Liz was keeping Nellie's Hooray Hubert school friends at bay so it would be just the six of us.

I threw the wedding invitation onto the table and tried Kat's mobile, but it rang out. She was probably having her interview. I left her a message. So, what else was I going to do with myself today? First thing was to open the rest of these envelopes, next was food shopping. Turning my attention to the former, I read one of the letters; it was from Allen at Race Engineering. Apparently, my Siren was overdue for its first service. If I whizzed it up to the factory, he and I could have a catch up whilst they saw to it. I opened the rest of the mail, mainly offers of work. I'd look at those later.

What was the matter with me? I was usually more revved up than this. The answer came back as quick as a flash. Lovesick bastard. I wanted that girl with me. We were great together. Well, my next chance – Liz and Nellie's wedding – was in the diary, and that meant I had six weeks to prepare. On which note, I rang Allen Race and arranged to pop over in an hour.

I'd only just hung up again when my phone started ringing. But it wasn't Kat. 'Morning David, how are you?'

'I'm splendid, Jake. More to the point how are you? My old friend the Chief Constable has been telling me what you and one of his brightest Detective Sergeants have been up to.'

David Lansdowne was my ex-boss and mentor who'd set me up with Race Engineering and provided me with invaluable background on Matravers' finances. I gave him the lowdown on my trip to Prague.

'Tell me, was my report useful?'

'Priceless, David. I was able to use it to steer through the nightmare he'd created. Although now he must be in an almighty financial mess.'

'That's why I'm ringing you. He's been in contact with our associate's office in Glasgow. He's on the point of bankruptcy, with creditors he can't pay and nothing coming in.'

'Thanks for the tip-off. I'll ring him now.' I boiled the kettle once more and did the magic trick with the coffee granules. Memo to self: now I could afford it, I'd have to get one of those fancy coffee machines like Allen Race had.

Sitting comfortably at my crappy old dining table once more, I peered across the miniature wasteland that was my postage stamp-sized garden, which Kat had restored and I'd ignored. I just couldn't get away from her, could I? Sighing, I picked up the phone again. It rang out for quite a long time and, in fact, I'd almost given up when Matravers answered.

'Matravers,' I said. 'Where's your sidekick, Andrew Blair?'

'Hello, Jake. I had to let him go.'

'I hear things are tight.'

'I'm sorry I was slow in answering the phone. Everyone wants money and there's nothing coming in.'

'You'll have Liz's auction in December.' I knew that Liz was determined to hold the auction for the painting before the wedding, which would come as a relief to Tomáš.

'I can't hold on that long.'

'So I hear,' I said.

'You thought you might be able to help, once we had the fake auction out of the way. Is there any chance?'

'Yes. I've an idea but I'll need to understand the exact situation before we can finalise it. Will you be in your office later? Good. I'll book a flight, although I'm guessing it'll be late afternoon by the time I can get there. Why don't I buy you dinner afterwards? I'll book a room at a hotel for the night.'

Then it was off to see Allen. The last time I'd arrived in Race Engineering's car park, I'd been car-less and on foot. The place had been rammed full of their unsold stock of Sirens as the business teetered on the edge of bankruptcy. This time, my lovesick, sorry-for-myself face actually cracked into a smile when I saw the building again. I remembered that when I first saw it, I'd thought it looked like two white cruise liners had collided simultaneously with an Art Deco lighthouse.

I walked up the short flight of white marble stairs and pushed against the polished aluminium and glass doors, dropped my car keys at reception and took a seat on the wine-red leather sofa. Last time I did this, I'd been here to be briefed by David Lansdowne before facing the board. It had been a difficult meeting but I'd won through with David's help and now, with Allen running the place, things were very different.

I could feel the energy fizzing around me. There was a complete lack of miserable faces and slouched shoulders; only determined, cheerful expressions and people walking in and out with a sense of purpose.

Allen came barrelling down the stairs and rushed across to greet me.

'Jake, it's so good to see you.' No shyness now, just a proper bear-hug and a big smile. He was still on the slim side but no longer looked like he was on a supermodel's diet. He'd let his blond hair grow a little, making him look less like a squaddie.

'You've got this place buzzing, Allen.'

He smiled. 'We have but we couldn't have done it without your help.'

Together, we walked across the light-filled lobby, mounted the marble staircase to the first floor – where I noticed the parquet flooring had been restored – and continued along towards Allen's hideaway. But I was in for a shock. It still had a Deco feel but all the offices were gone, the partitions taken down. Now it was open plan and *all* the staff who worked up here had the benefit of the view of the Welcombe Hills through the Crittal windows.

Allen saw the look on my face. 'Do you approve?'

I smiled. 'I do. One team; not us and them.'

'We've made changes in the factory as well. Every employee in the business has a voice, regardless of their role. Each area has a morning meeting where they discuss yesterday's performance and objectives for the day, and I get everyone together once a month to tell them how we're doing and get their feedback.'

'You've worked wonders.' I couldn't believe how much he'd achieved in a few short months. 'Congratulations, mate. I can see you have a success on your hands.'

He looked pleased. 'Coffee?'

We walked across to his desk. The coffee machine he loved now had pride of place in a small kitchen area off to the right, letting anyone who felt so inclined help themselves. He came back with two steaming mugs.

'What's all this?' I said, pointing to the electronic gizmo and instruction leaflet on his desk.

Allen took his seat. I'd never seen him look so relaxed. 'Have you heard of Moore's Law? The number of transistors on a circuit board doubles every two years and it's driving the pace of change.' He held up a mobile phone about the size of a glasses' case. 'This is my latest acquisition, the Nokia 9000. I've been waiting to get my hands on one.' He snapped it open to show the screen on one side and the QWERTY keyboard on the other. 'This single device is a phone, a web browser and a personal organiser. I can email, take notes and keep my diary up to date.'

'Making your Palm Pilot redundant.'

'Do you want it?'

I pulled out the Motorola Startac he'd given me back in May. 'Thanks but I wouldn't be without my Filofax and I'm still getting used to this.'

'How's Kat?' he asked.

'Fine,' I said. I didn't feel like getting into a long conversation about my dysfunctional love life. 'She's being interviewed for a promotion at the hotel where she works. Any news on Carina?' Carina was Allen's sister, and had been the MD here before Allen.

'Not a word.'

'Let's hope it stays that way.' Carina hadn't exactly had the business' best interests at heart.

'Indeed. I could do without the negative publicity we'd get if she reappeared.'

Allen's desk phone rang. 'Great, thanks, Tom,' he said and then, looking at me, 'your car's ready.'

I finished my coffee. 'In that case, I'd better get on my way. I have a plane to catch.'

Allen escorted me back to reception, where my keys were waiting.

'Great to see you, Jake.'

'You too, mate.'

'Don't be a stranger.'

'I won't.'

At Birmingham Airport, I dropped the car in short term parking and wandered into the terminal. I had minimal luggage in my carry-on bag, so I was straight through to airside in a few minutes, giving me time to grab a sandwich and admire the gathering rain clouds.

My phone rang.

'Hello, Jake.'

'Kat, how are you?'

'Confused. The job's mine if I want it.'

'And do you?'

'It wouldn't start until the New Year, so I have time to make my mind up.'

'That's good.'

'Where are you?'

'Airport. About to go and see Matravers to see if I can get him out of the financial mess he's in.'

'Poor Jake. Always looking after other people.'

'It's not so bad. At least they're always grateful.'

'So they should be.'

'Did you get my message about the wedding?'

'That's fine.'

'I could look after you too, you know. Just say the word.'

'Oh, Jake.'

They called my flight.

It was raining in Glasgow. I had a quiet, competent taxi driver who made his way through the traffic, giving me a chance to inspect the rain-washed streets and turn stuff over in my head. What was I looking for? Two things. Domestic bliss with Kat was number one, of course, but right now I needed to figure out what I was going to say to Matravers in a few short minutes. It was time to think it through. Liz had made a deal to sell Tomáš' painting. She'd been less than candid as to what she thought it was worth, but it sounded to me as if it was going to be a couple of hundred thousand pounds. It would be a straightforward gig – quite boring after the last one, with no funny business – just seller, auction house and buyer.

My research had shown me that auction houses normally charged the buyer *and* the seller for the privilege of their services; the commission from the seller was maybe 10%, plus there would be a 'premium' for the buyer that could be as much as 25%. So, on £200k that could comfortably put around *£70k into* Matravers Fine Arts' account, give or take the VAT. The question was – would that be enough?

It was after five when I got to Matravers Fine Arts. I knocked on the door and the man himself opened it. He didn't look great, I thought, as he shut and locked the door behind me and led the way into his office.

I looked around me. He had clearly been working his way through a stack of bills and paperwork had spilled over from his desk onto the floor. There were fewer pieces of furniture in here than last time I'd visited, and two of the portraits had vanished, leaving a shadow on the wallpaper around where they used to be – like the line they draw on the floor in American cop shows to show where the body was lying.

Matravers felt the need to explain. 'I was able to barter my way out of a couple of large bills using some of my collection.'

'I see Grandad's still here.' The sour-faced, be-whiskered portrait still hung above Matravers' desk. 'Yes. No one wanted that one.'

'Can't think why,' I responded. 'Suppose you lay out the current situation for me.'

'I'd love to, but I've had so many interruptions, and I can't make head nor tale of some of these invoices...'

I took my jacket off and slung it across the back of my seat. 'Tell you what. Make me a coffee, get me a fresh notepad, a pen and a calculator and I'll see what I can do.'

Matravers found what I'd asked for, adding a bottle of whisky and two cut glasses to my list. He poured drinks for us and settled down beside me, providing answers to questions when I needed his help to decipher the chaos. It took me back to the early years of my career, going through shoeboxes full of receipts to put together the accounts of local small businesses.

A couple of hours later, and a few inches off the level in the whisky bottle, and we had some answers.

All the outstanding invoices were in one pile with a schedule of what was due, and when, on the top. A couple of the items that Matravers thought were bills represented money owed to him. But the big problem was the massive debt he had with Quentin Bailey, his tech man.

I decided it was time to pull the rug up and look at the floorboards. 'Tell me, Matravers, what is it about this business that you enjoy?'

It didn't take him long to reply. 'Meeting and greeting the sellers and running the sale. There's nothing like an auction. I'm the ringmaster, making it all happen. Everyone is hanging on my every word. It's pure theatre.'

'And the bits you don't like?' My eyes flicked across the now neat piles of paper on his desk.

'I'm sure you've worked that one out, haven't you?'

'Here's an opinion for you. You have a role to play here. No, don't interrupt me yet. This is a family business of which you're the third generation. But you shouldn't be running it. That's not what you're good at. You're an ideas man – look at the internet auction project you initiated with Q. You should focus on the things you enjoy, where you can add value – those will be the areas you're best at. Get others to pick up the rest.'

'How can I do that when there's no money?'

'Simple. We sell the business. You retain a small stake and a title – how does Deputy Chairman sound? And we bring in the talent to pick up the pieces.'

'It's bust. Who's going to buy it?'

'Your big debt, the one that's causing the real problem, is the one you owe to Q. But he's let it mount up and he hasn't chased it, which suggests to me that he's not desperate for the cash. And then there's Liz. She has all the admin skills you're lacking and she's focused; she really wants to succeed. And it just so happens her father is a recently-retired successful businessman. He'd make the perfect Chairman. What if I could pull together a deal that brings those three in as shareholders, allowing *you* to do what you excel at?'

Matravers was keen on the idea – perhaps unsurprisingly since it was that or declare bankruptcy. He declined dinner – leaving me free to head back to the Central Hotel – but looked happier than I had when I'd arrived.

Tired by now, I ordered room service, then I rang Q and asked him if he could meet me at the hotel for breakfast in the morning. Liz was my next phone call. I took her through the conversation I'd had with Matravers.

'The finances aren't great, Liz, but they're not disastrous. There's no way the business can carry on as it is, but with you, your dad and Q there, and with Matravers contained and doing what he's best at, it'll blast through the auctioneering firmament.'

'I like the idea, but how much will it cost me?'

'That depends. Right now, the business has very little in the way of net assets and its current reputation is rather flaky, but it has a strong history and one very considerable asset: the new auction site Q built. I'll sound him out in the morning and then I'll come back to you. All I'm looking for tonight is an indication of interest from you and your dad.'

'You have it.'

'You don't need to ask him?'

'I'm my father's daughter.'

'Fair enough.'

It was getting late, but I wasn't ready to sleep. I put my jacket on and went down to the bar. It was pretty quiet in there, so I ordered a large Speyside and took a seat at a small side table. I thought about Liz and our time at Burgh Island and what fun we'd had. And Nellie's face when I'd wound him up about that night's activities. He really did love her.

17 | WEDNESDAY 29TH OCTOBER

Being an early riser, Q was there for breakfast at 7.30. He ordered a full Scottish, while I went for my usual scrambled eggs and toast with lashings of coffee.

'What's this about, Jake?'

'I'll cut to the chase. Money. Matravers is brassic. He owes you a pile of cash and he hasn't got it. If you push for it, he's likely to go bust and you won't get a penny.'

'The software is mine till it's paid for.'

'Agreed. But hear me out. Internet auctions are going to be big business and not just in art and antiques. With your technology on board, Matravers Fine Arts could be the perfect launch vehicle for a broader-based business addressing all sectors where internet auctions could lead the way.'

'I could take back the software and do it myself.'

'That's one option – or you could become part of something larger, and the Fine Art sector with those big margins would be a great place to start. Why not swap your outstanding invoices for a shareholding? Matravers would make an excellent front man, drawing on the family history. He can keep a small stake but I'll make sure your fellow shareholders are up to the mark.'

'Would you come in?'

'Not my game but Liz Lowsonford – Matravers' number two – and her dad, Brian, will.'

'Liz and *the* Brian Lowsonford? I'm in.'

I'd taken copies of all the outstanding invoices against Matravers Fine Arts so that I could get in touch with each of the creditors. Apart from Q, none were particularly big or overdue, so I figured a holding letter that offered a part payment now and the balance before the end of the year would buy us enough time.

When I got back to Glasgow Airport, my flight had been cancelled: technical problems, which probably meant the pilot was having trouble with his guide dog. I had to join a long line of tetchy would-be passengers to get a seat on a later flight – which would have been brilliant news if I enjoyed plane spotting.

I rang Liz. 'How are you getting on?'

'Splendidly,' she gushed. 'Nellie and I have met the vicar. We're going to church this Sunday to hear the banns read and I have my first fitting for the wedding dress tomorrow. I've organised the people to decorate the barn; I just have to get Daniel – that's my uncle – to clear it. Siobhan is having the cottage you and Kat are staying in spruced up. Which reminds me, same room or separate rooms? I never know with you two.'

'Makes two of us. We'll share,' I said with my fingers crossed.

'Spill the beans. How did you get on with Q? He's a good man, isn't he?'

'I like him. He's in, if you and your dad are.'

'Well, that's good and timely. If Dad stays retired much longer, my parents will be divorced before I'm married.'

'How's Devon?' I asked.

'It's years since I was here. I'd forgotten just how big the house is; it's a proper country mansion. Siobhan's returned the place to its former glory and Daniel's written the cheques. They've even bought back the land, so she could have the deer park she was mad keen on. And I tell you what – she has strapping men with rippling muscles around the place. Nellie will have to sharpen up his act or I might stray.'

'How's Nellie doing?' I asked.

'Starting to get bored and miss his office. I'm going to send him back to London shortly and it sounds as if I should go back up to Glasgow and stiffen Langdon's sinews for our next auction.'

We finished the call with a promise that Kat and I would be there by the 5th December; I was hoping Kat would come up to Stratford so we could drive down together.

And there I was again. Stuck in the Kat conundrum. Obsessing over the one question I couldn't find the answer to. It happened every time: just when I thought I was making progress with her, we'd slide down a snake and be back near the start of the board.

Sitting there in the airport, with nothing better to do, I fell to contemplating what I knew about the woman I loved. Kat's domineering mother had been in charge when she was growing up. Kat had been close to her dad but it didn't sound as if he had stood up to his wife – which left Kat swapping a strict mother for a possessive, ambitious lover. Vanda had set out to win Kat's heart, showering her with attention but then, as soon as she believed Kat was hers, she'd switched her focus back onto her long-term agenda and begun to treat Kat as a servant. Had Kat's attack on the nightclub's basement been because of the drug factory or was it a more personal revenge? After Vanda, Kat had moved on – was this a theme in her life and, if so, should I take it as a warning? – and met Carina in London. All she had to worry about then was staying in Carina's good books. Until one day, that changed. Was that *more* payback or a genuine desire to do the right thing?

What conclusions could I draw? That Kat was used to being dominated by strong women from childhood. Twice, when she'd fallen out of love with her partner, she'd exacted her revenge. What would happen if she split up with me – assuming we ever got together properly, that is? I couldn't answer that, of course, but I told myself I was different to her previous partners and not just in the obvious way. I wasn't interested in calling the shots and having her tag along behind me. She was a bright, dynamic, talented individual and we made a great team. Of course, it helped that I fancied her something rotten. The bed department seemed pretty good – despite her gags about *converting her sexual preferences* – when we weren't too distracted by events or lack of sleep.

Frustrated and no nearer an answer, I was relieved when the flight was called and I joined the hordes of tetchy travellers trailing across the runway to catch the plane back to Brum. The flying bus was heaving and I sat squashed up by a window, my bag under the seat in front and barely enough room for my legs as I stared out at the sky. Perhaps the truth came to me on a passing cloud? Who knows? But it struck me suddenly that there was no point in trying to guess what was in Kat's head. I was just going to have to be patient and wait until she was prepared to tell me what she thought. And, for the moment, I'd just carry on being lovable old me and maybe it would work out and maybe it wouldn't. As my mum would say: *we'll see*.

***

I arrived in Birmingham just in time for the daily rush hour on the M42. And to make things more exciting, those lovely clouds I'd been staring at had decided to drop their rain all over the road. Seeing the backed-up traffic on the motorway I opted for the "slow roads" to Stratford. It was somehow calming and therapeutic after the tiring trip and frustrations of the flight delays.

It was dark and still raining, but much more gently, when I parked up my Siren in the street round the corner, blipped the key fob, saw the lights flash in acknowledgement and walked to my front door. It was only when I got into the house, and saw the posh wedding invitation lying on the table, that I remembered that I hadn't made time to do any shopping yesterday. I checked the fridge, just to make sure some passing good fairy hadn't filled it with grub – but no such luck. It would have to be a takeaway then. I turned on my heel and was soon back in the street under an umbrella.

It was when I headed home again – the pleasing aroma of fish and chips from the container I was carrying making me hungry – that I noticed my tail. They were easy to spot, even though they were staying well back and out of the light, as there weren't many people about on a night like this. I changed direction, walking across to the next road, round the block and then up from the other way. My shadow stayed a discrete distance behind. When I got inside the house, I pulled out my phone and dialled Cooper.

'Do you want me to come over?' he asked.

'Wait. Let me see who it is. But if I don't ring you back in twenty minutes, send a squad car.'

I put my fish and chips in the oven to keep warm and waited, keeping the lights off so I could watch for their approach. A figure in a long black riding coat, hood up, walked slowly and deliberately towards my front door. There was something distinctly feminine about the walk. Too tall for Kat and it couldn't be Liz.

The bell rang.

I opened the door. The hood was deep and I couldn't see her face.

'Hello, Jake.'

The gravelly voice. Vanda. She spoke quietly.

'What the hell are you doing here?'

'May I come in?'

'Not until you tell me why you're here.'

She lowered her hood and looked straight at me. Her dark hair was short now and there was a cut in her lip. One side of her face looked swollen and was covered in a livid bruise, extending up around her eye –as if Mike Tyson had taken up cosmetic surgery. I stepped back to let her in. But it was only when she struggled to unzip her sodden coat that I realised her left arm was heavily bandaged. She wore a loose-fitting woollen dress underneath.

'Who did this to you?'

'Luganov.' She smiled weakly and flinched with pain.

'The buyer? You said you didn't know who he was.'

I knew she'd behaved badly but I had to admit that she'd treated Liz with kindness and respect. She'd tried it on, but during the time I'd known her she'd not played rough even though those around her had. I must be going soft.

'You're soaking wet. Let me take your coat. Come and sit and I'll make you a hot drink.'

'You'd better hear what I have to say first.'

I took her coat and hung it over a radiator. We passed my

low, slouchy sofa and reached the dining table. 'I think one of these straight-backed chairs will be easier for you.' I helped her to sit. 'Why would he do this to you?' I asked.

'He says I've cost him twenty million dollars and he wants it back. They've given me seven days to find the money or they'll finish the job.'

'But all he has to do is talk to the police to reclaim his money. It was a fraudulent action. It's waiting for him.'

'They'd love that if they knew who he really is.'

'What *can* you mean?'

'He has a dark past.'

My head was spinning. 'An acquaintance of Hendak's. I guess he was bound to be a villain. Why come to me?'

'You're my only option. You know where the money is and I don't.'

'What makes you think I'll help him get his money back?'

'You love Kat.' She coughed pathetically. 'And I'm desperate, Jake. I have nowhere else to go.'

'Let me call Interpol. Let's put a stop to this now.'

'No, Jake, I daren't disobey him. There's a car waiting for me outside.'

She stood. I remembered the first time I met her. She'd seemed so strong, invincible even. 'There's one more thing he told me I must do before I leave. You need to understand the sort of person you are dealing with.' Tears of shame rolled down her cheeks as, with her one good arm, she pulled at the front of her dress, ripping the fabric. She stepped free of the now crumpled garment and turned slowly through 360 degrees to show me her poor, tormented body: there were bruises and fierce-looking red welts on her back and chest, and a single word inked across the top of her breasts.

'It's pronounced *predatel*,' Vanda said. 'In your language it means traitor.' She circled slowly once more, reminding me of the damage they'd done to her.

I picked up my phone.

'What do you think you're doing?' she asked, alarmed.

'I can have a squad car outside in five minutes. Describe their car to me, I'll have them arrested.'

She smiled sadly. 'It's too late for heroics. You must help me or face the consequences.' She shrugged herself back into her coat. 'Will you zip it up for me? I don't think I can manage.'

I did as I was asked. 'What will happen to you?'

'If I do everything he says, he will let me heal and put me to work. Goodbye, Jake, and heed what I have said.'

I waited until she'd gone then slipped out of the back door. There was a passageway along the back of our row of gardens, which we used to put the rubbish bins out. I was just in time to see Vanda climbing into the front passenger seat of a smart black Mercedes saloon before it took off. I memorised the registration number. There was something very odd about all this.

I went back into the house, turned off the oven, threw my supper in the bin, grabbed my wallet, trusty leather jacket, phone and car keys and dived out of the door again. I stopped when I reached my car – the distinctive, upmarket Siren. Still it was a filthy night, dark and wet, like a cloak of invisibility, and mine wasn't the only low slung silver two seater on the road. I *could* do something about those distinctive number plates though. I swiped my hand through the gutter, picked up a handful of mud and smeared it over the front and back plates.

Once in the driver's seat, I pulled out my phone to send a quick text to Cooper.

I'm OK but developments to tell you – call you tomorrow.

The second one, I sent to Kat.

If you're not in the hotel, get there as soon as you can and please, please, please, stay where there are other people. I'm coming to get you.

I fired up the Siren and screeched out into the road, grateful that Allen had organised a timely oil change and service for me. I stuck to the speed limits in town but put the pedal to the metal once I was on the open roads. The Siren was enjoying it, lots of red-lining and snarly exhaust notes as we tear-arsed our way to the M40.

Once I was on the motorway, I gave it everything I'd got, keeping my eyes peeled for that black Mercedes: if I saw them, I'd force them off the road – anything to stop them reaching Kat before I could. Now and again, I slowed right down, crawling along in the slow lane, making sure I hadn't been followed.

I looked at my watch; just after eleven. I'd never done the journey from Stratford to London so quickly before: I must have almost halved my normal journey time. The fact that it was late and raining heavily had probably helped me avoid incurring the wrath of the traffic cops.

Once I was in town, I stuck within the limits. There'd been no sign of the Mercedes. They might have had no intention of going after Kat – I remembered the couple in the cemetery; Vanda had hinted they would abduct Kat as soon as she gave the word, yet the pair turned out to be there simply to visit a relative's grave – but that was a chance I wasn't prepared to take. I pulled into a car park and turned off the ignition, hearing the tick of cooling metalwork around me. I took out my phone. Kat had replied.

I'm here. Will do X.

I rang her; she answered straight away.

'Jake. What's wrong?'

'I've had a visit from Vanda in Stratford. She came to warn me that Luganov is after me and she implied they're going to snatch you if I don't cooperate with them.'

'What makes you think they know where I am?'

'Because in every phone call I ever had with Hendak when I was in the UK, he knew exactly where I was and who I was with.'

'Where are you now?'

'The NCP off Bloomsbury Square.'

'How do you know you weren't followed?'

'Because I kept watch for their car.'

'What do we do?'

'We'll disappear for a while, to give the authorities time to sort this mess out.'

'Where?'

Good question. 'Not sure, but I have an idea.'

'Come into the hotel. I'll meet you in the Cocktail Bar.'

It was warm and plush inside the brick-built, Edwardian building with its high ceilings, deep-piled tartan carpets and walls of pale oak panelling under neutral tones, jazzed up with scenes of bonny Scotland in bright, unreal colours. I asked the smartly-uniformed receptionist where I'd find the Cocktail Bar and he pointed me along the corridor.

It was quiet and snug in there, with a few residents enjoying a late night tipple. I walked up to the bar.

'I'm looking for Kat Dominova.'

'And you must be Jake.' He smiled. 'I'm not psychic; Kat described you perfectly. She's in the office behind here. Come through. Can I get you a drink?'

'Would there be any chance of a coffee?'

'Of course, I'll bring it through.'

He opened the door and I went in. Kat stood, a concerned expression on her face. She threw her arms around me, then took a step back and looked into my face. 'You think this is serious, don't you?'

'Yes. Vanda was making out she'd come to see me under duress, but I'm not sure. When she got to their car, she jumped in the front seat and was laughing. Why would she laugh when she was covered in the most awful bruises and welts, her face was all swollen and they'd tattooed her?'

Kat made a face. 'Vanda taught me everything I know about stage make-up. Bruises and red welts? Easy. Swollen face? Padding in the cheek. A tattoo? Probably a transfer.'

I thought. 'Which would mean she's in cahoots with Luganov.'

'And they want you.'

'And you. I couldn't take the risk that they'd do anything to you because of me.'

'I bet you say that to all the girls.'

My face broke into a smile. 'Only the special ones.'

'Oh. I'm special, am I?'

'Very.'

'Well, now you've got my attention, Mr Elderfield, what are you going to do with me?'

There was a discreet knock at the door, and the barman came in bearing my coffee.

'Thank you, Stuart,' Kat said, nodding at him. 'Now, Jake, have you eaten anything this evening? I thought not. Stuart, will you see if the kitchen can rustle up some sandwiches, please? Enough for two and more coffee.'

Stuart nodded. 'Certainly, Miss Dominova,' he said, closing the door behind him.

'He was very respectful,' I said.

'That's because he thinks I'll soon be his boss.'

'Is he wrong?'

'That rather depends on you, Jake.'

'Why?'

'Well, you see, I'd reached a decision about my future. I couldn't live in Stratford again; I'd need to be somewhere new, somewhere that doesn't have a host of bad memories attached to it. I thought the promotion would allow me to explore and see what the future might bring.'

'Where does that leave us?'

She pulled a face. 'You haven't changed.'

Confused? I was.

She looked up at me. Big eyes, concerned face. 'I mean, you've always been the same with me: kind, caring and not too pushy. I know there have been times when I've frustrated you but really, you've been very patient.' She came close, put her arms around my neck and looked deeply into my eyes. 'And here you are again, having driven through the howling rain to look after me.'

'I have to stop you there,' I said quickly. 'There was no howling.'

Her smile was infectious, but then she gave a heavy sigh. 'I'm trying to be nice and you're just not taking me seriously, are you?'

A knock on the door interrupted us again. Kat dropped her arms and stood back just in time. Stuart and a colleague, bearing a jug of coffee, an extra cup, some side plates and a large platter of assorted sandwiches came in.

'I told the chef the gentleman didn't look like he'd eaten for a week.' Stuart left grinning. His knowing smile said it all.

Kat resumed her stranglehold on me while I eyed the sandwiches greedily.

'Yes, yes, I'll let you eat in a minute. My point is this. You've shown you care about me in a way I could get used to. What if I could find work closer to you?'

'If I say yes, can we eat?'

'I promise, but there's something else.'

'What's that?' I said, my attention wandering.

'I want to make sure we have an opportunity for your third attempt.'

Ham, cheese, beef, this was a feast. 'Third attempt?' I said.

She looked into my eyes. 'You know, try before you buy, a road test. Don't you want to seduce me again?'

'Yes, but let's eat first.'

18 | THURSDAY 30TH OCTOBER

I woke early. Kat was still asleep. I looked at her sleeping face. I must love her, mustn't I? Otherwise, why would I dash down the motorway in the pouring rain on a winter's night?

We'd taken a room in the hotel but neither of us had slept very well. And not just because of the sex, although there was certainly some of that. Afterwards, though, we'd lain there together and although Kat had soon drifted off, I'd barely got a couple of hours. There was too much going on upstairs: my brain felt like a TV that kept swapping between two channels. Channel One was the situation we'd got ourselves into. Channel Two – you guessed it – was me and Kat. Neither was straightforward.

I hated the idea of running away and hiding but equally, how could I take on an adversary if I didn't know where or when they'd come or how many they'd be. The only sensible thing to do was to give the powers that be as much information as we had and a clear run at apprehending them. In the meantime, we'd hole up, out of the way and keep safe as houses.

Vanda might be deceiving me, of course, but either way, there'd been another person in that Mercedes. She'd got out of Prague, despite the police looking for her, *and* she'd found me in Stratford – which proved she had some kind of organisation behind her. I *had* to keep Kat out of her clutches. And that gave me one terrible, shameful thought. This was the perfect excuse to get Kat to myself.

'What time is it?' One blue-grey eye opened and her voice crept out from under the quilt.

'It's half seven. Shall I make us a coffee?' I said.

'That would be good. I'll just use the bathroom.'

It still gave me goosebumps when I saw her beautiful naked body slide out of the covers and her rear view as she walked elegantly across to the bathroom door. And the best news was, in a moment, I'd get to see the front.

With the coffee made I got on the phone.

'Who are you ringing?'

I looked up, just as the call was answered. 'Morning, Liz,' I said.

'Give her my love,' mouthed Kat.

'My plus one sends her love. Yes, she's here with me now,' I listened. 'She sends her love back,' I mouthed to Kat. 'Yes, that's why I'm ringing. I was hoping we could come sooner if that's OK? Well, today. No, no, we're happy to muddle through, nothing special. Yes, yes it'll be lovely to see you too but there's a reason for us forcing ourselves on you now. We need to get away from our usual haunts. I've had a visit from Vanda. Yes, Vanda Brazda, she made it very clear that we're in danger unless I involve myself with their nefarious schemes. I figure six weeks will be long enough for the law to mop this whole mess up and then we can get back to normal life. Are you a sure? This evening? It'll be late. Say about midnight with you? That's great, What's that? Car reg? Its J4KE.E. Liz, thank you. And can you fax us a map?' Kat passed me the hotel's fax number. 'Yes, see you soon.'

'So, you're whisking me away to Devon?'

'Liz's aunt has quite an estate down there. There's a big

old house, cottages, a barn and a fair bit of land. It's been in Liz's family for a long time and they know everyone around there. If anyone new turns up, they'll stand out like a bouncy castle at a funeral. It's the perfect place to hang out while this blows over.'

Kat gave me a long hard look. 'Running and hiding is not in your nature.'

I returned her look. 'There are times in this life when it feels right to take chances. But I only gamble with things I'm prepared to lose.'

'What would you do if I weren't here?'

'But you are. And I got you into this mess, so I'll damn well get you out of it.'

'Promise me something, Jake?'

'What?'

'That we'll face this together.'

'Deal.'

She shrugged, got into bed, reaching for her coffee. She sniggered. 'Anyway…'

'What?'

'If we're down there until the wedding, you'll have plenty of time to convince me, won't you?'

I was just enough of a gentleman to let her put her cup down before I hit her with my pillow.

We didn't rush. I figured it'd be best to wait until dark – there'd be less on the road, so easier to spot any signs of a tail. And Kat needed to have a meeting with the hotel's manager and explain what was going on. With this in mind, we decided to leave at 5pm. We'd go over to the flat she was sharing and pick up her things on the way. I'd raid a department store during the day for some essentials and see what I could beg, borrow or steal off Nellie when we got down there. In the meantime, I briefed Cooper on what had happened last night.

It was just after 7pm by the time we got onto the M3 with a full tank of petrol and some essential supplies: fuel station sandwiches – you know the ones, after you've eaten the sandwich, you wonder if the box they came in would have tasted better, some coffee and Crunchie bars. I'd checked the map while Kat had packed her bag and I'd been waiting in the car: the M3 would become the A303, then the A30; there was a quick blip down the A386 and then we'd hang a right on some little lanes to a place called Wytchtor Ferrers.

The journey was dark and damp for most of the way. We kept a sharp look out to begin with, watching for any sets of lights that started to look familiar. And I used the same trick as the previous night, bowling along at a fast pace, overtaking everything that moved, then, when the road behind us was empty, tucking in front of a truck and dawdling along at a steady fifty to see if anyone came screaming past.

Nobody did and we started to relax. We'd eaten the cardboard sandwiches, knocked back the coffee and demolished the chocolate. As the adrenalin wore off, our conversation turned to the forthcoming wedding, Liz's family and the place we were going to. I shared what little I knew, warned Kat about Liz's mum's inevitable line of questioning and we settled into a comfortable silence. I turned the radio down when I realised Kat had fallen asleep.

The roads got progressively emptier as we continued along our route. With about an hour to go, I stopped to fill the tank and wipe the number plates clean, taking a moment to look across at the sleeping girl half lying, half sitting in the bucket seat next to me. I could almost thank Vanda for putting us in this predicament, forcing us to face this together. Almost but not quite. If I ever got my hands on her… The night air was cool, rather than cold but all the same I was glad to get back into the sanctuary of the Siren.

'I fell asleep,' said Kat unnecessarily. 'Where are we?'

'Exeter services. Not far now.'

The Siren roared into life and we took off with a gentle burble.

Kat sat upright in her seat, pulling down the sun visor so she could inspect her appearance in the mirror. 'Will I do?' she said.

'You look fabulous, as always.' I paused. 'Although, it might have been better if you'd eaten the Crunchie rather than spreading it over your top.'

She laughed – a genuine, carefree laugh.

I took Liz's faxed map from my jacket pocket and passed it to Kat. 'I'm hoping you can guide us in.'

She gave me a mock salute. 'Aye Aye, Captain.'

It was just after 11.30pm when we turned off the tarmac and onto a semi-circular area of gravel backed by two granite pillars, one of which had a sign saying *Wytchtor House*. At least we were in the right place. Wrought iron gates blocked our way, but a smart single-storey granite cottage stood to the left of the driveway and as we pulled up, a tall, muscular-looking chap in his forties emerged from it, wearing a green wax jacket and bearing a shotgun under his arm. He took a moment to examine our car before breaking the gun and swinging the gates wide open. Before I could move off, he came up to the driver's side and I pressed the button to drop my window.

'Welcome, Mr Elderfield and Ms Dominova,' he said. 'Mrs Healey's niece gave me your description. Go straight up the drive and you'll see the house right in front of you.' The gravel crunched as the car edged forward; I looked in the rear-view mirror as he closed the gates behind us. I was liking the idea of this as a hide out. Our headlights illuminated open grassland to each side of the long drive. I'd get a proper sense of the place in daylight, but it seemed unlikely that anyone could get in here without being seen. We climbed a low rise and, as we came to the top of the slope, we saw the house for the first time.

'It's huge,' exclaimed Kat.

I must admit, it wasn't what I'd been expecting. It looked more like a country hotel than someone's home. It was a three-storey Georgian building, with a contemporary ground floor extension to one side. It was well lit and immaculate looking, rendered and painted in a pale cream colour. A barn stood some distance off to the right. I drove up to the house and swung round to face outwards, parking next to an Aston Martin and a Range Rover. Nice to leave the Siren in such fine company. The front door opened as we stepped out of the car.

Liz and Nellie descended the front steps, followed by a young man in dark trousers, matching waistcoat and open necked white shirt.

'Hello, you two,' said Liz. 'Come in, you must be exhausted after driving all that way.' She gave Kat an affectionate hug, then it was my turn.

Nellie gave me a manly handshake. 'Liz's right. If only you had a decent motor, you'd have got here much quicker.'

'Ignore him, Jake. He thinks he's being funny,' said Liz.

Nellie's face broke into a grin.

'Behave, or I may not marry you,' she scolded.

'Honestly, can't a bloke have a laugh with an old mate?'

I couldn't help smiling, tired as I was. 'C'mon you two, play nicely.'

'Quite right too,' said Liz, 'Leave all that, Jake; Adam will bring it in for you.'

They walked us up to the house.

'This is quite a place,' I said.

'You can have the tour tomorrow.' She glanced back at Kat walking alongside Nellie and lowered her voice. 'We'd planned to put you two in one of the cosy estate cottages, but you might feel more comfortable in the main house with everyone else.'

'That's kind, Liz, thank you. But I don't want to over play this. The main thing was to get Kat and me away from the action and give the police time to round Vanda and the others up.'

'Well, Daniel's very security conscious. I've briefed him and he's made his men aware. No one's going to get in here uninvited – it's a purely private affair.' She gave me a searching look. 'You're serious about this girl, aren't you?'

'Yes. I am.'

'Well, if that's the case, once the decorators have finished in the cottage I've chosen for you, we'll move you in there, to give you some time alone. It's still quite close to the house. How does that sound?'

'Perfect, thanks, Liz.'

Wytchtor House was quite something. A huge chandelier dominated the light, bright entrance hall, which was more like a ballroom than a place you'd hang your coat. They'd certainly spent some money here.

Liz followed my line of thought. 'Uncle Daniel is a merchant banker.'

'I hope he's left them some cash.'

'Can I get you anything to eat or to drink?' asked Liz.

Kat shook her head.

'I think we just need to sleep,' I said.

'Then I'll show you to your room.'

We crossed several acres of marble flooring to reach the stairs. The first flight ran up the right-hand wall to a half-landing at the back. Above the landing was a large window. It was too dark outside to make out the image portrayed in the stained-glass – but I guessed it was some kind of coat of arms. From the half-landing, the stairs then ran up the other side wall to the first-floor landing, where a line of bedroom doors faced the front of the building. Kat and I trudged up behind Liz and Nellie; Adam followed with our bags.

Nellie peeled off. 'I'll say goodnight. See you in the morning.'

Liz led us up to the second floor, opening one of the doors in front of her.

'You'll be comfortable in here,' she said.

The room was bathed in soft lighting. An Art Deco style lamp stood on each of the low cabinets either side of the King-sized bed. Pairs of wall lights glowed warmly around the room, and an ornate standard lamp projected a pool of light around a coffee table and two sofas in front of the window. Kat's attention was drawn to a dressing table displaying an expensive-looking range of vanity products. I peered out into the darkness. In daylight there would be a commanding view of the grounds – and I'd be able to reassure myself that we were safe here. Adam dropped our bags on the bench at the foot of the bed and drew the curtains.

Liz opened a door on our left. 'The bathroom's through here.'

Marble floors and walls, a shower big enough for a bus queue and a bath large enough for a modest pool party.

'Shouldn't it be you two in the honeymoon suite?' I said to Liz.

'I owe you both and I pay my debts. Besides, Nellie and I aren't married yet.' She smiled. 'Sleep well. And there's no rush in the morning. Come down when you're ready and anyone will show you towards breakfast.' She closed the door behind her.

19 | **SATURDAY 1ST NOVEMBER**

Kat and I slept well. It was after 8am by the time I crawled out from under the quilt. I left Kat dozing and pulled back the curtains. The sun was shining weakly and a gentle rain was drizzling down on the wide expanse of open grassland. Apart from where there were a few clusters of trees, I could see all the way to the boundary wall at the edge of the road. Below me, in the parking area at the front of the house, a group of men were talking. As I watched, three of them, in jeans, fleeces and work boots, climbed into a long wheelbase Land Rover and moved off, leaving the fourth, wearing a shirt, braces, shiny shoes and suit trousers, to come into the house. I felt calm and secure for the first time in weeks. Kat crept up behind me up and put her arms around my shoulders. I turned and kissed her on the forehead.

'Shall we try the shower out?' she said.

Another hour passed before we emerged from our bedroom and made our way downstairs, where we were directed to the spacious family kitchen at the back of the house. The kitchen – which was actually more of a kitchen/diner/sitting room – filled the entire single storey extension I'd noticed when we arrived last night. At one end, there was a large shiny stainless steel cooker, lots of cupboards, and a couple of sinks in one of those islands. A chap in a chef's hat was stirring things in a saucepan, while Liz and another woman were sitting at the table. 'Good morning, you two,' said Liz. 'Kat, Jake, please meet my aunt, Siobhan.'

'Delighted,' said Siobhan. 'I should thank you for rescuing my favourite niece.'

'I'm your only niece,' said Liz.

'All the more reason why you're my favourite,' said Siobhan.

'I'm curious,' I said. 'You're Siobhan and Liz's mum is Shona. Unusual names considering you grew up in Devon.'

'Our Father had a love of all things Gaelic.'

'He must have been delighted when Shona married Brian,' I said.

'Well, not at first, but he warmed to him as Brian's bank balance grew,' she replied.

Liz poured coffee for us and the chef conjured things up for us to eat. Just then, the guy I'd seen talking to the chaps in the car park joined us, coming straight over to Kat and me.

'Hello, Jake, Kat; I'm Daniel.'

'My husband,' said Siobhan.

'We're very grateful for your hospitality,' I said.

'It's really no trouble,' said Siobhan.

Daniel smiled and shook my hand. Having worked so closely with David Lansdowne, I could sense Daniel's army background straight away; he had the same bearing as David, straight-backed, and that easy, officer class, way with him. His relaxed, open expression made a statement: *throw me a problem and I'll fix it*.

Siobhan was also interesting. And not what I'd been expecting after her sister: she was older and, I thought, wiser than Shona; less overtly glamorous and more serious minded; not so inclined to ask embarrassing questions or make statements that would make a nun's toes curl. These were generous and genuine people.

'Now we're all here, it's time for a planning meeting,' said Liz, seeing Nellie wander in. She patted the seat next to her. 'Come and sit,' she told him, pulling out a notepad from her handbag. 'Right, I'm calling this meeting to order.'

'Order, order,' shouted Nellie.

Liz hit him with her notepad. 'Kat, you and Eva are to be my bridesmaids. My dressmaker will meet us later today with her sample book. I'm hoping you know Eva's size? Nellie, you'll take yourself and Jake to Daniel's tailors to see about suits and I suspect Jake will need a few more things to supplement the meagre luggage he brought with him. Daniel, a question for you: when will the barn be ready?'

Why did it not surprise me that Liz could be so forthright?

Daniel cleared his throat. 'I've briefed the team this morning and they'll start clearing the barn today. We'll check the electrics and plumbing and the heaters will be here in plenty of time to make sure they're powerful enough. The people who are going to dress the barn are coming to measure up tomorrow morning. I'll have to be in London…'

'I'll see to them,' said Siobhan.

'And I'll join you. Now, what about caterers?' said Liz.

Nellie made a face and spoke in my ear. 'If you've finished your breakfast, we could hoof it out of here.'

'I'll just grab my jacket,' I whispered.

Kat followed us out. 'Now Nellie, Jake – Liz and I have agreed on colours for you two. We're thinking blue silk-linen for the suits, white shirts, brown shoes and pale ties.' She glanced at me and then back at Nellie, addressing her next words to him. 'And look after Jake.'

Nellie nudged me. 'Be careful, Jake, she's starting to sound like Liz. Don't worry, Ms Dominova, I'll bring him back in one piece.'

***

Nellie had the keys to the Range Rover. 'Before we take off, I'll give you the tour.' He reversed the car round and followed a gravelled track that led through the grounds. 'There are thirty-eight acres now,' he said. 'It was in a sorry state when Siobhan inherited it. The land had all been sold off and the house was falling down. Daniel fixed all that.' He stopped the car. 'Look over there.'

There was a group of deer clustered together near some trees.

'Red deer. Very hardy.' He put the Range Rover into gear and we took off again. 'How much trouble are you in with this Vanda woman?'

'Honestly, I'm not sure. I've seen her three times since the auction. The first time was a gentle *let's do business together*, the second was a straightforward empty threat and the third was the most interesting. She looked like she'd had a good beating. But it doesn't stack up. I'm convinced it's a set-up. It sounds to me like she's now in league with Luganov, the guy who forked out for the painting. He wants his money back but he's not prepared to go to the police and reclaim it – which is where, I think, they've decided I come in. There's something very shady going on, whichever way you look at it. And Vanda definitely left me with the impression that if I didn't find a way to refund the twenty million, they'd snatch Kat. I wasn't going to take that chance. That's why we're here.'

'What do the police say?'

'Very little so far. The most worrying aspect is the way Vanda has been able to get over from Prague to catch up with me in Stratford.'

'You'll be fine here. Time to relax, mate.'

***

I thought hard as Nellie drove us down to Launceston. Everything that Vanda had said *had* been empty threats so far. So what was she up to? I could see how, if Luganov had been in league with Hendak, he might reach out to Vanda to find out why he couldn't contact him. And if Hendak and Luganov were in some money laundering scheme together, it would explain why Luganov wouldn't go to the police. How was Vanda involved, though? Just because she had the idea of auctioning the painting, it didn't mean she knew what Hendak and Luganov were up to. She probably just wanted a cut of the vast profit. But with Hendak off the scene, it would make sense for Luganov to question Vanda. He'd want to know where his money was and, of course, she'd know it hadn't gone further than Matravers' bank; in fact, I'd confirmed it to her. And she'd probably have told him all about my involvement in the raid on the club – which was why I was now in the frame. Vanda was probably on a percentage for helping him get his money back and thought the best way of motivating me was to threaten Kat. Not that in reality, I *could* get my hands on the dosh.

Still, with Kat and me out of the way for the next month or so, there'd be plenty of time for Interpol, the British and Czech police to sort things out before we were back in circulation again.

I didn't realise how wrong I could be.

20 | A MILD REST OF NOVEMBER

As winters go, this one was mild in every sense of the word: rainy and not too cold. But being in Devon, at Wytchtor Ferrers, after the madness that had been my life for the last month, felt like being in a rest home. It was too much for Nellie, of course; as soon as he'd complied with Liz's orders and carried out his few tasks to her satisfaction, he was off to his usual profligate lifestyle in London. Meanwhile, Liz spent most of her time developing and delivering a masterly marketing campaign that would yield a solid result for Tomáš' painting.

Kat became good friends with Siobhan, and she was able to use her hospitality skills to help with the organisation of the wedding reception – which left me at something of a loose end. Not that I was complaining. With the temperate weather, towny that I am, I was able to join Daniel on his walks around the estate and for a weekly trip into Tavistock. Through Daniel's and Nellie's generosity, I'd acquired a whole wardrobe of outdoorsy clothing suitable to this rural life I was suddenly living. I was even getting used to Daniel's two Golden Retrievers, who had viewed me with a certain suspicion initially – perhaps sensing I wasn't really the country type.

As the month progressed, I picked up a little admin for Matravers Fine Arts, helping to manage their flaky finances until new money arrived. I was also able to keep my hand in with a couple of small projects that I could complete remotely, and, thinking about my next paying job, I started to follow up on the various enquiries I'd received since Race Engineering. I must admit, though, Daniel's company drew me like a magnet: he was so calm and in control, and reminded me so much of David Lansdowne. By the third week, I was spending much of my time alongside him and his three guys, working on the barn. We cleaned and repainted the empty building ready for it to become a wedding venue. It was a real novelty for me to carry out a task where you could stand back at the end of the day and see what you'd achieved, and it felt both different and therapeutic when compared to my normal life.

Two sightings of Luganov had been reported but both had turned out to be false. Beyond a photograph and brief description from a Russian passport we knew nothing more about him. There had been no sightings of Vanda after her visit to me, and Lambert's investigations had drawn a blank. Cooper briefed me weekly and promised he would stay with it until it was resolved. Daniel, too, made sure his guys stayed alert to any possibility of danger, and regular contact with neighbours ensured we were always aware of any new faces in the neighbourhood.

As for Kat and I, we got to enjoy some quality time in each other's company. Once the decorators had finished in the cottage, we moved in and enjoyed some quiet evenings sitting in front of the fire in the sitting room. We cooked together. And that wasn't the only thing we did to pass the time – if you take my meaning.

21 | THE START OF AN ACTION-PACKED DECEMBER

A chauffeur-driven car picked Tomáš and Eva up from Heathrow on Monday 1st December, which was also the day that Brian and Shona arrived. I knew that Liz and Nellie had held a shore to ship phone call with her parents but, beyond that, I had no idea of what had been said or left unsaid. Someone should have briefed me, it occurred to me, so I didn't put my foot in it – especially as Liz and Siobhan were out at the florists when Brian and Shona pitched up; Nellie had gone off somewhere with Daniel; and Tomáš and Eva were in transit – which left Kat and me in the hot seats.

We'd been in the sitting room of the main house drinking coffee and chatting, when: in walks Shona with a face like thunder. 'Where's Elizabeth?'

I found myself standing, politely. Some people just have that effect on you, don't they? 'Hi, Shona. She's with her aunt in Tavistock, sorting out flowers. They should be back soon. Would you like some tea?'

'Bugger tea,' she said. 'Get me a gin and tonic.'

Brian wandered in, looking his usual affable self. 'Young Adam is taking our bags up. I'm gasping for a cuppa.'

Shona harrumphed and sat next to Kat, then stabbed a hand towards Brian. 'He's just told me he's going to buy that disastrous Fine Arts business where my daughter works. I thought he was going to retire.'

Adam put his head around the door. Brian amended his desire for tea to a large scotch and Kat and I ordered more coffee.

I held my hand up. 'I confess, that was my idea. I've arranged things so that Brian and Liz can take over Matravers Fine Arts. Brian will be able to do as much or as little as he likes as Chairman. Liz will run it; Matravers will stay on as a minority owner, bringing all his contacts and auctioneering skills to the party; and a very bright chap who built the new online auction facility will join the board.'

'What's all this going to cost?' said Shona.

Kat smirked when she saw me cross my fingers. 'That's the best bit,' I said. 'Quentin Bailey, the tech guy, is going to swap what he's currently owed – for building the website – for a shareholding, and the *great* news is Liz has already secured a deal to auction a valuable painting from a friend of ours, Tomáš Novák. Did you enjoy your cruise?'

Placated, and with a gin and tonic in her hand, Shona became dangerously affable. 'Cheers, everyone.' She started chatting to Kat, volume set to broadcast. 'So you're with Jake, are you? Last time, I saw him he was on his own. I thought he must be gay. He said he wasn't and as Neville had gone off somewhere, I rather hoped he and Liz would get together.'

I decided I'd better take one for the team while Kat was still talking to me. She and I swapped places, giving Brian the opportunity to ask her about Prague.

'Do I take it Liz has told you all that happened whilst she was in Prague?' I asked Shona.

'That Neville finally proposed to her? In a nightclub in front of all those people? I couldn't believe it. After all these years. And, of course, when Neville inherits the title, Elizabeth will be a lady. Who'd have thought it?'

Fortunately, before life became any more complicated, Liz and Siobhan returned. Kat excused herself as soon as it was polite to do so, and I took Brian and Liz off into a corner for a catch up.

'Brave question to Shona, Jake, and carefully handled,' said Brian. 'Well done. Liz and I have decided to keep the more complicated end of the Prague business between us.'

'Of course, and that's your call,' I replied. 'Are you both happy with the plan to take over Matravers Fine Arts? I'm suggesting that the commission from the sale of Tomáš's picture goes to Matravers in payment for his shares, and you keep the buyer's premium as working capital. Funds will be tight for a while but I'm hoping the publicity you've generated around the sale will quickly lead to some new business.'

Liz butted in. 'I'm really excited about the auction. Tomáš' painting has really stirred up interest in Kaintz. The number of bidders we have lined up is growing by the day and I've been offered two more of his pictures to sell.'

'That's great news. Brian, I believe the website that Q developed has wide applications beyond Fine Arts. I can see it being used for all sort of auction situations.'

'I agree, Jake. It's an interesting market place. One for the future, eh love?' he smiled, turning to Liz.

'We're very grateful, Jake,' said Liz.

So was Matravers, I thought – but didn't say.

Kat was back in our cottage lying on our bed. 'Are you OK?' I asked.

She propped herself up on one elbow. 'I was just thinking,' she said. 'Your life would be so much simpler if you were with Liz. You two get on so well.'

I sat next to her. 'We do and we always have. But I'm not sure I could stand Shona as my mother-in-law.'

She laughed. 'No, but Brian's nice. You can talk to him and he listens.'

'Anyway, it's all decided: Liz is going to marry Nellie, I'm not gay and there's only one girl for me.'

'But what if there's only one girl for me too? What if you and I get together and in three months I meet her and break your heart?'

I smiled. 'That's a risk I'll have to take. I've never met anyone like you, and I don't suppose I ever will again. I really think we can make each other happy.'

She hugged me then, in a way that made me think she'd never let go. But when we parted there were tears in her eyes. She shook her head. 'I don't know, Jake. I just don't know.'

The phone on the bedside table rang and I got up to answer it. Tomáš and Eva had arrived, and dinner would be served in half an hour.

Tomáš and Eva were staying in the cottage next to ours. It was great to see them again. Eva had really come out of herself, and Tomáš never stopped smiling. He and I walked up to the house together, Kat and Eva skipping along in front of us and singing in Czech at the top of their voices.

Dinner in the kitchen/diner was an informal affair: loud, happy, with lots of wine poured and drunk. Everyone except Shona knew about Liz's adventure in Prague, leading to lots of semi comprehensible asides that went completely over Shona's head. I almost felt sorry for her. Nellie found a suitable CD for Kat and Eva to dance to – showing us an excerpt from one of the routines they used to perform together in Prague. Brian ended the evening by leading us in some traditional Scottish folk songs. It was truly a great night.

Tomáš, Eva, Kat and I walked back to our respective cottages under a star-filled sky. There was much giggling as we shouted goodnight to each other. I opened the door with the latch key and a tipsy Kat fell into my arms. We staggered up the stairs together and sat on the bed looking at the night sky. Kat got up and leaned on the window sill, gazing up at the stars.

She turned to me. 'I don't know if the love I have is enough for you.'

I stood and held her in my arms. 'Of course it is. You are everything I ever wanted.'

She frowned. 'Then you don't want much.'

'Come to bed,' I said.

'In a while.'

I woke in the middle of the night when I felt her get into the bed. I turned to face her.

'Hold me please,' she said.

I wrapped my arms around her and we both drifted off to sleep.

Our cottages had small, fully-equipped kitchens and there were plenty of comestibles in the cupboards, fridge and freezer but pretty much every meal was taken together in the main house, in the extension. There were grander rooms to eat in at Wychtor House – I'd been on a nose around one morning and found the formal dining room, with a polished dark wood table large enough to seat twenty people – but the family kitchen was a warmer, friendlier place to gather.

Daniel's guys finished off the barn over the next few days and the decorators moved in to dress the place. Some machinery had also arrived to extend the drive and create a parking area large enough for all the wedding guests.

On the Matravers Fine Arts front, the publicity for the

auction kept building as the number of noted collectors signing up grew. Lawyers had drawn up documents for the transfer of ownership of the business, and all parties had agreed to finalise the deal on the 9th, the day after the auction.

I was still checking in with Cooper and Lambert but there hadn't been much to report. The police had kept an eye on Luganov's house and, armed with a court order, had searched the premises for any clues as to his background or whereabouts. An attempt to get into his computer resulted in software installed on the machine wiping all his files. The Mercedes that I'd seen Vanda get into that night in Stratford was hired in London using a false name and forged driving licence. A speed camera had caught the car going back into London the following night and Cooper was working to get his hands on the photograph to see if it might provide any clues.

Saturday 6th of December broke bright and fair, a sunny day for a "Stendo" – which was just as well, when we found out what Nellie had booked for us. The Dartmouth Steam Railway and River Boat Company ran something called the Round Robin. Nellie read us an outline over an early breakfast. 'Here goes. I've hired a limo to take us to Totnes where we catch a double decker bus to Paignton Railway Station. From there it's the steam train for a scenic seven-mile journey to Kingswear. We'll ride in the Observation Car at the back of the train, with splendid views of the country-side and coastline. Then there's a short ferry ride across the river from Kingswear to Dartmouth, where I've booked a relaxed, gourmet lunch at the Carved Angel – one of the first restaurants in this country to earn a Michelin star. And finally, we catch the river boat which will bring us back up to

Totnes. Our chauffeur will meet us and we'll return home in time for a wee drinky.'

'But not too much,' said Liz. 'We're all off to church tomorrow morning to hear the banns read for the last time.'

'Please – what is banns?' asked Eva.

'It's an old tradition in the Church of England. Before a wedding, forthcoming marriages are announced within the Sunday service on three separate occasions. It's to allow time for any legal objections before the event,' said Liz.

'Are you thinking of objecting?' I asked Nellie.

'The thought had crossed my mind,' he said.

Adam came up and whispered in his ear.

Nellie stood up. 'That's us, ladies and gentlemen. Be outside, please, in five minutes and be ready for some fun, fun, fun.'

As usual, with any event Nellie was involved in, it turned out to be pretty over the top. He had props for each of us for every stage of the journey, including flying helmets to wear on the bus – to which he added large moustaches and silk scarves when we got on the train. And whether we were at the front of the top deck on the bus or appreciating the view from the Observation Car, we were drinking Champagne. We *were* allowed to remove the head gear in the restaurant – only to have it replaced by pirates hats and black beards for the boat journey. He'd also brought a couple of kid's plastic swords with which he and I were to fight a duel on the upper deck.

'Well, I can honestly say, I haven't had this much fun since my Gran's funeral,' I said. Tomáš was with the girls drinking coffee inside while Nellie and I were sitting in the sunshine on deck and indulging in a spot of red wine.

Nellie put his serious face on. 'You'd tell me if I wasn't doing the right thing, wouldn't you, Jake?'

''Course, mate,' I replied. 'And I promise you, you are absolutely doing the right thing.'

'It's just… She's quite bossy, you know. And they always say look at the mother, don't they?' He shuddered. 'And I don't want to be married to Shona.'

'That would be bigamy, mate. She's married to Brian.'

'True, true. Shhh, the law's heading this way.'

'You two must be freezing out here. Why don't you come in and drink some strong, black coffee?' said Liz.

'That's an excellent idea, Liz. Liz, Liz, I was just saying to my very old friend, I don't want to be married to your mother.'

'Then it's just as well you're marrying me, isn't it?'

We took an arm each and Liz and I manoeuvred Nellie inside. There was just enough time to pour a bucket load of coffee into each of us.

Kat had been a bit distant since last night and it was fair to say I was feeling more than a little sorry for myself. I went and sat next to her.

'Have you had a good time?' I asked.

She smiled weakly, 'Yes, it's been fun. I'm sorry, Jake, I don't mean to be difficult, it's just…'

'I know.' I patted her hand. 'It's cool. Don't worry.'

The boat docked, we disembarked and piled into the waiting limo.

Nellie slept all the way back to Wychtor House.

We were all up bright and early for church the next morning. After the service – and the all-important reading of the banns – and once the congregation had left, we had a brief rehearsal for the big day. Then it was time to escape back to Wytchtor House for a traditional Sunday lunch.

In the afternoon I spent some time talking to Brian explaining why I had so much faith in Q and the online auction site. Liz, Brian and I then had a call with Matravers and Q, a final briefing before tomorrow's auction.

'I've added the other two Kaintz pictures to the catalogue, and we now have nineteen bidders registered,' said Matravers.

'What terms did you agree for the two new paintings?' asked Liz.

'Our standard terms – fifteen percent commission to the seller and twenty percent buyer's premium.

'What do you expect them to make?'

'I've estimated each at two hundred thousand pounds.'

'If your guess is correct, that could net us an extra one hundred and forty thousand pounds.'

'I'm assuming all the commissions will come to me in exchange for my shares, with the buyer's premiums going into the business?' said Matravers.

'That's what we agreed.'

'Excellent.'

'Are you still planning an eleven am start?' asked Liz.

'All is ready. I'll hand over to Q to talk you through it,' said Matravers.

'Good afternoon, everyone. I've set all the equipment up here in the offices and I've run the usual tests. We're good to go.'

Brian gave me a thumbs up.

Later, Tomáš, Eva, Kat and I, along with Liz's parents, were summoned back to the main house for early evening drinks and to meet Nellie's parents, William and Sarah Bosworth, who'd just arrived back from overseas to attend the wedding. I'd met them just once before, at Nellie's and my graduation ceremony, a long time ago, and they'd aged, the pair of them. Well, it *had* been a while. William still had most of his hair but was very grey now and had a slight stoop, as many older, tall men do – but he'd kept the weight off and looked fit and active. Sarah was the same lovely, quiet lady I remembered: she had an elegance that defied age. In fact, if anything, she was better looking now than the memory I had of her at the travesty they call Coventry Cathedral on a clammy day all that time ago. She was also lovely with Kat, engaging her in conversation and making her laugh.

It was interesting to see the variety of reactions provoked by meeting His Lordship. Shona, completely dazzled by the whole event, barely spoke and wasn't sure whether to curtsy or shake hands. It was quite awkward until Brian made them laugh and everyone relaxed. Siobhan and Daniel started off very polite and formal until Nellie's old man offered his hand and said, 'Please, Sarah and William will be just fine.'

He met me with the same warm, open smile that I remembered. I went to shake his hand, but he threw his arms around me. 'Jake, my boy, it's been a long time. Your graduation, you and Neville. How many years ago was that?'

'A good few,' I replied.

'Neville tells me you've been busy and that you had something of the role of matchmaker in this wedding.'

'I wouldn't go that far. Let's just say, I oiled a few wheels.'

'That's the Jake I remember. Always modest. It was a first you got, wasn't it? And I know you helped Neville to his 2:2.'

I caught up with Nellie before we left. 'Well, that seems to have gone OK,' he said. 'I'm so glad you, Kat, Tomáš and Eva were able to join us tonight.'

'Is this your subtle way of telling me this was the first time the parents have met?' I said.

He chuckled. 'Apart from a quick hello at our graduation, yes. That didn't go so well. Shona spilled her drink over Dad.'

'No wonder she looked petrified when they first met tonight. She probably thought she'd end up in the Tower.'

Tomáš and Eva were coming round to us tonight. Kat and I had gone through our stores and decided on a simple supper, after the enormous lunch we'd had earlier. We opted for pizza slices with a generous salad. Just the four of us. It would be nice to be in a smaller, more intimate group for a change. Eva, with her infectious laugh, was so different now to the cool professional I'd met in the hotel. Tomáš was the same quiet, slightly reserved chap but the two seemed really good together – and they were both excited about tomorrow's auction. Who could blame them?

'So, Tomáš. What's the first thing you're going to buy?' I asked.

'A new bed,' replied Eva, laughing.

'No, no,' said Tomáš, grinning shyly. 'More plasterboard. Then a new bed.' He put his glass up in the air and we all drank a toast. 'You know, Jake, you and Liz have changed my life in so many ways. Before this, the only thing I did that I was proud of was to help Kat escape.'

'Don't say that, Tomáš. You looked after your sick mother for all those years. Not many men would have done that,' said Kat.

'Yes, but I had to bury my own feelings and work for Vanda and Hendak. It was wrong but I needed an income.'

'Not anymore,' I said. 'With the painting sold, you'll be able to restore your house and make your own money.'

Tomáš lifted Eva's hand and kissed it. 'And I will have help.'

Eva blushed.

We drank a toast to a successful auction.

Kat had folded into herself after the drinks do. She'd sipped her wine and smiled weakly when something humorous came up but she hadn't said much all evening. I knew she was unsure about us but there seemed to be something more. The guys left quite early, so I refilled our glasses and sat down with her.

'You've been quiet all day. What's on your mind?' I asked.

'I feel like I'm under pressure on all sides.' She threw her arms up in frustration.

'I'm sorry Kat. The last thing I want…'

She put her head down and then looked up again. 'Oh, it's not you, Jake. You've been very patient. The hotel are on my case. They need a definite answer by tomorrow night on the job they're holding for me.' She put her elbows on the table and her head in her hands. 'I don't know what to do.'

'Aah. OK. Then we have to think this through. You have two things that don't seem to be compatible and you feel under pressure to choose between them.'

I got up from the table and went over to the sideboard and rummaged in the drawers.

'What are you looking for?'

I came back to the table with some sheets of writing paper and a pen. 'There's only one way to tackle this.' I put two sheets of paper and the pen in front of her. 'I want you to define the two things that are competing and make two columns underneath for each one: for and against.

She frowned at me.

'Don't think about it,' I said. 'Just do it, top of the head stuff. Everything is solvable but I want to capture your frustrations and see if we can knock them over. I'll make myself scarce for half an hour and then we'll go through your answers together.'

I left her sitting at the table, glass in one hand, pen in the other. I grabbed my leather jacket and pulled the door closed behind me: before I could help Kat, I had to make sense of my own head.

As usual with me, the motion of my legs seemed to spark up the brain cells. How was I feeling about life? I ran through the list. Liz was safe now. She and Nellie would be married in a couple of days. The auction tomorrow would clear up another couple of issues. With new ownership and firmer direction at Matravers Fine Arts, not only was Matravers' future secure but Liz would have plenty to occupy her mind while Nellie gadded about town and went on his travels. And money would enable Tomáš' and Eva's lives together. Which left three things to think about: Vanda's threats, me and Kat, and my future. I went through them, almost as if I were making a physical diagram, the same as Kat's.

Vanda's Threats: it was hard to believe a word she said and with two police forces and Interpol on her tail would she really have the time to come after me, Kat or any of us? Once this wedding was over, I'd head for home and get on with my life.

Which brought me back to Kat… No, future first – what did I want?

I'd trained in accountancy with the naïve belief I'd make a living that way. But that's not what seemed to be happening. Twice now, I'd got myself into situations that involved failing businesses. Some nice, genuine people, trying to do their best but being screwed over by the ones after easy money, who were prepared to go to any lengths to get it.

I walked on. It was colder tonight. The sky was clear again, filled with twinkling stars and, this time, there was a light frost on the ground. My breath hung around me in great clouds of steam as I walked. This was helping. I was feeling much calmer than when I left the cottage. I stopped and looked around me. The red deer were clustered around a small group of trees on my left. Most were asleep but one beady eyed individual was keeping a watch on me, looking out for the others.

And that's what he and I had in common. I was good at spotting trouble, working out who the villains were and how to sort the jigsaw pieces to build better, workable answers.

I was good at the numbers – honestly, there was no one better – but it was the people I really enjoyed. So that was it. I should fully embrace this exciting, adrenalin-filled lifestyle I'd fallen into. Who knows where it would take me? And it could be lucrative – look at Race Engineering where I'd earned a fat fee and a car. Only one way to go – follow the path and find out.

And now, finally, Kat. But this walk had given me the clue I needed.

She rushed to my side as I came in, throwing her arms around me. 'Why are you so wise? You always know the right thing to do. I've put my thoughts on paper.'

'Have you come to any conclusion?'

'Yes, but I don't think you're going to like it.'

'Then let me speak first. If you don't take this job, you'll always wonder. And that could so easily come between us in the years to come.'

'But what about you, Jake?'

'You're part of my life now, Kat, and that's never going to change. We're both discovering new things about ourselves.

It's exciting and a bit scary but, you know, as long as we keep talking and sharing our journey, we'll be fine.'

'Really, Jake, do you mean it?'

'Absolutely. My life has changed for the better since I met you. I'm no longer just an accountant. I've learned so much with this dangerous art business, and before that, Race Engineering. I'm solving problems and helping people in a way I never realised I could. I'm going to carry on. And one more thing.'

'What's that?'

'I can still care for you if you decide you prefer girls. Love and sex aren't the same thing.'

That made her grin. 'You'd be willing to share me?' She was incredulous.

'Well,' I said, 'left with a choice between no Kat and a half share – who knows?'

She threw a cushion at me. 'Who said you'd get half?' She stopped laughing then though and looked suddenly serious. 'You're saying we could still be together even if it's not all the time?'

'Whenever we get the chance and – who knows? – there'll probably be other escapades I want to drag you into.'

And with that, we turned out the lights and went upstairs. And yes, it was one of those nights where we didn't just sleep, well, not straight away.

I got up just after midnight. It was a clear night still and the moon was bright. It looked cold out there. I bid a silent goodnight to my friend, the red deer, before returning to bed, wrapping my arms around Kat and falling asleep.

22 | MONDAY 8TH DECEMBER – AUCTION DAY

With the air cleared, our cottage was a much happier place to be. Kat got on the phone first thing to firm up her job situation, while I went for a walk around the park, stopping off on the way back to take a peek inside the barn. From the outside, this was your regular brick-built, common or garden barn, to be found on just about every country estate in the land. On the inside, it was becoming one woman's Christmas wedding fantasy.

There was a stage at one end, with curtains of white and silver on either side. The inside walls of the barn were hidden by white and silver mesh veils draped from the overhead beams, with a line of four large candelabras hanging down the centre of the room. In front of the stage was an area left clear for dancing. Roughly two thirds of the rest of the space was taken up by eight large round tables – and Liz was standing in the middle of them, having a disagreement with two women about floral decorations. I looked across at her, pointed to my watch and mouthed *time*, before heading back to the main house – wondering as I did how Nellie was going to cope with married life.

Daniel had vacated his study and allowed Brian, Liz and me to commandeer his desktop and speakerphone so we could follow the sale. Liz – who had switched from bride-to-be to professional mode – came though carrying a tray with a pot of coffee, biscuits and three mugs.

'I thought Tomáš would be here,' I said.

'He said he wouldn't be able to stand it. He'd rather you pop in at the end to tell him how it's gone,' replied Liz.

'Are you there, Jake?' Q's voice came through the phone.

'All present and correct.'

'We're just about to start. We're up to twenty-four bidders signed on. Langdon is just typing up his opening words. We're putting Tomáš' painting up first. And here it goes.'

Matravers' words appeared on the screen alongside a picture of Tomáš' painting.

'He's inviting the first bids and they're coming in thick and fast.'

We watched the display clocking up as each bid was replaced by the latest.

Liz looked ecstatic. 'I knew it,' she said.

It didn't slow down until it reached £265k.

'Langdon thinks it'll top three hundred thousand pounds.'

As we sat on the edges of our respective seats, Matravers kept prodding and the bids kept going higher, albeit at a much decreased pace now. He didn't call time until it reached £317k. The other two Kaintzs made £225k and £247k respectively.

'Let's see, Matravers is on ten percent commission for Tomáš' picture and fisteen percent for the other two, so he's just made himself one hundred thousand pounds. As the new owners of Matravers Fine Arts, you're on twenty percent buyer's premium for all three and that puts over one hundred and fifty thousand pounds in your bank account. Not a bad morning's work. I'll go and tell Tomáš,' I said.

'Take him this,' said Liz, handing me a bottle of Champagne.

'Will do.'

I picked up Kat on the way round and the four of us had a celebratory glass of fizz – although the girls had to knock it back as the dressmaker was coming for Liz's and their final fittings. Tomáš just kept grinning to himself.

'I can't believe it,' he kept saying, wonderingly. 'To think it's been in my attic for all these years.'

'Liliana's letter was prophetic. The picture has brought you luck when you needed it most.'

'Yes. I can make plans now.'

All was good with the girls' dresses, and Nellie's and my suits got dropped off, so we were set for Wednesday. More of Liz's family turned up to fill Wytchtor House's nine bedrooms, and Tomáš and Eva asked us round for dinner so we could let Liz's lot mingle unmolested.

It was when we got back that I had the phone call from Cooper. 'I've just heard – your house was broken into last night.'

'What's been taken?'

'Nothing as far as we could see and that's the funny thing.'

'What do you mean?'

'A neighbour saw lights in there but knew you were away. A window had been forced but with minimal damage, as if someone didn't want you to know. We've had a locksmith round there and he's made it secure. No footprints or fingerprints to speak of. Everything as clean as a whistle. Nothing out of place.'

I frowned. As a numbers man, I'd never trusted coincidences – and I didn't trust this one *at all*. Something was going on. I just didn't know what.

Yet.

23 | TUESDAY 9TH DECEMBER

Two things to report today. The first was the closing session for the takeover of Matravers Fine Arts. Matravers walked away with a nominal shareholding in the company and his hundred thousand pounds, Q swapped his debt for a twenty-five percent stake, with Liz and her dad picking up the rest, leaving the business with a healthy bank balance.

But the big news came through another phone call with Cooper.

'I've finally got the photo from the speed camera. We were lucky it was one of the new Truvelo forward facing cameras that captures an image of the driver and – in this case – the front seat passenger. It's Luganov. And that's not all. Lambert came up trumps with an old passport photo of Dmitri Petrov. Change his hair style and add ten years, and it's him. And guess who's sitting next to him? She matches Vanda's description.'

I had to think this one through. 'So Luganov is really Petrov – the guy who was Hendak's boss when Kat left Prague eight years ago. He disappeared soon after and must have set up shop in London under his new name.' I stopped talking and mulled it over. I'd just connected all the dots.

'What are you thinking?' asked Cooper.

'Their scheme was cleverer than we first realised.'

'How so?'

'To begin with, I'd thought this was a simple fraud: buy

a likely painting on the cheap, falsify its provenance, take advantage of a buoyant art market and make a pile of money. But this was much smarter than that.'

'Explain.'

'Lambert was interested in the Dark Goddess because he believed the club was connected in some way with money laundering, but they had no hard proof. But if Petrov and Hendak were money launderers, they'd make their money by nefarious means and then find a way to clean it through the banking system. But that's complicated and could easily cost them thirty percent of the face value.'

'What's the answer?'

'They buy their painting back with their own dirty money. They feed cash into the banking system, accumulate it into an offshore account then use it to buy the picture.'

'But they already own the picture…'

'Yes, but if they go through this process, they *still* own their picture *and* they get clean money back from Matravers' bank less the slice for Matravers' fee – five percent instead of thirty. They've saved up to five million pounds.'

'That's clever.'

'And that's not all. By putting the painting through a public auction, they add that record to the painting's history, helping to justify why, if they ever put it up for sale again, it's worth at least that much.'

'Doubling their money.'

'Very nearly.' I thought more about what Vanda had told me. How much of it was true though? Was any of it relevant? 'With Hendak dead, Vanda is now working directly with Petrov. He wants his twenty million dollars and they think I can unlock it. And they know I'll do anything to protect Kat.'

'What will they try next?' asked Cooper.

And then something so obvious that I could have written *fool* with a felt pen across my forehead struck me. What if it was Vanda who broke in last night, snooping around to see what she could find? A cold chill ran through me. Had I left the wedding invitation on the dining table?

If I had, it would mean she'd know where I was and that Kat was with me.

'Let me think. I'll call you back.'

What the hell was I going to do? I looked at my watch. It was half ten in the morning. The wedding service was at 11.30am tomorrow, so I had a little over twenty-four hours to work out a *just-in-case* plan. They might even be on their way now. OK – this starts with objectives: what would theirs be? Vanda had told me Petrov wanted his $20M back and I expected she was in for a slice for helping him. I was coming to the conclusion that she was a liar and a heartless bitch too. She'd be looking to pressure me into finding a way to release the money, using my relationship with Kat as a crowbar. I shuddered at the thought. There's no way they'd come to the church; the police station was just over the way in Guildhall Square. That meant they might turn up here today or at the reception tomorrow. But how? They couldn't just walk in. Better check the security arrangements.

Daniel was on the phone in his office. I took a seat as he finished his call.

'Morning, Jake. I hear all went well with the acquisition of Matravers Fine Arts.'

'It did but I've just had some very disturbing news.' I quickly explained the situation.

'How likely do you think this is?' said Daniel.

'I can't be sure, but we need to be prepared, just in case.'

'What do you have in mind?'

'The guys you have on site look pretty handy. How many are there?'

'They're all ex-military from an agency I know in Plymouth. We had problems with poachers when we put the deer in. I can warn the ones we have here now; generally there are two or three, but I can get more if we need.'

'Any weapons?'

'I have shotguns.'

I thought aloud. 'The last thing I want is to disrupt Liz's and Nellie's big day but I think we should be cautious.'

'Agreed. We should keep those in the know to a minimum. I'll speak to the agency and see if we can get some extra help tomorrow. What else?'

'Suppliers? There'll be lots of coming and going tomorrow.'

'Indeed there will. Let's see. The florists have two teams, one for the church and one here, for buttonholes, the bride's flowers, the house and the barn. We've known them for years, no issue there. Caterers – they're providing food and wine for the wedding breakfast. That's a late lunch to you and me. And a buffet for the evening do. All the tableware, cutlery and glasses are coming from them too. The bar for the evening will be run by our local pub. The only one we've never used before is the company supplying the fireworks, Sparkling Skies.'

'How did you find them?'

'Yellow Pages. But we took references from previous customers and they were excellent.'

'Thoughts?'

'I suggest we have a guest list at the gate and check off arrivals. Likewise with each supplier; we'll ask for a list of their staff. I'll boost our security numbers to six for tomorrow, which will give us enough resource to patrol the grounds as well as man the gates.'

'Thanks, Daniel. It's great to have your support on this.'

'Don't worry, Jake. If these people turn up, we'll deal with them. You have enough to do, making sure my niece marries her man tomorrow.'

I left Daniel speaking to the agency and rang Cooper back to tell him about the invite and our precautions.

'Good,' he said. 'I'll ensure Devon Constabulary are aware that these two might be heading your way. They'll keep a look out for the car and pick them up if they're spotted. If you need their help, they'll be just a phone call away. And so will I.'

I found Kat standing in front of the mirror in our bedroom, practising being a bridesmaid.

'That dress looks amazing.' The shade of pale blue would tone nicely with Nellie's and my suits, but the real bonus was the way it brought out the colour in her blue-grey eyes.

She flounced in front of the mirror, examining the way she looked from every angle. 'Do you like it? My hair is too short really, but Liz has a hairdresser coming in the morning and by the time she's worked her magic, it'll look fine.'

I told her my news. 'It's just a precaution. I don't want anything to interfere with Liz's and Nellie's big day.'

'Will you tell Nellie this evening?'

'No. That's the last thing I want him worrying about.'

Liz was a stickler for old customs, including the one that says it's bad luck for the groom and bride to see each other on the night before the big day – which meant Nellie had been banned from the house that evening, and Kat and I had invited him to join us for dinner and to sleep over in our cottage. Now, we decided to ask Eva and Tomáš to dinner too so we could keep Nellie focused on the wedding.

'And I'll ask Tomáš to keep Nellie occupied first thing in the morning while I check through all the arrangements with Daniel.'

'That's my man,' said Kat, smiling.

24 | WEDNESDAY 10TH DECEMBER – WEDDING DAY

Daniel and I met the security team in the barn at 6am to brief them. It was going to be a long day.

It was like the Snow Queen's Winter Palace in the barn, with everything draped in silver and white. On a long side table, baskets of gleaming stainless-steel cutlery and orderly stacks of white crockery waited to be laid out on the eight round tables, already covered in pristine white table cloths. The tables, each with twelve seats placed around them were positioned towards the back of the barn; a wooden dance floor had been laid between them and the stage, and large vinyl snowflakes in – you guessed it – silver and white, had been glued down at random intervals. Despite my nerves, it made me smile to think how different it felt in the barn compared to the *actual* weather outside, which was quite mild with the odd rain shower.

We seated ourselves at one of the tables and Daniel explained the timetable for the day. The catering and floristry teams would arrive from 7am to get everything ready. Daniel's daughter, Stefanie and her band, Iconic Box, would arrive from London shortly to set up. There would also be a hair stylist coming to the house. The service at the church would start at 11.30am, so we'd all be on our way by 11am. Two of the guys would come with us and keep their eyes open while acting as ushers – but we didn't anticipate any issues there.

The wedding service would be forty-five minutes, followed by photography outside. The only possible change of plan was, if it rained, we'd be back early and have photos in the barn. The family would line up to greet the guests on their arrival, there'd be a glass of Champagne and lunch was to be served at 1.30pm. Speeches to follow. Music, dancing, then a break at 4pm. The caterers would clear up and set up for the evening buffet. Evening guests to arrive at 7.30pm, music and dancing again then fireworks at 10.30. During the afternoon break there'd be more coming and going – fresh food arriving for the buffet, the fireworks people arriving and setting up. Daniel fell silent as I addressed the guys.

'We don't expect trouble but we want to be prepared just in case. There are two individuals who may see this as an opportunity to target me and my companion, Kat Dominova. The people after Kat and me – Kat is a bridesmaid, the one with the short blonde hair – are wanted by the police internationally for a complex crime involving money laundering, kidnap, fraud and blackmail. They're dangerous and should be treated with caution.'

I read out a description of each of them.

'If they do arrive, they're to be detained and the police summoned. But there's a good chance that if they try to get here, they'll be detained on the way.'

Daniel passed around typewritten sheets of paper.

'Daniel is handing out two lists, suppliers and guests. Please check off people as they arrive and keep a watch during the day.'

Daniel joined in to drive the point home. 'I would

emphasise that, if these people do turn up, you're to use whatever means necessary to restrain them. I want them taken so the law can deal with them.'

It was 7.30am by the time I returned to our cottage. Tomáš was sitting at the table drinking coffee and Nellie was in charge of the frying pan.

'Where are the girls?' I asked.

'In the main house, breakfasting, hairstyling, applying war paint then dressing. I expect they'll be ready by tea-time,' said Nellie. 'Grub's up.'

By the time we'd finished we still had a couple of hours until we needed to get under way. I left Tomáš and Nellie making more coffee and went back to the barn to see how things were progressing. I was greeted by Daniel, who, already dressed for the occasion, was keen to introduce me to his daughter, whose band was setting up on stage.

'Stefanie,' she said, 'but everyone calls me Steve.'

She was the lead singer and spoke beautifully, which was both evidence of an expensive education and in complete contrast to her appearance: she wore fishnet tights, work boots, a short, skin-tight leather skirt and a sleeveless biker's jacket. Long unkempt hair, mad make-up and a token safety pin in her jacket completed the look. The other three band members were clearly on board with the punk dress code too, the keyboard player's and guitarist's leathers decorated with long lines of safety pins and the drummer displaying an impressive collection of tattoos on her muscled arms.

'What do you play?' I asked Steve.

'We'll start with a little full-on punk and then move into some softer stuff. Now and then, we'll do another nice loud, jarring track, just to make sure the oldies are still awake.'

'Great,' I said, as enthusiastically as I could manage. 'Could you do a special number for me?'

'Say the word.'

I returned to the house to boss Nellie into a presentable state and, with us both suited and booted, we climbed into the Siren and shot off into Tavistock. Liz had put Siobhan in charge of making sure everyone else had a lift. The light rain that had been falling eased as we arrived in the town. It was bustling with shoppers but we managed to get parked and legged it across to the church in good time. The sun came out.

'See, it really does shine on the righteous,' said Nellie.

'And us, surprisingly.'

I stopped him on the way in and reached into my pocket for the hip flask I'd secreted there. 'A small stiffener before you do the deed.'

The two ushers were already on post. With buttonholes affixed, Nellie and I wandered inside. Quite rightly, we were first here. The flowers were magnificent, especially given the time of year, and a little gentle organ music set the tone for the event – in sharp contrast to the noise I expected Iconic Box to be making later. Not for the first time, I made sure the rings were safely in my pocket.

We took our seats. I wondered what Kat was thinking right now. Would today affect her views about us? I looked at my oldest friend sitting next to me, and reached over to touch his hand. 'OK?'

He smiled. 'Never better, mate. Glad to be here, with you at my side.'

The church was filling up. I looked at my watch. Nearly time. And then it *was* time. As the organist struck up Purcell's "Trumpet Tune", Brian and Liz appeared at the top end of the aisle. I nudged Nellie and we stood. Feeling in my pocket for the rings had become a nervous tic, but I couldn't forget that moment in *Four Weddings and a Funeral* when the best man reached into his pocket and came out with… nothing. But it was okay: the rings were still there; great.

And then Liz was processing slowly down the aisle on Brian's arm followed by Kat and Eva.

'All set?' I asked Nellie.

He tapped his head. 'Solid as a rock, mate.'

We stood and the bride-to-be joined us. The ceremony started and Brian stepped back, while I remained at Nellie's side. Eva and Kat stood behind Liz, and I snatched a glance at Kat, who looked amazing. The pale blue dress really suited her skin tone and blonde hair. The cut of the fabric was just right – close but not too tight. She looked sophisticated yet good enough to eat. Her make-up, her hair, even the shoes: everything was perfect. She saw me looking and smiled. Her eyes were moist and I knew how she felt. It was that sort of occasion. Now more than ever, I knew we belonged together. I wanted her with me but I was determined to let her find her own way to me – to us. Let's call it patiently impatient.

I handed over the rings, witnessed the happy couple's signatures and then I was accompanying Kat along the aisle behind the bride and groom, and we were outside in the pale sunshine, under photographer's orders. Pretty soon, we were loading up and shipping out. Nellie was, of course, now with Liz and I was enjoying the company of the chief bridesmaid, Kat, back in the Siren.

'That was fun,' she said.

'Glad you enjoyed it,' I said.

'You never know, one day I might want to go the whole way and get married.'

I started the car, temporarily speechless.

She laughed when she saw my face. 'What's so strange about that idea?'

'You? Married?' I asked.

'No one has ever asked me.'

'Will you do me the honour?'

She smiled enigmatically. 'I'll think about it.'

We were on the top table, with the shortest walk to the dance floor and stage – which would be handy for the speeches. If only I knew what the hell was I going to say… A quick look at the seating plan had me wishing I had time to move the place cards around a little. Shona arrived and took the seat next to me. Kat was my cavalry, seated on my right, and Daniel was next to her.

The band struck up with a Ramones number before moving into "White Wedding".

'Ah,' said Nellie's father. Don't you just love Billy Idol?'

Shona looked at him askance.

Once the band had moved into a quieter track, Shona placed her hand on my thigh and leaned across me to speak to Kat. 'When are you going to make an honest man of our Jake, dear?' Shona winked at me.

'It's funny you should ask,' she said. 'He proposed to me in the car.'

Shona's expression reminded me of the kid's story about a cat with eyes like saucers. 'Did he?' she replied in the same voice as Lady Bracknell's "a handbag?" in *The Importance of Being Earnest.*

'Yes, I said I'd think about it,' said Kat, struggling not to laugh.

Shona looked me up and down, 'I think he's quite well off, you know.'

'He'll have to be. I have very expensive tastes.'

The starters arrived and everyone tucked in, saving me from further embarrassment for the moment. Now, that speech. I'd got plenty of stories from our time at university together, but would they work with this crowd? I looked at my watch. The time was going on. Did I really think Vanda would come? Eight tables of 12. That was 96 guests, plus all the staff knocking around. It would take some front to show up with this crowd. And if she didn't, what was I going to do? Hope that the police finally got their hands on her? I hated to admit it but there was nothing else I could do right now. Like a fisherman on a river bank with his baited line in the water all I could do was wait. But I was the bait. Try to relax and enjoy myself. Act natural, whatever that means.

Kat saw my face and squeezed my hand. '*Whatever will be, will be*,' she whispered. I ate one-handed and hung on to her.

'Brian was telling me about this deal you set up for him and Liz. It sounds like it could be quite lucrative,' Shona said.

'I hope so. Liz will be in her element and Brian can swan around and look important.'

'He's already booked another six-week cruise as a peace offering. The Caribbean again. I enjoyed it so much the first time. So did he – lots of young women in bathing suits to look at.'

I was glad when Daniel rescued me from this tangled web. 'How do you like your Siren, Jake?'

'She's fabulous,' I said, looking at Kat. 'And the car's not bad either.'

'Cheeky,' said Kat, grinning.

Shona went into a sulk when Daniel launched into a lecture about his Aston Martin. Fortunately it was interrupted by the arrival of the main course – venison – who'd have guessed? By the time we'd dealt with the sweet, I was seriously concerned. What the hell was I going to say when I had to get up on my hind legs? Well, I had one trick up my sleeve.

Brian got up from the table and went to the stage. Steve announced that the band would take a break and Brian took over the microphone. 'So, here we all are. My girl's finally done it. She's married the man of her dreams. It took long enough to get him here. But, to be fair, he's a great fella and I'd like to welcome him into our family. And we're honoured to have Neville's parents with us today. They've just flown in from sunny South Africa so they're feeling the cold.' He spoke for a little while longer – though not *too* long, and then concluded. 'Doesn't my girl look beautiful today? Please be upstanding and join me in a toast to the bride and groom.'

Nellie's turn came next and, unusually for him, he didn't have much to say for himself, finishing with a toast to the bridesmaids and calling them up to join him on stage to each receive an engraved silver locket as a memento of the day.

Nellie stepped down from the stage as I walked up to the mic. 'Well, Ladies and Gentlemen, how do I follow that? Two such brief speakers. I'm guessing that makes me the main entertainment. Apart from our fabulous band, that is – so would you please put your hands together for Iconic Box?'

As was expected of me, I then asked the crowd to join me in thanking a long list of people, including: the guests for attending; both sets of parents; Siobhan and Daniel, for hosting; the bridesmaids; and the staff. I made a couple of jokes about Nellie, then – just in time – from the back of the stage, two members of the catering crew appeared with a small round table topped with a conical shape covered in a cloth. They positioned it in front of me. 'Hello, what's this?' I said, adopting a puzzled expression as I pulled the cloth from the table. Underneath was a colourful cylindrical object about thirty centimetres high and twelve centimetres in diameter, with a blue touch paper sticking out of the top. Next to it was a box of matches. 'What do you think, Ladies and Gentlemen – should I?'

People clapped and shouted. I picked up the matches, lit the touch paper and stepped back. There was a whistling noise, like a roman candle, and a stream of metallic silver confetti, followed by blue glitter, then multi-coloured sequins and streamers, shot high up into the air. At the same time, the band struck up with their own wild, punk version of "Get the Fire Brigade" – originally a big hit for The Move in 1968. As the indoor firework died down, I snatched a hand-held fire extinguisher and pretended to be putting it out. You guessed it: I'd organised it through the chap Daniel had hired to do the fireworks later.

I grabbed the mic again. 'Excellent,' I said, as the applause and laughter died down. 'I wanted to do something that shows you how I feel – how I hope we *all* feel – about Liz and Nellie getting together. Unlike *this* little performance, though, I predict that no one will ever be able to put out the flame of their love.' I ended by asking everyone present to toast the bride and groom and then – much relieved to have got it over with – I left the stage to wild applause as the band struck up in a series of melodic numbers, starting with "Love is All Around". Their version was more like The Troggs' original than Wet Wet Wet's cover from *Four Weddings and a Funeral* – but that didn't stop Liz and Nellie from getting up onto the dance floor, and they were soon joined by smooching couples.

***

By 4pm, the daytime guests had all drifted away, and those who were staying had largely, it seemed, decided to take a rest until the evening do. Even Tomáš and Eva had gone back to their cottage, although Liz and Kat were still in the barn chatting over a coffee. The staff were clearing the debris and getting everything ready for round two. A chap from the pub was carrying in crates of drink and setting up the bar. Some of the glitter from the indoor firework had worked its way into the back of my shirt collar while I was dancing so I thought I'd go back to our cottage and sort it out.

I bumped into Daniel outside.

'Great speech,' he said.

'Well, you know how it is, I wanted to leave them hungry for more.'

He grinned. 'No unwanted guests so far.'

'No, I can only assume they've decided against it or the police have picked them up. No trouble at the gates?'

'No issues. There was just one query. The usual chap from the pub has the flu, so he sent a replacement. It's the pub's van though, and it was full of booze. He's in the barn now setting up.'

'Then I'll see you this evening for more fun and frolics.'

'See you later.'

I got all the way to the cottage before I remembered that we'd decided to be more security conscious today: we'd locked the cottage and Kat had the key. So I turned around.

I looked for Kat when I got back inside but she and Liz had moved away from the table where they'd been sitting. I gave the barn a quick scan. All the tidying up and setting out had been completed now; there was just the food to bring out later. The band were on stage, working on a couple of numbers, focused inwards, looking at each other and their instruments. I was just about to ask Steve if she knew where the girls were when I spotted a group near the bar in the far corner: Liz and Kat with two other people – who I didn't recognise, although that might be because they had their backs to me.

I walked towards them. As I got closer, I saw the dark-haired man was holding a gun. The second figure turned as I approached.

'Hello, Jake,' said a familiar gravelly voice.

I addressed the man. 'And you must be Dmitri Petrov.'

'He said his name was Phil Griffiths and he was from the pub,' said Liz. 'He asked us to help him with the ice machine, then he pulled this gun on us and told us to get in his van.'

'Jake is right. This is Petrov,' said Kat quietly.

'This is no time for introductions. We have to go,' said Petrov.

'I thought you were a Cockney,' said Liz, affronted.

'What can I say?' he said in his own, distinctly Eastern European, way. 'I'm good at accents. Like your friend Kat, here. C'mon, Vanda, we must move.'

'In a moment,' said Vanda. 'Jake. Listen to me. Liz and Kat will come with us. You will arrange to release the twenty million dollars. I will have Kat contact you with the details of where to send it. As soon as we receive the money, we will release these two.'

I stepped back. 'That's not going to work, Vanda. The money is in a special escrow account. The only people that can release it are the police.' I took another step back.

Kat – my beautiful, brilliant, clever Kat – had caught on to what I was doing. 'I'm going to faint,' she said weakly, diving to the floor. Liz got down next to her. 'Are you alright Kat. Kat, can you hear me?'

I leapt at Petrov, making a grab for his gun, but he was quicker than me. He brought the gun up then dropped it down quickly against the back of my head and the lights went out. The last thing I heard was Liz screaming.

I came to in the back of the van, which was being driven hard on the driveway towards the main gate, bumping and shaking all over the place at this speed. There was another vehicle in pursuit.

'That's Steve,' said Liz. 'There'll be hell to pay when she catches you.' She glared at Vanda who was holding the gun and directing its muzzle at us. There was another man lying comatose in the corner, his wrists tied to a bracket on the floor.

'That's Dave from the pub. It's his van,' said Liz.

We three were sitting on the floor propped against the side. Our wrists were tied behind us and we were doing our best to hang on to whatever we could to stay upright. Vanda was sitting in the front seat next to Petrov, facing back into the van and keeping her pistol trained on us.

'Look,' said Petrov.

'Damn,' said Vanda. 'They've locked the main gate.'

I craned my neck to see. The gate had been padlocked closed and four men were there with shotguns.

With Vanda and Petrov distracted, Kat whispered, 'Hold me.'

I watched in confusion for a second until I realised what she was doing. She let go of the side of the van, dropped her shoulders as low as she could and brought her wrists down to just below her feet. I grabbed a handful of her clothes to stop her sliding across the floor as she brought her wrists up to her mouth to bite at the knots securing them.

Petrov yanked at the steering wheel, skidding the van off the drive and onto the open grassland. Through the back windows and the dust behind us, I could see Steve closing in. Behind her was a Land Rover. Vanda, I realised, was no longer watching us; she was using both hands to stop herself being flung around – which meant the gun had disappeared for now. Kat was working at her ropes, grabbing threads between her teeth and pulling. It was as much as I could do to hang on to her and stop both of us sliding across the van.

Just then, two things happened at once. Kat's hands came free and one of the van's front tyres burst and Petrov lost control. The van careered into a tree.

The next thing I knew was when the rear doors were practically wrenched off their hinges and Steve and her muscle-bound drummer were pulling us out of the wreck. About four milli-seconds later, the Land Rover behind screeched to a halt, the front doors of the van were yanked open and shotguns were trained on Vanda and Petrov.

In the distance I could see blue lights arriving at the main gate.

25 | IT'S A WRAP

Liz would be fashionably late for her evening do but surprisingly composed. Vanda and Petrov were carted away by the authorities and then a taciturn police inspector accompanied us to the main house so we could unpack the events of the afternoon for him. So there we were, sitting round the big table in the kitchen/diner: Nellie, Liz, Eva, Steve, Steve's drummer, Siobhan and Daniel, the inspector, Kat and me. Some had coffee, others brandy. We didn't involve Liz and Nellie's parents – we figured that was best tackled tomorrow.

Once the inspector had assimilated the background, we took him through what had happened.

Steve piped up in her beautiful speaking voice. 'The band were practising a few numbers. We were up on the stage, sitting in a circle, minding our own business when I heard a scream—'

Liz interrupted. 'That was when Petrov hit Jake on the head.'

'I don't understand how I ended up in the van,' I said.

'They were concerned you'd recover in time to stop them,' said Kat.

Steve carried on. 'I turned around and saw these two' – here she pointed at Liz and Kat – 'walking out of the back door with that man holding a gun on them, and the woman had her arm round Jake and was dragging him along. So we dashed out of the front doors and saw them putting them in their van. We ran to our van, in the car park. I was just reaching for the keys when I saw Dad returning from walking the dogs, so I yelled to him and described what I'd seen. Then I took off after them.'

Daniel picked up the story. 'I'd kept my short-wave radio by me all day, just in case.' He looked at me and smiled. 'So I contacted the front gate, told them to lock it and set up a welcome committee. Then I went into the house and dialled 999.'

The inspector exuded a natural air of authority. His pristine uniform helped but it was more than that. He had an aura of quiet competence – solid, reliable and unfazed by anything. He clicked his ballpoint and closed his notebook, looking up. 'I was able to ascertain a few facts from Vanda Brazda before she was taken to the station. She'd been in the area since Monday, watching the comings and goings and noting down details of your suppliers from the signs on their vans. She obtained a schedule of the day's activities from someone who works for your caterers; I'll get more details when we question them at the station. Then today, she and Petrov flagged down the publican's van, pretending they had a puncture – and it looks like they gave him a real going over. We've taken him off to hospital to be checked over but I'm assured he'll be fine... which is more than I can say for his van.' He looked at us all then smiled. 'That'll do for now. We'll arrange to have someone come up here and take formal statements from you but, in the meantime, enjoy the rest of your day.'

Kat and I went to the cottage to get a shower and change.

'It's finally over,' I said, slipping into a different outfit.

'And I've laid all my ghosts to rest,' said Kat, putting her arms around me. 'We can focus on our future.' She stepped back and looked into my eyes.

I snuck a quick look in the mirror. Pale blue open-collared shirt, close fitting but smart jeans, a light grey linen jacket with a blue stripe in it, stylish brown brogues on my feet. The bump on the back of my head didn't show and, thanks to Kat's judicious application of witch hazel, it hadn't got any bigger. Clean, tidy, shortish dark hair and steady brown eyes.

Kat shook her head. 'Who'd have thought it? Me, with such a handsome man.'

'You look fabulous like that – but don't you think you should put some clothes on?' I said, given that she was still in her underwear.

She smiled sweetly. 'I just have to do my make-up and then I'll put my dress on. Tonight is the first party of the rest of your life.'

I returned her smile. 'I know. And I can't wait,' I said.

AFTERWORD

As I sit here today, printing off the final draft of *Dangerous Art*, many thoughts are rocketing through my head. First point – this is fiction: my life of crime only extends to writing about it, not practising it. So, as always with me, a fair bit of research has hopefully made the criminal elements of this story credible. But, I should caution you, that this story is pure invention and there are elements of it that just wouldn't happen in the real world. What I've tried very hard to reproduce faithfully are my feelings for some of the places that I love. The fabulous Art Deco Burgh Island Hotel at Bigbury-on-Sea, the fine old city of Prague, just a touch of the fair Glasgow and – the real showstopper – my home town, Tavistock. Wychtor Ferrers, Wychtor House, the Goldcrest Hotel and the Dark Goddess are, sadly, complete fabrications but hopefully, each in their own way help to give this story life.

And whilst writing this manuscript has been a largely solitary occupation, I am hugely grateful to my support team without whom *Dangerous Art* would never have made it to publication. First amongst these is Gary McBar who, I can honestly say, is the only completely real person in this tale. I first came across Gary mixing a mean cocktail in the Palm Court Lounge at Burgh Island – only to realise when we moved to Tavistock that he lives here too! As Jake says, 'life is full of coincidences!' He's since retired but a few lucky people get to see and talk to him at the occasional events that he participates in on the island. I owe a special thank you to the management and owners of the Burgh Island Hotel for allowing me to set the start of *Dangerous Art* there.

My advisors at BeRead Ltd continue to patiently help me to take my writing to market in a way I can be proud of, and have introduced me to a broader spectrum of supporters, namely: Paul of 25 Design for my fantastic covers; Andy, amazing typesetter at Andy Barr Books; and, of course, Sam Humphreys, my one in a million editor, who tunes up my offerings and has helped me enormously. Then there's the team at Brookfield Digital, who have built my amazing website and continue to actively help me to promote my work. And a special mention in the Brookfield team must go to Quentin Faulkner, who is my inspiration for Q. His knowledge of the workings of the internet in the late Nineties was pivotal to the telling of this story. Unlike Q Bailey, I've never heard that he did a spell in the submarines but – who knows? – perhaps he's a darker horse than he appears to be. Next, we have Hayley Perring, who continues to unpack the mysteries of social media and provide me with a presence that I could only have dreamt about. Then there's my many 'beta readers', as the trade calls them: real people who like crime thrillers and have taken the time and trouble to read *Dangerous Art* and give me their honest (and sometimes forthright) views of it. Theirs is a contribution I value greatly.

And yes, I have saved the best to (nearly) last. Inside the title page it says the following:

To Sharon, whose love, commitment and red pen have made Redline *and now* Dangerous Art *a reality. I am truly, madly and deeply grateful.*

Nothing I will ever write could possibly be more true.

And finally, thank you dear reader, for taking an interest in this book. I hope you enjoyed reading it as much as I enjoyed writing it.

Have you read my first book in the Jake Elderfield series, *Redline*?

Here's what it says on the back cover:

Betrayal, mystery and sabotage collide – can one man uncover the truth before it's too late?

When former racing star Rod Race is killed in a hit-and-run, his family's company spirals into crisis. A devastating test crash raises suspicions – bad luck or something more sinister? Jake Elderfield, fighting his own demons, is determined to save the business. But as secrets unravel and trust shatters, he realises Rod's death was no accident.

Fast-paced and full of twists, *Redline* is a high-octane thriller perfect for fans of psychological suspense and corporate intrigue.

READER REVIEWS

'A REFRESHING NEW TAKE ON A CRIME STORY.'

'NICE TO HAVE A CRIME STORY WHERE THE LEAD CHARACTER ISN'T A DETECTIVE.'

'A FAST-PACED PAGE-TURNER.'

'A FRESH, ORIGINAL AND GRIPPING THRILLER.'

If I've tempted you – you'll find the first three chapters on the following pages.

Go to my website www.terry-green.co.uk to buy *Redline* or to sign up to my Newsletter and receive a free copy of Kat's backstory, *The Velvet Revolutionary*.

REDLINE

AN EXTRACT

1 | MONDAY: START YOUR ENGINES

5th May 1997.

There's a phrase that's supposed to keep the noses of us have-nots pressed firmly to the grindstone. You know the one, it's often attributed to smug, successful bastards as they grin at you from the pages of the latest business magazine. It goes something like this: *People say I've been lucky but the harder I work, the luckier I get*.

Well, here's the truth. Luck needs hard work like a rabbit needs a space-hopper. Seems to me some fortunate types have everything good land in their lap while the rest of us poor fools get to put up with the dross life throws at us.

Do I sound bitter? Bloody right, I do. Accused of a crime I didn't commit, obliged to leave a promising career with a well-respected firm before I was booted out and, the real kick in the aspidistras, broken-hearted after the love of my life deserted me without so much as a *bye, I'm leaving*.

A phone call at half seven in the morning wasn't going to improve matters. Which is why I let my ancient Panasonic answer machine pick it up. Anthony Browne's nasal, upper-class bray filled the room.

'Morning, Jake. Listen chap, our vacancy's been filled so you don't need to come in today. Back to bed for you, old fruit. Sorry and all that. Ciao.'

The tape whirred in rewind and the answerphone reset. Bastard. The Panasonic's winking red eye mocked me from the top of the oak-effect sideboard until I reached across and hit the button, erasing the mendacious Browne from its memory and my Christmas card list.

Now what?

I left the scatter of unpaid bills lying across the heavy set, dark wood dining table and took all of three steps across my "compact kitchen stroke diner" – rental agents have such a way with words, don't they? – to the sink. There, I peered despondently through the window at the small, tousled square of unkempt lawn with its neglected borders.

Filling the kettle, I flicked the radio on in time to hear the eight am news. Blair again, sounding smug and earnest now he'd become Prime Minister. Lucky bugger, *he'd* be earning. A robin caught my attention as he landed on a gnarled rose bush, staring back at me belligerently. Clever though, the way our Tony had snatched the centre ground from the Tories while keeping a lid on the unions.

Still, as long as there's coffee there's hope. I spooned instant into a mug, squeezed out the last drops of milk, chucked the carton in the bin and placed the dirty spoon in the sink. Back to my makeshift workspace to mastermind my next move.

What the hell was I going to do? All my usual contacts had stopped answering the phone since the court case. Accusations – even false ones – have a way of putting people off. Even Anthony Bloody Browne's book-keeping job, hardly a role for a fully-qualified accountant, had disappeared as soon as they'd realised it was me. The letterbox rattled, signalling the arrival of another wodge of envelopes. More bills? Replies to my latest job applications? I perched my coffee on the table and made the dozen strides through the small, under-furnished sitting room to the front door of my terraced Victorian cottage. I scooped the mail from the mat and took a quick flick through. Strictly bin fodder.

A familiar, if unexpected, shadow loomed through the opaque door glass. Too curious for my own good, I snatched the door open to confront my ex-boss, his clenched fist raised to a knocker no longer within his reach.

'Morning, David. What can I do for you?' Best to be civil, at least until I knew what he wanted.

David Lansdowne always made me feel underdressed. He stood, straight-backed and immaculate as ever in sports jacket and twill trousers, his regimental tie precisely squared against his carefully pressed, pale blue shirt. Brown brogues held a mirror finish. He slowly lowered his arm as if completing a salute. Clear blue eyes, under bushy salt and pepper brows, studied my face. His professional smile hinted at his purpose; a man who was here to do business. Interesting.

'Morning, Jake. Thought I'd see how you're doing.'

'You'll be wanting coffee,' I said, standing back and ushering him towards the kitchen. He joined me at the sink as we waited for the kettle to boil. The rose bush quivered as the robin launched himself into a fly past in David's honour. Time to make polite conversation.

'Do you think my garden needs work, David?'

A broad smile graced his lips and softened his eyes. 'I'm no gardener, I'm afraid, I leave such things to Mrs Lansdowne. Tilda.'

'Perhaps you could send her round here?'

David guffawed. In all the time I'd known him, I'd never heard him make such a sound before. We really were in new territory. I poured steaming water onto coffee granules in a second mug.

'There's no milk.'

'No matter. Black will do the job.' He added a touch of cold water from the kitchen tap and followed me to the dining table.

Taking a seat opposite me, his eyes strayed to the notepad where I'd been working out the grand scale of my debts. I gathered up bills and jottings and dropped them into a single pile on the floor. My business, David.

'What can I do for you?'

'You didn't have to leave, you know,' he said sympathetically.

'*Any hint of suspicion sticks like gum to a schoolboy's desk*. Your words not mine.'

He had the grace to look uncomfortable. The silence between us was broken by the familiar sound of next door's toddler colliding with the furniture and landing with a thump. Over-cheery maternal tones gradually overcame the sound of wailing.

David cleared his throat. 'I've come with a proposition. One that I believe can take you past your recent difficulties. It concerns Race Engineering.' He took a mouthful of coffee and swallowed reluctantly.

'The sports car people,' I said. 'Flashy toys for well-off boys.'

Laughing at David's expression, I relaxed a little. 'I worked on a couple of their audits when I was first with you.'

'Indeed. And now they're in trouble. On the verge of bankruptcy.' He lifted his coffee mug, hesitated, then put it down again, untouched. 'I want you in there. Find out what's gone wrong, then show them how to get out of the hole they're in. You'd be their consultant.'

'With my reputation? Why the hell would they hire me?'

David leaned in, smiling. 'My influence will get you

through the door. Then – well, I know you. You'll do your research and come up with a convincing plan to get them out of trouble. All you've got to do is use your charm.'

I sipped my coffee and made a show of enjoying it. 'You don't think landscape gardening's for me then?'

'Not if you want to eat. So, how about it?' Why would David put me up for this when he'd got a plethora of talent to choose from. Did he think he owed me?

He pursed his lips impatiently, then looked at his watch, the prized rose gold Jaeger-LeCoultre Reverso presented to him last year, marking twenty-five years of loyal, lucrative service. 'I won't lie to you. They're difficult people and it's a messy situation. Most of my colleagues would run a mile rather than get involved. But, you're tenacious and now you've something to prove.'

This was my chance to get back in the game; to put the disasters of the past months behind me, prove my honesty and get on with my life. What had I got to lose? Absolutely nothing. 'I'll need a day rate, first week up front.'

'I'd expect nothing less.' Standing, he placed his nearly full mug in the kitchen sink. 'I have to go.' He paused by my front door, though, frowning, 'They'll take some saving. Especially from themselves.'

2 | WARMING UP

David had lingered just long enough to be convinced I would turn up for a meeting with the directors that evening before striding off to his waiting Jaguar. He needn't have worried; what with the legal bills I was facing for my defence and no salary coming in, if he'd suggested popping up to the moon to fetch some green cheese, I'd have offered to get my rocket out. And besides, after my career had stalled so dramatically, who was I to refuse a bump start?

Within the hour, a courier arrived at my door with a couple of large boxes. I had my orders: read the paperwork, then report to reception at Race Engineering, six pm sharp, ready to be grilled.

The files drew an eloquent picture of a company on its last legs but I wanted the narrative that went with the numbers – and I knew just the man.

It was lunchtime when I left the early May sunshine behind on Union Street and sauntered down shady steps into the dimly lit subterranean bar known as the Glovemaker's Arms. A handful of earnest drinkers were already in occupation, if you included the barman and two blokes playing pool.

I didn't see him at first, his slim form half-hidden in the gloom. Ned Drake, editor, reporter, advertising salesman and – for all I knew – head of toilet cleaning for the *Stratford Courier*, sitting alone in his usual booth, poring over an advance copy of this week's edition, checking for any howlers before his readership's critical eye got the chance. I'd known him for years and we'd helped each other out from time-to-time, swapping snippets of information as we'd progressed through our respective careers. I'd never thought I would one day be the subject of one of his columns, but the last time I'd seen him was three months ago, across a crowded courtroom.

His expression didn't change as I approached but he flicked his head up quickly in a kind of nervous tick, acknowledging my arrival. A gasp of ambient light caught the sheen in his short, black, slicked-down hair. I walked up to the bar, ordered a pint and put down a handful of change. I took the seat opposite Ned, placing the beer on the table in front of him. They call it reciprocity. Offer something up before you go for the gimme. Of course, a little threatening behaviour always helps seal the deal.

'All right, Jake?' he asked, a smug look behind his watchful eyes.

I smiled, 'Oh, I'm fine, Ned, couldn't be better. But you have a small problem.'

He drew smoke from his slim panatela, carefully blowing it sideways, away from my face, as he balanced the cigar back on the ashtray.

He returned my smile, 'What's that, then?'

'Me,' I said.

I picked up his cigar and stabbed the hot end down towards the back of his hand, stopping a hairsbreadth above it.

'Jesus,' he muttered under his breath, examining his heated flesh carefully. 'What d'you wanna go and do that for?' Stress brought out his Black Country accent.

'That's the difference between us, Ned. I could have burnt you but chose not to. You, on the other hand, lost me my job without a second thought.'

'I heard you resigned,' he whined.

'No choice after the way you covered the story.'

'You was the one in the dock.'

'I was innocent,' I responded.

'Like I haven't heard that before,' he smirked. 'The public had a right to know.'

I'd made my point. Time to get on with the job. 'I want a favour.'

Ned watched me balefully and started in on his pint. 'I'm listening.'

'I'm after everything you have and everything you've guessed about Race Engineering.'

He took a long pull at his beer, his dark eyes unblinking over the rim of his glass, then tapped the side of his nose. 'You're on to something, aren't you? OK, but let's get one thing straight. If you pick up even a hint of a story, it's mine. Do we understand each other?'

'We do,' I said.

He held up his half-empty glass and waggled it towards the bar, followed by a polite two finger salute. The barman made a house call, placing a beer in front of each of us. I took a mouthful from my glass as Ned spilled his story.

I already knew Race Engineering had been started a couple of decades ago by Roderick Race, an ex-racing driver – although I hadn't realised he'd got his nickname, Hot Rod, in honour of his supposed conquests in the bedroom. Ned reminded me that James Bishop, the ex-chief engineer of his racing team, had joined Race in the business. Together they'd launched a sports car called the Vixen. And they'd done well. A race series across Europe and lots of private sales. But, as always happens, after a while the market started to look around for the latest shiny thing and, in consequence, sales started to decline.

Before things became critical, however, a well-placed rumour about the development of Race's next car, the Siren, led to the company being showered with speculative deposits from the affluent anoraks who follow the brand.

Ned continued, 'Race's finished last year with a full order book and Hot Rod was having a whale of a time, jetting all over the world, doing deals with his cronies.' He finished his first beer and made an impressive inroad into the second. 'And then, back in February, while you were otherwise engaged…'

'Fighting off trumped-up charges, you mean.'

'They found him lying in the car park out at their test track.'

'Heart attack?'

Ned leaned in and took a final pull at his pint. 'Bloody hell. Don't you ever read my paper?'

'I wasn't much in the mood for comics back then.'

'He'd been hit by a car.'

'What happened?'

Ned shrugged. 'No witnesses, no tyre tracks. The ground was as dry as old Mother Shakespeare's bones and the car park surfaced with loose gravel. Left the forensics people scratching their heads.'

'Accident?'

'If that were an accident, my Aunt Nell's a badger.' He stopped talking long enough to look at his mobile phone, jot a note on the edge of his paper, tear the strip off and pass it to me. 'This copper's on the investigation team. You can mention my name if it helps.'

I examined his barely-legible scribble – *DS Guy Cooper* – and a phone number.

'The test track's out at Long Marston, you know, the old

airfield?' he said. 'Inquest was adjourned for further evidence. Buggered if I know where they're going to find that.'

'What happened then?' I asked.

He chuckled, 'That daughter's a feisty one. Hard as nails. Took charge of the business and got the new car launched. It started well but there were more bad news to come. I should know, I broke the story.'

'You're like a vulture sitting in a tree, waiting for something to die, aren't you?'

Ned chuckled thickly. 'It's not me, it's the dear old paper-buying public. Nothing sells like a wealthy local family going tits up.'

'And then there's the valuable public service you perform, I suppose?'

'Do you want to hear this or not?'

I gestured for him to continue.

'Couple of Sirens were out on the test track. One of 'em went sideways and took the other one out. Wonder no one was killed.' He started laughing and shook his head.

'What's funny about that?'

'Not a lot. But what happened after was. Thing is, no one would likely have known about it – but it were last Monday, I'd just got the paper ready and were in here having a quiet pint when I got a call from the office. An urgent special delivery. Prints, negatives and the bare bones of the story. Anonymous, like. I rang Race's and got hold of the daughter, Carina, to check it out. She rubbished it and gave me an earful so I sent copies of the pictures across. Ten minutes later I got some garbled nonsense on a fax from her lawyers admitting it was true but offering no explanation. I ran the story in last week's paper. It's been a good earner, been syndicated round the nationals.'

'How come you're not more pleased then?'

He frowned. 'It was a tuck up. Like finding a rat's bum floating in yer pint. I mightn't have a clue as to who did for old man Race but it was me as finished off the Siren.'

On the way home, I stopped to buy milk, so I could have a coffee – which was much needed after that lunchtime beer. Then I dialled the number Ned had given me and left a message.

The thought of Race's body lying in a car park put my own troubles in context. Why hadn't David mentioned it? And now, three months later, the new car had disgraced itself at the same circuit. Coincidence? I hoped so. I pushed the thought to the back of my mind. Time to get ready for the grilling.

It had been a while since I'd worn the Hugo Boss. Donning it increased my confidence a little, my charcoal pin-striped persona forming a protective veneer over the bundle of nerves within me. What if these people wouldn't listen to David? What if I fluffed the pitch?

My image stared soberly back at me from the full-length mirror of the wardrobe door. I could just about see the top of my head without bending at the knee. I pulled in my belt a notch. It would have been nice if the suit had shrunk a little to match my new, leaner profile. In some ways, being away at "college" had been good for me. Twelve weeks of disciplined routine and regular exercise had curbed bad habits and eliminated my recreational consumption of alcohol, forging a sharper, fitter me. And my always galloping ambition had been honed into a steely determination to prove myself.

I finger-combed my dark locks into some sort of order,

straightened my tie and the shoulders, discovering that if I tweaked my shirt sleeves up a little, no one would notice the slightly frayed left cuff. I tried a rakish grin. Not bad.

Back at the dining table, I dropped my papers into a battered leather document case, adding my slim Filofax before zipping up. I stepped into the street, closing the door behind me.

I'd quickly settled into Old Town on my return to Stratford. Before all this happened, Ella and I had been renting in one of the posh roads on the other side of town. Here, the rows of terraced Victorian houses in their modest streets were somehow comforting. Originally built for the workers who'd brought the railway to the town, the area had matured into a fashionable, bohemian district peopled by the middle classes. One or two darlings of the stage living quietly among the teachers and retired professionals, with an occasional radio producer thrown in. It was handy for the theatre and the shops. Back in the 1860s, it would have been a tight-knit community, self-reliant and hostile to outsiders. Round the corner from me, in Bull Street there had been four pubs in one relatively short road. My cottage was in Narrow Lane, then called Love Lane; an excellent address if you happened to be in the bliss business.

I'd lived quietly these last weeks, nursing my wounded pride, screened by the self-absorbed bustle of life around me. But here I was stepping back into the everyday stream of events. A semi-colon in my life; not the end of the sentence but definitely a new beginning.

Late afternoon sunshine anointed the buildings, warming the red brick and reflecting off the densely parked cars lining the street. At the top of the road, casually abandoned Volvo estates and people carriers signalled the imminent escape of squadrons of small people from the prep school. I felt a sense of camaraderie with them; after all, I knew what involuntary incarceration felt like after my brush with the law.

My thoughts turned to the task ahead of me. Directors of failing companies aren't generally noted for their calm manner and positive outlook. At one end of the scale would be the garrulous confessions of a profligate board. At the other, inarticulate misery. I hoped for something in the middle. Either way, as father confessor, I had a duty of care, which meant giving them enough stick to test their resolve. Well, you have to get your kicks where you can, don't you?

I crossed the street and turned north, walking past the end of Maidenhead Road, where my old life used to be.

My lips moved in a calming mantra: *when the going gets tough*. I caught a glimpse of my reflection in a nearby shop window, and tried out a confident grin, catching the attention of a passing "yumai mumai," as Ned would say. I noticed her straighten her shoulders and push out her chest, tossing her red hair.

The tourists who come to view "Will Spokeshave's" birthplace, to catch one of his plays, or simply to stroll by the river and feed the swans, probably never notice the small but thriving manufacturing base tucked away to the north of the town. Prospero Road Industrial Estate stays largely out of the limelight of Stratford's international reputation. Race Engineering had been, until recently, the one notable exception, its image underpinned by the fast, stylish sports cars it builds for rich, glamorous customers, lending it something to shout about. Till it lost its voice.

The building I was heading for was something out of the ordinary. Built in the 1930s, the two symmetrical, white-painted wings of offices, each with a double row of steel-framed Crittal windows, met in the middle, joining a rectangular tower which reached above the roof line. A clock at its apex proudly bore Race's logo. At the base of the tower was a short flight of white marble steps leading up to a pair of polished aluminium and glass doors, over which projected a flat canopy porch. The whole looked rather as if two white cruise liners had collided simultaneously into an art deco lighthouse. The clock showed five minutes to six.

High gates at the entrance to the car park were firmly closed, a huddle of reporters gathered on the pavement outside. A uniformed security guard stood just inside, with arms folded and a *not on your nelly* look of firm defiance on his face. A car approached, and he moved forward to unlock the gates. The driver edged forward gently, not looking left or right. A man in his mid-forties, accompanied by a colleague sporting a fancy camera, gestured a *wind down the window* motion. When the driver didn't comply, the reporter banged on the roof and shouted his question at the impervious glass.

I approached the back of the group and gently but firmly pushed my way through. At first, they ignored me but, as I reached the gate and explained to the security guard I had an appointment, they turned on me, firing off a myriad of questions. I kept my expression in neutral and walked through. The gate closed behind me and I found myself standing in the car park.

A wide expanse of tarmac stretched in front of me. In normal times, it would have easily provided enough parking space for the workforce, visitors and any attention-seeking celebrity who insisted on picking up their latest acquisition under the glare of the waiting paparazzi's cameras. Today was a different story.

Every parking space and even the grass verge between the fence and offices was occupied by a low-slung sinuous shape. But it was as if an artist with a bad hangover had captured the scene. Each car's paintwork was embalmed with a thick layer of wax. Every roof, windscreen and set of side windows was obscured by a fitted cover of drab, oatmeal coloured canvas. Each wheel was shrouded in thick layers of translucent plastic. Unregistered, unsold Sirens. Lots of them.

Only one car in the place had plates and shiny paint and it was right in front of the steps to reception. I edged my way carefully around the gleaming metallic blue bodywork and black soft top, noting the registration plate: *S11REN*. The interior was, of course, trimmed in tan leather and walnut, the perfect executive plaything for the man or woman who didn't care about the cost.

Once inside the building I approached the front desk. Unanswered telephones rang out intermittently in the background. The receptionist looked as if he'd had a hard day.

I smiled pleasantly. 'Hi. I'm Jake Elderfield. I'm here to meet David Lansdowne.'

He pulled his careworn face into a pale imitation of a greeting, 'Certainly, Mr Elderfield, I'll let him know you're here. Please take a seat,' he said.

I walked across the light-filled, double-height lobby, admiring the severe, clinical décor and the way it set off the building's simple aesthetic. I settled into a wine-red leather sofa and channelled positive thoughts.

A door at the back of the lobby opened, admitting the faintest smell of engine oil and I recognised the familiar strains of D:Ream's "Things Can Only Get Better" playing through the factory's public address system, over the low mechanised hum of machinery. How appropriate. A man in smartly pressed motor racing overalls walked through. He looked tired and thoughtful as he left the building.

An array of two-week old motoring journals lay on the coffee table in front of me. I picked up a magazine that was full of macho praise for Race's new car, billed as *the seductive Siren, a stylish masterpiece with plenty of grunt.*

The slap of leather soles descending the marble stairs alerted me to Lansdowne's arrival. David glided down with the simple grace of an accomplished ballroom dancer. Still attired in this morning's ensemble, he looked fresh and eager for the coming confrontation.

'Jake. Glad you could join us this evening.'

I stood and we shook hands. 'Well, here I am, David. How are things?'

'Challenging, but there are grounds for optimism, not least because you're here.'

I grinned as he ushered me towards the grand staircase, leading up to the first floor.

'I've borrowed an office. We can talk there.'

We climbed higher in the airy central atrium. Early evening sunshine pooled across the floor below us, projected from the four elongated, vertical windows in the building's front elevation, like the claw marks of a very large cat.

At the head of the stairs, we turned right into a parquet-floored corridor. Windows to our left looked down across the factory floor. To our right lay individual offices. The clear glass in the top half of each door allowed a glimpse of oak-panelled interiors and the opportunity to spy the rural view, beyond the edge of the industrial estate, that each occupant could enjoy from their desks. We came to an office with *Chairman* written in gold lettering across the door glass. David ushered me inside. A collection of wall-mounted photographs caught my eye; a shrine to the ego of one man. Blond, blue-eyed Roderick Race shaking hands with a minor royal during a factory visit. Another showed Race on the podium, his face grubby and hair dishevelled, spraying champagne over adoring onlookers. A third had him in black tie at a film premiere, accompanied by an attractive blonde, glass in hand, chatting companionably with several familiar Hollywood faces of twenty years ago. A glass-fronted cabinet displaying racing trophies and memorabilia sat against the far wall. An oak battleship of a desk occupied the central area of the office, with an ancient executive chair parked behind it. A scale model of the Siren, crafted from solid aluminium and perfect in its detail, sat in the centre of the otherwise empty desk.

It felt like trespassing, being among so many of the dead man's personal effects.

'Take a seat,' said David, gesturing to the two guest chairs and perching on the edge of the desk facing me. 'You've looked through the papers I sent across?'

'In detail.'

David moved behind the desk and settled himself into the comfortable-looking, faded leather seat. He reached for the model of the Siren, turning it slowly in his hands as he spoke.

'And what do you make of the situation?'

I frowned. 'They started well enough and had some good years but relied on the one model for too long. Still, credit where it's due; it was impressive, the way Carina and her team knuckled down to get the new car launched after Race's death. But this crash at the test track has left them teetering on a cliff edge. Have I missed anything?'

'I should say not. A good summary. I should tell you that they're minded to call in receivers but I'll make them listen to what you have to say first. There's a lot of emotion flying around in there and you'll need to dial down the heat and shine a light on the facts.' He placed the model car back on the desk.

And then he said something more prophetic than I could possibly have realised.

'You know, we had a saying in the army,' he said.

'If it moves salute it?'

'Not the one I'm thinking of. When you're thirsty, everything looks like an oasis.'

I smiled, 'No, you've lost me.'

'Beware the simplest solutions that appear to fit the facts.' He checked his watch, 'Shall we go through?'

3 | APPEALING TO THE CROWD

A head-and-shoulders portrait of the late Roderick Race posing in his racing overalls dominated the period-panelled, plush-carpeted boardroom, his middle-distance stare was on you wherever you stood. Proudly posed, he was a caricature of a nineteenth century industrial magnate in twentieth century overalls – although I wasn't sure the artist had taken his commission entirely seriously. It made the flamboyantly-tiled, art deco fireplace below seem positively staid. The full-width window at the far end of the room provided an excellent view of the ranks of slumbering Sirens awaiting the outcome of our deliberations. A long, highly-polished table occupied the centre ground. Five chairs were clustered around the near end with more lined up against the wall, should anyone feel the need to host a banquet. The seat at the head of the table was empty – reserved for David, no doubt. The other four were already occupied. A side table held a collection of thermos jugs, milk, sugar, mugs, a carafe of water and glasses. No biscuits. Things must be bad.

David placed his briefcase on the floor and rested his hands lightly on the back of the chair. I stood next to him, studying the four impassive faces turned towards us.

'I'd like you all to meet an old friend of mine, Jake Elderfield,' said David. 'Jake, may I first introduce Carina Race, managing director?'

She was a year or four older than me, maybe late thirties.

Attractive certainly. A generous mouth and long nose dominated her features. High cheek bones, large expressive eyes, full red lips and a determined chin. Her lightly tanned skin radiated health. When she spoke, her voice was surprisingly deep and inviting. Shame her greeting wasn't.

'I thought this was to be a private meeting, David? No place for hangers-on, surely?'

'Please think of Jake as a specialist to whom I've referred you.'

Nice touch, David. Carina didn't respond straight away. My eyes followed her as she went to refill her coffee mug. Graceful yet precise. Well-dressed, business-like but elegant in her double-breasted, navy-blue suit. A silver slide in the shape of a Celtic knot positioned at the nape of her neck kept her mane of auburn hair under control. She was gripping her coffee in her right hand as she came back towards me, her long, slim fingers displaying red, talon-like nails and a very large diamond solitaire ring. She'd have been tall even without her heels but with them, we were almost the same height. As she came in close, I could see her expression was amused, confident.

'Here to see what you can grab at our expense, no doubt. I suppose I could get a couple of my burliest chargehands to throw you out?' She seemed to consider the idea as she sipped her coffee. 'On reflection, it might be more amusing to hear what you have to say first.'

Returning to her seat, she directed her next words across the table to a chap with the look of a young plant in desperate need of sunlight and a kind word. 'It all seems so obvious to me, I don't know why we're even discussing it.'

The plant looked angry. 'It's not your decision to make, Carina, I…'

'Oh, save it,' she snapped. 'When I want your opinion, I'll tell you what it is.'

Her victim lowered his eyes and said nothing.

The well-groomed, fifty-something man sitting next to Carina was striving to appear younger in his fashionably-cut suit with a white, open-necked shirt. The "stress highlights" in his collar-length, dark, wavy hair somehow enhanced his sophisticated bohemian look. The faint pink pinstripes in the charcoal fabric of his suit added a touch of colour to his otherwise monochrome appearance. He remained seated and waved a languorous left-handed greeting in my direction.

'I've always had a fond regard for a happy ending, however unrealistic. You know, unlikely hero rescues the leading lady from the burning building just as the roof collapses. Welcome, Jake. I'm James, engineering director of this humble manufactory and owner of Berrington Pressings, supplier of parts to car makers large and small. Glad you made it before our closing down sale.'

I generously awarded him a half smile. 'You're not beaten yet.'

'The fat lady may not have burst into song but she's certainly taken a deep breath.'

Opposite James was a familiar-looking blonde woman of about the same age. Her pale blue dress and cream cardigan were understated elegance itself. She wore an expensive watch but no rings. I recognised her from the iconic film premiere photo on Race's office wall.

'Helen Race, Mr Elderfield. Please excuse my daughter's hostility and James's flippancy. This is a very trying time for us all. I, for one, am very keen to hear what you have to say.' She spoke like a BBC radio announcer from a different era, precisely articulating vowels and clipping sentences. Her handshake was cool and dry. I noticed her clear-varnished, closely-cut finger nails as she reached for a clearly expensive eyewear case. The steel-framed glasses she put on lent her an air of calm authority. I felt like a shy five-year-old, facing a scary doctor for the first time.

The plant – actually a slim young man with close-cropped blond hair – unfolded his long lean body and stood, seemingly genuinely pleased to see me. 'Allen Race, Mr Elderfield. Finance director.' He reached out a pale hand and gripped mine, pumping it enthusiastically, his blue eyes conveying sincerity.

James smirked. 'And I thought you just made the coffee round here, Boy Wonder.'

Ignoring him, Allen took up a chair from the side of the room and placed it between David's and his own, gesturing to me as he set it down.

'Call me Jake,' I said, taking the proffered seat.

He smiled and placed a glass of water in front of me.

David brought the meeting to order in a calm, confident voice. 'Thank you all for making yourselves available at short notice. We're here to consider Race Engineering's current difficulties and decide on our course of action. If everyone agrees, I will act as your chair this evening. Any dissenters? No? Good. Allen, may I ask you to record the minutes?'

Allen nodded quickly, unscrewed the cap of his fountain pen and sat ready with his notepad.

David continued. 'Jake, perhaps you would start us off.'

I opened my Filofax and leafed through the notes I'd made earlier. I'd already piled my other papers on the table in front of me, their purpose to intimidate my audience.

Carina sat back, arms folded, lips pressed tightly together. James doodled myopically on his pad. Allen waited with pen poised while Helen emanated calm discipline.

In my world, the call for help usually comes in so late the only option is to pay the workers off and put a for-sale sign on everything that doesn't move. That made this a novel experience: the chance to fix a business before it hit the wall.

'How does our charge, ladies and gentlemen; do we have a pulse?' I asked.

Allen opened his mouth to speak but Carina beat him to it.

'Shouldn't you be telling us?'

'I've only just arrived and I'm interested in your opinions.'

James jumped in. 'Sales have tanked since the *Courier*'s article and there's nothing left in the bank account. I'd say we're done, wouldn't you?' He shrugged and went back to his illustrative works.

Allen looked up from his papers, his brows furrowed into a frown. 'You're the reason we've no money, James; you've spent every last cent.'

'Perhaps if we'd had this conversation *before* we committed the expenditure?' said James.

'We did, if you remember. Repeatedly.'

'I'm afraid the miserable bleating noise you made didn't register. Perhaps you should have tried harder.'

'Enough,' I said, directing my gaze at Helen.

'I have nothing to say at present,' she said.

'How very Helen,' said James. 'When she finally shows up for a meeting, she has nothing to say.'

'Nevertheless, as a director you have a voice,' I said.

'And when I have something to add you shall hear it.'

'Ok. Let's try a different tack.' I smiled pleasantly. 'Anyone been through an insolvency before?'

Blank faces, dismissive shakes of the head.

'Thought not. The law says if you're unable to meet your

obligations, you should call in an administrator who will take control of the business. Their job will be to recover as much money as they can for your creditors. They'll be all sympathy at first but it's just a ruse to extract information – which they'll use against you if they think it'll lead them to more funds.' I leaned forward for emphasis. 'You'll be under the microscope. Any mistakes or signs of fraud and they'll be at your throats.'

Carina was dismissive. 'Nothing to find here. The quicker this is over, the sooner we can get on with our lives.'

I shrugged. 'It'll be thorough and unpleasant. It'll take weeks but will feel like months. If I was appointed, the first thing I'd look at would be your handling of the Siren.'

'What specifically?' asked Helen, her icy blue eyes lasering in on me.

'Let's start with the crash. What was the cause, James?'

James smiled. 'It's my turn in the tyre bath, is it? Well, bring it on. I say driver error.'

'Why would two professional drivers make such a dramatic mistake?'

'They're used to hacking around the circuit in Vixens. The new car is a completely different proposition, with a larger engine and different handling characteristics. Any powerful car requires one's full concentration to get the best from it.'

'If an experienced driver could lose control, it must call your design into question.'

'Should a knife manufacturer be held responsible when one cuts oneself preparing dinner? I don't think so.'

'So, what then? The driver just took his eye off the ball?'

James smiled, 'Or, in this case, the road.'

'Where's your evidence?'

'You asked me what I thought and I've told you.'

'Where's your analysis? Interviews with the drivers? Have you even examined the wreckage?'

James stared back impassively.

Carina shrugged dismissively. 'Let's move on. We saw no point in a detailed investigation after the *Courier*'s article. Everyone had their money back and none of the cars got into the open market.'

'So, no investigation. And without any actual evidence James decided it was the driver's fault. I don't suppose you bothered to discuss this with the other board members?'

'James and I made the decision together,' said Carina reasonably.

'Three black marks so far,' I said. 'Firstly, when your finance director suggested you were overspending, you ignored him. Secondly, you failed to investigate the crash, bringing about the current crisis. And finally, the two of you took a key decision without consulting your fellow directors.'

Carina shrugged. 'Why are we even bothering to talk about this? The outcome wouldn't have changed.'

'Not the point. You didn't follow due process.'

'Anyone can be clever after the event. You're supposed to be advising us. Why don't you get on with it?' she retorted angrily.

'I'm not done yet. Let's move on to this fateful press release, shall we?' I took a single sheet from the top of the pile in front of me and waved it under their noses. 'This admits the crash happened but there's no attempt to explain it. And now we know why, don't we? You don't actually know.'

James grinned and shook his head, while Carina stayed silent, her eyes flashing at me.

'What could you possibly believe this would achieve?' I said.

'It's called damage limitation. Our lawyers advised us to keep the release to a minimum,' said Carina sharply. 'The offer to refund customer deposits demonstrated our confidence in the car,' she added.

'Incredible. You emptied your bank account for no benefit. Did you *all* sign up to this?'

Helen spoke. 'It was Carina's decision.'

'I was told afterwards,' said Allen.

I shook my head.

'There wasn't time to drink tea and debate the mysteries of the universe,' said James.

Carina was emphatic in her agreement, 'Someone has to face up to the difficult decisions around here and I don't see any other volunteers.'

'But you didn't go about it the right way. You're vulnerable. Let me tell you what's going to happen if you make that call. A team of expensively suited vandals will come calling. As I said, they'll be nice as pie to begin with. They'll sit you down individually and the questions will start. They'll demand an office for their exclusive use from which you'll be banned.'

Helen sipped water from her glass.

'They'll exclude you from their conversations. They'll bury you and your team with requests for information, wearing you down and keeping you guessing. And then the threats will start: disqualification as a director, fines, losing your house, maybe even a prison term. Signing up as a company director is far too easy; people don't realise what's at stake if they don't do the job properly. And guess what? Ignorance is no defence.'

Allen had been watching me intensely. I paused to let him speak, but he looked down at his papers.

'They won't spare your blushes when they start looking for a buyer. Your friends, neighbours and everyone in the trade will know you've crashed your company.' I plucked a set of their accounts from my pile and flung the papers into the middle of the table. 'There won't be any obvious takers with these liabilities so it'll mean a break up. Your workforce will be paid off at statutory minimums – that's poverty wages. Your fixtures and fittings will be put up for auction – anything that doesn't sell will go on the scrap heap. Some of your people may be lucky enough to get a job stacking shelves in the supermarket that will almost certainly get built on this site. By then Race Engineering will be just a fond twinkle in the eye of a few enthusiasts and you'll be pariahs.'

'Jake's right,' said David. 'You should listen to him. I've known these situations become quite difficult. Smashed windows, unpleasant scenes when you're out for a quiet dinner. One managing director was beaten up by an aggrieved supplier.'

An awkward silence ensued. I let them sweat.

'There's plenty of ammunition here to give you a hard time.' I directed my words at James and Carina. 'Especially for you two.'

'Yes, yes. We understand it's not an attractive option but what choice do we have?' Helen's steely gaze caught my eye.

'None,' said Carina.

David smiled, watching me.

'What if I can show you a better way?' I leaned forward, 'Tell me, why do you think this company has been around for so long?'

James looked up from his pad, 'Oh, I know this. Some of us were stupid enough to be taken in by Roderick and we made quite a success of it despite him.'

'Must you always reduce everything to a joke, James?' said Helen acidly.

James shrugged, 'I've always believed it's better to see the humour in life than dwell on its tragedies.'

'Anyone else? What about you, Allen?' I asked.

'Because the Vixen's a good, dependable sports car.'

'This is a waste of time,' muttered Carina.

I shrugged and made to close my Filofax. 'We don't have to do this. The powers of darkness are just a phone call away.'

'Please continue, Mr Elderfield,' said Helen.

'Jake, please. And the answer's simple.' I gestured towards the leery portrait over the fireplace. 'Your founder's reputation became the essence of your brand. It made a promise that the Vixen fulfilled, allowing you to profit from selling cars your customers love.'

'Oh, so that's what marketing's all about, it is?' asked James.

'Why don't you just shut up and listen? You might learn something,' said Helen sharply.

I ignored the interruption. 'You've as much chance of reaching Mars on an armadillo as selling a Siren right now. But there's an alternative, if you're willing to consider it.'

James had stopped sketching. Was he the artist who'd produced the masterpiece over the fireplace? Unlikely. I'd say he was a man of taste. 'You've a hardcore of loyal fans who've bought Vixens from you. They can help.'

'Preposterous,' said James. 'They're hardly going to rush out and buy another one, are they?'

'James has hit the nail right between the eyes. Those cars are up to twenty years old. How many of them could do with a little TLC or maybe even a complete rebuild? And who better to reinvigorate your beloved motor than the people who made it? Upgrades, you know, tuning, suspension, retrims, hi-fi, you name it.' Was I getting through to them? At least I had their attention. I continued the pitch. 'You'd make money while restoring your reputation. Every Vixen you've ever sold would become a sales opportunity. The owners would thank you for increasing the value of their investment while they enjoy a better driving experience. Everyone wins.'

No smiles. I really must work on my delivery.

'You'll need to cut your costs to make it work; suspend directors' salaries, send home all non-essential staff and make it harder to spend money round here than finding a unicorn's tooth.'

'You expect us to work for nothing?' snapped Carina.

I shrugged. 'It's your call but unless you reduce your outgoings now you may never see another penny out of this business.'

'Shouldn't we make redundancies?' asked Allen.

'Common mistake. Redundancies burn cash. Better to agree lay-offs. Besides, when this plan works, we'll need them back pronto.'

He nodded, adding to his notes.

I continued. 'Once we've stabilised things, we'll see if we can't reduce your working capital by selling off anything you don't need and reducing your stock-holding. So, there's the plan. Four steps to solvency, ladies and gentlemen, cut costs, generate more sales, repay short term debt and then restructure the finances.'

Rock solid principles, detail to come later. James sat back in his chair, legs stretched in front of him, hands behind his head and a smug expression on his face.

I continued. 'If we're going to make this work, we'll need to stay so close even our sworn enemies couldn't slip a stiletto between us. I suggest we meet daily until we're through the worst of it, making all our key decisions together.'

And then the punchline. 'And let's see if we can't get your shipwrecked Siren off the rocks while we're at it.'

David took over.

'It would be helpful to hear everyone's thoughts.'

It wasn't going to take an Einstein to work out Allen was up for it but James and Carina would rather swim the channel pursued by killer whales. Helen was a puzzle. Which side was she on? And did it matter? If she *was* in favour of the plan, the best I could hope for was stalemate. Unless I was wrong about Carina, who was now staring at me with a half-smile on her lips.

'We build cars, we don't service them.' she said. 'That's what dealers are for. Think again or go away. I don't care which.'

Even-stevens then. I couldn't see this working.

Helen removed her glasses and appraised me carefully. 'What reassurances can you give?'

I made ready to pack away my papers. There seemed barely any point in answering.

'I can offer you only one certainty: unless you sign up for this, the company will fail,' I said.

'Think of our people and their families, Mum. Don't we have a responsibility to them?' asked Allen. 'Jake's proposal would allow us to protect some of their jobs at least.'

James laughed and shook his head.

Ignoring him, Helen nodded thoughtfully. 'Yes, I see.'

'What about you, James?' asked David.

'I'd say the fun's over, ladies and gentlemen. High time for a dose of reality.'

Carina came back into the discussion. 'I agree with James. Let's make the phone call.'

David gave an almost imperceptible shake of his head, forestalling my response.

'Thank you, Carina. I propose a motion for the board's consideration. Race Engineering should hire Jake to report to me, working closely with the directors to create a survival plan. I would ask each of you now to vote on the motion. All those in favour?'

Allen raised his hand.

'Thank you. All those against?'

James and Carina raised their hands.

Two to one against. Tied vote at best. Was it back to the situations vacant for me?

Helen still hadn't spoken. David looked at her expectantly. 'I've supported Carina in every decision she's made here.'

Carina smiled triumphantly. 'Thank you, Mother—'

Helen held up her hand, 'Let me finish. But this time I can't. I have to agree with Allen. We must take every opportunity to save Race Engineering, however slim its chances of success.'

'Which means the four directors are deadlocked, with two votes for the proposal and two against,' said David. 'Let's examine the situation with respect to shareholdings.'

David leafed through his papers, displaying a confidence I didn't feel. Was I still in with a chance? A shareholder's majority would outrank a director's vote every time. The one document I hadn't seen was a list of who owned what.

'For the proposal, Helen has twenty per cent of the shares, Allen ten.'

Helen's face was unreadable. Allen looked nervous, refusing to meet anyone's gaze.

'That makes thirty percent for. Against… Carina has thirty-five per cent.'

She was trying hard not to smile. Like a snake trying not to hiss. Elegant but deadly.

'James has ten. Forty-five percent in total.'

James snorted. There was a chunk of shares floating in the ether. David held up a piece of paper.

'This is a proxy form from the trustees of the Race Engineering Pension Fund authorising me to vote their shares. The fund holds twenty-five thousand shares or twenty-five per cent of the equity. 'I vote in favour of the motion. The proposal is carried fifty-five per cent to forty-five. Congratulations, Jake, consider yourself hired. You and I can sort out the details.'

Carina's smile was more of a grimace. She clapped her hands sarcastically half a dozen times.

'Apparently, we've had a boardroom coup. I suppose under the circumstances, I should offer the board my resignation.'

'Don't minute that, Allen,' said David. 'Perhaps Carina should reflect before such a move.'

Gathering up her belongings, she stood. 'I'll say good night, for now.' She banged the door closed behind her, the staccato clicks of her stiletto heels receding through the office.

There was a moment's silence, none of us quite sure how to react to Carina's abrupt – and I assumed deliberately antagonistic – departure. Then David and Helen stood together and James sauntered casually over to me. He seemed sanguine about losing the vote, offering me his hand to shake.

'Congratulations, dear boy. Welcome to the sinking ship.'

I shook the proffered hand but didn't reply.

'I'll go after Carina,' he added. 'Once she calms down, I'm sure she'll see the logic of working closely with you, even if it's only to keep an eye on what you're up to.' He chuckled, shaking his head as he walked away.

Helen chatted quietly with David before returning her glasses, notebook and pen to her handbag, offering me a brief nod of acknowledgement. I went over to them.

'I'm so sorry, Jake. What must you think of us?' she said.

'No issue. I'm just here to do a job.'

Helen left, and Allen joined David and me.

'I'd like a copy of those minutes to sign first thing in the morning and then, Jake, you and I need to go and have a chat with the bank and outline our intentions,' said David.

'Of course,' said Allen.

'I hope you didn't have any plans for this evening?' I asked.

Allen looked puzzled. 'No, why?'

'I want to go through all of your costs, line by line and build a new cash flow model.'

'No problem. And you'll need somewhere to work. There's Dad's office. It's hardly been used since he died. All his things are still in there. I'm only next door so I'll be on hand for anything you need.'

'Great.'

David looked grim-faced as Allen left the room. 'Well, we carried the day, my lad, but you're going to need to work on Carina and James. You must take these people with you, even if you have to chase them along with fixed bayonet. I want to see a real grip on the detail by the time we meet the bank tomorrow.' He smiled thinly. 'They won't be fooled by those superficial headlines you presented tonight and neither will I.'

He began to move away and then did an about turn to my side.

'Here's an idea, why don't I bring in breakfast tomorrow at seven am and you can demonstrate to me precisely how you are going to keep these people out of the brown stuff.'

ABOUT THE AUTHOR

Many of you already know me as "Cashier Number Three!" – and over the last twenty years or so, around twenty-five million shoppers every month have heard my voice summoning them from the queue in banks, shops and post offices everywhere.

My career has taken some interesting twists and turns – from cars to queues – cellular phones to celebrity chefs.

But I needed something more, which is why I turned to a life of crime.

A reader commented that my first business book, *You're Next*, read like a thriller. That got me thinking. Could I come up with a twist on the classic detective story? Could I write an entertaining, compelling series of novels set against the background of my career? Oh sure, there would have to be lies, fraud and murder, along with some delicious scandal and just a touch of romantic intrigue – in short, all the elements you'd expect in a compelling, page-turning thriller. And how about serving those up on a bed of gritty business challenges for our hero?

So here, from my base, on the Western edge of Dartmoor in delightful Devon, I'm plotting the career of Jake Elderfield. I hope you can join me on the journey.

Asking questions can be a dangerous art . . .

Jake Elderfield didn't come to Prague looking for trouble. But when his old friend Liz vanishes while working on a newly discovered masterpiece, he's pulled into a deadly game.

As Jake digs deeper, the picture quickly cracks. With a high-profile auction looming and fortunes on the line, Liz's disappearance is only the beginning. In a world where appearances deceive and money talks, someone is willing to do whatever it takes to keep the truth hidden. It's not just Liz who's in danger.

From the luxury of Burgh Island to the dark heart of Prague and a nail-biting finale in Tavistock, *Dangerous Art* is a fast-paced thriller packed with twists, danger, and deception.

PRAISE FOR *REDLINE*:

'A fast-paced page-turner.'

'A fresh, original and gripping thriller.'

For more information visit:
www.terry-green.co.uk
@terrygreenauthor
@terrygreenauthor

HUMAN AUTHORED

Cover design:www.25design.co.uk
Cover image:shutterstock and
www.figurestock.com

£9.99

ISBN 978-1-0682313-2-2